BETWEEN
THE
DRAGONS

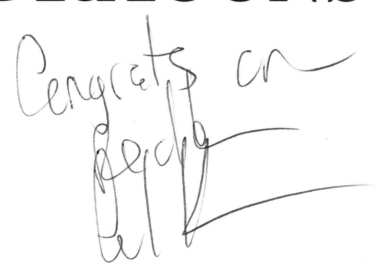

RIKO RADOJCIC

Fulton Books, Inc.
Meadville, PA

Published by Fulton Books 2021

ISBN 978-1-63710-062-2 (paperback)
ISBN 978-1-63710-063-9 (digital)

Printed in the United States of America

Contents

Acknowledgments

This book—a fictional novel—is a second attempt by the author to metamorphose from an engineer in the silicon chip industry to a writer. From counting electrons in a lab, analyzing arcane data and managing engineers, to imagining tales and telling—writing—fictional stories. In this tenuous state, any encouragement from family, friends, and colleagues was invaluable. Even absences of snickers—real or imagined—were appreciated and interpreted as signs of support. And actual hard and honest feedback, based on plowing through all of the author's attempts at writing, was totally priceless. Thank you.

The author was especially touched by the support, effort, comments, and suggestions from

- ✓ Matt Nowak, who had the patience to read and comment on every chapter in its rawest form, as it came off the press;
- ✓ Prof Andrew Kahng, a.k.a. ABK, whose honest feedback defines what the author aspires to—someday;
- ✓ Natasha Radojcic, a.k.a. # 1, who had very wise advice that she always delivered with such loving tact;
- ✓ Dan Perry, who gave such detailed, balanced, and to-the-point feedback;
- ✓ Vesna Niketic, who plowed through the book and assessed the veracity of all the assumptions;
- ✓ Dejan Radojcic, who faithfully slogged through a draft and made good comments even though he hates fiction and reading it must have been painful;
- ✓ Taravat Khadivi, a.k.a. TeraWatti, who has an eagle eye for spotting the smallest of errors or inconsistencies and is cursed with a sense of humor like the author.

Thank you, one and all! This book would not be what it is without you. I hope y'all like it.

Preface and a Note to the Reader

This is a work of fiction. Names, characters, businesses, places, events, locales, and incidents, other than the ones mentioned below or explicitly identified in the exhibits and footnotes, are either the products of the author's imagination or used in a fictitious manner. Any resemblance to actual persons, living or dead, or actual events is purely coincidental.

The work does use some real events as a framework for this fictional story—such as the trade war between China and the US, the blacklisting of Huawei, and so forth. Furthermore, in order to create a framework that is realistic, the work also refers to some real technologies used in manufacturing of silicon chips, as well as to some practices characteristic of the business side of the semiconductor industry. Several real technology companies, as well as a few public figures, have also been named.

This story does aim to describe a series of events that *could* happen and to create characters whose motives and decisions *are* realistic. The intent is to construct a set of situations and circumstances that mirror the reality of the high-tech industry, under which the decisions and actions taken by any of the characters is something that an average reader could reasonably relate to. Reading this story should not call for total suspension of disbelief. Furthermore, it is hoped that while enjoying a fictional story, the reader may also get a peek at some of the amazing wonders of modern high-technology and maybe even get an appreciation for the techie "nerds" who made it what it is.

Since the intent is to construct a story where the border between reality and fiction is fuzzy, the factual background used, whether it is historical, cultural, or technical in nature, is highlighted in the exhibits, clearly identified in separate numbered boxes, and the footnotes, scattered throughout the text. Note that these are not a part of the story and may be readily skipped.

Although laid out as a mostly linear sequence of events and told in third person, note that the story is actually presented as an interleaved narrative of the three main characters. To help the reader keep track of their different points of view, the narrator of each chapter is named in the section title, along with the date and the location where most of the given scene takes place.

And lastly, note that in this story the Chinese State, or people acting on its behalf, are presented as the "bad guy." In truth, the author does not believe that the use of any and all means for getting an upper hand in the global competition is limited to the Chinese state actors. Not at all. There is plenty of evidence that all sides play equally hard—and dirty—using whatever means they can find.

This can take a relatively benign form of government favoritism, ranging from blatant financial support for select companies or industries to various forms of selective tax shelters and on to state subsidies for Research and Development in targeted arenas. Or a state may use the usual import/export laws to shelter some industries and/or technologies. To the best of the author's knowledge, some version of these support mechanisms is practiced by every country on the planet.

Or it can take the form of more selective and perhaps biased enforcement of regulations when it is deemed to be in national interests. For example, in 2018, China blocked the merger of Qualcomm and NXP—two large western companies—on the grounds that the monopoly power of the merged entity would have put some of the Chinese industry and/or consumers at a disadvantage. This from a country where state-owned enterprises have virtual monopolies in telecom, oil and gas, and many other major industry sectors? Arguably. Coincidentally, in that same year, the US government blocked a takeover bid from Broadcom—then a foreign entity—for that same Qualcomm on the grounds of national security, presumably threatening the interests of American industry and/or consumers. This from a country whose companies have well-established global dominance in key sectors, such as software, server hardware, information technology, fintech, etc.? Arguably. Ironically, both countries claimed to be protecting free trade.

Nor is the use of the underhanded methods limited to China. For example, the US is accusing Huawei of building a back door in their equipment to support state-sponsored spying and thus of being a potential security leak. But some would say that the United States knows this only too well because it is the US, with its Five Eyes Intelligence Alliance, involving several western democracies, and multiple telecommunication companies, that has engaged in massive public surveillance programs as leaked by Edward Snowden in 2013.

Similarly, China is often accused of state-sponsored hacking, but it is the US (and Israel) who are credited with the notorious Stuxnet worm that was first uncovered in 2010. Stuxnet was a cyberweapon supposedly responsible for targeting industrial control systems that has infected over two hundred thousand computers worldwide and that has damaged thousands of machines. Ultimately, Stuxnet did destroy almost one-fifth of Iran's nuclear centrifuges—supposedly the real, and some would say a just, target.

Finally, many states and corporate entities are concerned about China acquiring Intellectual Property using unfair practices that sometimes include extortion and/or outright theft. But it is the American CIA and the German intelligence services who have recently been outed as the secret owners of a Swiss company Crypto that misled 120 governments around the world into buying its supposedly private encryption services—thereby enabling theft of their state secrets. If a company from the good, proper, and neutral Switzerland—a country perceived to be above the underhanded and illegitimate means supposedly used by other, presumably less scrupulous, entities, cannot be trusted—then who can be? (In the interest of full disclosure, the author is proud to be a [dual] citizen of Switzerland.)

The examples listed above are extreme cases that happen to have come into the public domain. Surely, those cases are the tip of the proverbial iceberg. Surely, there are many more cases, possibly motivated by the industrial policy rather than the grave national security concerns. And surely, most of these would be successfully kept quiet and would never surface to become known to the public. Maybe something like a situation described in this fictional story...

Part 1

THE RED DRAGON WOKE

Junjie Wu

Thursday, February 7
Liuxiaguan Teahouse, Dongcheng, Beijing, China

Junjie had to admit to himself that he was nervous. Maybe just a bit. It was not like him. Normally, he had no difficulty mixing with all kinds of people and was even quite comfortable relating to the Westerners—an attribute that was still somewhat rare among the Chinese.

He ascribed it mostly to his upbringing. He was endowed with a healthy dose of self-confidence thanks to the loving parents he was blessed with and the stable and secure home that they provided—even through the turbulent times of the Cultural Revolution.[1] He did not remember much about that time—he was way too young then—but knew all about it through the family lore. And thanks to the good years he spent in the west. He successfully completed his studies there—a Master's at the University of Manchester, England, and a PhD at Vanderbilt, United States, followed by a few good years working in the chip industry there. And, of course, thanks to the achievements and successes in his personal and professional life that he met with here, ever since he returned home.

---

[1] **Cultural Revolution**: See exhibit 1.5 below.

Or, on the other hand, it may just be due to the physical presence he was blessed with. He was taller and more robust—not fat by any means—but more solid than the average Chinese kids he grew up with. And he had matured into looks that even the western women found alluring: tall, slender, quite muscular, with pronounced cheekbones that gave his face a sense of depth and strength. Sometimes he was told that he looked a bit like that actor from *Hawaii Five-0*.[2]

This always caused him to smirk—not so much because of the complement but more because he knew that Daniel Dae Kim was Korean. *Westerners really are so bad at telling apart the entirely different Asian ethnicities.*

In any case, life has been good to Junjie. He was able and confident, and he normally dealt with people easily. Normally.

But this was Professor Lao! *The* Professor Lao.

Maybe a part of his nervousness was due just to the usual mixture of fear and respect carried over from his undergrad days when Lao was one of his lecturers. A natural mix of veneration and awe, intimidation and fear, respect and even love that students tend to feel for their professors. Especially for someone like professor Lao who seems to have been an omnipresent institution for just about every Tsinghua University[3] Electronic Engineering grad that Junjie met or heard of—forever…

Maybe a part of the apprehension was due to Professor Lao's reputation: venerable—seemingly eternal. Highly respected—well beyond the usual Confucian respect naturally due to old academics. And extremely well-connected. Rumors had it that Professor Lao held a record of having a larger number of his graduates in the Politburo

---

[2] **Hawaii Five-0**: An American action police television series that CBS ran from 1968 to 1980, and again for ten seasons, starting in 2010. The cast of the 2010 series included Daniel Dae Kim as Detective Lieutenant Chin Ho Kelly, HPD.

[3] **Tsinghua University** (abbreviated Tsinghua): A top-research university in Beijing, and a member of the C9 League of Chinese universities—an official alliance of nine universities initiated by the Chinese Central Government that account for 3 percent of the country's researchers, but receive 10 percent of national research expenditures, and produce 20 percent of the nation's academic publications and 30 percent of total citations.

and even in the Standing Committee[4] than any other professor in China—ever. That may have changed with the Party's Eighteenth National Congress[5] that seemed to favor engineers less than the previous one, but Professor Lao's connections have persisted—seemingly as always.

Or maybe Junjie was on edge just because the meeting was so unusual. It is not often that someone like the exulted Professor Lao invited him for an informal meeting. "To have tea and a chat," he said. Junjie was sure that Professor Lao was much more accustomed to turning down invitations than making them, especially from his old students and certainly from unimportant old students like himself—just a regular engineer and entrepreneur working in the industry. Not a princeling[6] or someone important and connected. And only two days after Chinese New Year: the time that people normally dedicate to their family and most intimate friends.

Must be something important, Junjie thought. *What could he want with me? Maybe "a favor" for me to hire his proverbial nephew? Maybe…*

Junjie positively resented being asked for that kind of favor and usually refused to hire anyone based on their connections. But this was professor Lao! This was different.

---

[4] **Standing Committee**: A committee consisting of the top leadership of the Communist Party of China. Historically, it has been composed of five to eleven members. Its officially mandated purpose is to conduct policy discussions and make decisions on major issues when the Politburo, a larger decision-making body, is not in session. In practice, it is the real seat of power in China—the inner cabinet of the chairman.

[5] **National Congress**: Theoretically the highest body within the Communist Party of China that meets every five years, typically in the Great Hall of the People in Beijing. In the past two decades, the National Congress of the CPC has been pivotal at least as a symbolic part of leadership changes and, therefore, has gained international media attention. The Eighteenth Congress was held in 2012.

[6] **Princeling**: A slightly derogatory name for a descendant of prominent and influential senior communist officials in the People's Republic of China. It is an informal categorization to describe the offspring—the second generation—of the CPC leadership that was close to Mao, and that has leveraged these connections to amass wealth and/or political power in modern post—Mao China.

Junjie knew that *if* that turned out to be the nature of this tea, it would be a knife with two edges. On one hand, he would be breaking his own rules—he always hired people only for their skill and ability and absolutely nothing else. On the other hand, if Professor Lao—and by extension—somebody powerful in the Party, does ask, that would mean that his business has been noticed. That his business is about to be blessed by the powers-to-be. That it has been deemed worthy of placing someone—a set of trusted eyes and ears—in it. That kind of a privilege—hiring an anointed someone—usually came with benefits: easy credit, more open doors, bigger opportunities.

If *that is what prof Lao wants*, he reminded himself.

"Ah, Albert! There you are. How are you?"

Professor Lao shuffled to the table that Junjie was sitting at—the corner table that Lao reserved—with the view of the pond and the garden and discretely separated by a beautiful silk screen from the rest of the teahouse. He was a bit stooped over and walked slowly with ever so slight a limp.

But looking good for his age. He must be what, seventy-five... eighty... by now, Junjie thought.

Junjie stood up, respectfully bowed, shook the bony and somewhat clammy hand that Professor Lao offered, and helped him to a chair. The usual expressions of respect for one's elders—especially befitting in that setting. Liuxiaguan Teahouse was a hidden gem—a rare oasis of traditional Chinese ways lost in the modern bustling Beijing. Serene and quiet, decorated in the old style with bamboo wood floors and replicas of famous ink prints, infused with the smells of tea, and with a view of a traditional manicured Chinese garden—pond and all.

"Professor Lao, an honor. Thank you. But please call me Junjie, my proper Chinese name."

He noted that Professor Lao was only seven minutes late. Convention would dictate that someone of Professor Lao's status may be even thirty minutes late without being considered rude.

"Ah. So you have not forgotten your Chinese name in all the years you spent in England and America?" Professor Lao asked. But, it seemed to Junjie, teasingly so; with a smile and a crinkle in his sharp eyes.

"No, of course not, Professor. Why would I? I am not ashamed to be Chinese," Junjie protested.

"Don't mind me, Junjie. I am just playing with you... Although it seems that many of my students who, like you, went abroad to complete their studies, often stay there, and forget where their home is... Do you think it is just the money? Even now that we have grown enough to be able to offer comparable standards of living for our brightest engineers? Or do you think that there are other reasons?"

Junjie was too experienced with the realities of Chinese life to be drawn into a conversation on topics that may have political overtones—not with relative strangers and especially not with someone like Professor Lao. So he just responded with, "Oh, Professor. I do not know. All I know is that *I* came back because *I* am from here," stressing the "I." "This is my home. My family is here."

"And because the SARS epidemic blocked your return to the US?" Professor Lao asked pointedly, alluding to the events back in 2003, when Junjie came to China to renew his H1B visa and was caught up in the SARS travel embargo that prevented his return to the US and ended up staying.

"Well, yes. But that was just the timing. I always knew I would come back. The only question was when, not if," Junjie protested.

"May I ask why?"

"Hmm, well. The family... The people and the culture... I feel so much more comfortable here. And I do believe that the future is here, not there. For me. For all of us in the semiconductor business. There is so much energy here. America is more...tired, I think."

The waitress came bringing not the menus but a steaming pot of water, a set of china cups, a tray with all the usual tea accessories, and a couple of platters of scrumptious-looking petit fours—presumably specially ordered in for the occasion.

"Ah, yes, the tea. I hope that you do not mind that I have ordered for both of us. Junjie, try this tea. Delicious. I know that you have developed a taste for imported English teas, but this domestic

Da Hong Pao[7] is special. In my opinion, Chinese tea is the very best," Professor Lao said in his slow and ponderous way while waiving the waitress away and preparing the tea himself. "On the other hand, *some* imports from the west are also excellent. Like for example, the games of bridge and soccer or ballroom dancing. Or like these French patisserie snacks. I hear that you have a sweet tooth, so I have asked for some glacé kind. Although, at my age, I find I prefer the salé style. Please...," he added, waving at the trays.

Junjie's antennas were ringing with all sorts of alarms. *He is being so...nice. Too nice. Almost obsequious. And Da Hong Pao. Wow! What is going on here?* It would be far more appropriate for him to be buying expensive tea and pouring it for the professor—not this way around.

And the professor seems to know a lot about my personal preferences, he noted.

After the usual polite niceties—health, well-being of the family, and the like—they slipped into an easy conversation about...everything. The professor asked this and that—smoothly and readily skipping from subject to subject. About CHARM Inc., Junjie's current technology company. About the semiconductor industry business cycle. About the recent developments in Silicon technology. About the cost of Silicon Chip foundries.[8] About the last Beijing Symphony performance of Dvorak's 'The New World'. About the cultural life of younger people in Beijing and the current fads... Everything.

He appeared relaxed and to be enjoying himself although his eyes were sharp and watched Junjie keenly.

Alert and animated—as always. Looking, and acting, the way that Junjie remembered him from thirty-odd years ago—the way he looked when trying to find a weakness in students' presentations.

---

[7] **Da Hong Pao** (Big Red Robe): A Wuyi rock tea grown in the Wuyi Mountains. It is a heavily oxidized, dark oolong tea. The highest quality versions frequently sell as the world's most expensive tea (up to US$1,025,000 per kilogram). In China, it is often reserved for honored guests.

[8] **Foundries**: A type of semiconductor fabrication facilities (typically called "fabs") used to manufacture external clients' (often referred to as "fabless" design houses) Integrated Circuit designs. The cost of the foundries capable of manufacturing the latest kind of chips runs to around US$10B or more.

Professor Lao paused only for a short while to pointedly admire a beautiful but somehow out-of-place western woman that walked by, proudly jiggling her assets, enticingly revealed by her tight white dress.

Who is he kidding? At his age? I bet that he has not been with a woman for forty years and probably would not know what to do with one by now, Junjie thought.

There has never been any talk of Professor Lao favoring some of his female students or anything of the kind. Supposedly, women were just not his thing.

This exhibition of a kind of familiarity that is normally shared only between old men-friends was out of character for someone like the venerable Professor Lao—even in male chauvinist China.

As if we were old friends? Why this informality? What is going on? Nah, this must be some kind of theater. But why? Junjie wondered.

Professor Lao continued the conversation unperturbed—seemingly relaxed and at ease. But never losing his presence—his gravitas—somehow amplified by his patient, unhurried, and monotonic speech pattern, sounding just like he did when delivering his lectures. Eventually, the conversation drifted to more benign topics: the weather, the pollution, the recent news.

"Did you read about Meng Wanzhou arrest?" he asked as if the thought just occurred to him.

"The Huawei CFO in Canada? Yes. It is horrible. I thought that taking hostages was something that civilized governments have stopped doing in the eighteenth century. Nowadays, that is practiced only by the triad and the terrorists. And here is the American government doing nothing short of taking a hostage. Outrageous and barbaric. So disappointing. This Trump is such a…pig," Junjie erupted.

The recent news was genuinely upsetting to him, and he allowed himself the outburst. Perhaps he was feeling more relaxed and at ease with Professor Lao? Perhaps he was caught off guard despite himself?

"And this after that shameful ZTE debacle last year. Arrogant extortion, I would say. Unfairly bringing a champion company like ZTE to its knees just to demonstrate his power. Spitting in our face," Junjie added hotly.

EXHIBIT 1.2   ZTE and the US: Everything you need to know

By: Brenda Stolyar and Christian de Looper July 13, 2018

Chinese telecommunications giant ZTE, which makes smartphones, telecommunications gear, and other mobile gadgets, has had a tough time recently. Its troubles began last year with a massive fine for working around U.S. sanctions that prevented sales to Iran and North Korea. The U.S. Department of Commerce then announced a ban preventing American companies from selling components to ZTE.

American-made microchips and software, notably the Android operating system, are essential to making its products. Couple this with also being targeted by the U.S. government as a potential security threat, and ZTE's survival has been in question.

The U.S. has recently lifted its ban on U.S. suppliers selling to ZTE, effectively allowing the Chinese company to resume business. The lifting of the ban comes just a day after the Commerce Department said that it would remove the ban if ZTE paid a $1 billion penalty and places $400 million in a U.S. bank escrow account. However, the lift itself comes with a 10-year suspended sentence clause, which along with the $400 million and a Department of Commerce appointed watchdog, is expected to keep ZTE — and other potential rule breakers — from breaking agreements again in the future.

ZTE has changed in order to smooth the path towards returning to business. Immediately after the ban came into effect, ZTE issued a statement to the Hong Kong Stock exchange, saying it would "take steps to comply with the denial order. The company is making active communications with relevant parties and seeking a solution." The actions include a committee focusing on compliance, overseen by ZTE's CEO and experts in the matter, along with additional training for staff. ZTE said it has learned from "past experiences on export control compliance."

From: https://www.digitaltrends.com/mobile/commerce-bans-zte-from-exporting-technology-from-the-us/

Junjie was passionate about this—perhaps unusually so among the Chinese urbanites who tend to be relatively reserved on political topics. He took some of the moves in the global game of chess that was played between China and the US personally. It was not because he was particularly patriotic—he wasn't at all. It was more that he felt strongly about globalization. He believed it to be an avenue to real and lasting world peace and prosperity. His time in the west—where he met all sorts of people from all sorts of places—has changed him. It taught him that smart, talented, and even nice, friendly, and interesting people can come from anywhere in the world. And vice versa. In contrast to what he picked up in his own monolithic and, yes, classist and racist China. He believed in internationalism. In contrast to the Chinese smug traditional tendency to view itself as the center of the world, the Middle Kingdom,[9] and to look inward. He believed in globalization and looked to the West—all of its many imperfec-

---

[9]   **Middle Kingdom** (or Middle Country): Chinese name for China dating back from circa 1000 BC (Mandarin: Zhongguo).

tions that he was fully aware of notwithstanding—as a leader in pursuing those ideals. He believed in free trade and open borders, in liberalism and democracy, in multiculturalism and multiracialism, in equal opportunity. The right and lofty goals to strive for. Or so he believed. And now Trump was pissing all over those ideals. Trump's overt boorish xenophobia and isolationism was offensive, disappointing, even hurtful. And embarrassing since Junjie was known in his circle of family and friends as being pro-West. Junjie feared that the trade war would end the golden age and resented it all—personally and passionately.

Professor Lao said nothing but has registered the reaction with a slightly raised eyebrow and an amused glint in his eyes.

After about an hour and a half, with the tea and treats all gone, Professor Lao rose slowly and said, "Junjie, this has been a real pleasure for me. Catching up with you, with someone from your generation, has been invigorating…and not just because of the obscenely pricey Oolong tea that I get to charge to my expense account." He added the last with a shrug in a kind of a self-effacing joke. "Please do send my regards to your parents and, of course, the rest of the family. And could you come to the university? My private office in the Provost's building, not the labs. Next Monday? Shall we say about 3:00 p.m.? See you then."

And he shuffled off, looking just like another frail old man. Like so many others found in all the parks of Beijing.

The invitation was not stated as a casual invite that it appeared to be—more like an order, a summons.

But to what? I seem to have passed some kind of a test, Junjie thought. *This meeting was not so that he could ask me for a favor. It was a test. But of what?*

He was still as confused and surprised now as he was when he initially received the invitation to tea—three days ago, just before CNY.[10] Still leaving him with all the questions unanswered.

Sometimes I miss the western—the American—ways, he mused. *They are open and up front. Almost brutishly simple. Not wasting any*

---

10 **CNY**: Chinese New Year.

energy or time on these subtle but significant symbolic-symbolism-games that we like to play in China. Especially old-school people like Lao. Nothing is what it seems to be on the surface.

He thought that he may have understood some of the messages. The comment about the Western imports like soccer, ballroom dancing, and bridge—known passions of the current and past chairmen of the Central Committee—was a clear message that some western imports are not only condoned but are desirable. That isolationism was not the objective... The petit fours were also not a coincidence. Maybe there just to inform him that they—whoever they are—knew everything about him. Down to his weakness for French pastry... The woman in the white dress was probably a plant—also some kind of a message. But he was not sure of what. Junjie worried that his own proclivity for women—especially the western women—might not be a secret after all. He liked to flirt with women—even to take advantage of the best escort services—when he could on his business trips to Europe and the US and such like. But he has always been discreet and careful. Maybe the woman in the white dress was a threat of exposure and a warning for him. Maybe...

Still, nothing here is what it seems to be on the surface. Other than that, Lao—or the powers to be behind him—clearly wants something.

Monday, February 11
Tsinghua University, Haidian District, Beijing, China

A guard led him to the Provost's building. Junjie did not even know it existed—at least when he was a student there. A secretary that looked like she was with Lao throughout his eternal career met him in the lobby and led the way to Lao's office suite. She pointed him to one of the usual red-stuffed armchairs lined along the wall—seemingly the obligatory Beijing Tiantan Furniture Co.[11] kind that is found in all the government offices—and assured him that professor Lao will be available shortly. In a few minutes, a buzzer sounded, and the secretary led him to the inner sanctum: Professor Lao's office.

"Ah, there you are, Junjie. Thank you for coming. Sit down, please. I have something to show you."

The office, dominated by a heavy red rosewood desk that made the prof look even smaller than he was, smelled of jasmine or some other fragrant flower. The large window next to him offered a view of a traditional Chinese garden, including a small pond and the typical arched bridge, in the atrium of the building. *Very zen*, Junjie thought. The office walls were, however, lined with floor to ceiling shelves filled with books, plaques, award certificates, and a few framed photographs. *Professorial...*

Professor Lao selected one of the several rolls of paper protruding from a waste-paper basket next to the desk and unfurled it across the tabletop, patiently weighing down the corners with random objects sitting on his desk. It was approximately a three-foot-long scroll that looked like a family tree chart with many little boxes, tiny writing, and arrows.

Junjie peered at it, and after a moment said questioningly: "It is a chart of the Silicon Chip Supply Chain, or some version thereof?"

---

[11] **Beijing Tiantan Furniture Co**. **Ltd**: The only Chinese state-owned enterprise in the furniture industry, with products that include commercial furniture for offices. Tiantan Furniture has won many important honors and is favored by government and related entities. Its furniture (e.g., the typical straight-backed red-stuffed chair) is often seen in photographs of visiting dignitaries and such like.

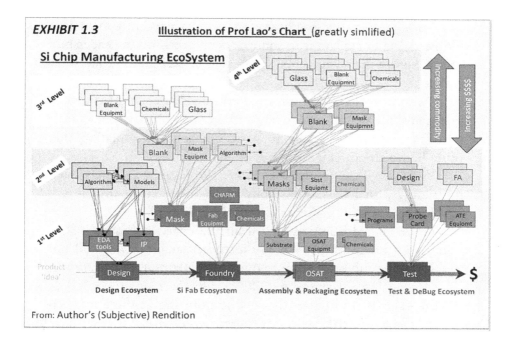

EXHIBIT 1.3 Illustration of Prof Lao's Chart (greatly simlified)

From: Author's (Subjective) Rendition

He was puzzled. Flavors of charts just like this one were ubiquitous—showing various players in the industry and where their products fit in the overall flow of manufacturing silicon chips. Versions could be readily found on the web, summarizing something that was pretty much common knowledge for experienced semiconductor professionals like himself. Nothing special.

Has the old prof lost it? Getting excited about rediscovering a wheel? he wondered inwardly.

"Yes, yes it is. Very good," Professor Lao confirmed. "But look at it closely, Junjie. One of my students just spent eight months compiling this one in a very particular way. What do you really see?"

"Oh, Professor. I would have to study it in detail to find a supplier that was missing or one that I have not heard of or a relationship that doesn't fit the normal paradigm," Junjie protested. There must have been hundreds of boxes and thousands of arrows on the chart, and he would have needed a magnifying glass to read all the writing.

"True, Junjie, true. But bear with me. I have recently spent a lot of time trying to explain it to some nonengineers in the Leadership. That is harder than you think. Look at it closely and tell me what you see."

"Well, the chart segregates the entire value chain into several ecosystems. For design, silicon fabrication, assembly, and test," Junjie started, questioningly trying to parse out some information that would be worth noticing.

"Yes, yes. That is not the point," Professor Lao interrupted impatiently with a wave of his bony hand. "Look at the overall pattern, Junjie. Look at the forest to spot the odd tree."

Junjie looked questioningly from the chart to Professor Lao, feeling a bit resentful. He was not a student anymore and did not need Lao to be subjecting him to one of his infamous oral exams.

"If you look past the details," Professor Lao proceeded to explain—slowly and patiently—while pointing at the appropriate sections of the chart with his finger, "you will see that we have organized the supply chain into a hierarchy. In terms of levels of removal from the actual chip production flow. There is the zeroth level that contains the entities that are directly involved in chip manufacturing. Design houses, silicon foundries, OSAT[12] providers, and so on. Typically, big entities with revenues of tens of billions of dollars. Then there is the first level. These are the suppliers to the zeroth level. Makers of the fab manufacturing equipment, photomask shops, makers of design CAD tools, producers of bare wafers and various specialty materials used in chip manufacturing, etc., usually with a turnover of a few billion dollars. And the second level is the suppliers to the first level, things like, for example, makers of E-beam writing equipment for photomask shops or design of probe cards for test equipment makers. Third level is the suppliers to the second level. Raw materi-

---

[12] **OSAT** (Outsourced Semiconductor Assembly and Test): A type of a merchant vendor company that provides IC assembly, packaging, and test services to other third-party companies (i.e., not for its own internal product).

als, glassware, generic chemicals, and the like. These are typically valued in millions of dollars. And so on. You see?"

"Yes, Professor. So?"

"Well, if you look closely, you could notice that as you go up from the zeroth level, the number of suppliers of a given type of a tool, material, or service typically increases. There are more of them at the higher levels of hierarchy."

"Hmm, yes. I guess that makes sense," Junjie responded, eager to demonstrate that he got it. "The further up the supply chain hierarchy that you go, the more you reach into the commodity zone where the level of knowledge and expertise required to produce a specific thing is lower? And so there should be more suppliers capable of producing that particular product or service? And I suppose each tends to be smaller and will operate with a lower margin?"

"Yes, very good, Junjie. Exactly. That is the normal trend."

A little pause.

"Except." Professor Lao held up a skeletal finger, indicating that he was getting to his point.

Finally, thought Junjie.

"Except in a few isolated cases. In some cases, up in the second or third or even the fourth level of the supply chain hierarchy, sometimes you can find a single specialized supplier. A pinch point." He used the expression in English and gesticulated with his hands as if to underline the term.

"A pinch point?" Junjie asked, not sure what Professor Lao was getting at.

"Yes. A single supplier. A sole source of some specialty tool, skill, or material with no existing or qualified alternatives. Like you and your CHARM Inc. is virtually the sole source of the kind of test wafers that you provide. In some cases, if that source was to be shut off, the whole supply chain would splutter or maybe even grind to a halt…a pinch point."

"I see."

"So," Professor Lao continued, "in a trade war like the one we are fighting with America, everyone is focused on the capabilities in the zeroth or maybe the first level of the supply chain hierarchy."

His unhurried, monotonic droning reminded Junjie of his student days. *Back then, his slow pace was actually a good thing*, he reminisced. *It allowed us to take notes. Now it is just tedious*, he thought, wishing to hurry the professor on.

"As you correctly pointed out," Professor Lao carried on, "that is where the differentiation is, and most of the value. Hence, we, and the US, are focusing all our energies there. Foundries, OSATs, Design Houses. Maybe some fab equipment makers..."

He let that sink in. Then, finally, he came to his point, "So right now, they have some and we have some... Fine... But owning these high-profile and very expensive capabilities ends up ensuring only parity. At best, we can be mutually independent of each other. Fine."

After a second or two, he added, almost as an afterthought, "Fine, of course, only as long as there is no disruptive change in the technology. Paradigm-shift kind of changes that might make some of these companies obsolete."

"Something that Americans tend to be better at than we are," Junjie inserted, voicing a common observation—perhaps a common fear. He actually believed it—based on his personal experiences of working in America and China.

"True. Our culture tends to emphasize respect for tradition. Theirs tends to glorify breaking rules," Professor Lao shrugged slightly, as if describing something obvious and unimportant.

Then, after a short pause, he got to his key point, "On the other hand, pinch point companies are different. If you own a pinch point, then you control the whole supply chain. Indirectly. Owning such a pinch point, well, that is more than just achieving parity. That could be an offensive weapon. You can choke your opponent."

There was a strange shine in Professor Lao's eyes. *Maybe a bit like a typical mad scientist in American cartoons*, Junjie thought, like

Professor Frink or Dr. Nefario. But perhaps he was just imagining this.

"Oh, I see," Junjie hesitated. He reflexively shied away from "offensive weapons." He wanted the trade war to be over and things to go back to normal—not to make it worse or to choke his competitors. Some of those competitors were friends and colleagues of his. He wanted to win by being better—like he has done with CHARM Inc.—rather than by being on the right side of someone powerful.

It is again like hiring people for who they happen to know rather than what they know, he thought automatically. This was his regular pet peeve.

"But," the professor raised his finger again, "as you said, the higher tiers of the supply chain are characterized by lower margins and lower revenues. Less money. And with less money, the motivation—and the capability—for innovation is lower. While the rest of the chip industry is dominated by frantic disruptive development—which, as you said, is America's strength—there are few revolutionary innovations at the higher levels of the supply chain hierarchy. Most of the focus there has been on improving the quality and driving the costs down through economies of scale. Those are *our* strengths. The industry uses pretty much the same tweezers and vacuum wands as it did thirty or fifty years ago. Or wafer baths. Or wafer carriers. Or glassware..."

"Hmm. I guess that makes sense. I never really thought about it," Junjie commented noncommittally.

"So," the professor continued, "companies at the higher levels of the supply chain hierarchy are at lower risk of being obsoleted by a disruptive change. Therefore, you would find that pinch point companies, even at the third or fourth level of the hierarchy, are actually very stable and robust." Professor Lao stopped, checked that Junjie was following him, and concluded, "So controlling these pinch points would be a lasting weapon that would give our side not only independence from the US but also a capability that could be used for offensive purposes. Shutting off only a few suitable pinch point companies could wreak real havoc in their supply chain. We could potentially cripple a targeted enemy. All for a few million-dollar investments."

"I see," Junjie repeated. He looked at Professor Lao with renewed respect. It was clear that Lao has spent some time thinking through the various scenarios that could come up in a trade war. Trump's actions did not seem to have caught *him* by surprise, like they did most of the rest of the industry.

"Good. Like I said, it took me a while to explain it to the Leadership. But I think that they have got it. There are well-publicized initiatives focused on making our national semiconductor industry independent of the US. Like the Made in China 2025[13] initiative and the Big Fund. Mostly focused on levels 0 and 1 of the supply chain hierarchy. That is all right and good…"

---

[13] **Made in China 2025**: One of the strategic plans of the People's Republic of China. With it, China aims to move away from being the "world's factory" (producing cheap goods due to lower labor costs) and move to producing higher-value products and services. It is in essence a blueprint to upgrade the manufacturing capabilities of Chinese industries into a more technology-intensive powerhouse. A major part of the initiative is focused on increasing the domestic share of manufacturing the semiconductor ICs.

EXHIBIT 1.4 The 'Big Fund' ▌South China Morning Post

Li Tao, 10 May, 2018

The recent move by the US government to ban the sale of American technology to Chinese equipment maker ZTE Corp has exposed the soft underbelly of China's technological ambitions. At the center of the technology gap is semiconductors: the integrated circuits that power everything from smartphones to super computers and driverless cars.

In light of the growing tensions in the US-China trade and economic relationship, China has sought to accelerate its efforts to gain self-sufficiency and parity in semiconductors. Back in 2014, the central government set up the China National Integrated Circuit Industry Investment Fund. This fund is so low profile that it does not have its own website. But it is leading the national effort to catch up in the global semiconductor industry by

Big fund

China National Integrated Circuit Industry Investment Fund

Established: **2014**

Registered capital: **98.7 billion yuan (US$15.5 billion)**

Chairman: **Wang Zhanpu**

First funding round: **138.7 billion yuan**

Prominent investors: **China Development Bank Capital, China Tobacco, E-Town Capital, China Mobile, Guosheng Group, China Electronics Technology Group Corp, Beijing Unis Communications Technology Group and Sino IC Capital**

Recent investee companies: **Semiconductor Manufacturing International Corp, ZTE Microelectronics, Tsinghua Unigroup and Yangtze Memory Technologies**

Sources: MIIT, Bernstein Research, regulatory filings   SCMP

raising funds and backing semiconductor start-ups and research and development. The goal: help China become self-sufficient in chips. It is a key part of the 'Made in China 2025' Initiative

The state-backed investment entity known as the "Big Fund" represents the Chinese government's primary vehicle to develop the domestic semiconductor supply chain and become competitive with the US.

From: https://www.scmp.com/tech/enterprises/article/2145422/how-chinas-big-fund-helping-country-catch-global-semiconductor-race

---

China's 'Big Fund' Phase II Aims at IC Self-Sufficiency

By Luffy Liu 10.30.2019

China's "Big Fund" is rolling out its second phase of funding armed with $28.90 billion in its capital. The Phase II's goal is to build an independent, self-sufficient and "controllable" industrial chain for the Chinese IC industry. China's "Big Fund" is rolling out its second phase of funding through a just-incorporated company called the National Integrated Circuit Industry Investment Fund Phase II Co., Ltd. (National Big Fund Phase II). Compared to its Phase I that began five years ago, Big Fund Phase II is twice as big at 204.15 billion yuan ($28.9 billion), slightly exceeding market expectations. Phase II investment is anticipated to start as early as November this year.

From: https://www.eetimes.com/chinas-big-fund-phase-ii-aims-at-ic-self-sufficiency/#

"But," he continued in uncharacteristically earnest tones, "we now also have the full support of the Leadership to proceed with my plan—to *control* the pinch points…" He amplified the term by pausing for a few seconds. "Obviously, actual implementation may take years. Requires patience, discretion, and tact. But we do have the full and absolute support and commitment from the Leadership. We can proceed."

"We?"

"Yes, we. If this enterprise is to succeed—if we are to take control of these pinch point entities—it must not appear to be orchestrated.

Especially not by our government. We must operate below the radar. All moves must appear to be clean and above board. Any activity should appear to make industrial sense—to achieve higher growth or better synergies or whatever excuses you, industrial types, usually use for acquisitions. Full respect for intellectual property rights, labor and environmental laws, and so on. Obviously, we want these to be successful acquisitions and to end up with stronger and better companies. Only a thriving company makes a good pinch point."

He paused again and peered at Junjie, as if to make sure that he appreciated the points made.

"And," having satisfied himself that Junjie got it, he continued, "The Leadership has learned that not all decisions are best made at the top level. Some decisions—like picking winners and losers in the fast-moving technology field are best made the American way—by the people in the industry. People like…you. You are a good businessman. Very familiar with silicon technology and its supply chain. You have a good track record of starting and running technology companies. You even know how to build a pinch point company. So the Leadership would want you, or people just like you, to choose and acquire suitable companies that happen to be pinch points in your ecosystem. And if you do that…well…you would find the Leadership very supportive. Full funding for the venture. Support with business intelligence. Favorable treatment by the domestic industry. Understanding tax rules… Whatever is needed."

Professor Lao did not change his tone or modulate his intonations. There was no sense of anything clandestine or improper. He was just describing something that should be obvious to any A student.

"I see," Junjie responded, coolly and noncommittally. He was not sure how he felt about working with—or for—the government. He liked his sense of independence—being on his own, in charge of his own destiny. He would most definitely hate being a pawn in someone else's game or having to do someone else's bidding. But, on the other hand, government favors could be good. Easy money to grow his real business.

Still, collaboration with the government types is known to be awkward but necessary when—if—you join the big boys club.

He was unsure.

"Think about it, Junjie," Professor Lao urged—calmly and knowingly—like a parent guiding a child in making his own discoveries. "It could be good for your business. And it could be good for our industry. Insurance against a…what did you call him…a pig… like Trump. Here, take the chart. It may help you make up your mind," he concluded, rolled up the chart, and offered it to Junjie with an understanding smile.

He got up, indicating that the meeting was over, and walked Junjie to the door. And as they bowed to part, he patted Junjie on his shoulder and repeated, "Think about it, Junjie. Give me a call when you want to discuss it further."

Professor Lao did not seem to feel that there was any doubt that Junjie would cooperate, leaving Junjie with a vague feeling of resentment. Junjie had a gut-level urge to do exactly the opposite. He did not like to be, or be seen to be, predictable or as someone who can be manipulated to follow orders.

Tuesday, February 12
CHARM Inc., Haidian District, Beijing, China

Junjie was staring out of his window, idly watching the twilight-hour traffic inching along the street below. The view was full of bustle and color: shiny cars, brightly clad people scurrying in the cold, walking or riding the ubiquitous neon-colored bikes or E-scooters, and interminable traffic jams, pollution, and noise—feature that came with progress. Gone are the days of his childhood when the wide avenues of Beijing were filled by swarms of drab, monochromatic Mao-jacket-clad proletariat riding plain black bicycles. But he was not really paying attention to the scene nine floors below him or marveling at the changes that took place in Beijing over the last few decades. He was thinking…

In the morning, when he came to the office, he pinned Professor Lao's chart on his wall—next to the pictures of Feng and the kids from last summer holiday in Australia. Between the phone calls, meetings, and other activities that filled his day, it caught his eye and reminded him of the odd conversation with Professor Lao. But he was tired of looking at it. He knew that he needed to make bigger decisions first—before he delved into the details of the chart.

He had an intuitive reluctance to get involved with the government. Either because of his preference for independence, or the strong family lore that warned against it, or both. In any case, he has always been averse to working with the government types. He preferred to avoid dealing with the "functionaries" who, in his experience, were mostly uncouth, corrupt country officials who spouted whatever party line they thought would cover their butt and line their pockets.

"Wang ba dan!"[14] he muttered under his breath.

However, in the back of his mind, he knew that sooner or later, he would have to deal with them. *You cannot really succeed big in business without dealing with those wolves.* But up to then, he allowed his biases to dominate. And it really never became an issue that he had to handle—yet...

But Professor Lao was different. He may be connected with the government and the Leadership—but he was different. He was also of an old Beijing family. He was civilized—a gentleman. And not corrupt. Working with him—or through him—could be an opportunity to collaborate with the government and earn their approval while still avoiding dealing with the peasants? Maybe...

On the plus side, it could be an opportunity to grow his business. Easy money. He knew that with time, CHARM Inc. would grow into a business worth tens of millions of dollars—but not much more. Because he purposely set it up that way—selling test chips

---

[14] **Wang ba dan**: Literally an egg of a turtle in Mandarin. But in Chinese, an egg is a pejorative term for "offspring," and a turtle can be used to symbolize the lowest of the low, and is known as a species that also abandons its eggs. So much more derogatory than a combination of a "bastard" and "son of a bitch" in English.

and metrology[15] solutions to fabs to develop process modules and to maintain their equipment. He felt that there was a gap—especially in China—and hence an opportunity in that arena. And he genuinely enjoyed that field: bringing really fascinating physics to manufacturing technology development and in-line metrology. CHARM was a stable and steady business and would grow organically. But even as a company that Professor Lao would characterize as a pinch point, it would not grow beyond the size of its particular market—few tens of millions of dollars. It had no "scale." CHARM would never be a $1B business. To reach that size, he would need to find a way of scaling revenue in proportion to the number of wafers manufactured and not in proportion to the number of process recipes or different pieces of fab equipment. China produced millions of wafers. That is where the money was. And the way that CHARM was set up, he was not tapping into that flow of money.

But his people—the engineers and the staff who placed their faith in him—hoped that it would. They—more than Junjie—needed the business to grow. The proceeds from the sale of his previous company have set him and his family up pretty well—nothing extravagant but enough to guarantee some level of comfort and security. But his employees? He had a responsibility to them too—to repay them for their hard work and loyalty. Maybe this collaboration with Lao's scheme could be an avenue toward growing the business—and meeting some of their expectations. Maybe…

On the minus side, M&A[16] is a lot of work. Especially when buying a company abroad—in America. A lot of work. A lot more time in the airplanes. Many more nights in the hotels… The image of the woman in the white dress from the Liuxiaguan Teahouse flashed

---

[15] **Metrology**: A branch of science dedicated to measurement, defined as the process of comparing an unknown quantity with a standard of a known quantity. CHARM Inc. business develops the measurement methods and provides the standards used for calibration and maintenance of semiconductor manufacturing equipment.

[16] **M&A** (mergers and acquisitions): A general term used to describe the consolidation of companies or assets through various types of financial transactions, including mergers, acquisitions, consolidations, tender offers, purchase of assets, and management acquisitions.

through his mind. But he just shook it off… A lot of work. Was he ready for that? Did he really want to take on that extra load? Isn't he getting to the age when he should be thinking about slowing down and smelling the roses? He would be fifty next year. Almost an old man. Maybe…

On the other hand, buying a company in America may be an elegant way of establishing a foothold there. That may be good for his kids—if and when they chose to study abroad. Maybe also an insurance against an upheaval of some kind in China—like the ones his parents lived through. Maybe…

EXHIBIT 1.5 The Upheavals: WW2, Civil War, Great Leap Forward & Cultural Revolution

Second Sino-Japanese War (WW2): a military conflict primarily waged between the Republic of China and the Empire of Japan from 1937 to 1945. China fought Japan with aid from the Soviet Union and the United States. The Second Sino-Japanese War was a part of WW2 and the largest Asian war in the 20th century. It accounted for the majority of civilian and military casualties in the Pacific War, with between 10 and 25 million Chinese civilians and over 4 million Chinese and Japanese military personnel dying from war-related violence, famine, and other causes. The war has been called "the Asian holocaust."
From: https://en.wikipedia.org/wiki/Second_Sino-Japanese_War

Chinese Civil War: fought between the Kuomintang (KMT)-led government of the Republic of China (ROC) and the Communist Party of China (CPC) lasting intermittently between 1927 and 1949. The hostilities were put on hold during World War II, and resumed with the Japanese defeat. The CPC gained the upper hand in the final phase of the war from 1945–1949, generally referred to as the Chinese Communist Revolution. The Communists gained control of mainland China and established the People's Republic of China (PRC) in 1949, forcing the leadership of the Republic of China to retreat to the island of Taiwan.
From: https://en.wikipedia.org/wiki/Chinese_Civil_War

Great Leap Forward of the People's Republic of China (PRC) was an economic and social campaign led by the Communist Party of China (CPC) from 1958 to 1962. Chairman Mao Zedong launched the campaign to reconstruct the country from an agrarian economy into a communist society through the formation of people's communes. Mao decreed increased efforts to multiply grain yields and bring industry to the countryside. Local officials were fearful of Anti-Rightist Campaigns and competed to fulfill or over-fulfill quotas based on Mao's exaggerated claims, collecting "surpluses" that in fact did not exist and leaving farmers to starve. The Great Leap resulted in tens of millions of deaths, with estimates ranging between 18 million and 45 million deaths, making the Great Chinese Famine the largest in human history.
From: https://en.wikipedia.org/wiki/Great_Leap_Forward

Cultural Revolution, formally the Great Proletarian Cultural Revolution, was a sociopolitical movement in the People's Republic of China from 1966 until 1976. Launched by Mao Zedong, the Chairman of the Communist Party of China (CPC), its stated goal was to preserve Chinese Communism by purging remnants of capitalist and traditional elements from Chinese society, and to re-impose Mao Zedong Thought as the dominant ideology in the CPC. Estimates of the death toll in Cultural Revolution, including civilians and Red Guards, vary greatly, ranging from hundreds of thousands to 20 million. The exact figure of those who were persecuted or died during the Cultural Revolution, may never be known, since many deaths went unreported or were actively covered up.
From: https://en.wikipedia.org/wiki/Cultural_Revolution#Death_toll

Besides, he knew that M&A could also be exciting and fun. An exhilarating time when the air is filled with opportunities and possibilities and none of the day-to-day realities have come to roost yet. Maybe…

Maybe, you should stop being selfish just worrying about your foibles and give it…what is it that the Americans say…your "old college try." Do the right thing for the family and for your people. And maybe even for your country. Look at it with an open mind. Do it!

Junjie retrieved a magnifying glass from his desk—a gift from somebody or other that also happened to come in handy when admiring some customer's chip—got up and walked over to Professor Lao's chart. He knew that to get "scale" and grow his business he would need to move away from the process development and equipment maintenance arena and get closer to manufacturing operations. He followed the arrows on Professor Lao's chart, looking for suitable entities in the manufacturing ecosystem…

Maybe something in lithography? Scanners and aligners and other equipment used in litho? Manufacturing is all about litho. and it is the point where design intersects the manufacturing flow…

EXHIBIT 1.6 — Semiconductor PhotoLithography

Photolithography is a patterning process in Integrated Circuit 'chip' manufacturing. The process involves transferring a pattern from a photomask to a Silicon substrate. This is primarily done using machines equipped with optical light sources.

The word lithography comes from the Greek lithos, meaning stones, and graphia, meaning to write - literally writing on stones. In the case of semiconductor lithography, stones are silicon wafers and patterns are written with a light-sensitive polymer called photoresist. To build the complex structures that make up an Integrated Circuit, lithography and pattern transfer steps are repeated typically 20 to 30 times per chip. Each pattern being printed on the wafer is aligned to the previously formed patterns and slowly the conductors, insulators, and selectively doped regions are built up to form the final device.

Overview of the Lithography Process

Optical lithography is a photographic process by which a light-sensitive polymer, called a photoresist, is exposed and developed to form images on the substrate.
The general sequence of steps for a typical optical lithography process is as follows: substrate preparation, photoresist spin coat, prebake, exposure, post-exposure bake, development, and post bake. A resist strip is the final operation.

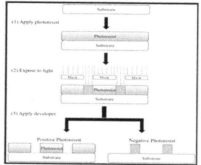

From:
https://spie.org/publications/fq06_p1-2_semiconductor_lithography?SSO=1
https://semiengineering.com/knowledge_centers/manufacturing/lithography/

Lots of money there. Could lithography be a way for him to plug into the manufacturing flow of money?

Maybe start a new company in the litho arena?

But he knew that it is a field that is way too competitive and complicated for a new entrant and that China is weak and unlikely to succeed in that space. A field dominated by few very large entities—like Nikon and ASML. He knew that the next generation litho technology—the so-called EUV—has taken more than twenty years to develop, costing God knows how many billions, leaving a single supplier in the field: ASML.

Aha! So ASML is a pinch point? Definitely! A big one.

EXHIBIT 1.7   **Extreme UV (EUV) for Lithography**

Extreme ultraviolet lithography is a next-generation lithography technology using light with an extreme ultraviolet (EUV) wavelengths, corresponding to about 13.5 nm. ASML is the sole EUV tool supplier.

<u>Few Quick Facts</u>

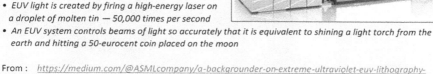

- *One EUV system contains 100,000 parts, 3,000 cables,40,000 bolts and 2 kilometers of hosing*
- *An EUV system weighs approximately 180,000 kg*
- *An EUV system ships in 40 freight containers, spread over 20 trucks and 3 cargo planes*
- *The mirrors used in an EUV system are extremely flat. If one was blown up to the size of Germany, the biggest bump would be less than 1 millimeter high*
- *EUV light is created by firing a high-energy laser on a droplet of molten tin — 50,000 times per second*
- *An EUV system controls beams of light so accurately that it is equivalent to shining a light torch from the earth and hitting a 50-eurocent coin placed on the moon*

From : *https://medium.com/@ASMLcompany/a-backgrounder-on-extreme-ultraviolet-euv-lithography-a5fccb8e99f4*

But that is a first-level activity on Lao's chart. Not suitable for me. Definitely not doing litho!

He followed the arrows in Professor Lao's chart to the next level of the hierarchy.

Photomask making? Photomasks could be an elegant way of side-stepping from a technology development base into volume manufacturing.

His gut feeling told him that the global market for photo-masks—including the captives—was probably worth somewhere around $5B to $10B—maybe even more with the complexity of lithography at the most advanced technology nodes. This area certainly had scale. He knew that photomasks are de facto a consumable item used by fabs. Regular wear and tear insured that they had to be routinely replaced for all existing designs in manufacturing—meaning, number of masks scaled with number of wafers as well as number of new designs.

He peered through the magnifying glass at the boxes corresponding to the entities that make photomasks for silicon manufacturing.

EXHIBIT 1.8   Photomask

A photomask is an opaque plate with holes or transparencies that allow light to shine through in a defined pattern. They are commonly used in photolithography – a key step in IC manufacturing process.

Lithographic photomasks are typically transparent fused silica – quartz - plates covered with a pattern defined in a chrome metal film. Photomasks are made by applying photoresist to a quartz substrate with chrome plating on one side and exposing it using a laser or an electron beam. The photoresist is then developed and the unprotected areas with chrome are etched, and the remaining photoresist is removed.

Quartz Photomasks are used with light wavelengths of 365 nm (mercury lamp), 248 nm (krypton fluoride laser), and 193 nm (argon fluoride laser). Photomasks have also been developed for other forms of radiation such as 13.5 nm (EUV), X-ray, electrons, and ions; but these require entirely new materials for the substrate and the pattern film. EUV photomasks for example work by reflecting light instead of blocking light.

A set of photomasks, each defining a pattern layer in integrated circuit fabrication, is fed into a photolithography stepper or scanner, and individually selected for exposure. The pattern is projected and shrunk onto the wafer surface. To achieve complete wafer coverage, the wafer is repeatedly "stepped" from position to position under the optical column until full exposure is achieved.

From: https://en.wikipedia.org/wiki/Photomask

Ugh! There must be a dozen of them. Dai Nippon, Applied, Toppan, Photronics, Hoya... Plus the captive shops that he knew large chip manufacturers like Intel, TSMC, and Samsung had... No major Chinese companies, though...

Most of the names were familiar to him—he has heard of them through industry gossip, magazines, conferences. Some of the bigger ones—the ones with internal R&D labs—were even his clients for the specialized metrology test chips. Well-known companies.

Definitely not one of Lao's "pinch points," he concluded.

Then, he did what Lao talked about. He peered at the chart through his magnifying glass, following the tiny arrows in the chart—

from the photomask makers up one level of the hierarchy—looking for companies that supply the photomask shops.

They buy equipment: electron beam writers provided by NuFlare, JOEL, Vistek, IMS—big companies. Big iron. Ugh. Not his kind of a thing…

They buy chemicals: photoresists and such. Provided by Merck, Dow, DuPont, Fuji, Tok, Sumitomo…and another dozen large chemical companies identified on Lao's chart. Clearly not a pinch point…

And they buy photomask blanks…

EXHIBIT 1.9   Photomask Blanks (Substrates)

A mask blank is a substrate for Lithographic Photomasks. Producing a photomask starts by producing the blank substrate:

1. *Create Quartz Substrate. The blank substrate is typically 6 inches square and 0.25 inches thick. It is made of pure fused silica - usually referred to simply as quartz. The surface of the substrate must be precisely polished to be extremely flat (~<10nm peak to valley) and defect-free.*
2. *Deposit Absorber Layer(s). A thin 'absorber' layer that can block the exposure light in a wafer lithography tool is deposited on the substrate. For binary photomasks, Cr compounds are the most common absorbers. For Phase-Shift Masks (PSMs), a special shifting material, such as Molybdenum ilicide, is used as the absorber, which is then coated with a pattern transfer film made of chromium.*
3. *Deposit Photoresist Layer. On top of the absorber is a thin layer of photoresist that a mask writer exposes typically using electron beam (e-beam) 'write' tools.*
4. *Etch, clean, inspect and pellicle*

From: http://www.appliedmaterials.com/semiconductor/products/photomask/info

Lithography process steps in advanced technology nodes use Extreme UltraViolet (EUV) light with 13.5nm wavelength (vs. traditional sources that use 193nm light wavelength (and/or above). EUV masks <u>reflect</u> light – as opposed to the traditional photomasks which <u>refract</u> (transmit) light. EUV photomask substrate is an extremely sophisticated multi-layer film stack. The films are deposited on a special 6" X 6" substrate. Between 40 and 50 alternating layers of Silicon and Molybdenum are deposited on the top of the substrate to act as a Bragg reflector that maximizes the reflection of the 13.5nm wavelength. This multi-layer reflector is then capped to prevent oxidation, typically with a thin layer of Ruthenium. A Tantalum Boron Nitride film topped by a thin anti-reflective oxide acts as the EUV absorber. The absorber has been engineered to have nearly zero etch bias enabling very fine feature resolution… An EUV mask blank with tight specs can cost more than $100,000.

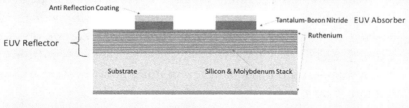

From: https://www.toppan.co.jp/electronics/english/semicon/photo_mask/

Aha! Look at that.

There were only a few companies identified as suppliers of blanks! And only two commercial suppliers of the EUV mask blanks! Toppan—big Japanese conglomerate. And BBI—a company he has not heard of.

Interesting… Maybe Lao has something here?

He returned to his desk, thinking…

Getting into mask making could be very valuable. Good area to be in. But moving directly into mask making would be difficult—highly specialized and prohibitively expensive. But moving into making mask blanks? Use mask blanks as a stepping-stone to progressively learn the mask-making technology and, overtime, assume a bigger piece of that $10B pie. Possible? Mask making was an area that China was weak at—so there was a long-term opportunity there. Meanwhile, masks, and hence mask blanks, were consumable items used by all the fabs, so there was a current steady and ongoing business there too. That felt analogous to his current business: a niche specialty that was essential to the mainstream with a steady ongoing demand for replacements. And it looked like making blanks for advanced EUV masks was also one of Lao's pinch points! Giving him access to cheap government money.

Interesting. Possible. Let's look at that. It would be free money from the government. What would I have to lose? Let's look at it—with an open mind, he reminded himself.

He picked up the phone, called Lao's secretary, and made an appointment to meet with the professor a day after tomorrow.

And he wondered if the message that the woman in the white dress from the Liuxiaguan Teahouse was not supposed to be a threat or a warning—but a temptation, a symbol of things that he coveted. Not just beautiful women, but, in this case, something else that he coveted: making his business into an international corporation worth a cool $1B. That was something he dreamed about—something that he coveted—in those delicious few minutes between sleep and wakefulness. Who knows?

Friday, February 22
Tsinghua University, Haidian District, Beijing, China

"Ah, Junjie! Come in, come in. Have a seat. I must say, congratulations!"

Professor Lao was positively beaming.

Not the usual scowl that his students are used to, thought Junjie wryly, still remembering that bubble-in-the-stomach anxiety that he used to feel when the prof would cross-examine him during the regular tutorial sessions he attended as a student.

But ever since that meeting at the Liuxiaguan Teahouse, Professor Lao has obviously chosen to reveal a different side of himself. This new Professor Lao has been kind, nice, cordial, supportive—even friendly. Junjie knew that this was because the prof needed him for this scheme of his, but he could not resist the charm. In fact, he reveled—positively glowed—in the attention of the omnipotent esteemed Professor Lao.

"Thank you, Professor... Congratulations for what? I have not done anything," he protested, taking his usual seat across the desk from Lao.

"Junjie, you always understate. But I like that... How about some tea?" Professor Lao smiled and toggled one of the switches on a small console built into the top drawer of his desk. It caught Junjie's eye because it looked like it was made in the 1950s.

Soon, a young uniformed woman appeared, pushing a tea cart, carefully poured the tea into two cups emblazoned with the purple-and-white university emblem, and silently left, leaving the room infused with the aroma of green tea.

"As per our chat last week," Professor Lao said with a smile, "I had a search done on this BBI company that you were interested in." He reached into another drawer and pulled out a thick folder. "I have read it... Junjie, I think you have picked a perfect pinch point company. So congratulations." He smiled and pushed the folder toward Junjie.

Junjie picked it up, hefted it to express appreciation for its volume, and quickly flipped through it—must have been hundreds of pages. A company profile report on Best Blanks Incorporated (BBI): a list of the principals, including personal and professional bios, list of clients, list of offices and employees, estimated company metrics—revenues, investments, profits, and losses—a copy of patents assigned to the company, copy of the news items mentioning BBI, list of publications, and all sorts of other data, it seemed…

"I know it will take you some time to digest," the professor continued, "but from what I can gather…and mind you, I am just an old academic. You may have a different perspective on it. It is a small and specialized company but apparently good. They seem to have more than 40 percent of the market for the photomask blanks. And much more importantly for us, we estimate that they have more like 80 percent market share for the EUV blanks. They are private— no public P&L data—so the business metrics are just estimates. But judging from their tax returns—yes, we had a peek at those—we are pretty confident of the numbers. Anyways, why don't you take it, read it, and then let me know what you think? But we are quite excited about this prospect… A pinch point—a choke hold—in litho-space. Perfect!"

Yes, the professor was positively beaming with satisfaction.

"Thank you, Professor. All right, I shall go through it," Junjie said, not quite ready to get excited. Experience has thought him that the old adage about the devil being in the details was, in fact, true. Also, intuitively, he distrusted a small company that remained small for a long time. Usually, that was an indicator of a poor business? Or poor leadership? Or a lousy market?

"And," the professor continued, "they seem to have all the characteristics of a classic pinch point company. I have been studying this kind of entities for a while. This Best Blanks Incorporated of yours is almost a textbook example." He smirked—a rare expression for him—and counted off on his fingers. "One, established and proven in the market. They supply just about all the mask shops. Two, high quality. Very few of their customers seem to have left them—ever. Three, small. Few tens of millions of dollar revenue per year. Four, very focused. They do blanks for photomasks for silicon chips and nothing else. Not even attempts to branch out into adjacent markets like, say, masks for flat panel displays. Five, a protective fence of a few key patents. They have some patents for polishing the glass and finished blanks. Six, apparently, some trade secrets. Tellingly, they seem to rely on homemade tools rather than commercial equipment. Seven, some specialized know-how. Their principals have been doing this since the nineties. All the attributes of a classic pinch point company. Perfect target, Junjie."

"Hmm. Well, I shall study it," Junjie repeated noncommittally.

"Yes, yes, please do," the professor concluded with a dismissive wave of a hand. He then deliberately reached for his teacup and sipped slowly.

Clearly about to change the subject, Junjie thought. He was getting to know the prof's habits and followed the lead taking a sip of his tea. *Hmm, good tea…*

Professor Lao cleared his throat, peered pointedly at Junjie over his glasses, and stated, "So, Junjie, from this point on, we will defer to you. You will take the lead with whatever you choose to be the next steps. Obviously, as you move ahead, we will need to maintain some…er…distance between you and the government or any of the government-affiliated entities. We do not want to raise any undue suspicions. So we have already…er…sanitized a few investment mechanisms that you can use. When you are ready, I will put you in touch with the right people, but you can assume that you have a very long credit line for this enterprise and access to some up-front cash flow to support the M&A expenses."

He then leaned forward in his chair and lowered his voice. *For emphasis?* Junjie thought.

"And obviously, discretion is essential. Here and especially abroad. There is no need to share with anyone whatever we talked about. That was just between us. Be careful. No one is to be trusted with the background story and the pinch point strategy. The whole transaction must appear to be a purely business-driven M&A. You will need to build a plan and a corresponding story that makes sense solely on commercial grounds. And after you acquire BBI, you will need to nurture and grow the company into a thriving business. But I believe you know that better than I do. So from this point on, everything is entirely in your hands. You are on your own, so to speak."

Professor Lao's obvious presumption that Junjie will cooperate again precipitated a sense of resentment in Junjie. But he let it pass and just nodded.

After a slight pause, Lao cleared his throat and lowered his voice in a way that amplified the sense of a conspiratorial bond. "On your own of course, until your country asks for your cooperation. Hopefully, it will never come to that, but if ever a time comes, I am sure that you will not forget, er, the favor," he trailed off, leaving the unstated obligation hover in the air.

Professor's hushed voice, and perhaps something in his verbiage, brought up the scene from *The Godfather* movie to Junjie's mind: "Someday, and that day may never come, I will call upon you to do a service for me…"

Then Lao added as an afterthought, "Perhaps you and I can get together and share tea on a more regular basis. Not here, though. Somewhere inconspicuous…," he trailed off.

"Yes, Professor. Of course. I shall study the report and think about it," Junjie said, not sure how to tell the professor that he is not committed. That he was not in. That he did not really care about the prof's pinch point strategy at all—not his cup of tea, so to speak. That he was mostly interested in an opportunity to fast track the growth of his company. That he still needed to think about the whole enterprise. But he decided to let it all slide—for the moment…

"Maybe we can meet for tea at Liuxiaguan Teahouse in a week" was all he said.

Professor Lao rose to walk Junjie out and added quietly, almost in whispers, "Look, Junjie, I know that you have been reluctant to work with the government in the past. Believe me, I understand your hesitation. Our families *are* similar in many respects. But over the years, I have had to collaborate with the paymasters of the university. After all, they *are* the guardians of our national heritage and are not all bad. Trust me, I will shelter you from the…er…crass and crude people in the Party. It will be all right. We have to be careful, of course, but this is the right thing to do, and I will guide you through the domestic political maze."

They bowed to each other and even shook hands as Junjie left, thick folder in hand, wondering how the professor knew so much about his reluctance to work with the government—down to his distaste for the country functionaries. And wondering what the professor meant by the last comment about needing to be careful. Was there a party faction that was against this strategy?

He did not think much about why the professor was so sure that he would cooperate with this scheme of his. He just wrote it off to Professor Lao being excited about the prospect—in as much as Professor Lao got excited about anything.

Ivan Jovanovic

Monday, March 4
Cortez Hill, San Diego, California, USA

Ivan woke, stretched, staggered out of bed to pee, made coffee, and crawled back under the covers. It was still dark outside, but he could hear the faint hum of an airplane overhead.

Must be six-ish, he mused idly, suspecting that it was one of the first flights of the day landing in San Diego Lindbergh Field. He turned on the radio and reached for his iPad to check his e-mails.

Some habits die hard, he thought.

Nowadays, there was never anything urgent that he would need to deal with before breakfast. He knew that he could enjoy his first coffee of the day in bed, admire the sunrise over San Diego through his window, listen to the *NPR Morning Edition* program, maybe even read an article or two in *The Economist*, all at whatever leisurely pace he chose and still not miss anything important. Standard morning routine, now that he was semiretired and did not need to rush to the office. But some habits die hard. He just *had* to scan through the e-mails, first thing. Or else, he knew that for sure a bolt of lightning would smite him dead.

Mostly the usual ads, PSAs, BBC, and Reuters's news briefs, *EE Times*, and Semiconductor Engineering dailies, and…and an e-mail from JunjieWu@CHARM.com.

Junjie? Is it our *Junjie? Interesting*, he thought clicking on it.

Ivan,

Hope all is well. It has been a while, and I hope
that you and the family are all fine. I am planning a biz trip to the US and was hoping that we
can get together. To catch up. And there are some
things that I would like your advice on. Will you
be in the Bay Area next week sometime? Or shall
I make a side trip down to San Diego? Let me
know.

Junjie

Junjie! It was *our Junjie—a.k.a. Albert!*

An image of Junjie of twenty-five-odd years ago conjured up
in his mind—young, eager, and confused. Ivan smiled remembering
hiring Junjie fresh from school—just after he completed his PhD at
Vanderbilt. And it turned out to be an excellent hiring choice. Junjie
was good: hardworking, talented, curious, eager to learn and with
a good feel for the technology—something that was relatively rare
amongst new grads. So Ivan brought him along when he moved from
Cadence to PDF.[17] Good talent was worth nurturing and preserving. All told, they worked together for six or seven years. And when
Junjie returned to China and started up his first venture company, he
tapped Ivan as an adviser. So they collaborated on a few projects and
stayed in contact till 2012 or 2013? Until Junjie sold that company.
And since then, pretty much nothing. *People get busy...*

Sure! Why not? he thought. *After all these years, getting together
with Junjie would be excellent.*

Ivan liked going up to the Bay Area anyways—always. To spend
some time, share a dinner or two, and maybe a walk in Shoreline
park, with Irina—his Russian girlfriend—who lived up there. To

---

[17] **Cadence** (Cadence Design Systems), **PDF** (PDF Solutions): Two real American
electronic design automation (EDA) software and engineering services companies. Note that their role in this story is fictional.

check on a few of his clients that he consulted for. To visit with his friends there and to catch up on all the gossip. Bay Area was the hub of the semiconductor industry, and inside gossip was always fun and interesting. The semiconductor business, the global powerhouse that it was, was still fairly provincial, so that an old guy like him knew, or knew of, just about everybody. That made the gossip that much more juicy and entertaining. Although now that he was out of the mainstream, and not sporting a badge of some known company, he found that his network was shrinking.

All the more reason to go up, he reminded himself.

Besides, now that he has taken advantage of a nice layoff package from Qualcomm—the last employer in his thirty-five-odd year career in the chip industry—he had nothing to hold him down. No day job to go to. And he lived alone—divorced and with all three of his kids grown up and gone. No family obligations to tend to. Nothing on his "worry list" to fret about.

He knew that if he went up to the Bay Area, all he would miss would be just his daily routine: forty laps in the pool, making up his one-kilometer swim; an hour or two bike ride, making up his ten- to twenty-mile route; and maybe some fave after-dinner TV program. Nothing particularly important or pressing… *Meh.*

Not too bad for a snotty-nosed kid from Belgrade, he commented to himself while pondering his current easy lifestyle and reminding himself of where he came from. He grew up in Belgrade, Yugoslavia. But due to a fortuitous set of circumstances, he avoided the wars and the disintegration of that country and all the misery that this brought to so many people back there—first by moving to England to complete his PhD and then by immigrating to America to enjoy what he thought of as a charmed life.

This then led him to go down his list of blessings. Good health for a sixty-seven-year-old body—although sagging a bit more than it used to and with a belly that was rounder than he would have liked. Three great children—now three wonderful adults, doing well on their own. In America—their safe, secure, and prosperous homeland. An exciting ride of a career—albeit now drawing to its sunset. A sense of security—boosted by a bank account that he knew could ensure a reasonably comfortable retirement. And living in San Diego—a place so beyond his reality that he first read about it in the "believe-it-or-not" section of his funny papers in Yugoslavia.

This was a part of his daily mantra that he repeated just about every morning and evening—aware of and very appreciative of the life he had. *Lucky, lucky doggie, you...* He laughed out loud but rapped on his head with his knuckles. This was his version of "knocking on wood" required to ward off provoking any mean spirits. Just a habit. *Sure, why not? Meh.*

He shrugged, checked the calendar on his phone for any appointments, and tapped on the Reply button on his iPad.

> Junjie!
>
> Great to hear from you! How ARE you?
>
> Yes, getting together would be excellent. I will drive up next week. How about drinks at the Red Lion bar—or for young guys like you the Doubletree hotel next to the San Jose airport? Tuesday at, say, 6:00 p.m.? Let me know if that works. Looking forward to it...
>
> Cheers!

Tuesday, March 12
Doubletree Hotel, San Jose, California, USA

They met in the lobby of the hotel—known as the Red Lion Hotel back in the Silicon Valley go-go days of the eighties and nineties—then a meeting place where many of the now-iconic chip companies were initially hatched up. Perhaps because it was within a walking distance from the San Jose Airport. They shook hands with Ivan resisting his natural urge to give Junjie a hug. He had paternal feelings for his old team, including Junjie. But he knew that this may be more appropriate in his native Yugoslavia than in Junjie's China. So he refrained.

They took possession of one of the tables in the lobby bar and ordered a couple of beers.

Ivan did not think that Junjie changed much but suspected that his western eye was not trained to pick up the subtle changes that aging brings to oriental faces.

Maybe a bit harder around the edges, Ivan thought to himself. *More chiseled.*

After they went through the usual superficialities—asking after family, health, and friends they had in common—they shook off the discomfort of a long gap in their familiarity and settled in for a chat, sipping their beers and munching on the nuts that came with the drinks. Like in the old times.

Junjie asked how Ivan was liking his new life of semiretirement with presumably a lot of free time. Ivan explained that it was not the free time but the flexibility that he was enjoying the most: the option to take on a consulting gig only if it was interesting, the freedom to drive up to San Jose to meet with a friend at a drop of a hat, the opportunity to juggle his gigs and spend three to four months a year in Montenegro, the ability to enjoy a bike ride in the middle of a day... They laughed about Ivan being a bit lost in the mornings without an office to rush to, given his lifelong habit of feeling obliged to be the first one in.

Ivan asked how was Junjie's new venture: CHARM Inc.[18] Junjie proudly described how he evolved the business from supplying just the charge monitoring wafers for plasma processing to selling wafers for all sorts of different process development and equipment maintenance needs and how he made CHARM a virtual sole source of a number of specialty test wafers not only in China but for the entire global industry and how he grew the business to a run rate of several tens of millions a year.

Yes, they chatted just like in the old times.

Junjie then sat up a bit and said, "Look, Ivan, that is what I wanted to talk to you about. I think CHARM is stable and steady. But as things are now, its growth is capped by the market that we are

---

[18] **CHARM Inc.:** A fictional company but somewhat modeled on and inspired by a real US company "Wafer Charging Monitors, Inc." See: http://www.charm-2.com/.

in. So I was thinking of growing by moving into an adjacent market…Photomask blanks… What do you think?"

"Mask blanks? Wow! Interesting! That is a big change from your current business, I would think?" Ivan blurted out his first reaction.

"Well, maybe so," Junjie responded, somewhat defensively, "but I feel like blanks are to photomasks like my test wafers are to silicon chip manufacturing. And so I do believe that there could be a lot of synergies and opportunities for growth, especially in China. I was thinking of acquiring BBI. Best Blanks Inc."

"BBI? Really?" Ivan asked, clearly surprised.

"Well, yes. Why not? I had an analysis done on BBI, and I noticed in the report that you were listed as one of their advisers. So that is the reason why I needed to talk with you," he trailed off.

"Really?" Ivan repeated. "I did not know that BBI had a Technology Advisory Board, and that if it did, that I was on it. I know Aki Roussos, their founder and CEO. Another old technology dude from San Diego. But I am not on their TAB."

"I just noticed your name mentioned in one of the reports—on a list of advisers. Not necessarily a TAB," Junjie clarified.

"Hmm. A while back—maybe ten years or so ago—at some conference or another, Aki sponsored a sort of a brainstorming session on the timing of EUV coming online. Apparently, he orchestrated this to help him gauge his investment in EUV mask blank technology. I participated in that. Maybe what you saw was some kind of a report that referred to that panel discussion." Ivan was thinking aloud.

"Maybe," Junjie confirmed. "So what do you think of BBI and Aki?" he pressed.

"Don't know much about BBI or its business. Like I said, Aki is another old technologist in San Diego—so I know him. We met a long time ago and overlapped for a while at Burroughs. But we were in different groups, so it is not like we are close friends or anything. Just people who know of each other and touch base at various industry events," Ivan explained with a shrug.

Then after a short pause, as random recollections and associations with Aki came to mind, Ivan added, "He is funny. You know his father is Greek, or Greek American, and his real given name is Archimedes. He says that when he was a kid, everybody in school called him Archie. Apparently, he hated this because there is a comic book series about a teenager named Archie[19] that everybody teased him about. But his mother is Japanese, and she called him Aki at home. So he switched to Aki and stuck with it. Interesting cross-cultural combo, Aki Roussos. And I do remember him mimicking his mother's attempt at pronouncing Archimedes in a strong Japanese accent. Very funny. Mind you, that was at some dinner or other, and we had a few," Ivan rambled on.

"So how about you let me treat you to a steak, and we talk about you being my agent for this…er acquisition enterprise?" Junjie asked pointing to Spencer's Restaurant across the lobby.

"Whoa!" Ivan laughed. "Steak sounds good, especially if you are buying—a drop in the bucket relative to what BBI will cost you. Sure." He then added, "As for being your agent, let's talk about that."

They drained their glasses and walked over to the restaurant, waited a few minutes to be seated, and settled into a booth. They ordered. Junjie commented that the one thing that he most missed in China was good American steak and serving size, which is apparently prohibitively expensive in Beijing.

This gave Ivan time to consider the offer, so he leaned forward and said earnestly, "Look, Junjie. I think of an agent," he made the air quotes, "as a sales guy who runs around, twists arms, and worries about all the loose ends so that he would get his commission. Like a lot lizard selling your house. That is just not me. So thanks, but no thanks… But if you like, I can introduce you to Aki, and you guys can take it from there? Cut out the middleman."

---

[19] **Archie Comics**: An American comic book series featuring fictional teenagers Archie Andrews, Jughead Jones, Betty Cooper, Veronica Lodge, Reggie Mantle, Sabrina Spellman, and Josie and the Pussycats. The initial Archie characters first appeared in Pep Comics no. 22 (cover, dated December 1941). The comic book series was very popular, and hundreds of issues were published all the way through to 2010s. Archie Comics characters and concepts have also appeared in numerous films, television programs, cartoons, and video games.

"I know, I know," Junjie responded with a smile. "Don't forget, I know you. I need you for the big-picture kind of things. For building the relationship. We can engage some lawyer to do the procedural stuff. That is not the problem. What I do need is someone that I can trust. Here. To initiate, guide, and oversee the effort. This kind of a transaction—if it is to take root—cannot be done from across the Pacific. I have a business to run in China, so I do need someone here focused on this effort. And you would be a perfect fit."

Ivan hesitated, and Junjie continued, "Also, I don't think that at this stage we should orchestrate a face-to-face. That will come later. It is too early now. People can get defensive when someone offers to buy out their business. I know I would. So if you could approach this Aki and sound him out…get a sense of how open he would be to selling his business or merging with CHARM. Get a sense of his goals and objectives. Develop a relationship. If he is open, then dealing with someone he knows—and presumably trusts—would make it easier for him too. He may view me as a hostile entity of some kind—especially at the outset. These kinds of transactions do need a middleman."

"Hmm. You clearly have more experience with M&A and have thought about this far more than I have," Ivan commented but still unsure.

"Yes, my friend, you would be a perfect fit to make this happen," Junjie reassured him.

The steaks were served, they shared the sides, and they enjoyed the rich flavor in silence for a while—both thinking.

"Look," Junjie pressed on, "in the long run, this M&A would not be successful without a lot of goodwill from Aki and his team. I don't want to just buy BBI assets. I want to buy BBI assets along with their intellectual property and know-how and client list and everything. I want to buy a functioning business—not a shell. For that, I am willing to pay a premium. And I want to grow it—not kill it. What I bring to the party is capital and a channel to the biggest growth market in the business, China. I need their technology and know-how and goodwill. So I need this to be implemented in a very friendly way. No hostility. I may need Aki to stay on—to ensure the continuity and to guide the transfer. To make his clients feel good. So the only way this works is if we handle the approach with tact and understanding. And they need to see someone they trust. So a middleman is a must. And you would be perfect. I know you. He knows you. You could be the impartial party who makes it come together."

"Hmm...," Ivan mumbled, still not sure. This was not like the normal consulting gigs that he engaged in.

"You would be perfect," Junjie repeated. "And, when—if—the deal does get done, a few percent middleman fee would definitely be appropriate. And I would carry your expenses in the meanwhile."

Wow. That money could be amazing. A middleman fee on a transaction like this could be a million or two. Wow. Half it, and it would still be amazing. No wonder lot lizards drive around in big fancy Mercedeses... But an agent? Ugh. On the other hand, why not? Ivan thought. *Nothing to lose in talking with Aki. One step at a time. It could be fun and interesting too. And it could end up being good for Junjie, good for Aki, and good for me. Why not...*

"Okay, Junjie, I will reach out to Aki, and let's see how it goes from there. But I am still not sure about being an agent. Let's shelf that."

For a moment, they were distracted by a woman, eating alone a couple of tables away, and talking loudly on her cell phone—disturbing the atmosphere of the quite dim-lit restaurant and looking somehow incongruous in a tight summery white dress.

Junjie suddenly glanced at his watch, as if reminded of something, and said, "Look. I have another...er, appointment. So I need to go. I remember you, years ago—back in Cadence—telling us that your grandma told you to never make an important decision without sleeping on it. So sleep on it. And then e-mail me in the morning and we can coordinate the details by phone. But I am so sure that you are the right fit for this, that I am not taking a no for an answer."

He waved the waiter down and asked for the dinner to be billed to his room, ordered a couple of after-dinner drinks, and said with a big confident grin: "In fact, I do believe that we should drink to it now."

Why not? Ivan thought.

"Let's drink to…aha…project Red Lion. How's that for a code name?" Junjie said with a smile and raised his glass. "Good name. Strong karma."

They clinked.

Why not? Ivan thought. *I'll talk to Aki when I get back to San Diego… Take it from there…*

Aki Roussos

Aki parked on the street about half a block from the edge of the cliffs facing the Pacific, took out the towel from the trunk of his car, and strolled slowly to his regular bench.

Other than a stiff, erect posture that seemed a bit unnatural—especially for a man who looked like he was in his fifties or sixties—to a casual observer, he would have appeared entirely unremarkable. Just a short older man strolling up to a bench and sitting down to admire the sunset over the Pacific. A closer observation would, however, reveal a striking square face with a hooked nose and a prominent cleft chin. Dark complexion: olive skin, jet-black straight hair, graying just a bit at the temples. A five o'clock shadow that even a close shave every morning did not hide by that time of the day. Hard to categorize: not Caucasian, not Latino, not Asian. Striking dark eyes—somewhat hooded, shining with intelligence, but somehow guarded and veiled. Giving a sense that there was more going on in his head than he let on. This was enhanced by a bolt-upright posture that gave him an air of formality—as if he was on a stage. But, in fact, it was just a habit that he developed since he was a child—trying to eke out all the inches that he could get from his five-foot-five stature that he was self-conscious about. Further observation would also reveal that he was a fastidious sort of a man. He wiped down the bench with the towel that he brought, folded it carefully to make a seat for himself, and gingerly sat on it. He placed his hands on his knees, and without slouching or appearing to relax in any way, he seemed to go into a kind of a yoga-like trance—breathing regularly, not moving, staring into the distance…

This was his thinking spot. A spectacular view—especially at sunset—of the Pacific and the soothing sound of the waves washing on the rocks below. Hypnotic. And very calming for him.

The beach below was his surfing spot since he was a kid. An easy walk from home when they lived in Point Loma—in the sixties and seventies—when he used to go and catch the waves every morning before school. Back then, surfing was more than a pastime for him. More than an escape from the bullying in school—for his relatively small stature, his mixed heritage, his nerdy ways… It was his touchstone. His identity. He kept returning to surf at this spot even after he moved north to Pacific Beach—first to attend UCSD then to have an easier commute to work in Sorrento Valley. Pacific Beach became a habit—and then his home. But he always came back to surf here. This was his spot.

Of course, it has been several years since he last went out. At first, it was because he just got busy—working while doing his PhD research—and found that he did not have the time every morning. Or even every second morning. Then it was because his mornings were filled with kid chores, and he found that sometimes he did not have the time even once a week—or once every two weeks. Then it was work and all the travel that it took to get his company going, and he did not manage to get here every month—or even every couple of months. And now—well, now he shivered and his sixty-year-old joints hurt just thinking about how cold the water would feel this time of the year—wet suit and all.

But he kept his spot. His bench. He found he could still get in the zone there—sitting on the cliff edge, listening to the waves, smelling the ocean and the kelp. His thinking spot. The spot where he, an introspective and an analytic kind of a man, made all the important decisions of his life.

And he had a lot to think about.

His normal equilibrium has been shaken up ever since that lunch with Ivan. He knew Ivan—well, mostly knew *of* Ivan—for years. When he got the e-mail last week asking to get together for lunch, his curiosity was piqued. It was odd. So he agreed, and they met on Monday at Sea Salt Del Mar with that great view of the Peñasquitos lagoon. And then Ivan dropped the bombshell and said that he had a friend who expressed an interest to buy his company and asked if Aki was remotely interested in something like that.

Sell BBI? What the fuck! Like someone asking him to sell his daughter. Really?

Or at least that was his first reaction—emotional. Ivan must have picked up on it and got defensive. He just kept repeating that he was only asking and that he was doing it as a favor to this friend of his. Nothing personal. Encouraged Aki to just think about it.

It was true. Aki has never thought about it. He has spent all these years—thirty years now—focused on building BBI. The idea of selling it was alien. He never really had the time for it. But even through the course of that lunch, as he recovered from the initial surprise, he realized that he should consider it—seriously and with an open mind. So he told Ivan that he needed to mull it over and that maybe they could get together in a week or two—one way or another.

So he came to his thinking spot. To consider for the first time the thought of life without BBI.

Life without BBI? Impossible!

BBI was his life's work—from inception on. After the few years at Burroughs, where he learned a bit about silicon chips; General Atomics, where he learned all about glass; and Photronics, where he learned about photomask making—he just knew it. In the pit of his belly. He knew that there was a gap in the industry—and hence an opportunity. That supply of high-quality blank substrates for photomasks was a problem that the semiconductor chip industry was wrestling with at the time—an opportunity for a company such as his BBI. And that it was the right thing for him. His vocation. And for the last thirty years, he has been nurturing it, growing it, caring for it. Made it into a business that it was then: they expected their production to reach a high of 250,000 blanks that year! Quarter million! With clients across the planet counting on it. With the best technology for making mask blanks—anywhere. Even the crazy EUV blanks. And with his people here and in Japan depending on it for their livelihoods.

Of course, BBI had paid back. Amply so. Gave him and his family a comfortable living. It did not make them into billionaires, but it afforded them a very good living. A house: first in Pacific Beach and then in La Jolla. Took care of all of Nicole's medical bills. Put her through college: private out-of-state school. A vacation abroad for Mary and Nicole every year—with him coming along when he could carve the time. Yes, BBI has been good to them.

On the other hand, he was getting on. He would be sixty in a couple of months. What would he do in five years? Ten years? Up to then, he has not considered an "exit plan" because he did not have to—yet. Maybe now was the time? And maybe this friend of Ivan's was an opportunity?

Truth be said, BBI has been like a member of the family—for him. Sometimes to the resentment of Mary and maybe even Nicole because it took him away so much of the time. When he was really honest with himself, he had to admit that he did use—maybe abuse—BBI as his escape hatch. To get away from the more painful things in life. It was so much easier to run and hide in the lab, in the airplane, in some business meeting or another than to deal with a child sick with leukemia. And with Mary's feeling stressed out and left alone to deal with all of Nicole's medical problems. He told himself—and her—that working and making the money was the best thing that he could do for their child. That this was his role—his duty. And with all the brilliance of hindsight, he was right. The very best care was expensive and paid for by the money he made through BBI. And it did cure Nicole. That was all behind them now. Thank God. But the walls that came up in their relationship then were still there, and given his reserved nature that made it impossible for him to discuss emotions, Mary still felt abandoned—possibly so forever. Truth be said, BBI was like a mistress for him. Like another, more constant and persistent "other woman." A lifelong obsession that has left him with no outside interests, no close personal friends, a somewhat distant relationship with his family… No life apart from BBI.

Maybe it was time that he came back? If it was not too late? Give Mary what she has so patiently been waiting for? If she would have him back?

And selling BBI—well, depending on the price—could set them up for good. There was no talk about the price that this friend of Ivan's was willing to pay, but when optimistic, Aki could imagine them walking away from BBI as wealthy people. Maybe even wealthy enough to set up Nicole for life. With an M&A multiplier[20] of three or four—hopefully—that could be as much as $50 to $70 million. After he paid off the loans and the options and maybe shared some of the benefits with his people, he could even end up with as much as $10 million. Enough. More than enough.

But even if wealthy—with money not a consideration—what would he do with his time? He has not developed any hobbies or any other interests. BBI has been all-consuming for him.

On the other hand, if he was to try and do anything else with his life, wasn't then the time? While he—and Mary—were still healthy and mobile? Do the classic things? Travel? Cruises? Proverbial drive across the country?

Grandkids? Wow!

Maybe use the money to help Nicole and Fred with something like IVF? Or adoption? Leukemia has affected Nicole's fertility, and they did mention that they would have liked to have children. Would be great to help.

And carrying on blindly, as is, didn't really make sense. Sooner or later, he did have to face the fact that he was getting old and that he needed to exit BBI some way.

Life without BBI? Possible… Perhaps possible, but is it desirable?

By the time he got up to go home, the sun has set, the last traces of orange glow were gone, the marine layer was moving in, and it was getting cold. He has not decided. He collected his towel and put

---

[20] **M&A multiplier**: In most simplistic terms, the ratio of company revenue to its sale price.

it back in the trunk of the car—where he kept it especially for these visits to his spot. He concluded that the right thing to do was to talk it over with Mary and Nicole. See what they thought.

He suspected that Mary would shrug and tell him that it was his decision—an aloof stance that she has assumed years ago. After she gave up competing with BBI for his time. So he knew that asking her was a form of procrastination. On the other hand, the fact that he would be underfoot all day, every day, was something that would affect Mary. She surely would have an opinion on that.

And Nicole? Nicole and Fred were on their own by then, of course. But she has had a rough life—with her leukemia. Maybe offering her a lifestyle of the rich while she was still relatively young would be some kind of compensation? Give her some joy that she missed out on. Maybe she would be the one who would like to go on those vacations and cruises and things. She was what…thirty-two… that year. Maybe she would like that. And then the kids? Maybe…

But on the drive home, a new thought came to mind—like a bolt of lightning.

What is the right thing for BBI? For the team and the clients?

He berated himself for thinking just about himself rather than doing what he preached and believed in: putting his company's and people's interests first. After all, he built BBI to be so much more than just him and his role in it.

He realized that the real question he should be asking was whether BBI was better off with him or without him—not if he was better off with or without BBI. In the long run. Was it likely to be better off with or without him ten or twenty years from then?

Despite his reluctance to allow it to percolate up to his consciousness, he knew the answer to that question—at the gut level. If BBI was to continue to flourish—if it was to survive him—then it was better off without him. BBI was a stable and steady business, and therefore, this was the right time to wean the company from his own personality and ego. Right time to nurture someone else to lead it into the future. To ensure that it survives him. With some kind of a graceful transition period while he still had the energy and vitality. To ensure that the new guy was right for BBI.

He realized that the idea of the end of his role in BBI—or even the end of his own life—was more palatable to him than the idea of an end of BBI itself. Up to then, he did not think much about abstract things like that. But it was clear to him that, emotionally, he related to BBI as a separate living entity. Not a thing. And that he wanted it to live on. After him. Maybe so that he would not be entirely forgotten.

So there, in his car, the answer became self-evident to him. He had to be open to this idea of selling BBI. Especially if the sale would lead to an infusion of capital that BBI needed to grow. He knew at the gut level that if BBI was to maintain its position in the market, then it had to scale up its capacity for manufacturing blanks for the EUV masks. Even though EUV blanks were not a big contributor to his revenue and bottom line up to then. But that was where the future was—EUV. And that required capital infusion—a lot of capital. Hence, for the sake of the company, he had to explore this offer. It was his duty and his responsibility to his team. He owed it to BBI.

Monday, April 1
Brigantine Restaurant, Del Mar, California, USA

"Hey, Ivan! How are you? And thanks for coming," Aki said as he handed the keys to the parking valet and walked up to meet Ivan at the entrance of the restaurant.

"Excellent, thanks. You?" Ivan responded shaking hands and questioningly eying Aki.

They were seated, admired the view of the Del Mar Racecourse, ordered, and exchanged other superficialities, apparently each reluctant to be the one to ask the question that was on both of their minds.

Ivan finally broke and asked, "So? Have you thought about it? Selling BBI?" Then he quickly added, "Or are you going to bite my head off for even asking?" The last with a big grin.

Aki was not in the mood to joke—this was his life they were talking about—and just said tersely, "Yes. And yes."

The blank expression on Ivan's face suggested that some elaboration was required.

"Look, BBI has been my life for the last thirty years. To me, it is a lot more than a place of work. So I did need to consider it from all sorts of angles. What would it mean to me and my family? What would it mean to my employees and clients? How would it work? I am still not sure. It would depend on how and when and all the other details. How much? But in principle, I guess I am open to listening."

"Oh, I must say I am a bit…surprised," Ivan reacted, raising his eyebrows and sitting back as if to take a better look at Aki. "I can imagine the feelings you have for your company. It is your baby. And for your people, I understand that you guys have been together for a long while. I myself get a bit paternal when thinking about some of the poor fools who worked with me for many years in many companies. I guess if I was in your shoes, I, too, would be reluctant… So if you do not mind me asking, what changed your mind? The last time we talked, I had an impression that you were closed to the idea."

"I was. Then I thought about it. I guess I am getting on in years. So it may be time. I am tired of living on airplanes. Maybe it is someone else's turn to take my place in that seat. And I don't know that I am ready to sell. I am just ready to listen," Aki repeated.

"I understand," Ivan said slowly. After a pause, he added tentatively, "You know, one of the few things I have learned in my life is that the thing to do is to always go *to* something, never *from* something," stressing the "to" and "from." "So if you don't mind me being a presumptuous self-appointed analyst, focus on what a sale of BBI would enable you to do rather than what it would free you of."

"Hey, I thought you wanted to help this friend of yours? Are you now talking me out of it?" Aki asked, only half-jokingly, somewhat surprised by Ivan's comments.

"No, no," Ivan protested. "I have no skin in this game. Asking you was a favor to Junjie—one of those 'poor fools' who used to work with me. But I really have no particular bias in the outcome. In the interest of full disclosure, Junjie did ask me to be his agent. But I turned it down and just agreed to broach the topic with you. Where and how this unfolds is up to you two. I will help if you guys want me to, but I will not be anyone's agent. Not my kind of a thing."

"Oh, I see. So how do you think you can help?" Aki was now not sure what was Ivan's role. Why was he even talking to Ivan about selling BBI?

"Frankly, I am not sure. I suggested to Junjie that after introducing you two, I should drop out, but he thought that a middleman is a constructive role in these transactions, so…maybe some kind of an adviser or a facilitator role. He thought that I may be able to help with…er…misunderstandings that could come up. He has been through M&A with his previous company, so he may be speaking from experience. I don't know."

They lapsed into silence for a while, concentrating on their respective lunches.

"You are right," Aki ventured slowly. "I don't really have a plan for life after BBI. And probably should. But…," he trailed off.

"But you thought that it may be the right thing for BBI," Ivan picked up the thread. "I am guessing that you are worrying more about your people, the clients, the company, your legacy, and other such things—rather than what you will do with yourself afterward. Like a parent sending off his kid to college. You may or may not be concerned about the empty nest syndrome, but you know that sending the kid away is the right thing to do regardless? I am just guessing."

"You are dead-on," Aki confirmed. "Yes, ever since you floated the balloon of selling BBI, I did think about what would be next for me. But in a way, that doesn't matter. The thing that matters to me right now is what would happen with BBI."

"Well, in that case, for starters, I will let Junjie know that you are open to a discussion. And then you two guys can explore all that," Ivan concluded. Then, seemingly as he started thinking about it, he added, "Up to you, but if I was in your shoes, I would insist that everything is done by the book from the very get-go. You should get some legal firm to advise you and represent your interests throughout the process… For starters, you need NDAs. You don't want someone like me blabbing and alarming your customers… You should also probably ask for some kind of a certificate of credit to verify the availability and the source of the funds. You probably don't want to sell BBI to some drug lord laundering his cash… And you need to set up some mechanism for managing the process. Something formal… Maybe you should consider some up-front commitment from him too—a break-up fee if things do not work out. After all, engaging in the process is going to cost you some BTUs…[21] Also, you will need to define some controlled mechanism that allows him a look into your business. He will have to understand your operations. Your customers. Your books… Come to think of it, you will end up sharing a lot of your secret sauce through the process, so maybe you need some noncompete commitment from him. In case things do not work out…maybe get a letter of intent first and only then engage in the M&A discussions. All in writing, of course…," Ivan rattled off items, between bites of his lunch, seemingly as they came to his mind.

"Hmm. Good ideas… Good points. How would you like to be *my* agent?" Aki asked, joking only partially. He had no experience with this aspect of business. An agent could be a guide and a teacher. Besides, he felt like Ivan got him. Seemed to understand his feelings about BBI.

Ivan laughed, put up his hands in a defensive gesture, and said, "No, no, no. Like I said, I don't want to be anyone's agent. Not my kind of a thing."

They talked on. About possible models of engagement. About Junjie. About what was important to Aki. About the various possible acquisition models. About what such a sale may mean for BBI's employees. And for its subsidiary in Japan. About mechanisms for assessment of the business value. About transfer mechanisms and timetables. About everything that came to mind…

By the time they finished, the restaurant was totally empty, and the waiters were pacing nervously around their table—willing them to go.

---

[21] **BTU** (British Thermal Units): A term used in engineering colloquialism to mean just generic energy of any kind.

Wednesday, April 17
BBI, Sorrento Valley, San Diego, California, USA

"All right, gentlemen, let's do this… Presumably the first of many teleconferences to come."

Even though only Aki and Ivan were present for the Skype call in the small conference room at BBI headquarters, with Junjie projected on screen—also alone in his office in Beijing—Ivan was actually standing. And wearing a jacket and a tie. Aki assumed that Ivan thought this would further amplify the sense of formality that he wanted to promote.

"I am guessing that you gentlemen have already done the searches on each other," Ivan opened, "and, therefore, that this may be somewhat superfluous, but why don't we begin with formal introductions? And take it from there. Junjie, would you mind going first?"

Following Ivan's lead, Junjie stood up, gave his brief bio, and then outlined his motivation for the proposed acquisition, describing his vision for the combined company.

."My big picture view of my business is that we bring specialized technical knowledge to solve niche problems of the semiconductor industry. At CHARM, we started by using programmable EEPROMs[22] to develop tools for controlling plasma[23] processes. We are now the biggest and possibly the only supplier of charge monitor wafers in the world. We then moved into providing all other types of test wafers. For process module development and calibration of fab equipment. And now we pretty much own that market too. We

---

[22] **EEPROM**: Electrically Erasable Programmable Read-Only Memory—a type of nonvolatile memory.

[23] **Plasma**: A state of matter consisting of ionized gaseous substance characterized by physical properties that are different from those of the usual solid, liquid, or gas states. Examples, neon signs, fluorescent lights, arc welding…

are now thinking about getting into MEMS[24] technology to expand our test wafer offerings and to become a truly unique supplier in the packaging market too." He paused to catch a breath, and then continued, tapping the table for emphasis, "If you zoom out, the common denominators are [a] good people with specialized technical knowledge, [b] the will to think out of the box and apply this knowledge in some new way, and [c] familiarity with the silicon technology and deep relationships with manufacturers, required to understand—really understand—their pain points where we can bring value. And where we can dominate a niche and make good margins."

He then pointed at Aki and made his point. "It seems to me that BBI fits very well into this model. You and your people, Aki, bring the specialized technical knowledge—in your case for making mask blanks. You have a great track record of applying that knowledge in new ways. For example, EUV mask blanks are entirely different from the transmissive quartz blanks that you grew up on, but look, you now own the market for EUV blanks! This is a known pain point. A real valuable niche... So I think of this conversation as merger rather than acquisition talks because I believe that there are real synergies. You bring the specialist technical knowledge, and I bring the relationships with the fastest-growing marketplace in the industry—China—and the capital that comes with that. All we need is the will and the imagination to leverage the combination."

He spoke very deliberately giving an impression that this is something that he has thought a lot about rather than some kind of a standard spiel.

Aki then followed suit and recited the blurb about himself and his company—well-practiced in all the meetings with the clients. He emphasized that his prime interests were the security for his people, the capital needed to scale EUV capacity, and the general wellbeing of BBI after the proposed acquisition.

---

[24] **MEMS**: MicroElectroMechanical Systems are miniaturized mechanical and electro-mechanical devices that are made using technologies analogous to the semiconductor chip technology. Examples include various type of sensors ubiquitously used in smart phones, such as accelerometer, gyroscope, proximity and touch sensors, microphones, fingerprint sensors, etc.

"Well, it sounds like you gentlemen see eye to eye," Ivan commented, probably to encourage the dialogue. "Certainly so, as far as the end goal is concerned. I hear words like infusion of capital and nothing about costs or efficiencies or economies of scale."

As the conversation developed and they all loosened up a bit, Aki felt...reassured. He saw a "kindred soul" in Junjie with similar attitudes and values, not some pushy, smug young pup with an MBA who thought that he knew it all but an experienced technologist and an innovative businessman. And somebody who seemed to care—really care—for his company.

Hmm, I like that... Emphasis on technical knowledge. And people. An interesting and unique spin on the business side, thought Aki, a bit surprised. He was prepared for some acquisitive, hard-nosed money type, not a technologist with an out-of-box business approach. *I like him*, he thought, despite himself. *If anyone is going to get their hands on BBI, someone like this Junjie is probably not a bad choice*, he concluded. But he warned himself that it was still early days and that he has to be cautious—not impulsive.

Gradually, perhaps subtly guided by Ivan, they eased into talking about the proposed merger.

They talked about the possible models and agreed that the simplest approach would be a straight acquisition by CHARM—rather than setting up a new combined entity. Aki would then pay off his obligations and wind down BBI, an independent entity—to be replaced by BBI, a subsidiary of CHARM.

They, of course, agreed on the continued employment of all the BBI people and on a transition period, where Aki would assume a role of an EVP of the Mask Business Unit for a period of at least a year or two—to reassure BBI employees and clients of the continuity of the business and to drive the synergies.

They agreed on some kind of a phased approach, with phase 1 focused on mutual fact-finding, phase 2 on developing a plan for the transfer of assets and know-how, and phase 3 on developing the postacquisition growth plans, including the required investments. They felt that the right way to start the relationship is to trust each other and so agreed that neither party would have any obligations toward the other until the final consummation of the deal.

They even addressed Ivan's role and agreed that his function would be to champion the interests of the future combined company-to-be. That way, he would not be an agent for either Junjie—presumably interested in minimizing the cost and biased in favor of CHARM, or for Aki—presumably interested in maximizing the price and biased in favor of BBI. They agreed that since both Junjie and Aki had businesses to run, Ivan would assume the role of an executor for the merger-related activities.

They discussed some of the mechanics and agreed that both parties should have a legal firm licensed in the US with subsidiaries in China and Japan to formally manage the substantive data exchanged between the parties. And they agreed to get together on regular basis to review the progress and ensure that the momentum is maintained.

They even agreed to keep the negotiations private until they were both ready to inform their employees and clients and that, in the meanwhile, they would use a code name "Red Lion." This was so as not to cause undue alarm and to be able to jointly shape the appropriate messaging.

The two hours that were scheduled for this introductory meeting flew by.

As a part of closing the call, Junjie commented, "I feel good about this. As I said, I do believe that the only way that this union can be successful is with a lot of goodwill and zero hostility. I feel this is a good start. Aki, I do look forward to a long and lasting collaboration. Thank you."

"Thank *you*," Aki responded. "I, too, feel good about it so far. And if I may add a personal comment, thank *you* for initiating this. Prior to this, I have not thought about an exit plan at all. And now I believe it to be essential for BBI's long-term future…"

That evening, after taking care of the daily business, Aki went back to his bench on Sunset Cliffs. To think about things. To digest the events of the day…

The beginning of the end, he mumbled, feeling sort of bittersweet. Maybe somewhat empty. Sad—maybe nostalgic—for himself and the life he had with BBI that is now winding down.

But knowing that it was the right thing for the company and its people—and maybe for his family too—buoyed him up.

The right thing to do, Archimedes, he encouraged himself. He always used his full proper name when talking to himself—especially when it came to making important decisions—just the way his father used to when he was a kid.

And…feeling relieved. The stress of the responsibility for BBI—a burden that he carried for so long that he was entirely unaware of it—was easing. Not gone yet of course—there were still so many things to be done to bring it off. But now that he had a defined path to exit, the stress was easing. He felt like…like the proverbial weight was lifted—or lifting. It felt good.

Just a matter of execution, he assured himself.

Part 2

THE BLUE DRAGON
SHRUGGED

The Snag

Ivan Jovanovic
Thursday, June 27
Cortez Hill, San Diego, California, USA

"Houston, we have a problem!"

"What's the problem?" Aki demanded the moment all three of them got on line. "At the last Red Lion call, you said that everything was on track."

"It was. Back then. Now, well, now we have the response from CFIUS," Ivan said flatly.

Up to that point—over the last eight weeks or so—it has been pretty smooth sailing. Just the usual M&A wrinkles to iron out. Easily done with both CEOs committed to the process and aiming for a similar end game.

Getting Junjie and Aki together outside their regular Red Lion weekly call was not trivial—they were both busy hands-on CEOs. Giving them only an hour's notice did not help—especially with the fifteen-hour time zone difference. But this was critical, and both Aki and Junjie were motivated and made the time.

"C-who? I am sorry, I must have not been paying attention," Junjie spoke up.

"CFIUS, the Committee for Foreign Investment in the United States, CFIUS. It is a part of the Treasury Department of the US federal government," Ivan clarified. "According to the standard procedures, we applied for CFIUS approval for the merger. This was supposed to be a procedural step. No one expected that the feds would have a problem with a small deal like the one we are talking about here. So we did not talk much about it at the regular Red Lion status meetings, which is why it may be unfamiliar to you. It was supposed to be just one of those standard forms that had to be filled out and that your legal firms completed as a part of a routine."

"And," Aki and Junjie demanded in unison.

"And CFIUS has issued a temporary injunction that bars the sale."

"WTF! Why? That makes no sense! Why does the federal government care if I sell my business as long as we pay all the taxes?" Aki burst out.

"Well, they do not clarify, nor, according to the lawyers, do they have to clarify their reasons. So no matter how much or little sense it makes to us—we cannot undo it. But," Ivan paused for the dramatic effect, "but, I just got off a call with this lawyer in DC—supposedly a CFIUS whisperer.[25] Apparently, dealing with CFIUS *is* his business. Anyways, according to him, there are some good news and some bad news for us in the CFIUS response." Ivan talked quietly, in steady and calm matter-of-fact tones, hoping that this would help to contain the outbursts of frustration that he anticipated from both Aki and Junjie.

---

[25] **Whisperer:** A person considered to possess some extraordinary skill or talent in managing or dealing with something specified. For example, in popular culture, a person who excels at calming hard-to-manage animals based on an understanding of the animals' natural instincts.

EXHIBIT 4.1   The Committee on Foreign Investment in the United States

 U.S. DEPARTMENT OF THE TREASURY

CFIUS is an interagency committee authorized to review certain transactions involving foreign investment in the United States, in order to determine the effect of such transactions on the national security of the US.

Members of CFIUS include the heads of:

- Department of the Treasury (chair)
- Department of Justice
- Department of Homeland Security
- Department of Commerce
- Department of Defense
- Department of State
- Department of Energy
- Office of the U.S. Trade Representative
- Office of Science & Technology Policy

Observer and Participants, as appropriate:

Office of Management & Budget
Council of Economic Advisors
National Security Council
National Economic Council
Homeland Security Council

The Foreign Investment Risk Review Modernization Act of 2018 (FIRRMA)
The Foreign Investment Risk Review Modernization Act of 2018 (FIRRMA) expands the jurisdiction of the Committee on Foreign Investment in the United States (CFIUS) to address growing national security concerns over foreign exploitation of certain investment structures which traditionally have fallen outside of CFIUS jurisdiction. Additionally, FIRRMA modernizes CFIUS's processes to better enable timely and effective reviews of covered transactions.

From: https://home.treasury.gov/policy-issues/international/the-committee-on-foreign-investment-in-the-united-states-cfius

---

"Bollocks!" Junjie exclaimed, very uncharacteristically for him. He rarely swore. "I thought that we had a cumbersome and corrupt bureaucracy here in China. I knew that dealing with the Japanese government can take forever. I worried that the state of California may impose some extra taxes. But I did not think that the US federal government would care. Why? Is it because CHARM is a Chinese company?"

"Maybe," Ivan responded, "given the political situation between the US and China, that is a possibility. But like I said, they do not clarify their reasons, and figuring out their motivation is pure speculation at this time."

"Okay, okay. So what are the good and bad news? What options do we have?" Aki asked, clearly trying to be constructive.

"Well, according to the lawyers, CFIUS can either clear a transaction or recommend barring it. If it flags a transaction, then the proposed deal is referred to the president, who can issue an executive order that permanently stops it."

"The president of the United States!" Junjie interrupted. "No way! You are kidding! He surely has more important things to worry about than our little deal." Junjie just could not believe that the president would get involved with any deal worth less than a few billion dollars.

"Or not," Ivan continued, ignoring Junjie's snarky comment. "The injunction we have received is a temporary order. They have neither cleared the sale of BBI, nor have they referred it to the president. We are in limbo right now."

"So?" Aki asked.

"Well, this CFIUS whisperer says that the way the committee operates is that they basically use the forms that we provided to fill out a checklist. That is step 1 in their process—apparently completed by the junior government staffers as a matter of procedure. Presumably, this checklist of theirs has been built up overtime and covers all the government concerns. If all the boxes are checked, then the transaction is cleared. Done. But if and when there is a box that is not checked, then the matter is referred to the senior CFIUS officials. Normally, these senior officials would then consult with their experts—either on their staff or with other branches in the government or even with outside trusted entities. That is step 2 in the process. Then based on the inputs of these experts, they make the determination to either wave, or flag, the transaction. Step 3 is when they flag a transaction and refer it to the president. This is normally based on national security arguments—typically if one of the parties is somehow associated with the Department of Defense or is deemed to be essential to the US economy. Step 4 is when the president signs the executive order that bars the transaction."

"Wow, Aki, congratulations! I bet you did not know that BBI is so very essential to the US economy," Junjie interjected sarcastically.

Hmm, this seems to have really gotten under Junjie's skin, thought Ivan, quite surprised with Junjie's negative attitude. *Very uncharacteristic for him.*

"Okay. So. We are blessed by a cumbersome government bureaucracy. And?" Aki asked, still trying to understand the issue.

"Well, our request is apparently stuck in step 2. Trump administration is a bit dysfunctional, and nowadays the government bureaucracy is empty. There are apparently upward of seven thousand vacancies in DC right now. So the CFIUS whisperer thinks that there is some checkbox in our application that has not been ticked, and that the committee is just sitting on the request because there are no experts that they can consult. Sort of like a pocket veto."

"So?"

"So we need to figure out what was the reason that might have caused the problem with that checklist of theirs. Back in step 1. And then decide what to do," Ivan concluded.

After a pause, he got to the key question, "So, Aki, has BBI done any business with DoD?"

"DoD? Department of Defense? Let me think," Aki ventured slowly while collecting his thoughts. "Well, yes and no. DoD has a little private fab in Maryland with a captive mask shop. They apparently use it to make some specialty stuff for the military. A few years ago, BBI has provided blanks for that mask shop... But this DOD fab is way behind the industry—maybe three or four nodes behind. When we worked with them, they were at something like the ninety-nanometer node when the rest of the industry was pushing twenty nanometers. So the glass we provided was run-of-the-mill kind of stuff. Nothing special. No particular sensitive or specialized technology. You could probably get something equivalent off Corning or some other regular glass provider for a dime a dozen. In fact, they probably did—because they have discontinued our engagement, and we have not dealt with them since...2012 or thenabouts."

EXHIBIT 4.2 **Silicon Technology Nodes**

Technology node (also process node, process technology or simply node) refers to a specific generation of silicon manufacturing process and its design rules. Generally, the smaller the technology node means the smaller the feature size, producing smaller transistors which are both faster and more power-efficient. Historically, the process node name referred to specific dimensions - including the gate length and M1 half-pitch.
Moore's Law is typically expressed in terms of the cadence of introduction of new technology nodes as a proxy to number of transistors per chip – one every two years or so...

Year	1971	1974	1977	1981	1984	1987	1990	1993	1996	1999	2001	2003	2005	2007	2009	2012	2014	2016	2018	2019	2021
Tech. Node	10 µm	6 µm	3 µm	1.5 µm	1 µm	0.8 µm	0.6 µm	0.35 µm	0.25 µm	180 nm	130 nm	90 nm	65 nm	45 nm	32 nm	22 nm	14 nm	10 nm	7 nm	5 nm	3 nm

Lithography Generation	Hg Lamp $\Lambda=400nm$	KrF Laser $\Lambda=248nm$	ArF Laser $\Lambda=193nm$	EUV $\Lambda=13.5nm$

Recently, the number denoting a technology node has lost the physical meaning it once held. Modern technology nodes such as 14 nm or 10 nm refer purely to a specific generation of technology and do not correspond to any feature size. Additionally, the size, density, and performance of the transistors are no longer consistent across different foundries. For example, Intel's 10 nm is comparable to tsmc's 7 nm. Nevertheless, the naming convention has stuck and is used to denote the relative advancement of a given technology.

From: https://en.wikichip.org/wiki/technology_node and https://en.wikipedia.org/wiki/22_nanometer

"Aha! That must be it!" Ivan exclaimed. He raised a finger as if to emphasize its significance—even though this was just a phone call and there was no one there to see him. "It is exactly the kind of a thing that the CFIUS whisperer mentioned. Apparently, he has dealt with analogous cases. The problem is that an expert is required to make the determination that a technology is not essential for DoD. And since there are no experts to be consulted, there is no determination. And so CFIUS is stuck."

"So?" Aki pressed.

"So according to this CFIUS whisperer, the options we have are the following—[a] we can try to file an appeal with CFIUS and attempt to convince them that there are no national security issues, [b] we can try to pull the political strings—representatives, senators, lobbyists, or people like that—who could pressure CFIUS to move on the request and hope that they make the right decision…"

"What? C'mon!" Aki interrupted. "BBI is a small company. We do not have lobbyists in DC or senators in our pocket or anything of the sort. This sounds like big government bullshit geared for large companies. It is just stupid for something like BBI."

"[C]," Ivan continued, ignoring Aki's outburst, "we can put everything on hold and wait for a time when we think CFIUS would be more reasonable and reapply." Ivan summarized the content of his conversation with the CFIUS expert—at the rate of whopping $1,200 per hour.

After a short pause, he added, "Or, I suppose, [d] we can try to figure out some ways of working around CFIUS altogether. There are always ways of working around the system. Loopholes and whatnot."

"This is ridiculous!" Junjie interjected, clearly angry and frustrated.

"Well, ridiculous or not, it is what it is," Ivan stated, still wishing to contain the venting. "Look, according to the CFIUS rules, we have forty-five days to file an appeal. Plenty of time. So this is what I suggest. We take a week to think about this. Do nothing in the meantime. Freeze everything and focus on pondering our options."

Silence. Ivan expected that neither Aki nor Junjie would be happy about the proposal. They—as usual for the type of people who end up being company CEOs—would have preferred the activity of attacking problems rather than the passivity of admiring them. But they did not seem to have a better idea and stayed silent.

"Okay, it is agreed then. Let's take the week to calm down, consult with the lawyers, and think about it. I will schedule a video call a week from now, and we'll take it from there," Ivan concluded.

They hung up with Ivan thinking that he should clear some time on his calendar to hold Aki's and Junjie's hands, consoling and counseling. *Probably individually—one at a time. This has got to be frustrating for them...*

Consequences 1

Ivan Jovanovic
Friday, June 28
BBI, Sorrento Valley, San Diego, California, USA

"Well, CFIUS sucks! The feds should all be lined up and publicly flogged, and California should secede from the union," Ivan joked in a hope of easing the tension that he expected from a pissed-off Aki. "So other than the CFIUS thing, how are you?"

"Good. Surprised, I guess. This sort of came out of the left field," Aki responded, reluctantly turning away from his PC and facing Ivan.

Clearly not in the mood for chitchat.

Ivan came to Aki's office. With Aki's full schedule, the meeting had to be pretty late in the day. At that hour, the BBI building was deserted and felt hollow. Presumably, most of the employees had better things to do on that Friday night than working late. The dimming gray light of the dusk was accentuated by the marine fog rolling in from the ocean and creating a somber aura. The canyon that Aki's window faced—one of the many that crisscrossed San Diego county—was looking almost eerie. Colorless with just shades of gray. Ominous somehow.

"Well, I thought we should talk about it some," Ivan ventured tentatively, feeling his way around the potentially emotional minefield.

"What's there to talk about?" Aki spoke in normal flat and even tones. "It is frustrating. By now, I have become quite attached to the idea of selling BBI, so I am feeling like my candy has been snatched away from me. Frustrating and irritating. Back to square one."

Hmm, he is clearly over the initial surprise and has already parsed his feelings. No need for a shrink session, Ivan thought, relieved that his concerns were misplaced and that he did not need to deal with Aki's emotions. *He is ready to move to the "action" part of SARA...*[26]

"Yes, understandable. It is a bummer that this came up, but I guess some monster had to rear its head. CFIUS is ours. Maybe it should be called Cerberus,"[27] Ivan added, hoping that Aki would get the reference from the Greek mythology. The blank look on Aki's face told him that he did not, so Ivan just moved on. "Okay then, are you ready to kick around some of the options you have?"

"Yes, tell me again what are those," Aki responded, sitting up a bit.

"I think you have basically three options. Clearly, you should consult with the lawyers and engage this guy in DC before you pick one, but in my opinion, I think it boils down to [1] you appeal the decision, [2] you wait them out until there is a political change, or [3] you ignore CFIUS and find a way around them." Ivan counted the options on his fingers.

"And? What does the Wise Old Man think? What are the pros and cons?" Aki asked, making the air quotes around "Wise Old Man," the title that Aki and Junjie jokingly gave to Ivan.

"I am glad you asked," Ivan responded with a wide grin—still trying to lighten the atmosphere. He has spent the day discussing the situation with the various lawyers and thinking about the feasibility of each option, so he was prepared for the question.

---

[26] **SARA**: An acronym for "Surprise-Anger-Rationalization-Action": sequence of normal reaction to bad news, as thought by some management courses.

[27] **Cerberus** (Greek mythology): A multiheaded dog that guards the gates of the underworld to prevent the dead from leaving—sometimes referred to as the hound of Hades (hell).

"Appealing the ruling seems like the right thing to do. But it would require someone on the other end of the conversation that is listening and *understanding*. If the guy in DC is right, the problem is that, right now, there is no such person at CFIUS. So in the absence of political muscle, this may be a losing proposition."

"Okay. Scrap that one. Next?" Aki responded sullenly.

"No, no. It is a valid option, and it is your decision. I am just giving you an opinion."

"Okay, and option 2?" Aki clearly did not seem to want to dwell on it.

Maybe because it involves political muscle, thought Ivan to himself but just moved on.

"Well, the problem with waiting it out is that it would be open-ended. Reading the political tea leaves, I would guess that you have to wait at least until Trump is gone. So either a year or, God forbid, five years. Plus whatever time it takes to actually staff up and change the direction of the government bureaucracy."

"Five years! Scrap that. I may be dead by then," Aki reacted, even more downcast.

"Well, you can also try to do it…er…let's call it the Yugoslav way," Ivan said. "Work around the system. I don't know the exact legalities, but in principle, I suppose that if you were a wily Yugoslav, you could think about transferring all the technology, IP, know-how, and maybe even the physical assets and the people to your Japanese subsidiary. And then sell that subsidiary to CHARM, leaving BBI–USA an empty shell. Or something along those lines. I suspect that a deal like that would end up in no-man's-land, so to speak. You would be selling a foreign subsidiary and therefore presumably would not be under CFIUS jurisdiction. And as far as Japan is concerned, you would be selling a subsidiary of a foreign company and therefore not subject to government approval. Or something like that…"

"Is that legal?"

"I believe that a solution along those lines could be found. But I am not a lawyer, and if I was in your shoes, I would not take my word for it. You need to consult with the professionals—people who know a lot more than I do about it. International and business law types." After a bit of a pause, Ivan added haltingly, as if thinking aloud, "However, even if it is legal or if it can be made to look legal, no matter which way you turn it, it would not be by the book."

"Ugh. Meaning?"

"Well, it depends on all sorts. But if I was in your shoes and I chose that path, it would cost me some sleep. And the question you have to ask yourself is whether selling BBI to CHARM at this time is worth that to you."

"Ugh."

"And, come to think of it," Ivan added, as a new idea came to him, "if you are set on selling BBI, the fourth option you could consider is selling to someone other than CHARM. A US-based company or maybe an NATO-country company or something like that. You would know the possible candidates better than I. We did not talk about that in our context," Ivan said, pointing to the two of them, "but if I was in your shoes, I would think about that too."

A long silence, with Aki leaning back in his chair, thinking, absorbing, and internalizing the options in front of him.

"This is serious. I need some time to think about it. Maybe on the next call with Junjie, we can sound him out on how long is his fuse. How long is he willing to wait for us to unravel this snag."

"Okay." Ivan pulled a pad of paper—ruled into metric based tiny squares—carefully selected one of the six neatly arrayed pens that he had in his old-fashioned laptop bag that he always toted about and jotted down a note.

"Ivan, thanks. These are all good and wise words... So there are no magic bullets to make CFIUS go away," Aki concluded, wistfully.

"Not from me, I am afraid. Hey, man, I am sorry we hit this snag, but you know, there are worse things. After all, the worst that can happen is that you end up at square one. The same place that you were at before our lunch a couple of months ago."

"True. But it is too late now. That ship has already sailed. I have changed. My expectations have changed. We cannot really go back," Aki trailed off.

"Now get out of my shoes," he added with a wave of a hand. The last was a joke but said without even cracking a smile. Aki had a sort of dry sense of humor.

Ivan left with Aki staring gloomily into the deep shadows of the canyon outside his window.

Aki Roussos
Monday, July 1
Sunset Cliffs, San Diego, California, USA

Aki purposely put off thinking about BBI and the CFIUS snag over the weekend. To put some distance between himself and the events. Hoping that this may bring some new insights. Hoping for a magic solution. Or he tried to, as much as he could stop thinking about work issues—a lifelong habit. Instead—much to Mary's surprise— he spent the weekend tidying the backyard, fixing up the BBQ, and restocking the outdoors wet bar, all in preparation for a Fourth of July party that they were hosting that year. Mary seemed pleased.

But he knew that he could not defer facing the problems forever. So on that Monday, he left work early and came to his thinking bench. It was still quite warm—almost unpleasantly hot—with more than a couple of hours to go to the sunset. And crowded with throngs of tourists walking the cliffs and even climbing down to the beach. He was extra diligent in wiping the bench down.

The nature of his meditation was different from when he was last at his bench. The question he was mulling was not if he should sell BBI but when and how to sell it. He loved his company and felt a responsibility toward his people. He has accepted that the right thing to do is to have someone else lead BBI into the next phase of its existence—for the sake of the company. He was warming up to the idea of merging with CHARM. He liked Junjie and felt that he could be trusted to take care of his baby. He was comfortable—confident even—that he was on the right track. And now this issue with CFIUS was blocking the path.

"*Goddamn, shit, and fuck!*" he muttered under his breath, allowing himself to vent his frustration and disappointment. And maybe even to feel a bit sorry for himself. In his daydreams—on the rare occasions that he permitted those to himself—he liked to imagine an all-employee meeting where he would announce the deal with CHARM and paint a picture of a bright and long future that he arranged for all of them. He liked that version of his exit—graceful and gradual—before he rode off into the proverbial sunset. But all this was now in jeopardy. Yes, he did feel like his candy was snatched away from him.

Archimedes, stop admiring the problem and focus on a solution.

He forced himself to concentrate. He found that sometimes just changing the order of issues helped him look at things in a different way.

All right. Ivan's option 4…sell to someone else?

In as much as he tried to force himself to analyze this option methodically and logically, he knew the answer to this question. In his gut. Yes, he was confident that some of his competitors, and maybe some of the clients too, would be glad to get their hands on his company. But he also understood that their objective would be to absorb his business and technology into their operations—and then to wind it down—rather than to invest in BBI expansion. That is what he would do if the roles were reversed. Definitely not a path to a long-term future for BBI. Definitely not the story that he would expect his people to applaud. Definitely not the way he would like to be seen: cashing out and riding off into that sunset and screw all the people who worked for him these last thirty years.

Besides, he was pretty sure that the most his competitors could offer is a multiplier of three or four. Not the six or eight that Junjie mentioned as a possibility for technology companies in China. The difference between a multiplier of four and eight would mean millions of dollars. Hard to ignore a difference of a few mils. Especially when doing the right thing brings the better price.

No, I am not selling out to a competitor. Not if I can help it. Scrap option 4, he concluded.

Option 3…the "Yugoslav" way that Ivan mentioned?

Something in him—something deep inside—rebelled against that option. He could not quite put his finger on it and articulate it fully—even to himself. It felt…smarmy. Wrong. Like he would be cheating. Even if the lawyers could find a way that was fully legitimate and legal, he would feel uneasy. Just as Ivan suggested that he might.

Damn, seems like Ivan is in my head too, not just in my shoes, he noted, smirking to himself.

Maybe it was Aki's upbringing—his mother was very Japanese when it came to teaching him the morality of rules. She drilled into him a sense that rules were good. That they were there to make sure that everything was fair. That breaking them—even the unstated ones or the simplest of rules like waiting in a line—is rude and disrespectful. That it showed that he thought that he was better or more important than others. Above everybody else. Rude.

Breaking rules—or even "the Yugoslav way" of going around the rules—would be an act of selfish egoism. Definitely not an attribute that his mom would approve of.

Interesting how she always emphasized the propriety of following rules and never the consequences of breaking them, he mused. *And curious that dad—a natural rebel—always seemed to stay quiet on the topic, apparently deferring entirely to mom. A case of opposites attracting?*

Aki shook his head to remind himself to stay focused.

He had many opportunities in his life when he could have gained some advantage by embracing one of those shortcut schemes. By doing something less than full-fledged following of the rules. From the innocent misrepresentation on his taxes or expense reports to charging more for his products based on things he might have heard through the back door. He could have benefited. He could have made more money. But he never did. He did not believe that those that do the right and proper things—the good guys—end last. The success that he has had to date proved to him that his beliefs were right. Beliefs that some would call naive.

He built BBI fairly—following all the stated and even unstated rules and regs. *Why change that now? Besides*, he thought, *you never know when some of these shady schemes might come back and haunt you. Bite you in the ass. Some irregularity could come to roost five years, ten years, down the road. Not a way to a peaceful retirement.*

On the other hand, he challenged himself in his head, *what if the choice boiled down to this shady option 3 scheme or scrapping the entire deal? That would be a bit harder.*

Would it be fair to his people—to BBI—that he walked away from a good deal just because he had some personal reservations about the propriety of how it was executed? Even if his lawyers assured him that it was legal? Isn't imposing his personal ethical values also an act of selfish egoism? Would implementing option 3 be the lesser evil than aborting the sale of BBI? And therefore, the greater good? And therefore, the right thing to do?

Shelf option 3, he concluded. *It is not clear.*

Option 2—waiting until CFIUS practices changed?

He considered this. He thought that it was possible that Junjie was right and that CFIUS was picking on this particular transaction because CHARM was a Chinese company. CFIUS may have been directed to exercise extra caution when scrutinizing all deals involving China. This may be a part of the trade war that the Trump administration was pursuing. Maybe…but if that was the case, then Ivan was probably right too, and it was unlikely to change until Trump was gone. At least a year—assuming that he gets booted out in 2020. Probably two—given all the things that the new administration would have to do to reverse Trump's policies.

Even if that was not the situation—and the CFIUS injunction was just a case of bureaucratic red-tape caused by the lack of suitable staff, as that CFIUS whisperer seemed to think—it would be a while until CFIUS staffed up and resolved its logjams. Even if they were to hire the experts that they were lacking that very day, it would be months until they were trained up and operational. He knew this would be the case even with a small company like BBI, let alone for a giant government bureaucracy.

Yes, Ivan was probably right, and it would be years.

And in business, years was a long time to wait. He, personally, was not in a hurry—he had the "years." He could carry on with BBI as is for quite a while more. But Junjie may not. Junjie may not be willing to wait. Maybe he should hold off on making up his mind about option 2 until a discussion with Junjie? But further consideration told him that even if Junjie said he was willing to wait—he could not commit to it. In fact, even if Junjie would be foolish enough to commit to waiting—it would be even more foolish for Aki to rely on it. Years is a long time in business. No one can commit credibly to what he may or may not be doing a year or two down the road.

Nope. Option 2 is a nonoperative option, he concluded. *Scrap that!* *And option 1—just appeal to CFIUS to reconsider?*

The more he thought about it, the more he liked this option. And not just because of the process of elimination—because none of the other options appealed to him. He liked this approach because it seemed like the right thing to do. Maybe Ivan, and this CFIUS whisperer of his, were wrong? Maybe they can reason with CFIUS and demonstrate that the questions of national security did not apply in the case of BBI. Yes, BBI did have some specialty technology and was very good at what it did. But it was a part—in fact, a tiny part—of a global supply chain. And try as it might, the government could not contain it all within the US. There was a lot more than mask blanks that went into making silicon chips. By then, much of the supply chain that enabled the silicon technology was abroad. In Japan and Korea. In Europe. Taiwan. And yes, in China. It was too late for CFIUS to try to force that genie back into the bottle, so to speak. It was not reasonable. Surely, with patience and a bit of time, they should be able to make CFIUS—or the people at CFIUS—to see that. They were, after all, probably perfectly reasonable normal people who put on their pants one leg at a time. Just doing their jobs like everybody else.

So why wouldn't we challenge the injunction? It is our right. What have we got to lose—other than the money and time required to file the appeal? That should not be too prohibitive. Especially if Junjie was willing to support it. Wait for it to work itself out and maybe even share the cost?

Yes, he was comfortable with that decision. He would pursue option 1.

It is the right thing to do, Aki declared to himself.

He got up, stretched, shook out and folded his towel, cast a last glance at the spectacular view of the Sunset Cliffs and the dusk settling over the Pacific and slowly walked back to his car. Confident and satisfied with his conclusion.

Consequences 2

Ivan Jovanovic
Sunday, June 31
Cortez Hill, San Diego, California, USA

"Hey, Junjie! How are things? You over the surprise present from our local friendly CFIUS by now?"

Ivan called Junjie on his office number, hoping that the weekend would have helped Junjie cool off a bit—it was Monday morning in Beijing. And as always, he joked—just in case things got tense.

"No. Every time I think about it, I get more ticked off. This Trump is such a pig. And a racist. I am sure that it is because I am Chinese. I bet none of this would be happening if I was British or something," he blurted.

Hmm, clearly not over it yet, Ivan thought. *Shrink session required. Funny that Junjie seems to be taking it so personally. Much more so than Aki.*

"Maybe so. I understand your frustration, man. It *was* unexpected. But you know, as much as I hate to be defending Trump, this is not his doing. So even if you were a blue-blooded Brit, we might be having the same conversation."

"Oh?" skeptical Junjie.

"I did some background search on CFIUS. In its current format, it was set up back in the eighties—so if anything racist is going on, it was probably aimed at the Japanese rather than Chinese companies."

"Doesn't change the fact that he is now using it against the Chinese," Junjie insisted.

"And," Ivan continued, "if you look at the history through the Bush and Obama years, roughly one in three acquisition deals were investigated, and only about one in a thousand ended up on a president's desk. So the odds of something like what we are encountering were not so long even before Trump."

"Hmm, really?" Junjie asked a bit suspiciously.

"Really. The only unusual thing here is purely the relatively small size of a deal that still seems to have caught their attention. We expected to fly under the radar, so to speak. Perhaps naively so. CFIUS seems to have gotten more diligent. Or if the guy in DC is right—it has just gotten stupider."

"Yeah, well…"

"It is true that the number of proposed transactions questioned by CFIUS has been increasing for years. In fact, last year, some of the laws were further strengthened. So yes, I am afraid that, in general, it is getting harder for foreigners to buy US companies. But this is neither because of, nor in spite of, Trump. Or the fact that you are Chinese."

Silence.

"Be that as it may, though," Ivan continued, trying to get to the point he needed to address, "we do have a problem. Right now, your M&A is dead in water."

"Clearly."

The terse responses conjured up a picture of Junjie—sitting back, arms crossed, pouting face. *Very unusual for him*, thought Ivan. *He is normally so gung ho positive.*

"I think the ball is now mostly in Aki's court. There is not much that you can do from your end. It is not like CHARM can change its bid to alter CFIUS's injunction or anything like that. Short of just walking away. Incidentally, over the last ten years or so, in about 40 percent of the cases questioned by CFIUS, that is exactly what the buyers decided to do. Just walk away."

EXHIBIT 6.1 CFIUS Stats & Notable Cases

Statistics for years between 2005 and 2015 (Bush/Obama)
- 1239 notifications
- 348 investigations (28%)   (46% in 2015)
- 139 withdrawals (40%)   (19% in 2015)
- 3 presidential decisions

Notable Cases:

1990: President George H. W. Bush voided the sale of MAMCO Manufacturing to a Chinese agency,

2005: The acquisition of IBM's PC unit by Lenovo was blocked by CFIUS but approved by Pres. George W. Bush

2005: a CNOOC Group (a major Chinese State-owned oil and gas corporation) offer was not opposed by the CFIUS but was blocked by the US House of Representatives

2006: State-owned Dubai Ports World's planned acquisition of P&O, the lessee and operator of ports for container ships. This acquisition was initially approved by the CFIUS but was opposed by Congress

2010: Russian interests acquired a controlling interest in Uranium One, with 20 percent of U.S. uranium extraction capacity. CFIUS voted in favor

2012: Ralls Corporation, owned by the Chinese Sany Group, was ordered by Pres. Barack Obama to divest itself of wind farm projects located close to U.S. Navy weapon facility

2016: a $2.6 billion deal by Philips to sell Lumileds division to GO Scale Capital, and GRS Ventures was blocked over concerns regarding Chinese applications of gallium nitride.

2017: President Trump blocked the acquisition by a Chinese purchaser of Lattice Semiconductor

2018: President Trump blocked Singapore-based Broadcom Limited from purchasing Qualcomm, citing national security concerns brought up by CFIUS

From:

https://en.m.wikipedia.org/wiki/Committee_on_Foreign_Investment_in_the_United_States#Notable_cases

Year	Notifications	Investigations	Notices withdrawn	Presidential decision
1988	14	1	0	1
1989	204	5	2	3
1990	295	6	2	4
1991	152	1	0	1
1992	106	2	1	1
1993	82	0	0	0
1994	69	0	0	0
1995	81	0	0	0
1996	55	0	0	0
1997	62	0	0	0
1998	65	2	2	0
1999	79	0	0	0
2000	72	1	0	1
2001	55	1	1	0
2002	43	0	0	0
2003	41	2	1	1
2004	53	2	2	0
2005	65	2	2	0
2006	111	7	19	2
2007	138	6	15	0
2008	155	23	23	0
2009	65	25	7	0
2010	93	35	12	0
2011	111	40	6	0
2012	114	45	22	1
2013	97	48	8	0
2014	147	51	12	0
2015	143	66	13	0

Ivan waited a bit to let that sink in.

"So the question for you is, are you ready to walk away?" Ivan asked, getting very specific.

Silence, followed by a mumbled, "No, not yet," from Junjie.

"Then whatever we do about CFIUS is mostly up to Aki. But you obviously have a stake in the outcome, and by now you and Aki have built a good relationship. So you may be able to influence him."

"Yes, I guess that is true," Junjie commented, sounding forlorn—like he is resigned to his fate. "What were his options again?"

"One, we appeal, two, we wait, three, we try to work around CFIUS," Ivan summarized the options.

"So what do you think?" Junjie asked, listlessly.

Not the usual opinionated and impulsive Junjie here, Ivan thought. *This has really got him down.*

"Well, in a rational world, I would suggest that we pursue option 1 and try to reason with CFIUS. But these are not rational times. On the other hand, if we choose to wait, we may be waiting for a long time. Even if Trump loses next year, it would take a while to alter the course of the government bureaucracy. Like steering a supertanker. So in my humble opinion, the waiting period would be of the order of years. Leaving us with option 3. Playing some kind of a shell game with BBI's Japanese subsidiary. Give it access to all of BBI's technology, people, and know-how, and then have you acquire just the subsidiary. That is what a good Yugoslav would do. But that could be a bit shady. Given these options, I suspect Aki will pick the first one. But I am just guessing. However, I do believe that you could influence him."

"I see," a flat, noncommittal statement from a resigned Junjie.

"So do you have any preferences from your end?" Ivan urged.

Silence.

"Junjie?" Ivan goaded.

"Let me talk to some people here. I don't know. Give me a day or two. Will let you know."

Hmm, Junjie is taking all this so personally and emotionally, Ivan thought idly to himself as they said their goodbyes. *Not like him. Curious...* They signed off without the usual chitchat.

Junjie Wu
Wednesday, July 3
Liuxiaguan Teahouse, Dongcheng, Beijing, China

"Professor Lao, we have a problem!" Junjie blurted out even before the old professor had the chance to sit down. He was so preoccupied with the CFIUS snag that they encountered that he did not even notice a young woman in a white dress whose high heels clip-clopped loudly on the bamboo wood floor as she made her way past their table. Unusual for him. Beautiful. Asian…

"Hello, Junjie. How are you today? Bearing up with the sauna that seems to have arrived a bit early this year? Or am I just getting older and less tolerant to the extremes in our weather?" Professor Lao spoke in his usual unhurried and deliberate way—possibly to calm Junjie down. Besides, it was very hot and humid outside, and he may have needed time to catch his breath in the reinvigorating cool of the teahouse.

"Oh, I am sorry, Professor… Please." Junjie caught himself and jumped up to help the professor to his seat.

Over the last few months, their biweekly tea has become a habit for the two of them, and they were meeting at their usual spot in the Liuxiaguan Teahouse. They even had a regular table reserved, and the staff has gotten to know them and their routine. The waitress appeared automatically with their usual tea and petit fours. Junjie poured the tea.

"Ah, that is so much better." Professor Lao smiled, sipping his tea and peering at Junjie. "Now then, what is the problem?"

"The problem is US federal government and the so-called CFIUS," Junjie began.

"Ah, CFIUS. Yes, I know about them. They have been rather erratic recently—seemingly blocking or waiving proposed transactions at random. Perhaps it is a symptom of the chaotic government under the current president," Lao opined in his steady monotone. Another sip of tea, and a nibble of his pastry… "But I am surprised that a small deal like yours caught their attention. That *is* unusual," he added.

"Well, we have received only a temporary injunction. So they did not block the transaction—just questioning it." Junjie explained, perhaps calmed down by Professor Lao's nonplussed behavior.

"I see." Another sip of tea. "So, Junjie…what are you planning to do?"

"Well, it looks like our options are either to appeal the injunction or to wait or to work around CFIUS," Junjie explained.

"Work around CFIUS? How do you mean?" Professor Lao arched his eyebrows—an expression that Junjie has learned to mean that the old prof was surprised.

"We think that it may be possible to transfer BBI technology and assets to its subsidiary in Japan and then for CHARM to acquire that."

"Hmm... Interesting"—sip of tea and another bite of the pastry—"you thought of that?"

"No, it was Ivan's idea," Junjie responded, a bit surprised at the question. *Who cares who thought of it?*

Over the last few months, during their afternoon teas, they have talked a lot about the BBI and the acquisition process. So Professor Lao was familiar with the principals involved—he knew all about Ivan and Aki.

"I see. He is from Yugoslavia, you said. That makes sense. Americans normally do not think about working *around* the system. Americans normally try to work *through* the system," Professor Lao said, stressing the "around" and "through." "Which is why they have so many lawyers and spend so much time and money arguing in courts"—another sip of tea and nibble of his pastry—"interesting idea," he stated, clearly intrigued.

"You think so? But we expect that Aki—the American among us—will choose to appeal the decision," Junjie explained, trying to get Professor Lao to focus on the issue. *American litigious ways are not the point now.*

"No! We do not want that. That must be stopped," Professor Lao reacted instantly, in short abrupt sentences. Extremely unusual for him. "Definitely not!"

"Why?" Junjie asked, taken aback by the sharp edge in prof's voice.

"Well," Professor Lao explained, "CFIUS has been erratic and unpredictable. Sometimes seemingly irrational. But we cannot rely on CFIUS—or the people in CFIUS—to be stupid. If we could figure out the pinch point weakness in the supply chain, they may do so as well. Someday. And we do not want to help them by forcing them to focus on that area. That may wake them up and they may end up blocking our moves. And it is too early for that. We are not ready yet." By then he seemed to have regained his self-control and was again talking in his usual unhurried monotone. "So no—we do not want to appeal their injunction. Appealing their BBI decision could possibly trigger a review, precipitating who knows what. It puts our entire strategy at risk," Professor Lao concluded.

"Oh, I see." Junjie understood the point and chided himself for not anticipating it. It made sense.

"Well, I suppose we should then walk away and abandon the entire deal with BBI," he conceded.

Disappointed. Over the last few months, Junjie warmed up to the idea of doubling the size of his company and operating in the sunshine cast by the Chinese powers-to-be. And he was enjoying the thrill of the M&A chase. He was disappointed to be going back to just running the old CHARM Inc.

"Yes, yes, we could. That would be the easiest option. We can always do that. But that would be unfortunate. BBI would be such a good pinch point to have. With it, we could potentially choke the entire litho flow. Especially for the advanced nodes using EUV. It is pivotal to our strategy. And the window of opportunity may not always be open," Professor Lao drawled pensively.

"True. Well then, I suppose that we could encourage Aki to pursue the option of working around CFIUS. Maybe force him to reconsider by limiting the term of our interest? Give him only a month or so. I understand CFIUS appeals can take a while, so a tight term-limit from us could in effect block the possibility of an appeal." Junjie fell into his problem-solving mode. He now understood the constraints and intuitively tried to figure out a path around them. A natural mode for him.

"Yes. Yes, that would be best. Let us not give up yet."

"But, knowing Aki," Junjie added pensively—slowly—as he was working it out in his mind in real time, "he is very proper kind of a man. By-the-book kind of a bloke... I doubt that he would be comfortable with working around CFIUS... Don't know... It may take him a while."

Professor Lao looked at Junjie searchingly and seemed to go into a meditative mode. After a long ponderous silence and another sip of tea, he mused, "Hmm. I am not sure that time is on our side… Waiting for many months would not be good…"

Junjie got a feeling that Lao was talking more to himself than to him.

Professor Lao then reached down for his beat-up old bag that he seemed to always have with him. It reminded Junjie of the typical schoolbags that children used back in Mao's years: rough reddish-brown leather, crude buckles, sturdy handle. Lao retrieved a large A4 size envelope from it and offered it to Junjie.

"In fact, I have something here that may help you convince Aki to…er…cooperate," he intoned hesitatingly. "To choose the right option and make up his mind sooner rather than later… If you need it."

Junjie opened the envelope and flipped through the contents. He was first shocked and surprised—incredulous. Then outraged and disgusted. And finally slightly nauseous. The envelope contained what seemed to be some kind of a report on Aki. Some pictures of him—looking a bit younger than now—with some woman. Japanese, he guessed. Intimate pictures. With the two of them in amorous situations: kissing in a bar, snuggling under covers of a large bed, holding hands on a beach, sitting together at a breakfast counter in their bathrobes… Some receipts for something that looked like apartment rental statements… Some text that he did not read…

A realization that the report was dirt on Aki bubbled up into Junjie's consciousness, precipitating the emotional responses that he was experiencing. Kompromat,[28] presumably to be used to blackmail Aki to cooperate. Junjie was dumbfounded. He quickly stuffed the contents back in the envelope and tried to rein in his emotions.

---

[28] **Kompromat**: Damaging information about a person used to create negative publicity or for blackmail and extortion. Source: Russian. Widespread use of kompromat has been one of the characteristic features of the politics of Russia and other post-Soviet states and typically included doctored photographs, planted drugs, videos of liaisons with prostitutes, and a wide range of other entrapment techniques—often of sexual nature.

Finally, after what felt like a long time to him, he collected himself enough and pushed the envelope back toward Professor Lao.

"No, Professor. I cannot. I will not use dirt to pressure Aki. He is a friend by now. I refuse to engage in this…this…" He was at a loss for words to describe what he felt about such a report. And about his disgust at the thought of confronting Aki with it. And about his disappointment in Professor Lao, who seemed to expect him to do so.

"I understand," Professor Lao said slowly. But it seemed to Junjie that his wrinkly face assumed a different look and that the color has gone out of his eyes. Not the usual benign grandfatherly look. More like a blank look of a snake entirely devoid of emotions. But his voice was the usual calm drone, sounding just like he was explaining something that should be obvious. Maybe he was just imagining it.

"Let me explain something to you, Junjie. Our society is a bit like a living organism. When an organism, such as our body, detects something new—a virus or a bacterium or some new tissue—it first ascertains if that new quantity is 'self' or 'alien'." Professor Lao underlined the "self" and "alien." "And if an organism determines that the new entity is alien, then its immunity mechanism kicks in and generates the antibodies that kill the invader. It is a natural mechanism that our body has evolved over the eons to protect itself. The immune system works automatically even if the invader is benign or neutral or even beneficial. That is why the doctors have to inhibit the autoimmune system before they do an organ transplant. If they don't, the body may see the new tissue as foreign and reject the transplanted organ. This response is autonomous so that even when a patient knows that his life depends on his body accepting the new organ, the immune system can destroy new tissue and, in the end, ultimately kill the patient. Very ironic, don't you think? On the other hand, of course, when the autoimmune system is inhibited, then patients can die from unrelated diseases. Even a common cold can be lethal. You see?"

"Er, I do not understand," Junjie said, staring at Professor Lao and wondering where is the old kook going with this diversion.

"Well, our social system—our government—operates somewhat like a living organism. The system has detected you and is now aware of you and your BBI acquisition. If you refuse to behave in a normal and expected way—if you do not continue with this enterprise—then they will decide that you are an alien matter. The immunity mechanisms will be automatically triggered. The equivalent of antibodies will be activated and will destroy you and those that they associate with you... Or if you behave in a normal way—sort of mimic what the people in the system expect—then they will recognize you as self and nurture you. In that case, the immunity mechanisms will protect you, not attack you. You see?"

Junjie was stunned and just stared at Professor Lao. Not sure if he understood correctly. Dumbfounded.

"Junjie, I have grown fond of you, so let me be perfectly clear. We need BBI, and the system will do what it takes to get it. With or without you. But you cannot hope to walk away unnoticed. Not anymore. The trade war has aggravated the system, and our autoimmune functions have been boosted—like a vaccine sensitizes the body to fight invader species. The government is concerned that the stress caused by the trade war does not lead to other problems in our society—like a patient killed by unrelated diseases. So our national autoimmune functions have been supercharged and are hyperactive nowadays. And much as with a human body, the immunity functions operate automatically—and are not fully under the control of the Leadership. So I may not be able to shelter you. Make no mistake, Junjie. The choices you make now will determine if this supercharged autoimmune system sees you, and yours, as self or as alien. Be very careful, Junjie. That is what is at stake now. You are with us or against us. There is nothing in between."

Professor Lao patted Junjie's hand in an unusual paternal gesture, rose slowly, encouraged Junjie to think about it, and shuffled off. He left the envelope on the table.

Junjie Wu
Wednesday, July 3
CHARM Inc., Haidian District, Beijing, China

Junjie went to hide in his office. He knew that he could hunker down there and avoid intrusions or interruptions by just slamming his door shut—more so than at home. And he needed some alone time after that tea with Lao.

His first reaction was that of shock and surprise. Incredulity. Did it really happen the way he recalled it? Did Professor Lao really ask him to blackmail Aki? And threaten him and his family if he did not?

Then that of anger and disgust…

Bloody hell! I knew it! I should have stayed away from anything that is in any way connected to the bloody government. Governments poison and destroy anything that they touch. Damn. Even Professor Lao seems to have been corrupted. My parents were right when they told me to avoid—to shun—anything to do with the government… Any government… But the fool that I am, I did not listen.

He paced around his office, aimlessly walking back and forth to the window, to the door firmly shut to keep the outside away, to his desk.

He wanted to break something. He wanted to scream. He wanted to hide.

Well, a lot of good that would do you, you idiot. Greedy stupid git. It is too late now—you are trapped.

He called Feng to tell her that something came up and that he won't be home until late. He was certain that she could take one look at him and know that something terrible has happened. She could always read him, and he was sure that right then, he was radiating fear—and possibly shame. And then he would have to explain things to her. And that was the very last thing he wanted to do right then. He did not want to talk about it with her. He wanted to shelter her. He wanted to hide from her judging him. In some hole.

You should be ashamed. Disgusting! Maybe the sewer is where you should hide, the rat that you are!

He could not even bear to think about facing his old parents. The very ones that told him to stay away from the government and all government functionaries. The ones who shared the family wisdom with him from the earliest times that he could remember. Wisdom that dictated that their family survived for many years—going way before Mao's Great Leap Forward and Cultural Revolution upheavals—by always following the three family rules: (1) be the best in whatever trade you pick: it is your only source of security; (2) hold your opinion of others to yourself: trust no one to keep your secrets; and (3) stay well away from the government: they do things to you for reasons that have nothing to do with your actions.

The Wu family rules seem to have worked for his parents. They survived all the turbulence of Mao's era as doctors that no firebrand revolutionary managed to accuse of any impropriety because they never said anything and that no one wanted to exile to the countryside because their services were sought after in the capital.

Later—when he was a teenager and it was again safe to espouse Chinese traditional values—they liked to cloak these rules in Confucian terms, by telling him that he was of "gong class" and not the "shi' class."

EXHIBIT 6.2   **The Four Traditional Occupations**

The four occupations or "four categories of the people" was an occupation classification used in ancient China by either Confucian or Legalist scholars as far back as the late Zhou dynasty and is considered a central part of the fengjian social structure (c. 1046–256 BC). These were the shi (gentry scholars), the nong (peasant farmers), the gong (artisans and craftsmen), and the shang (merchants and traders). The four occupations were not always arranged in this order. The four categories were not socioeconomic classes; wealth and standing did not correspond to these categories, nor were they hereditary.

The Gong were those who had skills to make useful objects. This was the class identified by the Chinese character that stands for "labor." They were like farmers in that they produced essential objects, but most of them did not have land of their own and so did not generate the revenue. However, they commanded more respect than merchants because the skills they had were handed down from father to son. Artisans could be government employed or self-employed, and those that were most successful could become wealthy enough to hire apprentices or laborers that they could manage. Besides creating their own enterprises, the artisans also formed their own guilds.

From: https://en.wikipedia.org/wiki/Four_occupations
          https://mmsamee.weebly.com/ancient-chinas-social-classes.html

And they celebrated Confucian dictums that emphasized work, morality, and respect for others. His favorite, displayed in beautiful calligraphy on the wall of their home, was

> Riches and honor are what men desire; but if they arrive at them in improper ways, they should not continue to hold them. Poverty and low estate are what men dislike; but if they arrive at such condition by improper ways, they should not refuse it.

No, nothing proper here. I do not deserve my riches and honor... I have failed to be a good son... To be a good father to my own son... No way I can tell my parents about Professor Lao and where this is taking me..., he lamented.

Junjie was deeply ashamed—not just of the dirt he was supposed to use against Aki or the dishonorable act of blackmail—but also of betraying the family lore. He allowed himself—a scion of an old Beijing gong class family of professionals—to forget all those lessons and to get entangled with the government types. Trapped into having to behave in a way that he knew was wrong and immoral. He was ashamed of having gotten himself into that situation—of dishonoring his family.

A tiny voice in his head reminded him how, while he was living in America, he thought that the emphasis on shame, family honor, and saving face was so antiquated. And yet somehow since he returned to China, these traditional values reasserted themselves. They burned then.

An hour, maybe two, passed. In his head, he ranted and raged. Against himself. Against the damned Professor Lao—that snake that masqueraded as an honorable man, a professor, and an academic. Against the corrupt government and its "autoimmune" system. Against the world he was living in...

The realization that he not only swallowed Professor Lao's lure but even enjoyed and reveled in it, only served to amplify his shame.

You were a vein sucker. Greedy. And now you have to pay for it and shall bring shame on yourself and on your family.

Hours later, all the voices in his head were exhausted, leaving him with a single one that told him only one thing: that he had no choice.

Rant and rave as you might—you must do what Lao told you.

Professor Lao made it clear. Either he was to behave like a good boy and do as he was told—or they will destroy him. Probably destroy CHARM. And possibly his family too. His family—and the people of CHARM Inc.—did not do anything other than trust and look up to him. They deserved better. So he had no choice. He had to play along to protect them. He had to become just like those government fat cats—corrupt, greedy, uncouth, dishonorable…

And Lao said that if he did not do it, someone else would. He had no choice. As much as he would like to, he could not walk away. The end result for Aki and BBI would be the same. If he walked away, they would find someone else to be the front for buying it—using God knows what other means. He suspected that Lao did not give him their ultimate weapon. That there could very well be other things in that briefcase of his that would pressure Aki even more. Bottom line: he could not save BBI from them. The only difference would be whether Junjie, CHARM, and his family would survive and blossom—or be rooted out. No choice.

He tried to imagine what his father would do in his situation. But, of course, this was no help—his father would have been smarter and would not have gotten into that position, to begin with.

No choice. I must become a looter.

He used a term that he borrowed from Ayn Rand's *Atlas Shrugged*[29]—one of the many books banned in China that he enjoyed

---

[29] **Atlas Shrugged**: A 1957 novel by Ayn Rand, considered to be her magnum opus. *Atlas Shrugged* contains Rand's most extensive statement of Objectivism: the philosophical system that she founded that claims that man's own happiness is the moral purpose of his life, with productive achievement as his noblest activity, and reason as his only absolute. The book depicts a dystopian United States in which private businesses suffer under burdensome regulations, enacted and enforced by "looters" who exploit the productive elements of the society. Atlas Shrugged has enjoyed enduring commercial success and has, for example, placed as no. 20 in PBS's study of the "The Great American Read" as recently as 2018.

reading when he lived in England and America. Forbidden books, like Orwell's *1984* and *Animal Farm*, or Ayn Rand's works, that opened his eyes to different social philosophies. Alternative to the state-sanctioned Marxism-Leninism-Maoism... He thought that the term "looter" was an excellent way of describing the corrupt government fat cats and burned at the idea of having to apply it to himself.

I must convince Aki to choose option 3—by any means. Any means at all. Including blackmail, or whatever they come up with to further amp up the pressure on poor Aki... No choice.

Amid all the noise in his head, he almost missed a glimmer of an idea—of hope—that twinkled faintly in his mind.

Maybe there is a way for me to wriggle out? Maybe there is still a way to refuse without losing CHARM or shaming my family? Trying to find it would be the only honorable thing to do now?

An idea—maybe just a hope—was working its way through his mind. Like a worm. A thought—an outline of a plan—was forming in his head.

Without analyzing it as thoroughly as he knew he should—he decided to act on it. It was easier that way. Maybe impulsively. Maybe because his intuition told him to.

He went to his desk, opened his laptop, logged on, and booked his flight to America.

He would leave the next day.

He made a mental note to pack that evening and to bring Sing along—his lucky stuffed panda. He was a meticulous packer who made sure that his socks and underwear were neatly packed in ziplock plastic bags, his shirts and trousers were perfectly folded and ironed along the seams, and all his toiletries were in separate baggies—in case one should leak. So, of course, he had a separate leather pouch for Sing. He was a bit embarrassed to admit to it—a grown man traveling with his stuffed animal. But he has had Sing since he was a child and never traveled without him.

Especially for an important trip like this. Why take chances?

Part 3

TRAPPED BETWEEN THE DRAGONS

Collateral Damage

Junjie Wu
Thursday, July 4
AA180 PEK-LAX flight, Somewhere over the Pacific Ocean

Junjie took his usual American Airlines flight to Los Angeles. He preferred flying American Airlines to Air China, partially due to his OneWorld frequent flyers mileage account and partially due to what he perceived to be its superior safety record. Despite the fact that the food and the service were inferior. And that the stewardesses were nowhere nearly as attractive and nice. He had no trouble booking a seat even on such short notice, probably due to his status with AA and that apparently most travelers preferred getting to States before, or after, the Fourth of July holiday.

After the meal was served and cleared, he first took care of the work chores. Leaving on such a short notice meant that in the morning—before leaving—he had to scramble to either move or delegate the various engagements that he had scheduled for the rest of the week and—to be safe—the first part of the following week. He pulled together the information packets, presentations, and background stories needed for these meetings into a series of e-mails that he would send out to his delegates; the people he selected to absorb his meetings. And then there were the e-mails that he had to catch up on. And the several technical papers that he has been toting around for the last few weeks—intending to read them but never finding the time.

The show must go on, he mused.

But his heart was not in it. He understood that all this was a form of procrastination. He knew that his people would manage the meetings just fine, with or without this help from him. And that the e-mails were mostly routine. And that the technical papers could wait for another few weeks. But taking care of the work chores was easier than dealing with the real problem that hung over him like a dark cloud.

He finally closed his laptop, walked back to the galley, procured a couple of those miniature bottles of whiskey, a can of soda, and a cup full of ice, and settled back in his seat—to think. A pretty lady in a white dress, sitting in a seat diagonally across the aisle from his, was only a minor distraction. She, too, was sipping on a drink, watching some movie. Seemed to be cold a bit—wrapped in a shawl of some kind. And small or lithe enough to be sitting with her feet tucked under her.

Lucky lady, he thought, *the seat is actually big enough for her. Quite pretty. Wonder how she would use that flexibility in bed*, with all sorts of X-rated images flashing through his mind.

He then shook his head and urged himself to stop ogling her and to focus.

C'mon, Albert! What are you going to tell them? Focus! He normally used his English name when chiding himself. It was the name that his strictest—and scariest—teachers used, and it still made him sit up and pay attention. More so than his Chinese name. That tended to come in gentler tones, like his mother used.

He would have preferred it if he could find a way to save face—to appear less dishonorable than he felt. To tell Ivan and Aki some abbreviated version of the story that would make him appear less of a fool or, worse, a snake. But after some thought, and maybe after finishing his first whiskey, he concluded that full disclosure was the only way.

Losing face is your penance, he admonished himself. *You deserve it.*

Yes, he decided that the only right and honorable thing to do is to tell them everything: the truth, the whole truth, and nothing but the truth. Regardless of how weak or gullible—or maybe even two-faced and dishonorable—he may appear to them. It was his only avenue to preserving a vestige of self-respect.

At that point in time, he did not consider the possible and the potentially dangerous repercussions of his leaking Professor Lao's pinch point strategy. He was more concerned about saving face—especially in front of Ivan, whom he considered as a kind of a father figure—than he was about guarding Lao's secret. Besides, for some reason, he did not consider telling Ivan and Aki as leaking. They were friends. Telling them did not feel like sharing a secret with an enemy.

He spent the rest of the flight fidgeting restlessly in that seat that was too small for him—unlike for the lady in the snug white dress. Between sleep and wakefulness. Pondering about the possible options that he may have. It seemed to him that Professor Lao held all the cards.

As he went over the events in his head, it became very clear to him that Professor Lao threatened him. Either he missed it, or he hid from it, but it was only then that the enormity of it ripened and fully crystallized into the ugly truth that it was. Lao threatened him! And his family!

The more Junjie thought about it—about Lao's readiness to resort to blackmail, to force, to threats, the more he suspected that Lao's so-called friends among the Leadership were the dark side of the government. The Chinese version of the deep state.[30] Probably involving the army and the secret police. Yes, Professor Lao may have a fine wrapping, a veneer of an academic, and he may have put a sophisticated spin on his messages, but he was also a brute who threaten Junjie and his family. No doubt about it. This was more like the methods used by the army and secret police, than, say, the Ministry of Industry or some other legitimate branch of the government. And certainly not like what one would expect from a professor and a gentleman. Wang ba dan!

---

[30] **Deep state**: A conspiracy theory that suggests that collusion and cronyism exist within the political system and constitute a hidden government within the legitimately elected government. The term was originally coined to refer to a relatively invisible state apparatus "composed of high-level elements within the intelligence services, military, security, judiciary, and organized crime" in countries like Turkey, Ukraine, Colombia, Italy, Israel, etc....

Again and again, he concluded that he—Junjie—had no choice but to comply with Lao's directives. Especially if the army and the secret police were involved. Lao was as clear and explicit about that as he possibly could be. Junjie could not believe that he did not see it before. Or was it that he did not *want to* see it before?

Bringing Ivan and Aki in on the truth would not change anything. All it would do would be to inform them about what they were dealing with. Then if Aki chose to walk away from the deal—and to take whatever ugly consequences may occur—then it would be on Aki's head. Then Junjie could almost wash his hands of whatever may happen to Aki. Almost.

Junjie knew that if Aki did choose to walk away, they—Professor Lao and his cronies—would perceive Junjie as a failure. At first, he thought that this may be good—at least they would not brand him as uncooperative—and might even leave him alone. But on further thought, he concluded that they would probably think that Junjie knew too much. So either he succeeded to acquire BBI and he became a part of that corrupt system, or they would—what is that word used in the movies—neutralize him. Being left alone was not an option for him. In fact, the consequences of Aki choosing to walk away could very well be more severe for Junjie than for Aki.

But what options do I have? He kept coming back to that question.

He did not come up with any plausible answers. At least not for the rest of his flight. Or during the car ride to the hotel. Or during his dinner and lonely session in the hotel bar... Even Sing did not have any helpful ideas or opinions...

Ivan Jovanovic
Friday, July 5, AM
Cortez Hill, San Diego, California, USA

Stunned silence! Following Junjie's revelations, the conference room suddenly felt different to Ivan. Sterile. Like an operating theater. With the overhead light glaring brightly and seemingly casting no shadows. To Ivan, they suddenly seemed to be two-dimensional: frozen at the moment with Aki staring at Junjie in stunned silence and Junjie standing and talking. Like an overexposed photograph.

The day before, Ivan was surprised when he received a terse call from Junjie who told him that he has flown to the US and needed a private face-to-face meeting with him and Aki rather than the teleconference that was scheduled. That was certainly unexpected.

Odd, Ivan thought at the time. *Not that Junjie decided to come to the US, but that he did not give us a heads-up of any kind. Odd.* Maybe somewhat disquieting.

Ivan immediately called Aki at home—it was the Fourth of July holiday—explained, and made sure that Aki was available to meet the following day. Then he booked the conference room in his condo building—an amenity of the building that he really appreciated and that came in so very handy when he met with his consulting clients.

Suitably private for Junjie, he wondered.

The meeting in itself was a good surprise. Very congenial. They met in the lobby of the building at the agreed time, and Ivan escorted Junjie and Aki to the conference room. Aki seemed very excited to be meeting Junjie in person for the first time. They shook hands warmly and exchanged bro-style backslaps. Given their—especially Aki's—rather reserved personalities and a shared bias toward the oriental etiquette that avoided physical contact, these were only slightly awkward. That was great to see.

However, all that geniality melted away the moment that the conference room doors were closed and Junjie started to talk. The pleasant surprise of the face-to-face meeting paled in comparison to the dark surprise brought by Junjie explaining everything. Everything!

The revelation that the ultimate source of Junjie's M&A funds was the so-called "Big Fund" was not necessarily unexpected or particularly alarming. Ivan read something about the Big Fund in the press only a few days ago and was vaguely aware of its connection to the Chinese government. He did not think much about it, and hearing Junjie explain it was no big deal.

Yeah, so? Understandable and not a secret—or a surprise, was Ivan's net take accompanied with a shrug. *Meh. Big Fund. So what…*

Junjie sharing his new insight that the funding source may in fact be controlled by some sinister organs of the Chinese state was however somewhat disturbing. His suspicion that it may be the PLA[31] or the MSS[32]—shared in hushed tones with all the disclaimers about it being just his personal opinion rather than a verified fact—was more alarming. Much more alarming. His elaboration of who and what the PLA and MSS were only served to amplify the concern for Ivan.

EXHIBIT 7.1   Tito's Yugoslavia

Josip Broz, 7 May 1892 – 4 May 1980, commonly known as Tito, was a Yugoslav communist revolutionary and statesman, serving in various roles from 1943 until his death in 1980. During World War II, he was the leader of the Partisans, often regarded as the most effective resistance movement in occupied Europe. He also served as the President of the Socialist Federal Republic of Yugoslavia from January 1953 to May 1980. While his presidency has been criticized as authoritarian and concerns about the repression of political opponents have been raised, Tito has been seen by most as a benevolent dictator. As the head of a "highly centralized and oppressive" regime, Tito wielded tremendous power in Yugoslavia, with his authoritarian rule administered through an elaborate bureaucracy that routinely suppressed human rights. The main victims of this repression were during the first years known and alleged Stalinists, but during the following years even some of the most prominent among Tito's collaborators were arrested. Milovan Đilas, perhaps the closest of Tito's collaborators and widely regarded as Tito's possible successor, was arrested because of his criticism against the regime. The repression did not exclude intellectuals and writers, who were arrested and sent to jail for, for example, writing poems considered anti-Titoist.

After the reforms of 1961 Tito's presidency had become comparatively more liberal than other communist regimes, but the Communist Party continued to alternate between liberalism and repression. Yugoslavia managed to remain independent from the Soviet Union and its brand of socialism was in many ways the envy of Eastern Europe, but Tito's Yugoslavia remained a tightly controlled police state. For example, outside the Soviet Union, Yugoslavia had more political prisoners than all of the rest of Eastern Europe combined.

Tito's secret police was modelled on the Soviet KGB. Its members were ever-present and often acted extrajudicially, with victims including middle-class intellectuals, liberals and democrats. Yugoslavia was a signatory to the International Covenant on Civil and Political Rights, but scant regard was paid to some of its provisions.

From: https://en.wikipedia.org/wiki/Josip_Broz_Tito#Evaluation

---

[31] **PLA** (People's Liberation Army): The armed forces of the People's Republic of China (PRC) and of its founding and ruling political party, the Communist Party of China (CPC).

[32] **MSS** (Ministry of State Security): The intelligence, security, and secret police agency of the People's Republic of China, responsible for counterintelligence, foreign intelligence, and political security. A document from the US Department of Justice described the agency as a combination of CIA and FBI.

Ivan had a reflexive fear of such "organs of the state." A fear that was drilled into his psyche from the earliest days of his childhood in Tito's Yugoslavia. His perspective was probably colored by the fact that a distant uncle from his mother's part of the family has been on the wrong side of Yugoslav politics in the postwar years so that the family lore that he grew up with dictated fear and wariness of the police. But it was also a general knowledge absorbed by just growing up there and then. Everybody knew it—instinctively. Do not mess with the police—especially the secret police. Turn the other way. Run and hide.

But perhaps a bit overblown in this case, Ivan thought. *Maybe it is just like the DARPA[33] connection to our DoD.*

But Junjie's description of their determination to complete the acquisition of BBI despite the CFIUS injunction and the ugly turn of events that forced him to use some kompromat to blackmail Aki into cooperation—that was positively frightening. Ivan was utterly stunned. And seriously concerned.

I am not messing around with the Chinese government, the PLA, or their CIA! No way! This is like Yugoslav UDBA.[34] No way.

His primary urge was to get up and walk away.

And judging from Aki's pale face, he was probably just as dismayed. And probably just as eager to walk away as Ivan was.

Stunned silence was all that either Ivan or Aki could manage in response to Junjie's revelations. They just stared at him.

"First," Junjie continued, "I want to apologize. I am ashamed. To be involved with dirt. With this kind of people. People who want me to blackmail you, Aki. I want no part of that. Believe me, I am deeply ashamed. But before you get up and walk away in disgust, please hear me out."

---

[33] **DARPA** (Defense Advanced Research Projects Agency): An arm of the United States Department of Defense responsible for the development of emerging technologies for use by the military. With a mission of "Strategic Surprise" and often credited for the invention of the internet, DARPA is a source of funding for very disruptive technologies tapped by many US research labs and academic institutions.

[34] **UDBA**: Serbo-Croatian acronym for Yugoslavia's secret police organization (like KGB or FBI…).

Ivan could see that Junjie was working hard to control him-self—to be as even and measured as he could manage. There was not a tremor in his voice or any other such overt sign of emotional turmoil. Just a steely stone face with maybe a slight jutting of the jaw and very measured—almost robotic—movements. And terse clipped sentences—as if he was reading down a list of items that he had to mention. Junjie kept his gaze mostly downcast, fixed on some spot on the table, but whenever his eyes flitted about, they shone in a way that Ivan has not seen before—in as much as he could read Junjie's inscrutable oriental[35] face. Shining with some strong emotions? Maybe…close to tears? Pleading for understanding? For forgiveness? Maybe shame? Ivan was not sure what Junjie was feeling, but it was clear that he was working hard to contain some strong pent-up emo-tions that seemed to be boiling beneath the surface. Holding himself on very tight reins.

This must be so hard for him—a proud man like Junjie, Ivan thought.

Aki, on the other hand, turned into a block of ice. Arms crossed. Hard face. Blank dark slits in place of his eyes. Proverbial shields up. Waiting.

Stunned silence.

"Once I finally understood the scheme, my first impulse was also to run away," Junjie continued, in an earnest and more animated way, now eagerly seeking direct eye contact. Seemingly trying to con-trol a flood of thoughts that he must have been chewing over for a while. "I don't want to be involved with anything as disgusting as blackmail. No way. But I was told in no uncertain terms that if I do walk away, it would be bad. For me, for my company, and for my family. After some thought, I realized that I have no choice. Being Chinese, with my whole family there, and with all my assets locked

---

[35] **Inscrutable oriental**: A moniker often applied to Chinese that is left over from the colonial times when the Europeans who, unable or unwilling to appreciate the diverse social customs of the region, more or less gave up trying to figure it out and simply wrote off all local people as "inscrutable" or mysterious/unread-able. The stereotype has been carried on to the modern times (e.g., in the mov-ies and media, usually with negative connotations).

in China, I have no choice. I must collaborate—or at least appear to cooperate—with the dictates of the government. Especially when those dictates come from PLA or MSS."

Stony silence.

"I would fully understand that you want to walk away," he carried on, now pointedly looking from Aki to Ivan and back. "I would if I was in your place. But!" Pause amplified by a slap of the table. "But I believe that they will continue the campaign to get BBI. And they may come at you with a lot more than the kompromat that they shared with me." He made air quotes and lowered his voice slightly whenever mentioning "they."

Silence.

"So I suspect that you too"—looking at Aki—"actually have no choice. I don't know—and don't want to know—what else they may have on you, but I believe that there is much more than this." He concluded, tossing an A4 size envelope on the table and sliding it toward Aki.

Aki just glanced at it, distaste written all over his face, as if it was something dirty and that he would not want to touch. He did not pick it up and said nothing.

"So, again, I must apologize to you. I have stupidly become an instrument that has brought this to your doorstep, and for that, I am truly sorry. I wish I could undo it somehow. But I cannot. So…," Junjie trailed off.

"So?" Ivan asked, finally finding his voice and recovering his composure.

"So I believe that the only decent thing that I can do now is to help deal with the consequences. I believe that the best, and in fact in my opinion the only, thing that we can do now is to join forces and figure out a way of stopping them."

Ivan got up, nervously paced the room, and argumentatively said, "Join forces to do what? What can three old engineers do against the People's Republic of China or, if you are right, the PLA and… what did you call them…the MSS?"

Aki said nothing. He has not moved a muscle since Junjie began.

"I have no idea," Junjie retorted, "but I do know that if we don't do something now, things will only get uglier. They will not let it go and magically drop everything. We do not get to just walk away from the merger talks and carry on as if nothing has happened. They will amp up the pressure. I believe that if we do not refuse now, in the long run, we will end up being just exponents of their corrupt schemes. And I believe that three heads are always better than one. Having brought it on him, I do not want to leave Aki handling alone whatever they choose to do next. So let's put our gray heads together and figure out something…"

Aki suddenly got up, picked up the envelope on the table, and said, "Give me twenty-four hours. I need to think about this—alone. Let us meet here tomorrow and then talk about it."

He barely waited for Ivan and Junjie to nod, perhaps somewhat hesitantly, before he walked out, leaving them staring at the door that closed behind him.

"Dog's bollocks!" Junjie muttered, looking desperately at Ivan. "Now what?"

Ivan shrugged, not knowing what to do or say.

They stayed in the conference room and talked for a few more hours with Junjie filling Ivan in with all the background. About Professor Lao. About the pinch point strategy. About the ways that the Chinese government works and the antibodies that Lao talked about. About Junjie's fears and sense of shame. About everything…

Aki Roussos
Friday, July 5, PM
Sunset Cliffs, San Diego, California, USA

Goddamn, shit, and fuck!

Aki was back at his bench, but this time, entirely unaware of his surroundings. He came there more by force of habit than because he consciously decided that he needed his thinking bench. The news that Junjie brought were disturbing, and he needed to parse them. It was not just the threat of dissolution of the BBI sale to CHARM—a transaction that he was by then quite committed to. Nor the threat of blackmail—something that did not scare him since he had nothing to hide. It was this talk of the various secret parts of the Chinese government: things that he heard about only in the movies and that had nothing to do with his world. Until then.

He finally forced himself to open the envelope that was sitting next to him—silently accusing him of something.

Keiko! Pictures of him and Keiko.

What the fuck? Where the hell did they get these? Are they for real?

His first instinct was to suspect that it was some kind of a fake. The kind of things you read about in the tabloids. He examined the photographs looking for some telltale signs of misplaced blurs or something out of place. Nothing. Or at least nothing that his untrained eyes could spot.

Why? Why the fuck would someone take these? And keep them for all these years?

It has been, what, more than fifteen years since then. Pretty much ten years since he even last thought of Keiko.

They—whoever the fuck they are—must have gotten them from Keiko? But that would be so very much not like her... Cannot be. I should double-check, though. But how?

He has entirely lost contact with Keiko since they split up. She left him, left BBI, left the city, and moved on. She disappeared, and even back then—while he was still trying to stop her from leaving him—she vanished without a trace. Finding her now: impossible. Probably a fool's errand that would take months at best. Besides, even if he found her, would he want to confront her? Would it resurrect all those feelings? He shied away from pursuing that thread of thought.

However they got these—from Keiko or whoever—does it really matter? Probably not. No, not really.

He was completely befuddled. Not so much by the pictures themselves—he had to admit that those looked real enough. On further inspection, he thought that he could even place each of the scenes in the photographs. Looked genuine.

It must have been Keiko. She was a bit of a shutterbug... She kept them? Wow... But how the hell did the Chinese whatchamacallit get them?

He was a bit flattered but mostly puzzled by the fact that Keiko would bother to keep them. And he was certainly confused and alarmed that they ended up in the hands of the Chinese government.

The thought of Keiko triggered a mixture of recollections that came at him in a kind of flood of mental images. Dredging up all the emotions from his time with her. The passion. The thrill and the exhilaration. And yes, the love. And the guilt. In fact—mostly the guilt.

Thoughts, feelings, and mental pictures that he has not revisited in years. But inevitably superimposed on the scenes of Keiko in Japan also came the images of Mary with Nicole in the hospital here. And the enormous sense of guilt.

Yes, he did have an affair with Keiko all those years ago. Back then—about twenty years ago—he realized that in order to capture the business from all the mask shops in Japan, he needed a BBI subsidiary there. Necessary to access, to get close to, more than half of the global photomask making market. So he was spending a lot of time in Japan. First to negotiate the bureaucracy involved, then to establish the office and the lab, then to hire the people and transfer the technology, then to develop all the relationships with the local suppliers and customers… A lot of work and a lot of time. Many lonely nights and weekends alone in a faceless anonymous megapolis.

At first, Keiko was just one of his hires. Then a colleague who would occasionally accompany him to dinner. Then a friend who would sometimes show him around the city during the weekends. Then a companion who came with him on his business trips there. Then a lover. Then an obsession.

He was ready to leave America and move to Japan to be with her. Every time he was there—with her—he swore that he would do it. Soon… Mostly to himself.

But every time he came back home to America, to a good wife—a woman whom he loved, a mother of his only child—and to a sick daughter fighting leukemia, he realized that he could not. Never.

Over the years, after Keiko left him and the passion faded, he rationalized that it was a kind of temporary insanity. It was the only way that he could explain why a man he thought himself to be— steady, cautious, and thoughtful—would get involved in such an affair. He rationalized that it was as if some kind of an evil twin—a doppelganger[36]—occupied his body. Not the real him. There were two people in one body. One loved Keiko—blindly and passionately. And one loved Mary—deeply and honestly. Doppelgangers. He lived with the excitement and anxiety, stress and euphoria—schizophrenia—of the double life for almost two years.

It was Keiko who finally freed him. Back then, she probably understood him better than he understood himself, and in a typical Keiko-fashion, with no recrimination or regret, she just accepted the situation as a fact of life. Accepted that no matter what he said, and indeed believed, he would never leave his American family. Accepted it as if some God-ordained reality was revealed to her. Her fate. Not something that either of them could affect or change. Fatalism—that was so very Japanese.

And so she did what she thought was the only honorable thing to do. She left. He, of course, tried to stop her. Needed to keep her close. Needed to be with her. Wanted to rage against the reality and fight the fates. Wanted to deny the truth… But she only smiled her tranquil and enchanting Mona Lisa smile and disappeared.

Leaving him with just a terrible sense of guilt.

Overtime, his passion cooled, and he was even grateful that she had the fortitude to leave him. His feelings faded. Except for the guilt. Even now, just thinking about it, the pangs of guilt were just as acute as they were back then.

In the months—maybe even years—that he took to fully pick that part of his life apart, he came to understand that his affair with Keiko was a coping mechanism for him. That, in a way, he used her like some kind of an opiate. To cope with Nicole's leukemia. An escape. None of that had anything to do with Mary or the love that he felt for her. And for Nicole. But that awareness did nothing to alleviate his sense of guilt that washed over him, like a wave, every time he dredged up the memories.

So he mostly didn't. He has not thought about Keiko and his double life in more than ten years. And he has never tried to explain

---

[36] **Doppelganger**: A nonbiologically related look-alike or double of a living person, sometimes portrayed as a ghostly or paranormal phenomenon. (Source: German mid-nineteenth century literally "double-goer.")

it to Mary. How could he? It sounded so lame even to him. "Look, dear, it was not really me who was with Keiko. It was my evil doppelganger who occupied my body." Really! So he didn't.

Mary may have had her suspicions at the time. Possibly. They say that women sense those things. But she did not say anything, and so they never talked about it. He just bottled up the guilt and all the feelings associated with that time in his life and buried them deep in the basement of his mind. The whole affair with Keiko was a dark secret locked away in his past.

This is all too crazy. Fuck it! There is nothing I can do about the past. I am just going to bury this.

He put the photographs back in the envelope and decided that he would treat them as if they did not exist. An act of will. Like one treated some kind of a nightmare. Like he treated the entire history with Keiko. Not real or relevant to here and now. There was nothing that he could do about them anyways.

He was a bit relieved with that decision. It somehow alleviated the pressure to make any choices or to act in any way.

Besides—it was years ago. It does not matter anymore, he told himself… He shook his head, as if to drive the memories and the guilt away.

But then, a mental movie played in his head and a scene of Mary looking through these pictures popped up. And in an instant, he realized that real or not, however they—whoever the fuck they are—got them, he had to keep those photographs, and the sordid side of his life that they revealed, from Mary. The source or the authenticity of the pictures was entirely irrelevant.

No way that Mary can see these. No way!

He assured himself that he did not have any feelings about the pictures and did not really care if they became public or about whoever may or may not see them—except for Mary. Mary deserved better than the man in those pictures. The man that he was back then. Confronting her with these pictures would only cause her pain. She deserved better.

If he was more honest with himself, he would have realized that it was not just the determination to shelter Mary that drove him. It was also his shame at how he behaved and his fear of having to face the truth that he has hidden for so many years. No way could he look her—or himself—in the eye again if it all bubbled up to the surface. He needed to keep his dark secret hidden to preserve his self-image almost as much as he needed to shelter Mary.

Gradually, he realized—accepted—that he would do anything to keep the pictures and everything they conveyed secret.

Anything at all. Yes, he would even sell BBI. Sell his baby to whichever devil they want him to. In whatever way they want him to. Sell his people—colleagues, friends—their jobs and their security. Anything...

No way is he taking Mary through the pain...

Having accepted that decision, he was ready to go. But he knew that there was another key loose end that he had to consider. That he could not just leave it at that and walk away.

There was a basic question of trust that he had to assess and analyze. Should he trust Junjie? And by extension, should he trust whatever Junjie said? After all, he barely knew the man.

Maybe all this is some kind of a lie? A fake? A trap? A mind game?

There was a voice of caution in his head, warning him to be careful. A voice that sounded somewhat like his mother and that he was used to heeding.

Careful, Aki, it said. *An introduction by a remote acquaintance— after all, what do you know even about Ivan? And Junjie? A few phone calls? And here he is now, threatening blackmail and all sorts of dire consequences. Careful, Aki.*

But there was also a voice of intuition in his head. Impulsive and perhaps somewhat emotional. A voice, sounding remotely like his father, arguing that he should go with his instinct.

Archimedes, your intuition has always served you well. Trust it. What does your gut tell you? Besides, why would Junjie lie? What would he have to gain by inventing all this? If anything, he only stands to lose...

Even though Aki was a cautious man, he often did rely on his gut feeling. But almost exclusively in the realm of business only. This was an arena where he felt that his experience and industry knowledge gave him all the background information so that subliminal decision-making could be trusted. But the situation he was facing then was different. Entirely alien to him. Caution was merited. Definitely.

So Aki tried to force himself to be disciplined and structured.

Make a list of pros and cons. Do not accept what Junjie says just on the face of it. Make a case for trusting him!

But he could not. He tried. But no matter how much he admonished himself to make a balanced list, he could not. He could not think of a single credible reason why Junjie would be inventing the dirt and the whole set up.

Firstly, it was obscure and only Aki knew it—the stuff about Keiko. Not something that could be easily manufactured or just made up on a whim. Something that presumably took a vast network—such as one would assume the Chinese government to have— to gather. Just like Junjie said.

Second, why? Why would anyone go through all the trouble to set up the kompromat? And again, the only rational reason that came to mind was to compel him to bypass the CFIUS injunction and sell BBI to a Chinese concern. It was the only sane reason that he could think of. Just like Junjie said.

And third, given just the little that Aki knew of China, it seemed to him that everything that Junjie was doing—trying to talk Aki out of simple selling out—could only hurt Junjie. Surely, the easiest thing for Junjie to do would have been to obey the orders of his government. The only possible nefarious reason that Aki could cook up for Junjie's behavior would be that he was trying to trick Aki into playing a role in some elaborate internal political scheme? Far-fetched? And it seemed rather irrational to Aki—since his own path of least resistance was to sell out. Why set it up, to begin with, if the intent is to scupper it? Made no sense. So it seemed to Aki that the only rational reason for Junjie's behavior was to try to untangle himself from a situation that he hated. Just like Junjie said.

No, Aki could not come up with rational reasons to distrust Junjie. And on top of that, his intuition—his gut feeling—was to sympathize with Junjie's predicament.

Well, then, Archimedes, he told himself, *proceed assuming that Junjie is trustworthy. But cautiously and carefully. Keep an open and wary eye…*

The Three Conspirators

"All right. I will do whatever the fuck they want," Aki stated resolutely the moment they gathered and closed the door of the conference room. "There is no way I want my family to see these," he added, tossing the envelope back toward Junjie. "Tell me again, what exactly is it that they want me to do?"

All business. No emotion. He was a rock.

"*They* want you to do it Ivan's Yugoslav way—transfer all BBI assets to its Japanese subsidiary and then sell that to CHARM, lock stock, and barrel," Junjie responded directly.

And then after a short pause, this time emphasizing the "I," "But *I* want you to fully understand what that would mean… Putting it bluntly, it would mean that they own you. Us. We would become cogs in their machine. Potentially putting us in an ever more compromising position in the future."

"Like what?" Aki demanded argumentatively. "What could they want with me after they got BBI?"

"You don't know them the way I do." Junjie was deadly serious now, leaning forward and staring directly into Aki's eyes. "Once you are tainted—and make no mistake—you giving in now would taint you in their eyes, you become an asset in their toolbox. Every time you give in a bit, you become that much dirtier and hence that much more useful to them. They would keep you on at BBI and milk you as long as they can."

"How? What would I have that they would want?" Aki persisted, clearly showing that he just could not conceive of someone pressuring him personally—once he was stripped of his professional cloak. In his mind, his sense of self-worth was very much tied to his role at BBI.

"I am just speculating now," Junjie continued, "but this could begin with something relatively benign. Like using you, the CEO of BBI, and your relationship with your clients to perturb the supply chain. Maybe suggest that you drop the price for some select customers and then once they are fully dependent on BBI, order you to shut off their supply. Or use you as a political pawn and tell you to break your contracts and cut off all clients from some targeted countries. Or force you to pursue BBI competitors in the courts on some kind of trumped-up patent infringement charges, just to harass a targeted company. Then after you complied with these benign demands, they could amp things up and use you to plant misinformation somewhere. Or maybe make you falsify your QA inspection reports in order to inject some kind of defect into specific BBI blanks. To infect a portion of the mask supply chain. Or to sabotage a specific product or a targeted company. And eventually, once you are compromised enough, make you commit outright illegal acts—things like stealing secrets, manipulating the markets, bribing people, recruiting other spies…" He counted off on his fingers the various ways that he heard MSS used in their game of industrial espionage or economic extortion. "Ultimately the kinds of things that people go to jail for…for a very long time," he finished.

Aki just stared at Junjie, saying nothing but presumably internalizing the threats.

"I don't really know. The thing that I do know is that they would own us. Me more than you, but you too to a great degree. Forever," Junjie concluded emphatically.

Sullen silence.

"Yeah. That sounds about right to me. From the little that I know, that would be typical of the kind of things that the secret police do. Anywhere and everywhere," interjected Ivan. To him, the scenario outlined by Junjie was credible. Reminiscent of the kinds of things that the secret police were supposed to have done in Yugoslavia. Kinds of things he overheard older people talk about in hushed tones... "But what choice does he have?" Ivan questioned, sounding as resigned as Aki looked.

"I don't know, but I believe that we must resist now. And that if we do not, we will regret it down the road," Junjie retorted defensively.

"Resist how?" Ivan persisted.

"You think we should reach out to the FBI or someone like that? The CIA? The police? Someone in the US government that is supposed to protect me," Aki asked, perking up a bit. Like he has seen a ray of hope.

"Yes and no," Junjie responded. "Maybe yes, if we had something concrete to show them. Something that was of value to your FBI. Right now, I have nothing. Nothing at all other than a generic chart, a report on BBI, that kompromat, and my credit line with the Big Fund. And my suspicions. Weak..."

Pause, with Aki and Ivan staring at him.

"And no, if a visit to the FBI leads to the awkward questions reaching wrong ears. All that would do is alert them that someone is looking. And I suspect that this, in turn, would lead to things spinning out of control and them amping up the pressure. Could be further blackmail. Could be just leaks of absurd stories to the press, causing embarrassment, or maybe some out-of-proportion political flak. Which would in the end make it much more difficult to extricate yourself from the mess. You, me, our reputations, our families, our companies, and people—all likely collateral damage."

Silence.

"Yeah, I guess that too sounds right," Ivan interjected. "With the trade war and the antagonistic atmosphere between the US and China, there can be no cooperation. So even if we take the most wildly optimistic view and assume that this whole thing is a scheme run by some rogue group within the Chinese government, it is not like the good side of their establishment would come to help. So even if we did have some kind of proof—what could the FBI do with it to protect you? Nothing."

Dejected silence.

"For what it is worth, I think—the sense I got—is that the only thing that they care about is premature exposure of their pinch point strategy. Professor Lao is scared that early exposure would lead to the US blocking his plan," Junjie ventured.

"Huh? Pinch point strategy? Professor Lao? What the hell are you talking about?" Aki demanded.

Junjie and Ivan exchanged puzzled looks and then realized that Aki was not in on that portion of the conversation the day before. They brought him up to speed with Junjie talking in brief fragmented sentences, presumably to get through the recap quickly. Having spent the day ruminating over the story, Ivan added explanations and elaborations whenever he felt that Junjie may be losing Aki. After about half an hour or so, Aki nodded, saying, "Okay, I get it…"

They sat there for several minutes in silence. In a dejected downcast mood. Then Aki picked up where they left off, "So maybe we can take that pinch point strategy to the FBI. Surely, that is something valuable for the US government?" He spoke up hopefully.

"True," Ivan opined, "true if we found someone in the FBI who [a] believed us with no proof and [b] understood it and appreciated it for what it is. There is a hell of a lot more to this than someone connected to the Chinese government using underhanded means to buy small US companies. The implications of this pinch point strategy of theirs are huge. If successful, China could potentially control the entire semiconductor industry. At least for a while. That is big. But not something that a regular schlub on the street, or for that matter, even a highly trained FBI agent, is likely to get. If he believed the story." Ivan was clearly skeptical of a government official—any nonengineer—appreciating the implications.

"But if that is the case, then surely, surely, we have a responsibility to alert the US government! If what you say is true, then this is bigger than just the three of us, and we have a, er, civic duty to report it," Aki persisted in somewhat demanding tones.

"Well," Junjie hesitated, as if thinking aloud, "even if we did find someone in the US government who appreciated it for what it is, I am not sure how they could protect you—us—though. Potentially, we could help the US block the pinch point takeover. True. But given the current animosity, I fear that you and I would get burned on the way. The Chinese side would definitely not forget or forgive being outed. They would release whatever they have on you if for no other reason than just for spite. And I don't want to begin speculating what they might do to me and my family—to punish me for leaking their secret. And I am guessing that the US government, in turn, would do whatever it took to stick it to China. I doubt that either side would be interested in protecting you and me."

"Not to mention that going to the FBI would probably only serve to exacerbate the relationship. Make the trade war worse," Ivan added.

"So you guys are saying that it is an either-or tradeoff?" Aki challenged. "Either we do the right thing and get burned on the way, or we protect our butts and let this Professor Lao do whatever he wants? Is that it?"

"Yeah. I am sorry, Aki," Junjie confirmed. "I believe so."

"Doesn't that then just boil down to a choice of how we get shafted?" Aki demanded.

But as he digested what he just said and with images of Mary looking through those photographs flashing through his mind, Aki sat up and protested, "Wait! I refuse to believe that that's it. Is there nothing in between! There must be. There always is."

Ivan suddenly got up, walked resolutely to the whiteboard hanging on the wall of the conference room, and selected one of the markers. "So why don't the three old engineers do what they are trained to do, the SWOT analysis?" He clearly got an idea of some kind.

"The what?" Aki and Junjie asked in unison.

"SWOT. Strengths, Weaknesses, Opportunities, Threats. Surely you have done that kind of formal analysis when making strategic business decisions."

"Humph. You forget that we are small company guys," Aki reacted dismissively, pointing to himself and Junjie. "We make strategic decisions mostly by gut feel. We do not have the time to screw around with the management bullshit like you, big-company droids," he concluded, alluding to Ivan's career with large companies like Unisys, Cadence, and Qualcomm with Junjie nodding and looking dubious.

"Okay. Bear with me." Ivan drew on the board a square subdivided into four equal quadrants. He titled the quadrants Strengths, Weaknesses, Opportunities, Threats, respectively, saying, "The top two squares, the strengths and weaknesses, refer to our internal attributes, and the bottom two, the opportunities and threats, to the external factors. This whole technique is just a way of breaking up a knotty problem into bite-size pieces to help us precipitate a plan. So let's just talk about each section separately and see what comes out."

Aki and Junjie leaned back in their chairs, suspicious of whatever Ivan was suggesting. Waiting.

"First, it is important to precisely define and constrain the problem," Ivan said and wrote in big bold letters above the drawing: "Objective: stop Professor Lao." "Let us focus on the specific local issue. It is not like we can solve the global trade war problems."

Ivan intuitively tended to personalize all problems. Probably due to what he felt was a genetic predisposition of all people from the Balkans—or maybe just the wisdom he picked up in Yugoslavia from his earliest childhood and on. Whatever the origin of this impulse, his lifelong experience told him that all problems—big or small— were solved by dealing with people, not organizations. This was at a subliminal level—not something that he was explicitly aware of. He just knew that it was useless to try to deal with something as amorphous and shapeless as the Chinese government and that it would be much more productive to focus on a specific individual who personalized or caused the problem—like this Professor Lao.

"Okay. Strengths?" he asked, turning to face Aki and Junjie. "What are the strengths that we—the three of us—have in this cat-and-mouse game versus Professor Lao?"

"Well, for one, we do know of his pinch point strategy," Junjie volunteered.

"And if I understand you correctly, this Professor Lao of yours is worried about showing his hand prematurely," Aki added.

"Excellent points," Ivan exclaimed, writing notes on the whiteboard. He was pleased that Aki and Junjie took to the process so readily. It was good—even therapeutic—to be doing rather than just worrying and feeling helpless.

Maybe this is also healthy for us, he thought to himself.

"Okay, and the weaknesses," he goaded. "Remember, we can always come back and elaborate as we go along. As things occur to us. In fact, that is how it normally works—a comment for one quadrant often triggers a thought for some other quadrant."

They stayed in the room, brainstorming and talking for most of the day, Aki and Junjie probably sharing in the comfort of activity. Of doing something. Anything was better than just sitting there and feeling helpless. They ordered pizza for lunch, and Ivan brought some beers down from his unit. All three of them were fully engaged, throwing out thoughts, discussing each of the points, adding ideas… It was dusk outside by the time they seem to have exhausted all avenues of thought. After many additions and erasures the chart on the whiteboard was smudged and messy but concise.

OBJECTIVE: Stop Professor Lao

	Strengths	Weakness
Internal	• Know of the Pinch Point Plan • Understand its significance • Aware of their overall plan • Aware of their need for secrecy • Aware of their sense of urgency • Have something they want (BBI & CHARM)	• 3 lone old guys • Not 'operatives' • Not hackers • Vulnerable (BBI & CHARM) • Vulnerable (families) • Not on either side (US or China)
	Opportunities	Threats
External	• No one aware of us colluding • We are Under the Radar • Surprise factor on our side • Time: We are not in a hurry • We have something they want (BBI & CHARM)	• Aki Kompromat leaking out • Yanfeng livelihood/safety • Busted and exposed • Lao wants to take over the world • US not aware of the PP plan • Treason if not reported

The three of them sat back facing the whiteboard and stared at it. Junjie put his feet up on the table and leaned way back, crossing his arms behind his head—thinking. Aki sat erect, arms crossed. Thinking. Ivan fiddled with the marker he used—thinking.

After a long while, Ivan broke the silence and volunteered, "All right. Here is a proposal. For something like a middle way. Between reporting it to the FBI and getting screwed on the way and giving in and letting Lao have his way with you. An outline of a strategy. Tell me why it is wrong…"

Pregnant pause with Aki and Junjie looking at Ivan expectantly.

"First, it is clear that there is nothing that we can do about the trade war. It is going to go as it is going to go. Agreed?"

Aki and Junjie shrugged and nodded readily. This was obvious.

"Second, I assume that neither one of you two wants to get involved with it—on either side. Agreed?"

Aki and Junjie took a bit longer to weigh this, but in the end, both nodded resolutely.

"Okay, good. I thought as much. So let me postulate a theory. In the long run," Ivan proposed, "given that you two guys do not wish to become weapons—or collateral damage—in a fight between the two dragons, the only way you and yours can be safe is if you distance yourselves from your respective companies. Surely, Professor Lao—and by extension, the Chinese government—is interested in you only to get to your companies. Same would presumably be true for the US government if and when it wakes up to Lao's ploy. BBI and CHARM are the assets in this game—not you two…"

Pause. Aki nodded slowly. Junjie shrugged slightly. Both agreeing—but grudgingly so.

Noticing their hesitation, Ivan reminded himself that Aki and Junjie were probably used to thinking of their companies as extensions of themselves—not as separate entities. *Like parents do when their kids are little. Maybe that is normal for company founding fathers?*

"Ergo," Ivan continued aloud, "you have to distance yourselves from those assets. Assuming that Lao is rational, he, and the dragon behind him, will focus on BBI and CHARM and the whole pinch point strategy. If you sever the link between yourselves and your companies, they will forget about you two. Same would be true for the feds—the other dragon. Overtime, any association between you and BBI and CHARM would dissipate and would presumably eventually be entirely erased."

Silence.

"That is the only way that I can see that you two get to walk away from this whole thing and live the rest of your sorry lives in peace and quiet," Ivan concluded, to drive his point home.

Silence.

"That means that you have to cast off your companies—cut the umbilical cord so to speak. Let some new management deal with the dragons. I assume you are ready for that," he clarified and waited for Aki and Junjie to confirm. This was a critical axiom of the strategy he was proposing. Ivan knew how they felt about their companies— their babies—and thought that this was pushing their nose into a reality that they may not have fully accepted yet. *Must be hard for them. Poor sods.*

Then, as if to encourage them, Ivan added, "If it makes you feel any better, I believe that this distancing would actually be good for your companies too. In this global power game that we are caught up in, you two have become a liability to your respective companies. That is why they are pushing on you personally. You are the weak links. It is very obvious in your case, Aki, but is also true for you, Junjie. So separating yourselves from the companies you founded is also a way of securing the future of your creations. It is the right thing to do for your companies too."

Aki and Junjie stared at him for a long time—digesting what he just told them. Probably looking for reasons to disagree. Finally, having found none, they nodded—still hesitating but consenting.

Ivan tried to relate to their feelings by making a kind of a parallel in his head. He tried to understand Aki and Junjie by imagining how a parent would feel. *Not easy feeling like a whole company—people, business, everything—depended on you. Big burden to tote about. For years. And then someone tells you to walk away. Must be like bringing up a child and then someone tells you that she is grown up and you should let her be. Hard. Poor sods.*

Having gotten their consent—however grudging—Ivan allowed, "But this distancing is going to take time. It is not like you guys can just walk away from your babies at a drop of a hat. You will need some time to elegantly separate yourselves from BBI and CHARM. Enough time to find a safe pair of hands to take over your companies. So we need a ploy to check Professor Lao in the near term—like right now..."

After a short pause, he continued with his thread of thought, "The way I see it, the only way to do this would be to get some concrete proof of Lao's strategy. We need more than just Junjie's suspicions. Once we got that, we do *not* give it to the FBI—that would only get us involved in a big game that we are not qualified or interested in playing. So we just threaten that we will release the information to the US government unless he backs off. That is his one weak point. So we have to push on it. We threaten him that we will expose his strategy if he picks on you two. That should make him pause for a bit. Hopefully enough of a delay to allow you two to implement the long-term strategy."

Silence. Long quiet period with each of them looking from the whiteboard to each other and back. They were clearly not on board with Ivan's proposal. Yet.

"So are you two sure that you are willing to part with your companies in order to disentangle yourselves from the mess that this has become? To protect your families, and presumably your legacies?" Ivan asked again.

Junjie and Aki looked at each other and started to speak at the same time. They both stopped and started again. Then Junjie fell silent and waved for Aki to go first.

"Yes," Aki spoke up. "I am clearly ready to sell and leave BBI. But given my druthers, only to, what did you call it, a safe pair of hands. I owe it to my people to put in place a transition to a good new leader who would ensure BBI's long-term survival. You can call it 'my legacy' if you like. I do not want to sell out to just anyone. Unless you hold a gun to my head—like this Professor Lao is doing."

Ivan and Aki turned to face Junjie, who after a pregnant pause just said, "Ditto. I feel very much the same about CHARM."

"Okay, good," Ivan concluded, tapping the table as if to mark the end of that topic. "Ergo, we should concentrate on the near-term issue. To remove that gun from your heads and give you the time to find a safe pair of hands for your companies. So we must obtain a concrete proof of Lao's pinch point strategy."

"Well... I guess all you say is true enough." Aki drew out. "The big question is, surely, how? How the fuck are we going to get that 'concrete proof'?" He made the air quotes with his fingers, adding, "It is not like Professor Lao will just hand it over to us if we ask him nicely?"

"True," Junjie interjected. "We would have to extract it from him somehow. By ruse or force? By tricking him? By extortion? Or by stealing it, maybe..."

Silence as the questions hung in the air. Verbalizing what they were contemplating—robbing and extorting Professor Lao—was sobering for each one of them.

"None of which are the kinds of things that any of us have had much experience with," Aki stated the obvious.

Silence.

"True. But even if we did have the right experience, the primary question is, *should* we?" Junjie opined. "Not can we? Should we get involved with theft and extortion with someone like Professor Lao—or the people behind him? That would be like poking a hornet's nest. Waking up a sleeping snake. Potentially a very nasty snake."

Pregnant silence. Given their life experience in the sheltered, and some would say the genteel high-tech world, this was so scary to them that it was abstract.

"Maybe another way of putting that is, why?" Ivan added. "Why would we—three old geezers—risk waking a potentially nasty snake? Is our motivation sufficient to justify such a risk?" And then after a short pause, he added, "Or is the risk sufficient to make us fold right here and now?"

Long pause as each one of them mulled over the questions—internalizing the seriousness of what they were contemplating. Making the tradeoffs in their mind... How far would they be willing to go? Why would they take the risks, and if so, how would they do it all?

Aki suddenly got up and said decisively, "All good and valid questions… Presumably, questions that we—each one of us individually—have to answer for ourselves. Let's do this. Let's take some time—twenty-four hours—to think it over. Why don't you, gentlemen, come over to my house for dinner tomorrow and we finish this there?"

Ivan Jovanovic
Sunday, July 7, AM
Cortez Hill, San Diego, California, USA

Ivan went up to the pool on top of his building earlier than normal—just as the gym area opened: 6:00 a.m.—for his morning swim and to do some thinking. The sun was peeking over the distant Cuyamaca Mountains in the east and casting a crisp yellowish glow over San Diego. The mist that separated the heated pool from the chilly night air still hugged the glassy surface of the water. It was very quiet and peaceful with the city below still mostly asleep, and only the sound of an occasional early-riser commuter car breaking the silence.

Probably too early even for Jonathan Livingston, he thought to himself. Jonathan Livingston was a name he gave to a seagull who, much to the chagrin of the cleaning crew, occasionally came and shared the open-air pool with the few morning swimmers before it got crowded.

Ivan got in and started swimming his laps, noticing only that the water felt a little bit colder than normal. After all, he got to enjoy the view every day, and none of it was particularly remarkable to him. One…two…three…

He found that other than with work-related issues, he was usually too fidgety to concentrate on a single subject for a long time. Normally, his mind tended to flit from topic to topic—following some bizarre web of associations. Except when he was busy doing something repetitive and mindless. Like swimming. That seemed to keep the part of his brain that generated the random thoughts quiet—maybe busy counting the laps and working out the associated derivative metrics.

Five...six... Usually, he averaged eighteen strokes per lap, which—according to the wall clock—took him about one minute. So for the twenty-five-meter pool length, he was doing about 1.4 meters per stroke in about 3.3 seconds...with a sigma[37] of about a stroke per lap, driven probably by the strength of his push off, his kick rate, and possibly the number of other swimmers... Seven...eight...

Freeing whatever part of his brain that was responsible for logical thought to focus and concentrate on the events that took place over the previous couple of days. Swimming was his Zen moment, and Ivan purposely put off all attempts to think about their problem until his morning swim. His mind could now focus on Junjie's revelations and Aki's predicament. And the gambit that they were contemplating.

During the initial few laps, while his mind was busy recapping, he mostly felt a sense of gratitude and maybe relief. *Well, none of it is really my problem. I am just a peripheral observer. Thank God I do not own a company that anyone wants. No one is trying to blackmail me. My family and I are entirely untouched by the whole sad story. Lucky, lucky doggie, me...*

The logical side of him instantly concluded that the only rational thing for him to do is to make sure that he remained uninvolved. *Duh. No-brainer.* Given the supposed entanglement of the Chinese secret police, all his instincts, honed by his Yugoslav upbringing, urged him to disengage from the mess. *Turn around and run. It is not my problem. Run Ivan, run...*

Nine...ten...

Somewhere around a quarter way through his routine, he started pondering about Aki and Junjie. How they may be feeling and what they might or might not do.

---

[37] **Sigma** (standard deviation): A measure of the amount of variation among a set of values in a normal bell-shaped distribution. A low sigma indicates that the values tend to be close to the mean while a high sigma indicates that the values are spread out over a wider range.

Eleven…twelve…thirteen…

Aki is in deep bandini,[38] *the poor bugger. Having to choose between family and BBI has got to be hard for him. Probably like those horror scenarios where you have to pick which one of your two kids you would save… Although whatever dirt they have on him seems to trump all his care for BBI and love of his friends, colleagues, and people there. Family wins. Poor guy.*

For a few laps, Ivan tried to imagine what that dirt might be. But he found it difficult. Aki was such a straight arrow. Other than his tendency to swear, which Ivan assumed is just a natural consequence of public education in America, Aki appeared to be so proper that it was hard for Ivan to imagine him getting into a situation that is even remotely blackmailable.

I bet he wouldn't cross a street on a red light even in the middle of a night with no one around, Ivan thought. *Must be the Japanese side of him.*

Yet there must have been something in his past—and the Chinese secret police clearly found it.

Ivan then tried to imagine Aki in some kind of a ploy to force Professor Lao to back off—and found it equally difficult to picture. He thought of Aki as a very deliberate and cautious kind of a man. Very analytic and not at all rash or spontaneous.

He probably ponders long and hard and takes his twenty-four hours to decide if and when to fart, Ivan thought.

Not the kind of a man who Ivan could imagine getting involved in—or successfully pulling off—any kind of an illegal scheme. It did not seem to Ivan that Aki had it in him. Too deliberate and analytical. Unlikely to cope well with surprises that may arise in an uncontrolled situation. Unlikely to be quick on his feet and to leverage some unforeseen opportunity. Likely to get wrapped around an axle over some irrelevant detail…

Fifteen…sixteen…seventeen…

Yet, Aki is in a pickle, and he must do something to save his BBI.

Ivan then thought about Junjie. He felt that he knew Junjie a lot better than he knew Aki. But what he knew of Junjie scared him.

---

[38] **Bandini:** A brand of fertilizer. Quite smelly. Old-time colloquialism for shit.

Junjie is probably on the other extreme, he thought. *Too impulsive and likely to leap first and think about it after…*

Unlike with Aki, Ivan could easily see Junjie getting involved with some risky scheme to extort Lao. But he could also easily imagine Junjie getting into trouble. Junjie was too confident—perhaps overly so for the kind of things that they were thinking of doing. Cocky. Not patient enough to plan ahead and compensate for his impulsiveness.

Yet, Junjie too is in a pickle, and he also must do something to save himself.

Nineteen…twenty…twenty-one…

Ivan spent the second half of his routine pondering what would be the right thing for him to do.

Do nothing? Admire the events from afar?

After all, none of it was his problem. Ultimately, it was just a gig for him, and Aki and Junjie were grown-up men who should be able to take care of themselves.

But on the other hand, he believed that Aki and Junjie would not be successful with the ploy they were contemplating. Especially in China. Aki was too cautious, slow, and rigid, and Junjie was too impulsive. They would get in trouble…

No! Doing nothing is not right.

Aki and Junjie were friends. Junjie especially was someone he was close with for almost a decade. A kind of a protégé. Letting them get into trouble and doing nothing about it was surely not the right thing to do. Not an act of a friend—or even just of a decent fellow human being.

Twenty-six…twenty-seven…twenty-eight…

Try to talk them out of it?

But trying to talk them out of doing anything was also not the right thing to do. It would be like proverbial sticking his head in the sand. Ignoring the fact that Aki and Junjie had a real problem that they had to deal with. Trying to talk them out of doing something about it would be no more than a transparent excuse to do nothing at all. Also not an act of a friend.

Thirty…thirty-one…thirty-two…

Try to get them to enlist some help? Maybe the professionals?

Maybe Aki was right, and they should call the FBI or the CIA or someone in law enforcement?

But everything in Ivan rebelled against that thought. *C'mon, Ivan, when did the police ever help anyone?* he challenged, again falling back on the biases from old Yugoslavia.

Not to mention that nothing has happened—yet. Normally, even with clean governments, the police get involved only after something took place—not before. Unless there was proof of a planned criminal act. And they had none. And it is not like the police are known for a sensitive touch that would be required to handle Aki's delicate situation. Even if they miraculously did develop a more humane touch—like the FBI might have—it is not like they would be looking out for Aki's best interests. They would be doing—probably rightly—whatever they thought was best for the US. And screw Aki.

No, he could not bring himself to believe that counseling his friends to go to the police would be either honorable or practical. Ever.

Thirty-three…thirty-four…

So join them in that ploy?

No! That would be too stupid, dangerous, and scary.

And it is not like he—Ivan—was any better equipped to deal with the kind of a situation that they were contemplating. *Of course, assuming that permanently borrowing books from a library don't count,* Ivan thought reflexively in the back of his mind. He was remembering a set of bound Scientific American books that he stole from his high school library—and that he felt guilty about ever since. That was the extent of his criminal experience remotely relevant to the kind of thing they were contemplating. Weak…

He would be as likely to fail as they were. So getting involved would be not just unhelpful but could, in fact, also be irresponsible—potentially only encouraging them to do something dangerous. Also not an act of a friend.

Thirty-five…thirty-six…thirty-seven…

So—no right answers? Doing nothing or encouraging them to do nothing would be turning a blind eye. A sin of omission. Joining them or getting them to call the FBI would be dangerous and stupid. A sin of commission...

But while doing the last of his laps, he concluded that, in fact, the righteous thing would be to help his friends. Give them the benefit of his knowledge and judgment—for whatever those may be worth—to make the best decisions. If he believed that the facts on the ground indicated that whatever they may be thinking was too dangerous, then an act of a friend would be to help them to reduce the danger. If the facts on the ground indicated that there was a chance of stopping Professor Lao, then a friend would help them to do it safely. As opposed to entirely washing his hands or telling them to do nothing. Only by honestly and constructively helping them would he have the right to counsel them to walk away—if he felt that it was not safe.

Thirty-nine...forty...

Also, he carried on with his musings, unconsciously exceeding his quota of laps, *if I were to drop out and they did get in trouble, how horrible would I feel afterward?*

Ivan thought that—God forbid—if Aki and Junjie did get caught in the act, the worst-case scenario could be quite serious. He suspected that under normal circumstances—even in China—breaking and entering would be punishable by a fine and perhaps a suspended sentence of a few months in prison. Two old guys. Respectable members of the society. First offense. One a foreigner. Etcetera. Not that bad, really. But he worried that in this specific situation, Aki and Junjie ran a risk of becoming a kind of a football in the political game between the US and China. Which could end up maximizing all the negative consequences. The Chinese side would likely want to make a point and might tag the crime as espionage, or God knows what else, and they could end up in prison for years. Or worse. Unthinkably horrible.

Surely, surely, he had an obligation to help avoid something like that. He could not live with himself if he just walked away, did nothing at all, and they ended up getting into that kind of trouble.

Not to mention that even if he were to drop out—if he walked away there and then—if Aki and Junjie were caught, he could very well be pulled into that pissing match: as a person of interest who presumably knew the most about the failed ploy. They—either the US or China—could paint him to look really bad. They could even come up with some kind of drummed-up charges against him too. He knew—well, he suspected—that in that kind of a situation, the public narrative rarely bore any relationship to the truth and was usually shaped by the political interest of whoever was telling the story. Regardless if he was actively involved or not.

So—if for nothing other than purely selfish reasons of covering his own butt—he had a stake in making sure that Aki and Junjie did not get in trouble.

Forty-six...forty-seven...forty-eight...

Besides, he carried on, deciding to push on to fifty laps, *what else have I got to do?*

He was in a phase of his life when he was entirely free and totally unencumbered. Living alone. No one depended on him. Anymore...

He sometimes felt that this was a double-edged sword. On one hand, it felt good to be so free that he could do whatever came to mind with no consequences on people dear to him. He could pack up and go to...Timbuktu...tomorrow, if he so chose. And nobody would know—at least for a while. On the other hand, it also meant that he could drop dead and no one would know either—maybe for a week or two.

So why not try to help? Why not use whatever time that he may have left on this earth to do something that was right? And surely, surely, stopping this Professor Lao from taking over the supply chain of the semiconductor chip industry has got to be the right thing to do. Surely.

So stay connected... Help to keep them safe and out of trouble... If it is too dangerous, you can drop out later. You can always walk away... Yes. That is the honorable course of action.

Forty-nine...fifty...

Junjie Wu
Sunday, July 7, PM
La Jolla, California, USA

"Beautiful home, Aki," Junjie commented, looking around as Aki led them through a hall to a large kitchen and a den. From the street, it appeared to be a relatively ordinary and typical two-story American family house—lacking only a basketball hoop over the two-car garage door. Nothing special. But this was somewhat deceptive. On the inside, it was a wonderful home, tastefully done up in the Spanish colonial style, rich with wood paneling, heavy ceiling beams, and a curved wood and tile staircase leading up to the second floor. The decor augmented by the light cast through a large stained-glass window installed above the front door gave it a sense of cool sanctuary.

Must be especially welcoming in hot summer days, Junjie thought.

Cozy den sunk a few steps below the level of the kitchen and the rest of the downstairs with a fireplace to one side, a flat-panel TV and an old-school sound system to the other, and with a set of French windows leading out to a tiled porch and manicured backyard. Junjie was impressed. He has, of course, been to the houses of his American colleagues and friends before but seems to have gotten used to apartment living typical of Beijing and was struck by the spaciousness and the sense of peace and security that this house projected. "Beautiful."

"Thank you," Aki commented, clearly pleased and maybe somewhat proud. "We could not afford it now, but when we moved in, before the neighborhood became so fashionable, it was a fixer-upper, and we did it up over the years. Actually, Mary did it up. I just get to enjoy it."

Aki introduced them to Mary.

"Gentlemen, come in, come in," she greeted them in her deep and strikingly calm voice. She repeated their names when they were introduced, as if deliberately concentrating to remember them.

A slight woman—maybe a couple of inches taller than Aki. Slim and fine-featured. Dressed simply in jeans and a white tee. No gaudy jewelry—just a small watch on her wrist. A pleasant California-girl face with medium-length blond hair pulled back in a ponytail and a bright ready smile that showed off perfect white teeth. Only a touch of makeup that did not attempt to hide the wrinkles around her blue eyes—or the age that they implied. Altogether a beautiful woman of a certain age…

"Make yourselves at home. You okay with some white wine? Sparkling water?" She exuded a sense of calm, a sense of being in peace and harmony with the world. Graceful, easy movements, and a slow and deliberate speech pattern. Confident and comfortable with people—readily establishing a personal and direct connection, emphasized by the ease with which she touched them. A touch on the arm when offering the wine. A tap on the shoulder when inviting them to come and sit.

Rare for an American, Junjie thought.

Aki grilled steaks and potatoes in a brick barbecue built to the side of the porch. Mary made a salad. They chatted easily, sipping cool white wine.

Perfect American Dream evening, thought Junjie. *Like in the Hollywood movies.* Which made him appreciate the irony of the situation. *Just like an opening scene in some drama film… Sinister topic in an idyllic setting. A contrast… No suspenseful music though*, he joked inwardly.

But his inner feeling of shame was amplified by a sense that it was he who brought the dirt and the ominous drama into this apparent Eden.

After dinner, Mary excused herself, saying something about leaving them to talk business and having a canasta game with her friends and left. Their dog, a four-legged mass of long black hair—a French Briard apparently—heaved a sigh of a martyr woken from a good honest sleep and padded off after her. She was clearly the alpha.

"That is my 'why'," Aki said after she left, making the air quotes. "Why am I willing to risk waking up that ugly nasty snake that we talked about yesterday. If it was not for her, I would tell this Professor Lao of yours to fuck off. But I have to keep that dirt away from her. I have to protect her from…well…from the mistakes I made in the past."

Ivan and Junjie nodded, understanding fully.

"Here are my constraints," Aki continued. "I want to protect BBI, its people, and its clients. It is my obligation—duty. But I will stop short of doing anything that hurts Mary in any way. That is my red line. So I am ready to participate in whatever ploy we come up with to stop Lao, but in parallel, I will initiate actions that will meet his demands. Transferring assets and IP to BBI KK[39] will take a few months. If we can stop Lao in that time—great. I want to. I am in. I will even consider doing stupid and dangerous things. But once the transfer is done, I will sell BBI KK to CHARM or whoever else they want me to. If that means that I am selling BBI people down the river and am doomed to be Lao's whore—so be it. If that is what it takes to keep Mary from being hurt. The way I see it, that is the only avenue open to me. I owe it to her," he trailed off.

"Understood," Junjie responded. "My constraints are somewhat similar. I do want to stop those bastards. It is the right thing to do. I do have an obligation to wash away the dirt I have brought. To restore my self-respect—or at least to limit the dishonor. So like you, I am committed to stopping Lao. But in the end, I, too, will have to comply with his dictates. I have to protect my family. And my employees. I also feel like, in the end, I will have no choice but to suck it up and comply."

They looked at each other with compassion and understanding shining in their eyes. Or so Junjie thought.

"And your schedule—a few months—sounds reasonable to me," Junjie concluded. "So I, too, am 'in' on...what did you call it, Aki...doing stupid things to stop Professor Lao. But only up to the point of hurting my family."

They turned and looked at Ivan.

"My stakes are obviously lower than yours." Ivan shrugged. "Thank God, no one is threatening me or my family, or anything like that. So unlike you two poor sods, I could actually walk away, and no one would be any wiser or any worse off. Probably."

---

[39] **KK**: A type of corporate entity in Japan—"Kabushiki Kaisha" commonly abbreviated KK, usually translated as "stock company." Analogous to US "Inc." designation. As opposed to "Godo Kaisha" abbreviated GK, modeled after the American limited-liability company (LLC).

Pause.

"But the way I figure it, what the hell. Why not? It seems to me that stopping Lao is the right thing to do. For me and my friends. For the industry that has been so good to me. And for the greater cosmos. Surely stopping the trolls from any secret police has got to be a ticket to heaven even for people like me. So being a Forrest Gump[40] kind of a guy, meh, why not?" He shrugged and added, "Sounds like fun that will break up the monotony of my semi-retirement. I am in."

They smirked but looked searchingly at him.

"Are you sure?" Junjie asked. "In your place, I think I would walk."

"Well," Ivan spoke slowly, "my kids are all grown up and gone. Doing well on their own…knock on wood," rapping his head with his fist. "I have no dependents—which is to say that the liability for me is much lower. So I can afford to risk doing the right thing? Besides, I am implicated in the mess, and if something goes off the rails and becomes a nasty fight between the two dragons, who is to say that Lao—or the feds—would leave me alone. I may know too much. If either side is anything like what the Yugoslav secret police were supposed to be, they probably would not. I could be a loose end for them. So I feel like I better help to make sure that the ploy works and things do not go off rails." After a pause, he added a joke, "Just to make sure that you two bozos don't do stuff that is too stupid or too dangerous…"

Aki and Junjie looked at him for a long while, finally nodded, and then raised their glasses to toast each other. But somber and serious—not jovial.

Junjie took this to mean that the three of them have agreed and that the toast was a way of sealing the deal. They were all "in" on the plot to stop Professor Lao. In on the plot they were about to cook up.

---

[40] *Forrest Gump*: A 1994 American comedy-drama film based on the 1986 novel of the same name by Winston Groom. The story depicts several decades in the life of Forrest Gump (portrayed by Tom Hanks), a slow-witted but kind-hearted man from Alabama who unwittingly stumbles into a series of defining historical events in the twentieth-century United States.

This was not a toast to celebrate. This was a toast to mark the beginning of…of something very serious and possibly dangerous.

They spent the rest of the evening sitting on the porch, admiring the world that at that point in time consisted just of Aki's backyard, subtly lit by the big moon and the strategically placed tiki torches. And discussing the "how."

Such a tranquil setting and such a disquieting topic, thought Junjie again. *Incongruous*.

How were they going to get the proof of the pinch point scheme—proof that is concrete enough to frighten Professor Lao into ceasing and desisting from pressuring Aki or punishing Junjie. Planning.

When it got cold, they moved inside into the den. Planning.

Mary came back from her canasta game, said good night, and went to bed upstairs. The dog looked at them questioningly, as if to say, "What are you losers still doing here?" and followed her up, morosely giving up what seemed to be his usual bed by the fireplace.

They stayed up until 2:00 a.m. Planning…

They applied their best engineering management skills and agreed on a typical phased approach—just like they would use when defining some project at work. They dubbed the stages of their crazy enterprise as the "plan," the "caper," and the "sting." They defined a schedule for each of the phases to be within the time line of their cover story: the transfer of the BBI assets to BBI KK in Japan. And they made sure that an owner was assigned for each task—just like they would at work. They focused mostly on things that had to be done in the first phase but also assigned responsibilities for the longer-term activities. And they agreed to have regular meetings to review their status. Maybe to pull the plug. After all, the whole scheme was crazy. They would decide in a follow-up meeting after they gathered some data—just like they would do with a work project.

As Ivan and Junjie picked up, ready to leave, Junjie ventured pensively, "You know, in some bizarre way, I am enjoying this…conspiracy. If it was not serious, I must admit, I think it would be sort of fun…this James Bond business."

147

"Yeah, don't let it get to your head dude," Ivan cautioned. "We are just three old guys, and anyone sane would tell us to get off it." And then after a pause with an ear-to-ear grin, he added, "But yes, I guess it is sort of fun. At least for now. In the safety of this...sanctuary," waving at Aki's beautiful backyard.

"Well, let's see what we learn between now and the next time," Aki added.

Either way, mission accomplished, Junjie thought to himself. *At least I am not all alone anymore. At least I tried, and Aki knows what he is in for. And who knows? Maybe, just maybe, we can actually pull it off...*

And they parted.

Part 4

WRIGGLING OUT

The Plan

Ivan Jovanovic
Monday, August 5
Prince Hotel, Shin Yokohama, Japan

They met again in a month—almost to a day. As they had planned in Aki's backyard.

They selected Japan as the meeting spot, partially to share the pain of the travel, and partially because it fitted well with their cover story. They actually did spend most of the day touring the BBI KK facility. It was necessary to familiarize Junjie with BBI operations. In case that their plot failed and Aki did end up having to sell out. And just in case Professor Lao had someone monitor their movements.

But their minds were not really on the technology and the impressive lab that Aki set up in his Japanese subsidiary. They were eager to get back to the hotel where they were to address the things that really brought them there: their clandestine enterprise.

Ivan was in charge of what they only half-jokingly termed "the counterespionage" activities. Basically, he was to be responsible for making all the arrangements while ensuring that their plot remained hidden from Professor Lao, and more specifically, from the Chinese deep state and its nosy and potentially very dangerous agents.

"These days, you never know who may be listening in on your calls or reading your mail, so paranoia has to be the rule...," Ivan declared a month ago while they were planning things in Aki's backyard, which was probably why they so readily agreed on his "counterespionage" assignment.

When psyching up for this role, Ivan encouraged himself to think like his brother would. His brother who lived in Serbia—the rump of Yugoslavia—was, in Ivan's opinion, somewhat paranoid about the proverbial big brother watching. Ivan knew that this paranoia was first stimulated by some of the police practices used in the communist ex-Yugoslavia and that this then blossomed in reaction to the large internet companies—Microsoft, Facebook, Google, and the like—who nowadays seemed to know everything there is to know about one's life. Just like the police in ex-Yugoslavia. Silly or not, Ivan thought that some paranoia may come in handy in this ploy of theirs. So he pretended to be—to think—like his brother.

He obtained separate laptops and open phones on Amazon and Alibaba. "To be used sparingly for our assignments only," he said. He subscribed them to anonymous Guerrilla Mail[41] service in order to obscure their identity in cyberspace, but he dictated that they use it only for what they just called "the project." "Nothing else," he insisted. He declared that all plot-related communications between them were to be face-to-face only. "The more we talk on the phone or e-mail, the more likely it is that someone will hear us," he said.

So they have not had any direct communications about their plan since that evening in Aki's backyard.

They used their normal laptops, e-mail, and phones only for their regular jobs and for the official Red Lion project business—which they continued both as a cover story and in order to be ready to comply with Professor Lao's demand to sell BBI. In about a quarter. In case they decided to abort their ploy.

---

[41] **Guerrilla Mail**: A service that provides disposable temporary e-mail addresses to obscure sender's identity. They provide a scramble address feature, which generates a random e-mail address. Guerrilla Mail also employs encryption software to ensure privacy.

And hard as it was, they contained themselves—even during the weekly Red Lion videoconference meetings—and said nothing at all about their plot. Other than the pre-agreed coded shorthand messages that they exchanged: just a thumbs-up or down hand gesture to indicate whether they were on track with their assignments and ready to meet and report the findings. Nothing else.

Junjie griped about, and strained against, the security restrictions that Ivan insisted on and that he thought were excessive and only slowed them down. He was impatient to get on with it. Aki just smirked about all the paranoid precautions but went along—partially to humor Ivan and partially because he, too, felt a need to be very careful since they were potentially messing with professionals. Not amateurs like he knew themselves to be.

When all three of them indicated that they were ready—pretty much on the schedule they agreed to in Aki's backyard—Ivan made the arrangements for the meeting in Japan. He booked their rooms in Shin Yokohama Fuji View Hotel—conveniently located for their meetings at BBI KK—for the week before the Japanese "Mountain Day" summer holiday. He thought that the three foreign businessmen would be less conspicuous during a working week. But he also reserved a private conference room at the Prince Hotel—about a couple of miles from their Fuji View. Via Skype using the dark laptop and bogus internet ID. Just in case someone was tracking them and tempted to bug their hotel and listen in on their private meetings...

But they hoped that there was no need for any of it since Professor Lao was supposed to be under an impression that everything was going according to his plan and hence would presumably not be watching them. Still...

They hurried through the day to complete the Red Lion business at BBI KK, took a train to Shin Yokohama, grabbed a quick bite at the Yakitori restaurant in the railway station, and walked over to the Prince Hotel—only a short walk away. Just three Gaijin[42] busi-

---

[42] **Gaijin**: A Japanese word for foreigners and non-Japanese. The word is composed of two kanji: gai ("outside") and jin ("person"). Some feel the word has come to have a negative or pejorative connotation while other observers maintain it is neutral or even positive.

nessmen going about their day. An old white guy with a gray short-cropped beard, a large nose and a crooked face, a bit of a paunch hanging over his belt, wearing pleated pants and a blazer dating back to mideighties… A middle-aged tall Chinese man, looking trim and fit, graying just a bit around his temples, and wearing a set of fashionable glasses that matched his fine suit… A short American geezer of Greek Japanese origin, stiff and erect in a dark suit, skipping along in order to keep up with the others. All three of them armed with the obligatory computer bags, sweltering in jackets and ties—the regular uniform of a typical salaryman.[43] Nothing particularly notable or unusual for that hot and humid midsummer evening in the business district of Shin-Yokohama.

As the clerk from the Prince Hotel bowed and left, closing the doors to their conference room behind her, Ivan heaved a deep sigh of relief and watched the other two let down their guard. Aki and Junjie both visibly relaxed—dropping their erect and formal postures, loosening the knots in their ties, taking off their jackets, and rolling up their sleeves. Getting comfortable in that small and stuffy meeting room—poorly air-conditioned to the usual Japanese standards of something like a sweltering eighty degrees Fahrenheit.

Maybe these security precautions are putting undue pressure on all of us, Ivan thought to himself. *Still…*

"All right, gentlemen. Who wants to go first?" Junjie asked eagerly the moment they settled around the conference table with coffees for jet-lagged Ivan and Aki and a soda for Junjie.

"Yes. I don't have much more additional stuff to report, so…," Aki spoke up. Ivan and Junjie sat back to listen. "In my role as 'the con artist,' I had two major tasks," Aki started. "The first one was to take care of the *cover story*," emphasizing "cover story" with air quotes. "We already talked about the status of the transfer of all company assets to BBI KK in the Red Lion meeting. Like I said, it is pretty much on track. I followed up with the lawyers, and yes, the shell game scheme that we are playing is legal. As long as the foreign

---

[43] **Salaryman:** Japanese colloquial term for a salaried white-collar worker (sararīman). Often also a slightly derogatory term for a Japanese employee who shows overriding loyalty to the corporation.

entity is listed as a separate company—even if it is majority owned by a US parent. BBI KK meets those criteria. Really, I should say that it is not illegal. Barely. But apparently, it is practiced often. We do need to be careful about keeping our motivations quiet in case someone challenges the sale. It would not look good if it came out in courts that after receiving an injunction from CFIUS we transferred all the assets to BBI KK just to sell them to some foreign third party. So to be safe, we commit nothing regarding the motivations for the IP and asset transfers to paper or in an e-mail. We stick to the story that we are doing the entire shuffle purely to enhance internal BBI efficiency and operational flexibility."

After a pause, he added, "As far as the few employees who are in the know, the official plan for the merger with CHARM is to challenge the CFIUS injunction. The lawyers are, in fact, preparing the appropriate paperwork for a CFIUS appeal. Good thing to do should we by any chance end up going that way."

"Altogether," he summed up, "there are no issues or snags that I can foresee. We are on schedule and could be ready to sell BBI KK in less than a couple of months from now." After a short pause, he added, "If I have to."

"And?" Ivan prodded.

"And nothing. The cover story is intact. Everything we talked about for the Red Lion project goes and also applies in this context," he said, pointing at the three of them to emphasize that he was addressing their clandestine plot then. "Nothing is permanent or binding or irreversible until we actually do pull the trigger and sell BBI KK to CHARM. So the things we are doing now can either remain purely a cover story if, or when, we abort the sale, or they can be real steps toward closing the deal if our ploy fails."

"Good. Good cover... And the second part?" Junjie goaded.

"Yes, my second task was to research the mechanism for reporting foreign *malfeasance* to the US government." He pronounced the word deliberately, implying that this is a part of the official jargon. "So that we would sound credible if or when we threaten Lao. It turns out that it's a piece of cake. You know, FBI seems to have gone a long way from the Efrem Zimbalist Jr. time..."

155

"Huh, whose time?" Junjie and Ivan asked looking blankly at Aki.

"Oh, never mind. There was a TV show about the FBI in the sixties and seventies that I used to watch as a kid. It was apparently a part of a campaign that gave the FBI a very positive image in America. The G-men were then these good, clean-cut, and proper all-American-boys chasing down the meanies and the baddies. I forgot that you two did not grow up in the States. Forget it. Anyways, counterintelligence is obviously one of the main responsibilities of the FBI. And industrial espionage seems to be a very high-profile aspect of that. You would be surprised about how much stuff the FBI posts about industrial espionage. I mean, KGB and mafia move over—as far as the FBI is concerned, it is all about protecting the US technology. So reporting something related to that type of activity is just an easy phone call away. They—bless their bureaucratic pointy heads—even have a form for submitting tips. The sense I get from those posts is that our case—this pinch point strategy of Professor Lao's—is not typical but that the FBI would certainly get it and have people who would appreciate it for what it is. And I am sure that at worst, if they did not, they would know who to call…"

EXHIBIT 9.2   The Federal Bureau of Investigation (FBI)

WHAT WE INVESTIGATE

| Terrorism | Counterintelligence | Cyber Crime | Public Corruption | Civil Rights | Organized Crime | White-Collar Crime | Violent Crime | WMD |

Inside the FBI's Counterintelligence Program

The FBI has been responsible for identifying and neutralizing ongoing national security threats from foreign intelligence services since 1917, nine years after the Bureau was created in 1908... While the Counterintelligence Division continues to neutralize national security threats from foreign intelligence services, its modern-day mission is much broader. The FBI is the lead agency for exposing, preventing, and investigating intelligence activities on U.S. soil, and the Counterintelligence Division uses its full suite of investigative and intelligence capabilities to combat counterintelligence threats... The overall goals are as follows:

- *Protect the secrets of the U.S. Intelligence Community, using intelligence to focus investigative efforts, and collaborating with our government partners to reduce the risk of espionage and insider threats.*
- *__Protect the nation's critical assets, like our advanced technologies and sensitive information in the defense, intelligence, economic, financial, public health, and science and technology sectors.__*
- *Counter the activities of foreign spies. Through proactive investigations, the Bureau identifies who they are and stops what they are doing.*
- *Keep weapons of mass destruction from falling into the wrong hands, and use intelligence to drive the FBI's investigative efforts to keep threats from becoming reality...*

Economic Espionage

Economic espionage is a problem that costs the American economy hundreds of billions of dollars per year and puts our national security at risk. While it is not a new threat, it is a growing one, and the theft attempts by foreign competitors and adversaries are becoming more brazen and varied.

According to the Economic Espionage Act (Title 18 U.S.C. §1831), economic espionage is (1) whoever knowingly performs targeting or acquisition of trade secrets to (2) knowingly benefit any foreign government, foreign instrumentality, or foreign agent. In contrast, the theft of trade secrets (Title 18 U.S.C. Section 1832) is (1) whoever knowingly misappropriates trade secrets to (2) benefit anyone other than the owner.

Historically, economic espionage has targeted defense-related and high-tech industries. But recent FBI cases have shown that no industry, large or small, is immune to the threat. Any company with a proprietary product, process, or idea can be a target....

From: https://www.fbi.gov/investigate/counterintelligence

Aki concluded by retrieving a folder from his laptop bag and tossing a bunch of printouts of the FBI web pages on the desk.

"Don't worry, Ivan, I used the dark computer and gorilla identity for this search," he added with a bit of a grin.

"So you think that we would just need to whisper 'FBI' in Lao's ear and he would take us seriously?" Ivan asked to confirm his understanding, ignoring the snide comment.

"Well, I don't know Lao, but FBI—or more specifically FBI counterintelligence unit—is the appropriate port for reporting his pinch point strategy, so it should be a credible threat," Aki responded, sounding quite definitive.

Junjie nodded, mumbling something about not knowing the ways of the US government, but that, if the roles were reversed, MSS would be the right port for accessing the Chinese authorities.

Junjie then sat up to do his bit. The plan was that Junjie would be in charge of what they termed the "intelligence" activities. He was supposed to find out whatever he could about Professor Lao: his daily routine, who he met with, where and when, his movements, and such like.

"Well, this was a lot harder than they make it out to be in the movies," Junjie started, "especially with all his paranoia constraints," nodding toward Ivan.

"Like what?" Aki asked.

"Well, obviously, I needed someone to follow Professor Lao around, 24-7. There are a lot of people for hire in China who would do whatever you ask them for a right fee, but I guess I agree that you cannot trust just any man on the street with something like this. Could be dangerous if it leaked out. So I needed a professional, a private detective of some kind. Finding one that is truly trust-worthy, sure not to be connected in any way with the police, PLA, or MSS, and guaranteed to not leak back to Professor Lao—well, that was harder. Let's face it—most private eyes are retired cops. Not like I could just pick anybody from the yellow pages. I certainly had no relevant experiences and there is no one in my family—who are ultimately the only people I can really trust—who does that kind of a thing. But one of my fifty-odd cousins currently living in Beijing is a lawyer who sometimes deals with criminal cases…" He paused and added an explanation, "I guess, coming from an old Beijing family helps. I have a lot of cousins who live in the area." He shrugged, grinned a bit, and carried on, "This one is all right and someone I felt I could trust. He is a bit older than me, but we were reasonably close when we were kids. And I know that he was quite active in '89 during the Tiananmen Square[44] protests—so I thought that it is unlikely that he would have any love for the PLA or MSS. Anyways, I thought that as a criminal lawyer, he might know someone suitable. So I approached him with a made-up story about needing a hush-hush search on a rogue ex-employee whose uncle was someone big in the Party. And he did. Apparently, he routinely used a private investigator company whose discretion my cousin could vouch for. That company turned out to be these three gay men—understandably bitter at the system that abused them. Gays are often treated horribly in China. So I hired them. They normally deal with the divorces, missing persons, and even criminal cases, so I thought that they would have the right skills for what we needed."

EXHIBIT 9.3   Private Investigators in China    **CHINADAILY**.COM.CN

2015-06-12:   *Chen Tianben of the People's Public Security University of China estimates that more than 100,000 people are employed in nearly 23,000 Private Investigative firms. Many of these investigators are former employees of the judiciary, law enforcers or lawyers. Private investigators first emerged in China in the early 1990s in Beijing and Shanghai, usually retained to assist civil, and occasionally criminal, investigations. Despite being unrecognized in China, private investigators have a role to play in litigation, both civil and criminal, as lawyers sometimes hire them to collect evidence. China's Civil Procedure Law stipulates that the burden of proof falls on the claimant. Lawyers say many claimants who cannot retrieve effective evidence on their own naturally seek help from "professional services."*
A lack of official recognition and clear legal guidance means upright and law-abiding investigators are often tarred with the same brush as those engaged in illegal undertakings. No professional code of conduct regulates their practices. Professionalism and legal compliance are patchy. No legislation clarifies what is off-limits. Most investgators are hired to find lost parents or runaway kids. Other services range from snooping on extramarital affairs to corporate profiling and debt recovery. Many advertise unique strengths and all pledge to keep their clients' information confidential. Their cases usually do not meet the minimum criteria for police to launch a formal investigation.

From: https://www.chinadaily.com.cn/china/2015-06/12/content_20979772.htm

---

"And?" Aki goaded.

---

[44]   **Tiananmen Square protests**: Student-led demonstrations held in China during 1989, calling for constitutional due process, democracy, freedom of the press, and freedom of speech. At the height of the protests, about one million people assembled in the Tiananmen Square. The protests were forcibly suppressed when the government declared martial law and sent the military to occupy central parts of Beijing.

"And it seems that Professor Lao leads what appears to be—at least on the surface—a pretty ordinary and boring life. Or he did so for the last, what is it now…three weeks that we had him tailed. He spends his days at the university, weekends included, and nights at his apartment. He lives quite near and walks to and from home. He lives alone. His wife passed away years ago, and his son lives in Shanghai with his family. Our investigators did some checking, and it really does seem that he has no one else that is close to him. He does not seem to have friends that he hangs around with or a social club or anything like that. He really appears to be all about work. And alone. He has an ayi who comes during the week to his place—"

"A what?" Aki interrupted.

"Ayi…A charwoman. A cleaning lady. A woman who does the cleaning and cooking for him and presumably all the other home chores like laundry and grocery shopping and stuff."

"Oh, okay. Go on."

"Anyways, like I said, he seems to spend all his awake time at the university. So far, he had no special visitors at either of his offices there. He has two. The private office in the Provost's block where I met with him, and one in the Electronic Engineering building—next to his labs—where he normally meets with his students. He does not seem to have an office anywhere else…"

"You mean no office in any of the ministries or anything like that?" Ivan asked for confirmation.

"Yes, exactly. There wasn't anything that we could find that would indicate another office anywhere. And even if he did have one, for sure, he has not been there in the last three weeks… Anyways, no visitors at the university, other than the biweekly meetings with his grad students in his lab. But…" Junjie paused here and tapped the table for emphasis. "But he did have a number of separate meetings off-site. Various public places—like teahouses and restaurants. One was with me for our usual fortnightly meeting in Liuxiaguan Teahouse."

"Your usual what," Aki interrupted again, "and where?"

"Fortnightly. Every two weeks. Sorry. When I was a kid, my English teacher was British, and I lived in Manchester for a few years—so my British-ism creeps back up every now and then," Junjie explained. "Anyways, I do meet with him every couple of weeks in this traditional teahouse he found." "But," he continued, a bit impatiently, eager to reveal his findings, "he had another three off-site meetings. My men did the check on the people he met with. Two are in the chip business, sort of like me. One I actually know of and might have even met at some conference or other. He is the CEO of Accelicon Inc.—a provider of device modeling software tools and services and such like. The other is the founder and CTO at Platform Design—a start-up in the test business. Both, actually I should say all three of us, are Tsinghua graduates and Professor Lao's ex-students. The other two blokes were a few years ahead of me. A definite pattern there…"

"Interesting! Very interesting!" Ivan exclaimed, clearly excited by Junjie's findings.

"The fourth off-site meeting was odd. The first three were, I presume, like mine—judging from the similarity in our profiles. The last meeting was with someone who does not exist. Which is to say, with someone that has no profile or any kind of footprint that my men could dig up. So possibly a PLA or an MSS kind of a person…I presume. I don't know, but c'mon, who in this day and age does not have some kind of a presence on the open web?"

He tossed on the table a report that included a set of photographs, along with what looked like dates, places, names…but all in Mandarin.

Silence while Ivan and Aki flipped through the photographs and the report digesting whatever information they could glean from the pages.

Aki stared at one of the photographs for a long time. Studying the face of the enemy. "Wow," he commented holding it up, "this Professor Lao of yours is ancient-looking—looks like he is a hundred if he is a day… Just lacks a Fu Manchu to look like an old master from some karate movie."

"Well"—Junjie shrugged—"evidently, looks are deceiving." This was a sore spot for him, and he did not seem like he wanted to talk about Lao's deceptive looks.

"Okay. Excellent. So what can we conclude from this?" Ivan posed the question walking over to the flip chart that was standing on an easel in the corner of the room. Before anyone said anything, he wrote:

1. Keeps a low-profile appearance. Just an old academic?
2. Runs PP (pinch point) projects through off-site meetings in public places?
3. Likely that he has three (or more—short sampling window) active PP projects going right now?
4. Seems to be recruiting from a pool of his old students?
5. Interface to the "deep state" is Mr. X (his boss or a contact to PLA/MSS)?
6. Meets with Mr. X off-site in public places?
7. Likely that he has a stash of paper documents somewhere?
8. Likely that these are in his office at the U (Provost block)?
9. …

He turned to face Aki and Junjie and looked at them questioningly. "I know that this is a stretch based only on what Junjie has seen in the last few weeks, but would you guys agree that these are reasonable conclusions from the available data?"

"Well, not really enough to go on to make any conclusions," Aki objected, "but I guess reasonable presumptions. Possible," he trailed off.

"True. Of course, we should get more data. Always. But as good engineers that we are, we have to create some kind of a model based on whatever data is available. This is a best-guess model based on what we have today. Agreed?" Ivan prodded, understanding the reluctance that engineers normally feel toward making decisions with incomplete data—something that he spent virtually his whole career managing.

"Why do you think that he has paper documents?" Aki persisted.

"No particular reason. He interfaced with Junjie via paper. I mean, he gave Junjie a printed report on BBI rather than sending him an e-file... He seemed to have that dirt on you readily available on paper. Besides, he is old. Probably prefers things on paper. Just an educated guess," Ivan explained with a shrug.

"Reasonable," Junjie nodded. "I have not seen Professor Lao compulsively checking his phone during our meetings—like the rest of us digital kind of people often do. Come to think of it, I am not sure if he even has a mobile phone. So I guess it is possible that he is paper-based. In fact, knowing him, I would be more surprised if he wasn't. Why do you think that these would be at his university office?"

"Again—just a guess. Process of elimination. I am guessing that the other two guys he met with are also engaged in a takeover of a targeted pinch point company. So it is likely that there are at least three sets of reports like the one he has given you for BBI, along with three sets of confidential files on the key people at those companies—like the one for Aki. At least. That is, of course, extrapolating from what we have seen him do with you and BBI. If so, I am guessing that he has a copy. And if so, he has to keep those somewhere. Sounds like home is unlikely with that, what did you call her, ayi, poking around. Ditto for his office next to the labs, where his students may be nosing around. And without a separate office in some secure building, he is either toting them with him all the time or keeping them at the University Provost building," Ivan rationalized.

"Well, he does carry a beat-up schoolboy bag with him wherever he goes," Junjie opined, "but three sets of documents like the ones he gave me would be quite bulky... Come to think of it, his bag never looked stuffed or particularly heavy. It would probably fall apart with anything more than a sandwich and a folder in it."

"Either way—good point." Ivan got up and added a note on his flip chart.

9. Possible that the documents are in the bag that Lao carries about?

"If that is the case," Ivan continued, "I would think we are home-free. That would be really the best-case scenario. We would just need to blanket him and go. Probably too easy. Too good to be true."

"Blanket him?" Aki asked.

"A Yugoslav tradition. You hire a few goons to toss a blanket on a guy so he cannot see anything, throw in a few punches for a good measure, grab his bag, and run," Ivan responded with a smirk and a shrug.

"Yes, probably too good to be true," Junjie reacted. "But if necessary, it would be easy to find yobos[45] in Beijing who would enjoy an assignment like that." The last with a sort of a funny evil look in his eyes.

Hmm. Junjie looks like his yobos are not the only ones who would enjoy that, thought Ivan. *Lao really got to him.* But he said nothing.

"Okay, okay. So?" Aki asked.

"So the most likely scenario is that Lao keeps whatever documents he has in his private office at the university. That would be consistent with his security model, relying purely on anonymity. Which is actually a pretty good strategy for him—he is not exactly a typical spymaster. Who'd think that he is what he is? Certainly, he fooled Junjie. So keeping the paperwork handy in the university is possible—maybe even likely…," Ivan explained. After a short pause, he added, "Ergo, if we are to do anything, we need to break into that office and take a look at the documents there. In my opinion, this would be good for us."

"Good for us? Why?" Junjie and Aki questioned.

"Well, with my counterespionage hat on, I did some thinking. If we are to go through with this crazy scheme of ours, we would have to deal with *their* security measures." Pause. They have not discussed this before. "If you think about it, the security measures could probably be classified into military-grade and civilian-grade security. Possibly also secret service-grade and industrial-grade security. And so on. We can only speculate what the secret service and military-grade security measures involve and—given that we are three old geezers

---

[45] **Yobo**: Someone, usually a male, who is uncouth, badly behaved, and obnoxious. Loud and drunk are also characteristics (Australia). A cruel and brutal fellow (UK).

and not James Bond—my gut feeling would be to abort our mission if we felt that that is what we are facing. But judging from our current understanding—our best guess operating model—with Lao's university office, we are probably dealing with civilian-grade security. At worst, this would involve things like CCTV cameras. Maybe even motion sensors and some kind of alarmed electronic locks on doors and windows—like some people have in their homes. A night guard trying to stay awake. That kind of a thing. Presumably defined mostly to keep unruly students from playing stupid pranks… We should, of course, double-check, but at least as far as I am concerned, that level of security would not be a red light," Ivan responded. "As opposed to needing to deal with military-grade security, professional armed guards, and God knows what else," he added to stress the difference. "What do you, gentlemen, think?"

Long silence, followed by Aki and Junjie nodding slowly. Hesitating. Not sure about Ivan's conclusions.

"So I suggest that we focus on Lao's university office. Concentrate on figuring out how, when—or if—we break into that office. Of course, in parallel, we should also continue watching him. To get more data."

"Agreed," Aki and Junjie spoke up readily. They were evidently more comfortable with getting more data.

"Good. Let's put a pin in that. For tomorrow's session. It is late, and jet lag is catching up with me," Ivan concluded.

Then tearing the flip chart sheet that he wrote on, he faced them with a straight face and declared, "Meanwhile, gentlemen, I need you to eat this paper. One-third each. Must destroy all evidence."

Aki Roussos
Tuesday, August 6, AM
"Marine Rouge" Boat, Yokohama, Japan

They started the day early—since two of the three of them were jet-lagged and unlikely to sleep in anyways.

"Plenty of time to catch up on sleep during the flight back," Ivan insisted. He was all energetic and fidgety, as if he had already had several cups of coffee.

Easy for him to say. I can't sleep on planes, thought Aki, somewhat grumpily. *And maybe a bit hard on Junjie too. His body clock is only an hour off from Tokyo time—in the wrong direction... Seems alert enough, though. Must be the adrenaline—enough of that to keep any one of us up.*

They met in the hotel breakfast lounge, armed with their roll-on bags—since they were flying out that evening. They ate, checked out of the hotel, and were at the BBI KK offices by 8:00 a.m. At that time, the place was pretty much deserted, but they needed nothing other than coffee from the local staff, so they met in the BBI KK boardroom and took care of the remaining Red Lion business. They were done by 10:00 a.m.

Ivan, with his paranoia in full bloom, suggested that they address the rest of their clandestine business while taking a tour of the Yokohama harbor. Not necessarily an unusual activity for visiting gaijin businessmen with some leftover time on their hands. And yet anyone who was prepared to follow them in the business district would stick out on a tourist boat. And an unplanned activity is unlikely to be bugged. Or so Ivan said.

The tour boat had a bar and a restaurant lounge on the first deck, and they settled in a booth with a nice view. They had plenty of privacy as most of the tourists were crowded on the upper decks, presumably due to the better view and better light for taking pictures. And it was a nice day and not too hot out on the water.

The three of them would eat lunch and talk on the boat, and Aki and Ivan would still have the time to catch their return flight. Junjie was in no hurry at all since his flight back to Beijing was scheduled for the following day. He had some other CHARM business to take care of in Tokyo. So they had a few hours.

"I was thinking," Ivan opened eagerly, seemingly all amped up, "we have to address at least three things this morning. And we have a decision to make." He retrieved a piece of paper from his jacket pocket and glanced at the notes he had jotted there.

Hmm, looks like Mr. Counterespionage here did not get a good night's sleep last night, thought Aki, turning to face Ivan.

Ivan dived right in. "We need to talk about the next steps for [a] the short-term plan, [b] the long-term plan, and [c] risk management." He counted off on his fingers. "Agreed?"

"Sounds reasonable. You are clearly ahead of me," Junjie spoke up. "Maybe I am not fully awake yet... Go."

Aki just nodded. *Seems like he has things well in hand,* waiting to hear what Ivan had to say.

"All right. Short term. As we talked about last night, we need to carry on getting the data"—making the air quotes around "data"—"and keep watching Lao. Agreed?"

"Check and done." Junjie nodded. "My men are on it."

"Good. Second, another thing that we need," Ivan continued, "is the plan of that, er, what was it that you called it...the Provost's building. Basic layout kind of a thing. Something better than what we could lift off Google Earth. Junjie, do you think that you or your guys could get your hands on that?"

"Mmm, don't know. Will check," Junjie confirmed and typed a reminder into his phone.

"Next, I think that we have to probe the security in Lao's office. Test it to see what is there. CCTV? Motion sensors? Locks? Guards? Whatever...I had a thought on that. Have you guys seen *How to Steal a Million*?[46] An old movie?"

"Er, no, not that I recall," Aki blurted. "Why?" But thinking to himself, *A funny time to talk about movies? C'mon, Ivan!*

Junjie just looked puzzled.

"Well, not important really," Ivan responded, shrugging, "I don't remember most of the plot, but the salient bit that popped in my mind—sometime around four o'clock this morning—was that these guys robbing a museum used a boomerang to repeatedly trigger

---

[46] **How to Steal a Million**: A 1966 heist comedy film, starring Audrey Hepburn and Peter O'Toole. The plot involves stealing a fake statuette from a museum. The protagonists repeatedly set off the security alarm using a boomerang until the alarm system is presumed to be faulty and is finally disabled. *Rotten Tomatoes* average rating of 6.9/10.

the alarm system until the embarrassed guards assumed that it was broken and turned it off. And then they just waltzed away with the prize."

"You want us to use a boomerang? What the fuck are you talking about?" Aki asked incredulously.

"No, no, no," Ivan waved away the question. "We can use something much better. A modern-day boomerang." Pause. "Drones!"

He seemed excited with an expectant grin on his face. But this was met by just blank stares from Aki and Junjie.

"I will have to do much more research on this, but my basic thought is that we could use drones to probe the security of Lao's office. See what we are dealing with before we do something stupid. Check if there are things like motion sensors—probably the hardest portion of the civilian-level security to defeat. Or if there are CCTV cameras, test whether they are monitored in real time or are just on autorecord. We could go in with drones and see what happens. If an alarm is triggered—at worst, they would find an untraceable drone there. No harm done. Then we could do it again and again until they get fed up and turn off the irritating alarm."

He is definitely very pleased with himself, thought Aki, noting Ivan's Cheshire cat grin. *The idea...well...sounds a bit hokey to me.*

"Perhaps," Ivan continued, "we could use drone-mounted cameras to observe Lao in his office. See if and how he arms or disarms any electronic locks or whatever other hidden security he may have. Or where he keeps his papers. Maybe he has some hidden box or a safe? Do all that reconnaissance before we actually go in there." He flashed one of his exaggerated big goofy grins—clearly satisfied with his idea. All amped up, waving his hands, and his eyes shining a bit. "Anyways, something along those lines... What do you, gentlemen, think?"

"We-e-e-ll," Aki hesitated, not sure what exactly would be involved. Seemed to him a bit naive. It is not like you can fly drones about without being noticed. "You think that Lao would not notice a drone buzzing over his head? In his office? C'mon."

"No, no, of course not. I was thinking maybe we could use a drone to park a camera in his office when he is not there—and watch him while he is," Ivan clarified. "Something like that?"

"Hmm, I don't know," Aki drew out slowly. "Let's think about it." Not sure at all.

"Well, it is an idea," Junjie volunteered. "Maybe daft but worth considering. In the meantime, how about I have my men check on the guards and suss out the building security measures in general?" He was clearly also dubious about using drones. "Just in case the drone idea bombs out."

"Good. Good idea. Excellent!" Ivan was definitely in a "taking-care-of-business mode." "You do that. And I will look into drones. Those are the assignments for the next phase. Agreed?"

Aki and Junjie nodded, unsure about the drones but willing to go along with it for now. *Let's see...worth a shot.*

"Good. Okay. So much for the short term." Ivan ticked off an item on his list. "Part two, the long-term plan." Pause with Aki and Junjie waiting to see what Ivan had in mind. "Seems to me that it is time to start poking around for that 'safe pair of hands' that we talked about a month ago"—making the air quotes—"I mean, if we are widely successful, break into Lao's office and get away with all sorts of proofs and actually manage to block Lao—then what? All that was intended to give you guys some time to find a way of distancing yourselves from BBI and CHARM. It may be time to think about how would you go about doing that? Seems to me that both of you are determined to ensure the viability of your companies after you leave... So how? Aki didn't seem to like selling out to a competitor. So who then?" Ivan explained his concern.

"Good point," Aki and Junjie nodded.

The waiter brought their lunches: simple bento boxes[47] and a large Sapporo bottle. They shared the beer and got into their meals. Bento box kind of food—bite-size morsels—was especially suitable for carrying on their conversation through the lunch. A piece of sushi between the exchange of thoughts. A bite of teriyaki chicken between some new ideas.

---

[47] **Bento box**: A single-portion meal—restaurant served, takeout, or home-packed—common in Japanese, Taiwanese, and Korean cuisines and other Asian cultures. A traditional bento holds rice or noodles, fish or meat, with pickled and cooked vegetables, typically packed in a box.

The waiter seemed to hover around their table—probably willing them to get on with it since the lunchtime rush was on and there was a line of people waiting in front of the restaurant. But they took their time and carried on. Rude, but...

Aki accepted that between his regular work and the focus on the short-term activities, he—and probably Junjie too—did not have much of a chance to think about their exit plans.

"So I think that you two gentlemen should start poking about on that," Ivan repeated. "I mean, if there is no viable long-term path that is attractive for you two, then there is absolutely no point in taking the risks of breaking into Lao's office. It would be stupid. You guys should have at least a list of attractive options before we do something rash or stupid. Something... What do you think?"

"Yes, agreed. Okay. Will do...," Aki said uncertainly. Not because he was unwilling—but because he was not sure how to proceed. But he had to admit that Ivan had a good point. They do need to—they must—invest some BTUs now before they bit the bullet and actually did something dangerous.

Junjie nodded. "True. No point risking a break-in if we don't have at least a plan for the long-term exit."

"Good... And the third point," Ivan continued, ticking off another item on his list, "is our risks. Specifically, Junjie, I am not sure how good an actor you are, but you said that you have a meeting with Lao every couple of weeks. We need you to continue these to make sure that he is not alarmed. But, on the other hand, knowing what you now know, you need to be good at lying to him. Really good. Must not alarm him or alert him to any changes. Your whole body language must be the same as before... That has got to be hard to do. So I think the more that you meet with him, the greater are the risks that Lao will sense that something is wrong... What do you think?"

Junjie sat up and shuddered a bit as if to shake himself awake and responded in short clipped sentences. "Yes. Good point. I was going to mention it. It is hard. I am not sure how long I can keep it up. The last time we met, I told him a partial truth. That I was very uncomfortable blackmailing Aki. He may have ascribed my behavior to that. Don't know. But I agree. It is damn hard. I want to spit at him. And instead, I just pour his tea and smile politely. Sooner or later, it will show."

Clearly not a topic that Junjie is comfortable with, Aki realized, noting the change in Junjie's posture, speech pattern, and body language. *He gets all tight-lipped and tense. On a very short rein...*

"Yeah, that has to be hard," Aki inserted aloud. "I keep forgetting that you are actually there—at the ground level—dealing with the enemy."

"The point is that we can fool Lao once, maybe we can fool him twice—but we cannot fool him forever," Ivan clarified. "Chances are that he will get a sense that something is wrong sooner or later. So I guess what I am saying is that our time is limited. We started out planning on something of the order of a quarter in total—to mesh in with our cover story. That would give us another couple of months. But that is also roughly four or five more meetings for Junjie with Lao. May be too risky. I am thinking that we need to pull in the schedule. Move much faster...," Ivan trailed off.

"Agreed," Aki responded, feeling for Junjie.

Junjie nodded readily. He clearly agreed with the concern and was eager to get out of his predicament.

Understandably so, thought Aki to himself. *It has got to be hard for him to play nice with Lao. Tough spot.*

"All right. Hang in there for one or two more meetings and let's see how fast we can get through the next phase," Ivan said definitively.

Seems like Ivan has somehow taken over this thing. Herr Kommadant here, Aki thought, feeling only slightly surprised. Ivan was normally such a laid-back kind of a guy, not a driver. *But on the other hand, Junjie and I do have full-time jobs running our companies. He doesn't...*

"And the final point," Ivan continued, "is the decision. Do we pull the plug on our ploy, or do we go on?"

Black and white. Yes or no, Aki thought and said, "Well, I am still in. Let's see what we come up with, but for now—I say we keep going. We have nothing to lose—yet."

"Yes, yes," Junjie confirmed. "Definitely. I am, in fact, a bit less frightened now than I was a month ago. Maybe it is just because the surprise wore off. Don't know, but yes, I say we keep going."

"Good. Me too," Ivan concluded. "Let's not get complacent, but so far so good."

With that, Junjie checked his watch, flagged the waiter, and ordered another Sapporo. They poured the beer and raised their glasses to toast the agreement—their bond.

By the time the tour boat docked, it was already 2:25 p.m.—ten minutes behind schedule that they expected. Aki and Ivan had to rush in order to catch the bus to Yokohama railway station—in time for their 3:00 p.m. Narita Express to the airport. They said hurried goodbyes and left.

Junjie Wu
Tuesday, August 6, PM
"Marine Rouge" Boat, Yokohama, Japan

Junjie did not need to hurry. Unusually for him, he actually did not have anywhere pressing to go. His meeting was scheduled for the next day, and all he needed to do for the rest of the afternoon is to make his way to his hotel in Minato—close to the TEL[48] Akasaka site. Normally, he would rush to check in and do some work in his room. But on that day, he felt like he needed the time. Some alone time to ponder. So he stayed behind in the boat restaurant to take care of the bill and on a whim decided to do another round in the tour boat—to sit in the lounge, drink some beer, enjoy an afternoon on Yokohama bay…and to collect himself.

The irony that Lao's money would be used to pay for their lunch and beers was not lost on him—since he was expensing the

---

[48] **Tokyo Electron Limited** (TEL): A Japanese electronics and semiconductor company headquartered in Akasaka, Japan, best known as a supplier of equipment for manufacturing of integrated circuits, flat panel displays, and photovoltaic cells. The company was founded as Tokyo Electron Laboratories, Inc. in 1963 and over the last few years TEL has consistently been one of the top 5 IC Fab Equipment makers in the world.

entire trip as a part of the cover story—the Red Lion M&A that Lao was funding.

He smirked to himself, enjoying that thought, sat back, took a good swig of his beer, and looked around. The lunchtime crowd that he was only partially aware of was gone. Most of the people seemed to be back up on the top decks. He was pretty much alone in the lounge other than a voluptuous woman in a summery white dress sitting alone at the bar and nursing some kind of a martini drink.

Odd, Junjie thought in passing. *A foreign woman, looks Mediterranean. Maybe Italian? Or Israeli? Drinking all by herself in the middle of a day in a bar on a boat touring Yokohama harbor. Odd. But sexy.*

He really did not think that much about it. He was more pre-occupied digesting the conversation he just had with Ivan and Aki.

Ivan is right—again. He usually is, Junjie thought, recalling the times, back when he first started working at Cadence, when Ivan jokingly used to assure his team that he was always right. He smiled with nostalgia. *Things were simpler back then...* Another sip of beer.

Yes, I really do have to develop some kind of an exit plan. C'mon, Albert! Focus.

He had two problems. Maybe more. One was to figure out his exit from CHARM. How would he engineer that without betraying the trust that his people placed in him? And the other was to figure out what to do with himself if—when—he did leave. He did not think that Lao or his cronies would allow him to start another business. They may not take any overt actions against him as long as he threatened to expose their pinch point strategy, but that did not mean that they would sit idly by and let him build another company. Unlikely.

And yet he was not ready to retire. Not so much because of financial reasons—he did have a sort of a nest egg that could afford them a reasonable standard of living. It was because of how he saw himself. He was not ready to join the army of old men, swollen by the growing life expectancy and with a retirement age still stuck at sixty. He was not ready for loitering in the parks of Beijing with nothing to do all day long other than buttonholing unsuspecting strangers to engage them in inane conversations. Bored out of their minds. No, he was not ready for that. Not yet. Which is why he has always been reluctant to even open the door to the idea of exiting CHARM. But now he had to.

The woman in the white dress made a bit of a show of herself—clumsily getting off her barstool and making her way probably to the ladies' room. Normally, in a situation like that, especially with just the two of them in the lounge, he would approach a woman like her. Offer to buy a drink. Engage in a conversation. Flirt a bit. *Tempting...*

But now—now he was preoccupied. So he just ignored her and gazed out at the big Ferris wheel on Yokohama pier. *Besides, she is not my type...*

Albert—how are you going to exit CHARM?

He forced himself to focus. To consider how would he distance—separate—himself from the company he started but without screwing over all the people?

Sell the company? To a domestic foundry user—like SMIC[49]—or some other State-Owned Enterprise[50] active in the technology field?

No!

---

[49] **SMIC** (Semiconductor Manufacturing International Corporation): A state-backed publicly held semiconductor foundry company. SMIC has wafer fabrication sites throughout mainland China, offices in the United States, Italy, Japan, and Taiwan, and a representative office in Hong Kong. It is headquartered in Shanghai, China, and incorporated in the Cayman Islands. It is the biggest and most visible Chinese foundry.

[50] **State-owned enterprise** (SOE): A business enterprise where the government or state has significant control through full, majority, or significant minority ownership. While SOEs may have a public policy objectives (e.g., a state railway company may aim to make transportation more accessible), they are different from government agencies or state entities. However, SOEs do typically have a political as well as a commercial purpose. Many large companies in China are SOEs, responsible for around 30 percent of GDP, and approximately 40 percent of net profits. The role of the Communist Party of China in SOEs has varied at different periods but has increased during the rule of Xi Jinping, with the Party formally taking a commanding role in all SOEs.

He was pretty sure that they would just screw it up and swallow the people. CHARM was too small and too specialized for something like that to work.

Sell to an existing partner company in China—like NAURA or AMEC—or some other fab equipment maker?

No!

Ditto. He thought that CHARM would also be lost in their much larger operations. Eventually, the team that he assembled would dissipate and his employees would have to start all over again.

Besides, Junjie thought that Lao could—and probably would—sabotage a transaction like that. Aside from spiteful reasons, Lao would probably object to having CHARM end up as a part of a larger corporation—state-owned or not. It would make using the pinch point power of CHARM harder for him.

In fact, Junjie thought, the only way to stop Lao from interfering was to make sure that there was no cover of darkness—that his exit from CHARM was public and visible. Suitable publicity would make his exit from CHARM less prone to interference. Less susceptible to Lao's corrupt or covert actions. Junjie knew that even though CHARM was a small company, high-tech got a lot of news coverage in China. In the gossip mill of the Beijing tech sector. On the Shanghai exchange. In the industry that was the battleground of the trade war. So he thought that getting some news coverage was a reasonable expectation—depending on how it was done. The rest of the Chinese government—possibly the only force that could counterbalance Lao—was sensitive to public appearances. Especially now, with this trade war going on. Eager to appear rational. Eager to project an image of a global good guy who played by the rules. In contrast to Trump.

Need to shine a light on it, he mused. *Must engineer a very public exit. Visible. Press releases and news briefs kind of visible...*

That train of thought and perhaps the effect of the beer precipitated a realization that was crystal clear to him at that point in time. That if his exit from CHARM is to succeed, he must use it to make the Party and the Government of the People's Republic of China look good.

Which then gave him an idea...

Restructure CHARM into a worker-owned cooperative kind of a company?

Maybe? Co-ops are politically very correct. Worker-ownership would fit well with the ideology. The government would like to point to a case of the old communist-like model working well in a new industry. It would look good. And co-ops are a popular way of working with foreigners. He could sell a minority portion to a foreign investor—or a partner of some kind—and the rest to his employees? Having a foreign partner would help with the visibility and maybe provide some immunity needed to fend Lao off. In these days of trade wars, the government would be eager to show off some foreign entity investing in a Chinese technology co-op. It would look good. There would be some good press. Good image for the Government and the Party. Even Lao might not want to mess with that.

EXHIBIT 9.4 Cooperative

A cooperative (also known as co-operative, co-op, or coop) is "an autonomous association of persons united voluntarily to meet their common economic, social, and cultural needs and aspirations through a jointly-owned enterprise". Cooperatives may include:

- *businesses owned and managed by the people who use their services (a consumer cooperative)*
- ***organizations managed by the people who work there (worker cooperatives)***
- *multi-stakeholder or hybrid cooperatives that share ownership between different stakeholder groups. For example, care cooperatives where ownership is shared between both care-givers and receivers. Stakeholders might also include non-profits or investors.*

Cooperative businesses are typically more economically resilient than many other forms of enterprise, with twice the number of co-operatives (80%) surviving their first five years compared with other business ownership models (41%). Research published by the Worldwatch Institute found that in 2012 approximately one billion people in 96 countries had become members of at least one cooperative. The turnover of the largest three hundred cooperatives in the world reached $2.2 trillion.

From: https://en.wikipedia.org/wiki/Cooperative

Chinese Industrial Cooperatives (Chinese pinyin: Gōngyè Hézuòshè) were organisations established to promote grassroots industrial and economic development in China. The movement was led through the Chinese Industrial Cooperative Association (CICA or Indusco founded in 1938. Also known by the nickname Gung Ho International Committee). The CICA was revived in 1983 in Beijing to promote cooperatives in China. Gung-ho is an English term, with the current meaning of "enthusiastic" or "overzealous". It is thought to have originated from the Chinese short-form of what were known in the 1930s as "Chinese Industrial Cooperatives", i.e. in Chinese official pinyin Romanisation of the acronym is gōng hé, meaning "work together".

From: https://en.wikipedia.org/wiki/Chinese_Industrial_Cooperatives#Revival

Yes! That could work! He would need to identify an appropriate foreign partner. Maybe some of the Japanese equipment vendors? Like TEL that he was due to meet with the next day? Better than an American company? Or Korean? Yes, that could work.

And sell the rest to the team?

His people—they would love it. He would have preferred to sell the entire company to them—they do deserve it. But that would not generate the publicity that he needed.

He turned that idea over in his mind, trying to imagine CHARM—his baby—without him. And the more he thought about it, the more he realized that CHARM was a small-enough company that some kind of committee management elected by worker-owners could, in fact, function very well. They all knew each other. They knew everyone's strengths and weaknesses. And he has put together an ace team—all of them top-notch kind of people. Real professionals.

In a way, he resented this conclusion. Emotionally, he would have preferred to conclude that CHARM could not possibly go on without him. That he was vitally needed. That without him, chaos and confusion would reign eventually leading to the inevitable collapse of the company. But intellectually, he knew that this was not the case. That CHARM could function quite well without him.

And the distributed management responsibilities—without any one person to pick on—would, in fact, make it harder for Lao to interfere with the company down the road. An added benefit of a co-op.

They—his people—would need to get a loan from a bank to fund, say 70 percent of the sale price—to pay him and the other investors off. With the other 30 percent coming from that foreign partner. The banks would likely support it. Partially because of that politically desirable image and partially because it could be structured to be a great deal for them. If the price was right. CHARM was a good, stable, and profitable business. Worth investing in.

And truth be said, he would be willing to take a bit of a haircut[51] to make that kind of a transaction work. To him, that kind of

---

[51] **Haircut**: In finance, refers to the discount—a reduction—applied to the value of an asset (e.g., landers who do not collect a complete repayment and interest on a given loan are said to have taken a haircut).

an exit would be worth missing out on the top dollar that he could get for CHARM on an open market.

What is there not to like?

Reward his people, exit CHARM very gracefully, and stick it to Lao. An honorable way to exit the company. Yes, he was pretty sure that he could price the deal to make it attractive to the banks.

That kind of an exit...hmm...would be worth a lot of money to me.

The more he thought about it, the more he liked that plan. He, of course, would need to ensure that a lot of things lined up just right. But the outline of the plan appealed to him.

Yes! That could work. And it would be the honorable thing to do.

He looked around, satisfied. A few more people in the lounge. The lady in the white dress was back, perched on her stool, enjoying her martini. Maybe a second martini. Or third. Still alone. *Tempting... Wonder what is her story*, he thought.

Albert! Pay attention! What is there for me after CHARM? He forced himself to refocus.

Retire? Stop working altogether? Travel around and take it easy?

No. He was not ready for that. He was still young enough to contribute. To matter. Only fifty. Besides, the nest egg notwithstanding, his major expenses were still ahead of him. University fees for his children. Grandkids' private schools—when they come. Income would be nice.

Give up on the profession and do something entirely different? Become a manager in some nonrelated business? Write? Become a commentator of some kind? Get involved with some nonprofit?

No. None of that sounded appealing to him. He loved the technology field. Technology was a part of him. Besides, he was too old to learn something like an entirely new trade.

Take a job as an engineer or an engineering manager? In some other technology company?

No. Working for someone else was just not him. Punching the clock? Doing a nine-to-five? Reporting and justifying his time to someone else? No, not his way. It would be frustrating and unsatisfying. That would not work.

Emigrate—to the US or anywhere outside China—and do his thing? Start another tech company?

No. It would be so disruptive to the whole family. His parents would not move. Too old. Feng and the kids would hate it. No, that would not work at all.

Teach? At some university? Hmmm.

This idea felt good. He knew that given Lao's opposition, it would be unlikely that he would be able to get a position at Tsinghua or any other of the anointed nine top-tier schools in the country. For sure, Lao would sabotage him there. But it is possible that Lao and his cronies would not block him from joining some other lower-profile institution. That would be more acceptable to them than him either starting another tech company or going to a really prestigious university. And there are around seventy universities in Beijing alone and about three thousand in China. Most of those would not be suitable, of course, but...surely, a seasoned professional, like himself, in one of the hottest fields of engineering, would be able to find a post at one of them. Probably. Teach engineering? Or entrepreneurship in some biz school?

He has taught a few university-level classes in the past—mostly as a favor to the various profs who asked him to and as a way of spotting new talent to recruit. And he has always found it very satisfying and rewarding. Yes, the image of himself as a professor at some technical university, teaching students and maybe even doing some research, really appealed to him. That is it!

Yes! I have a plan! I will convert CHARM into a co-op and become a university professor. I like it!

If he were alone, he might have even gotten up and pumped his fist. He felt so good about the plan. Well, not a plan yet. Maybe just an outline. A goal.

But instead, he just drained his glass and looked around the lounge. The lady in the white dress has disappeared somewhere. A few other people occupying random booths and tables, sheltering from the afternoon heat.

Contrary to the local customs that he was fully aware of, on leaving the lounge, he tucked an excellent tip under his empty glass.

He suspected that it might, in fact, cause all sorts of problems for the poor Japanese waiters. Take it or leave it? Keep it or share it? How to share it? It was not normal or customary…

Still, Junjie felt good about his afternoon well spent. He thought it would be good karma to share the joy.

Ivan Jovanovic
Tuesday, August 27
Lakeshore Hotel, Hsinchu, Taiwan, ROC

Three weeks passed. Ivan felt under pressure to act—before Junjie's predicament got out of hand and Lao sensed that things were going wrong. He knew that they must define a concrete schedule. If his managerial experience has thought him anything, it was that nothing ever happened unless there was a target date to work to. Intentions and goodwill counted for nothing without a target date.

He decided that if they were actually to go into Lao's office—still a big "if" in his mind—they would be best off doing it when there were a lot of disruptions anyways. So he perused through the list of Chinese holidays—thinking that holidays tend to be a natural disruption to any normal organizational routine—and hence the time when a security system would be least likely to be reliable.

He zeroed in on the midautumn festival, a.k.a. the Moon Festival, which that year fell on Friday, September 13.

EXHIBIT 9.5 Moon Festival

The Mid-Autumn Festival is a harvest festival celebrated notably by the Chinese and Vietnamese people. It relates to Chuseok (in Korea) and Tsukimi (in Japan). The festival is held on the 15th day of the 8th month of the lunar calendar with a full moon at night.

The Mid-Autumn Festival is the second most important traditional festival in China (the most important one is Chinese New Year). It's a family day in China - like Thanksgiving. There are many traditional and new celebrations:

Traditional activities included Fire Dragon dancing, enjoying the displays of lanterns, and eating moon cakes. Today, it is still an occasion for outdoor reunions among friends and relatives to eat mooncakes and watch the moon, a symbol of harmony and unity. A notable part of celebrating the holiday is the carrying of brightly lit lanterns, lighting lanterns on towers, or floating sky lanterns. The Mid-Autumn moon has also been a choice occasion to celebrate marriages. Girls would pray to moon deity Chang'e to help fulfill their romantic wishes.

From: https://www.chinahighlights.com/festivals/mid-autumn-festival-tradition.htm

A.k.a. the target D-Day, he thought. *A public holiday! Second in importance only to Chinese New Year. And Friday the 13. Perfect!*

He suspected that the Provost building—the place where Professor Lao had his private office—would probably be entirely deserted during a public holiday. No one was likely to be burning the midnight oil then. A time when the guards were most likely to be sleepy. And Moon Festival sounded like a holiday when students—assuming that Chinese students were like any other twentysomething-year-olds in the world—were apt to undertake unexpected and dumb antics. Lanterns, moonlight parties, fire dragon dancing, and girls potentially in a romantic mood all sounded just perfect. Plenty of opportunities for distractions. Plenty of opportunities for generating confusion.

But they had to have a final meeting before they actually did anything concrete. Or stupid and dangerous. They needed to agree to a specific plan and to recommit to it. And they needed time to prepare. So Ivan decided that a meeting a couple of weeks or so before the target D-day was merited. Someplace like Taiwan rather than

Beijing—partially because it would be safer than meeting on Lao's turf and partially because it could be made to fit in well with their cover story. And also a good excuse for Junjie to travel and to skip his biweekly meeting with Professor Lao.

So during a regular Red Lion videoconference, Ivan suggested that it would be appropriate to give a heads-up about the forthcoming sale of BBI KK to its principal clients. Officially, to sound out their reaction. Actually, to prepare them—since serving important clients with a fait accompli is the absolute worst sin in business. A taboo. As he expected, Aki immediately identified TSMC as a suitable prominent client. TSMC was known to be the largest consumer—and producer—of photomasks in the world. Junjie also mentioned Toppan[52] as an important local mask shop and SMIC as a flagship end user in China.

EXHIBIT 9.6   **Taiwan Semiconductor Manufacturing Corporation**

Taiwan Semiconductor Manufacturing Company, Limited (TSMC), founded in 1987, was the first and is now the largest dedicated independent (pure-play) semiconductor foundry, with its headquarters and main operations located in the Hsinchu Science and Industrial Park in Hsinchu, Taiwan. Annual capacity of the manufacturing facilities managed by TSMC and its subsidiaries exceeded 12 million 12-inch equivalent wafers in 2018. These facilities include three 12-inch wafer GIGAFAB® fabs, four 8-inch wafer fabs, and one 6-inch wafer fab – all in Taiwan – as well as one 12-inch wafer fab at a wholly owned subsidiary, TSMC Nanjing Company Limited, and two 8-inch wafer fabs at wholly owned subsidiaries, WaferTech in the United States and TSMC China Company Limited.
Most of the leading fabless semiconductor companies such as Advanced Micro Devices (AMD), Apple Inc., Broadcom Inc., MediaTek, Nvidia, and Qualcomm are customers of TSMC, as well as emerging companies such as AppliedMicro, HiSilicon, Spectra7, and Spreadtrum. Leading programmable logic device company Xilinx also make use of TSMC's foundry services. Some integrated device manufacturers that have their own fabrication facilities like Intel, STMicroelectronics and Texas Instruments outsource some of their production to TSMC. At least one semiconductor company, LSI, re-sells TSMC wafers through its ASIC design services and design IP-portfolio.
TSMC provides customer service, account management and engineering services through offices in North America, Europe, Japan, China, and South Korea. At the end of 2018, the Company and its subsidiaries employed more than 48,000 people.

From: https://en.wikipedia.org/wiki/TSMC and https://www.tsmc.com/english/default.htm

---

[52] **Toppan** (Toppan Photomasks Inc): A part of Toppan Printing Co., a Japanese conglomerate, and one of the premier manufacturers of photomasks for the IC industry. They have a large manufacturing site in Shanghai, China.

Hence, a meeting in Hsinchu in Taiwan—TSMC's home-town—was natural. And convenient for their ploy. To be followed by a week or so in Shanghai—officially to meet with Toppan and maybe SMIC. But also a fine place to acquire the necessary gear. And then a week or so in Beijing—officially as a final meeting at CHARM but actually to complete their plans and to do the deed.

If they decide to do it.

Ivan picked the week of August 26, as it gave them more than a couple of weeks to their target D-day. Aki reached out to his main contact at TSMC, who indicated that he would be available on Tuesday, the twenty-seventh. Convenient since this allowed them to spend the weekend at home and to fly out on Sunday night.

Like the month before for their meeting in Japan, Ivan made the arrangements. He booked his favorite hotel in Hsinchu: Lakeshore—not the most luxurious or prestigious, but Ivan was used to it ever since way back in the nineties when his work took him to Taiwan fairly often. Their EVA Air red-eye flight landed on sched-ule at 6:00 a.m. at what Ivan still thought of as Chiang Kai-shek Airport.[53] Following the usual hour or so limo ride to Hsinchu, they took advantage of the early check-in option that the hotel offered and had a quick shower and a short nap.

As agreed, they met Junjie, who arrived the previous evening, in the lobby at 10:00 a.m. A quick taxi ride to the TSMC Fab-12 site and they were in time for their meeting.

YS—their host and the director of the TSMC mask-making operations—listened patiently to Aki and Junjie explain the ratio-nale behind the merger of BBI and CHARM. The usual... Synergy. Capital infusion. Expansion of EUV capacity. After posing a round of questions and presumably receiving satisfactory answers, YS indi-cated that he did not have any issues with the proposed deal. The fact that both CEOs were in the room, positively asserting that the

---

[53] **Chiang Kai-shek Airport** (code: TPE): The main airport for Taipei, Taiwan, renamed Taoyuan International Airport in 2006. Originally named after the Chinese nationalist leader who served as the president of the Republic of China between 1928 and 1975, first in mainland China until 1949 and then in Taiwan until his death.

supply and quality of the BBI blanks would not be affected in any way, was an important factor. The fact that Junjie added his personal assurances in Mandarin, as opposed to the English used throughout the meeting, probably also counted. And the fact that both BBI and CHARM were already existing and highly rated suppliers to TSMC certainly helped. This avoided the need for additional bureaucratic procedures required to certify all new vendors—something that YS, like any good engineer, was probably eager to bypass. They were surprised—and humbled—that Burn Lin, a legendary guru on photolithography, dropped by to say hi during their postmeeting courtesy lunch in the TSMC cafeteria. That underscored the importance that TSMC attached to their supply of mask blanks.

Altogether, an excellent meeting. They were done by 1:00 p.m.

Ivan directed the taxi to take them to the Ambassador Hotel—not their own Lakeshore—practicing the same precautions as for their meeting in Japan. They settled in the conference room that he reserved and he dived straight in.

"Gentlemen," he said, "I did my homework on drones. And the one thing that I can say is, man, there sure are a shitload of them. Different types, sizes, ranges, applications…whatever. Hundreds… The hard part was selecting the right ones for our job. And the good news is that China turns out to be the world leader in drone technology. So I was thinking that we should just buy them there. Probably safer than ordering them by mail or transporting them with us."

EXHIBIT 9.7 Drones (Civilian Use)

An unmanned aerial vehicle (UAV) (commonly known as a drone) is an aircraft without a human pilot on board and a type of unmanned vehicle. UAVs are a component of an unmanned aircraft system (UAS); which include a UAV, a ground-based controller, and a system of communications between the two.

Size: cm's to m's
Weight: gm's to kg's
Range: ~m's to 10's of km's
Flight Time: min's to ~hr
Payload: 0 to ~kg's
Price: $10 to $10,000's
Control: manual to automated
Camera: none to Hi Res + IR + Video
Uses: Toys, Selfies, Reconeissance, Pics, Mapping, Remote inspections, Delivery, Fishing, Agricultural Spraying, Emergancy and Rescue Ops...

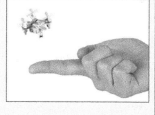

"Yeah, yeah," Aki interjected impatiently, "but what are we going to do with them? What's the plan?"

Aki sounded somewhat testy. *So uncharacteristic for him*, thought Ivan. *He is normally such a rock. Maybe it's the jet lag?*

"Good point. Sorry," Ivan responded, realizing that Aki and Junjie were not in the loop on all the things that he was planning over the last month or so. It was old hat to him, but Junjie and Aki were in the dark and understandably anxious.

Ivan took a deep breath and focused on rewinding the film in his head—unraveling his plan into its basic components so that it would be as logical to them after a few minutes, as it was to him after weeks of thinking about it.

He held up one finger and started. "First, I think that we need a sort of a base to operate from. It is not like the three of us—particularly the laowai[54] among us—can walk around and fly drones and expect to be unnoticed. Especially at night. And especially in Beijing—which is, legally speaking, a drone no-fly zone. I thought about trying to be obvious and hide in plain sight. Maybe put on lab coats and pretend that we are testing some new 5G antenna or something. But I suspect that this kind of ploy may work only in the movies. So we need a base. A hotel where foreigners would not be unusual or odd. I found one that would be suitable—the Holiday Inn on Shuangqing Road. But it is about a mile from Lao's office building. I could not find anything that meets our requirements and that is much closer. What do you think, Junjie?"

"Er, I guess." Junjie shrugged. "Probably…"

"And I checked, and their rooms do have windows that open, and some of the suites even have balconies," Ivan announced proudly.

"Er, so?"

"So second," Ivan responded, holding up two fingers, "we need a drone that can be operated from our base. And therefore, we also need a balcony or at least a window that opens for launching it. A rare feature in modern high-rise hotels." Big grin. He was clearly pleased with himself for having thought of this little detail. "You can get drones," he continued, "with an operating range well over a kilometer—maybe even tens of kilometers. Piece of cake. But these tend to be relatively big and bulky. For a range of the order of a kilometer, they are roughly the size of your big heads or thereabouts. Not the kind of a drone that you can park in someone's office without it being noticed."

"So?" Aki prodded again. He was anxious and impatient. Leaning forward in his chair. Antsy.

---

[54] **Laowai**: An informal term or slang for "foreigner" in Pinyin notation. It literally means "old foreign" with neutral or slightly impolite connotation. The term is typically used to refer to Europeans, Africans, Latin Americans, and Middle Easterners, and not to ethnic Han or other Asian ethnicities.

Pinyin is the romanization of the Chinese characters based on their pronunciation. In Mandarin Chinese, the phrase "Pin Yin" literally translates into "spell sound." In other words, spelling out Chinese phrases with letters from the English alphabet.

"So we need to set up a kind of a relay system. Have one relatively big drone that we can control from our hotel and make it act as a mothership through which we can operate secondary drones that we have in the building. See what I mean?"

"Can that be done?" Junjie asked dubiously.

"Yes, why not?" Ivan shrugged. "The joysticks that are used to pilot drones are just transducers to interface to humans. A drone actually receives a series of command signals encoded on an RF carrier wave. So think of it as a master drone whose payload is an RF emitter that sends out the signals to operate the slave drones plus a phone that can send pictures back to us. Or think of it as a kind of a Wi-Fi hot spot through which we transmit the control signals. After all, it is just an RF relay link with an incoming signal, some digital processing, and an outgoing signal. Make sure that the incoming and outgoing signals operate on the right channels and presto. Actually, in this day and age of digital-everything, it is not that hard to set up."

He paused there to let all that sink in. Aki and Junjie were engineers, but their field of expertise was on the other end of the spectrum of specialties. But Ivan was sure that they could get it by just dredging up some basics from their university courses.

"Okaaaay…" Aki drew out, hesitating and unsure. "Go on."

"We fly the mothership drone—the one with a long range—from the hotel and park it, for example, on the roof of Lao's building. No one is going to see it there—especially at night. It can act as our private local Wi-Fi hotspot that we can use to control little drones inside the building."

"Little drones?" both Junjie and Aki questioned.

"Yes. That is the third element," Ivan said holding up three fingers. "Drones that carry just a camera. These can be smaller with a shorter operating range and flight times. We could then use these little drones as our eyes in the building. They can send the pictures to the big drone that would then relay these back to us in the safety of our hotel room."

"Ah, I see! Or at least, I understand the principle." Junjie nodded. "But, but…how are you going to get those baby drones into the building?"

"Aha! Good question. Clearly, we would need to stage them in the building by hand. And then operate them from the hotel through our relay station. Makes sense?"

Dubious looks from Junjie and Aki.

"The question is if you," Ivan continued, pointing at Junjie, "or your detectives, or someone, can inconspicuously scatter a few smaller drones around the building. This kind of drone can be quite small. Good ones can fit in the palm of a hand. Not so good ones are the size of a thumb. The palm-sized one would be about right for our purpose—in terms of range, camera, battery life… And I presume at that size, they would be easy to hide. Leave them somewhere where they would not be obvious. If this building is anything like any other office building I have been in, there should be plenty of places where they could be left unobserved and unobstructed. Some tall shelf? Big filing cabinets tucked in a corner somewhere? Unoccupied cubicle? Behind some admin's flowerpot? Behind a water cooler or a coffee station… I don't know. We would have to play that by ear."

"Hmm." Junjie scratched his head. "Maybe. Possibly… That building is not exactly crawling with students, but there are still people who normally have business there. So it is not deserted during the working hours. Or at least it wasn't whenever I went there. We should be able to get into the building without causing undue attention. Especially during the week. Not so sure about finding suitable hiding spots for the drones though. But we can try…"

"Well, that will have to do."

"Oh, okay. I get it!" Aki exclaimed, finally grasping the plan. "Then at night, when there is no one around, we fly these baby drones and find suitable hiding spots for them inside the building—all from the safety of our hotel room. We can then use their cameras to observe daytime activities. We use the big mothership drone to relay the control signals and then when the baby drones are in place to relay the pictures back to us during the daytime hours. Right? Tricky, but I think I get it." He seemed excited—nodding, amused, and interested.

"Exactly. We use the baby drones to look around and probe the security systems at night. If we trigger some kind of an alarm—good.

Potentially we lose some drones, but we get to understand what we are dealing with. If we don't—still good. We end up with eyes in the building. All from our hotel room."

The three of them looked at each other. They were excited now—eyes shining, nodding, and grinning.

A bit like kids who have hatched a plot to steal some cookies or something, thought Ivan to himself.

"Agreed?" Ivan prodded.

Aki and Junjie nodded but still somewhat reluctantly.

Ivan expected that this was because the plan probably felt fanciful and farfetched to them. It did to him too—to begin with—until he convinced himself that it could actually work. *Why not?* Besides, it probably appealed to their sense of safety. It was a way of peeking into Lao's building from far away.

Like poking a nasty snake with a very, very long stick, thought Ivan.

"Good. It would help if we had a plan for the building. Junjie, any luck with that?"

"Yes!" Junjie retrieved a wad of papers from his computer bag. "That particular building was built in '08. No wonder I did not know of it when I was a student. Anyways, turns out that the university committee that was responsible for planning and permitting that building had all the plans. When the building was finished and inaugurated, they stashed the plans in the university library—since Provost's building is such a showpiece. My men just nicked them from there. Easy." He spread out copies of the specs and various sections of the architectural drawings across the table.

"Excellent." Ivan paged through the plans. "Excellent. These will give us the layout. There are still a lot of unknowns—rooms may have been remodeled, cubicles and partitions could have been built, furniture… We will have to navigate the drones around those in real time."

After a pause, Ivan concluded, "So that would be phase 1. The info we collect would give us a sense of the security procedures in the building. And eyes inside it. And we can watch. And doing all that would be relatively safe. All we would be guilty of is violating drone no-fly rules."

"And then?" Aki asked.

"Then we decide." Ivan shrugged and spread his hands in a universal gesture of not knowing. "We watch. Let's see how Lao goes in and out of his office. Where are the keys? Does he do anything to deactivate some hidden alarms? And so on. And then we make the final plan in real time. With some real data."

"Final plan?"

"Yes, my friends. That would be phase 2. The point of no return. Ultimately—if we are really going to do this—one of us has to go into that building, break into Lao's office, and photograph his papers." After a pause, he added hurriedly, "And get out, of course." The last with a bit of a grin. "I can see no other way. It is that, or we decide to abort the whole ploy."

Silence. That was the scary stuff. All this planning—drones and sitting in the hotel room—that was easy. Sounded like fun. But actually going in and breaking into Lao's office. That was scary. Sobering. They fell silent.

"Easy," Ivan concluded, trying to sound more confident than he really felt. "I believe that if successful, phase 1 would be all that we could do to minimize the risks. Which would presumably make phase 2 a reasonable undertaking—since we would know exactly what we would be walking into. But in the end, someone would have to actually and physically go in and do the deed. And—let's face it—the risks would not be zero. And the liability—if we do get caught—could be serious."

Aki and Junjie nodded hesitantly in the sober silence.

"However you turn it, that is the best plan that I could come up with," Ivan said in closing. Pause, to allow Aki and Junjie to protest or add anything. "Are we in or out?"

They looked from one to the other. They looked at the plans scattered on the table. They looked through the window. Finally, Aki and Junjie both nodded again.

Acquiescence rather than agreement, thought Ivan. *Okay, for now—since the final go/no-go decision will really have to be made the night before. That will be the point of no return. Up till then, we can still safely pull out.*

But all he said was, "Okay. We will acquire the drones and the rest of the gizmos and gear in China. Mostly in Shanghai when we visit Toppan. Some in Beijing. We don't want to attract too much attention by buying too many things all in one shop at one time. I believe that if we earmark the mothership drone for export, we get to bypass the government rules and won't have to register it with the police. Then we go to Beijing and check into our hotel. We do the drone thing. At night. And we watch… And then we make the final decision: to abort or to go in."

The Caper

Junjie Wu
Monday, September 9
Holiday Inn, Haidian District, Beijing

"Okay, guys, cross your fingers. This is it!" Ivan mumbled, very intent on the drone, the size of a large pizza, that was perched on the table next to him. Making sure that the cargo it was carrying—a plastic box containing a phone, several attachments with associated wiring, other electronic devices, and a spare battery pack—was securely zip-tied to the drone frame. Gizmos that Junjie, and probably Aki, did not quite understand but that Ivan specified with apparent confidence. He had a long list of requirements and insisted on seemingly unimportant factors—down to minutiae, such as the presence or absence of power-on lights indicating LEDs. All procured in the four shops in Shanghai and one in Beijing that Ivan demanded they visit.

They were on the balcony of Ivan's suite. It was just past midnight, and the constant buzz of a busy city was beginning to abate for the night. But they thought not yet so much that the whir of the drone would be overly noticeable.

Junjie had to push very hard to make sure that Ivan got a room with a balcony. This was a part of the last-minute room switch that Ivan, the paranoiac in chief, insisted on. Just in case someone was bugging them. Junjie made up a story about Ivan being a smoker and needing a balcony for a cigarette or two. The helpful clerk offered to put Ivan in a room on a smoking floor. Even at no added cost. Junjie had to backpaddle and explained that Ivan was one of those crazy Americans who only smoked outside. That did not convince the clerk who seemed intent on opening Ivan's eyes to the comforts of smoking indoors. But a couple of discretely slipped fifty-yuan bills—a huge tip by local standards—did the trick.

They spent quite a while debating the exact timing—down to specific days or even hours.

Aki argued that the sooner that they place the drones in their observation spots, the more time they would have to gather the data, and the better would be their intelligence. "No-brainer," he claimed.

Junjie thought that the quality of their intel would probably follow the eighty-twenty rule[55] and that spending much more than a couple of days gathering the data would not necessarily produce more useful information. He also worried that the longer that the drones sat in their observation posts, the more likely it was that someone would find them.

Ivan believed that there was a Goldilocks[56] point—not too soon and not too late but just the right day. "Not to mention that the longer that we leave the drones out there, the harder it is to manage their battery life," he added.

So they settled on Monday—which would give them three working days and three full nights of observation prior to the target D-Day.

---

[55] **Eighty-twenty rule** (Pareto Principle): A general observation that states that 80 percent of a certain task can be accomplished with 20 percent of the effort, and conversely, the hardest 20 percent of an endeavor takes 80 percent of the effort. For example, in computer science, fixing the top 20 percent of the most-reported bugs eliminates 80 percent of system crashes.

[56] **Goldilocks moment**: Named by analogy to the children's story *The Three Bears*, in which a little girl named Goldilocks tastes three different bowls of porridge and finds that she prefers porridge that is neither too hot nor too cold but has just the right temperature. The term is easily understood and applied to a wide range of situations.

"Well?" Junjie asked impatiently. He was anxious and nervous. Wanted to get on with it already!

Albert! Cool it, he cautioned himself but then quickly rationalized it. *Finally! Finally, we are getting down to doing something other than just talking and planning.*

"Here goes nothing," Ivan responded, RC controller—with its two joysticks, numerous buttons and switches, and a display screen—in his hands. Ready to go. His hands were trembling.

Wow? Ivan—nervous? Never thought I would see that, Junjie thought, slightly amused by seeing that even Ivan, who is normally so laid back, was succumbing to the tension. *Understandable, though*, he allowed.

Up to then, Junjie thought that Ivan seemed so sure of himself, readily assuming a lead role in this caper of theirs with himself and Aki mostly agreeing to whatever he proposed. Which Junjie ascribed to the fact that Ivan had the most time to think things through, as opposed to him and Aki who had full-time day jobs that kept them pretty busy. *Besides, this drone stuff is Ivan's thing...*

Ivan flicked a switch, and the four propellers hummed on. Making quite a racket. Or so Junjie felt—hoping that none of the guests in the adjoining rooms would notice it. The drone gradually rose to a few feet over their heads and hovered in place. Ivan pressed a button on his controller and the drone disappeared into the darkness—flying off in the direction of the university.

Ivan spent a big chunk of that day preprogramming a flight path. He must have loaded, tested, and reloaded it a dozen times, alternately checking Google Maps and his little notebook that contained the notes that he took on their walks across the Tsinghua campus. Ever since they checked into their hotel, Ivan and Aki walked it at least twice a day. The university was on the way to CHARM offices, so walking through the campus fit in well with their cover story. And Junjie made sure that they had some kind of an engagement at CHARM offices every working day—meeting with key people, lawyers from his legal firm, the investors, and the like. Just in case—should anyone be watching. Or should they abort their ploy so that the sale of BBI KK would have to go through.

The drone was to fly on autopilot up to the Provost's building at an altitude of sixty feet—high enough to clear the trees and structures that were on its selected path. Ivan did not want to fly above sixty feet—roughly equivalent to a six-floor building—and he had to navigate around the taller buildings. All to obscure the drone—just in case the authorities had a way of monitoring and enforcing the Beijing no-fly rules.

It was then supposed to hover there until Ivan took over in manual mode, selected a suitable perch for it, and landed it. Or at least, that was the plan.

The drone was programmed to fly at a moderate thirty miles per hour, and it arrived at its target in less than a couple of minutes. Of course, to the three of them, those minutes felt like excruciatingly long hours. No one spoke a word. No one dared to breathe. Aki and Junjie stood behind Ivan, looking intently over his shoulder at the screen on the controller that displayed a blur of barely recognizable bright lights and nondescript shapes that the drone was sending back.

"There," Junjie exclaimed as the characteristic doughnut shape of the Provost building emerged on the screen.

Judging from the plans that they studied so very carefully and from what Junjie told them, the Provost building was a two-story structure with a large open-air garden in the middle. This gave it a footprint that was easy to spot.

All three of them sighed and took a deep breath.

Ivan slowly pushed on one of the joysticks, and the Provost building grew nearer as the drone descended. All the usual equipment that cluttered the building's flat roof gradually came into focus: the various air-conditioning and heating units, all sorts of vents and pipes, the roof access and elevator equipment structure, and the like.

They knew the basic layout of the site: from the architectural plans and the various blogs about the show building. The whole west wing served as an entrance hall that was meant to impress. A two-story atrium, marble and glass, with an imposing reception desk in the center, a view of the serene Chinese garden behind it, and wide open staircase on either side leading up to the second floor of the north and south wings. And with all kinds of display stands scattered about—showcasing the special trophies and honors that the university won. Both floors of the north and south wings seemed to be the "prestige area" that included the private office suites along the inner walls, presumably occupied by the selected lucky luminaries of the school who just had to have the view of the garden. And more office suites and meeting rooms of various sizes distributed along the outer walls. Both floors of the east wing seemed to be the working area laid out like modern open-space offices with cubicles in the middle and walled rooms along the edges.

Junjie indicated that Professor Lao's office was on the second floor of the north wing of the building. So the intent was to park the drone on the roof of the south wing. Hoping to place it so that they could see into Lao's window.

The little dial on the controller was reading the altitude: sixty feet, fifty feet, forty feet... Ivan carefully navigated the drone to position it over the south wing and swiveled the camera to inspect the detailed layout on that portion of the roof.

Earlier, they had discussed—more like speculated—about the right parking spot for the drone. First of all, they agreed it must not be too obvious. So parking it on the very edge of the roof was ruled out. The parking spot then needed to be pulled back but sufficiently elevated to give the camera clearance over the roof edge required to see into Lao's office. Second, they were concerned about parking the drone on top of some piece of equipment—an air-conditioner unit or something—that might kick into operation and vibrate enough to disturb or even shake off the drone. Third, the parking spot needed to be reasonably clear of other electronic gear—various antenna, transformers, and the like—to minimize electromagnetic interference of any kind.

They pored over the building plans and zeroed in on an air duct—roughly two-by-one-foot rectangular shaft that was supposed to have elevated rims and a cap—presumably to prevent rain from getting into the duct. But they were looking at ten-year-old building plans. A lot might have changed. So they knew that they had to be careful with this last step.

"There," Aki said, pointing to one particular rectangular feature displayed on the screen and holding next to it the section of the building plan that included the targeted air shaft.

Ivan manipulated the camera and zoomed in. They waited a few seconds to get the full resolution in the low-light conditions. Yes, it did look like the drawing in the building plans. But no, the metal housing over the duct was steepled, not flat. Not a landing pad.

"Shit!" Aki swore. "Now what? I knew that we should have done at least a reconnaissance flight earlier. Now we are up a shit's creek without a paddle. I hate this last-minute stuff." He stopped short of saying "I told you so."

"Yeah, maybe…," Ivan mumbled without taking his eyes off the screen. "But we agreed that today was the Goldilocks day," he trailed off, as he flew the drone around, inspecting other air shafts and vents.

"I like last-minute stuff," Junjie inserted lightheartedly. "I find that I get more creative when I am under pressure. Adrenaline does wonders for my efficiency and creativity."

"There," Ivan said, pointing to a cylindrical pipe, about a foot or so in diameter, with a veined turbine extractor fan—looking a bit like a mushroom, but with a flat cap on top of it. "What is that?"

Junjie and Aki frantically leafed through the plans. Junjie found the appropriate structure and said hesitantly, "Er, roughly translated, it says here stink shaft."

"Ah, a fart-fan exhaust." Ivan giggled. "Some terms seem to be universal."

"From what little I know," he ventured tentatively—thinking aloud but focused on the screen, "these kinds of fans are meant to provide a slight negative pressure. They suck rather than blow… Presumably to assist the airflow or to prevent back drafts from fans that happen to share an exhaust duct. I guess no one likes the smell from one bathroom seeping into another one. Maybe providing every bathroom with its own vent pipe is expensive… Anyway, this type of fans—at least in America—tend to operate at relatively low speeds. So that they can last forever. Presumably changing out fans on a roof is not a popular idea. I guess it must be a pain in the ass—what with resealing and stuff… So let me make a stupid, wild-ass guess and assume that the vibrations from something like it should be relatively low. What do you gents think?"

Hmm, when faced with a choice he really does go on and on, Junjie remarked to himself, noting Ivan's habit of talking continuously whenever they encountered an unforeseen problem. *His mind is chaos… And his thinking process is so much birdwalking.*[57]

Aki and Junjie looked at each other uncertainly. "No idea," they responded in unison.

"Any better alternatives?" Ivan questioned.

"Er, not that I can see," Aki muttered.

"Do it," Junjie encouraged.

Ivan slowly maneuvered the drone directly overhead and ever so gradually descended onto the target structure. They knew that it was critical that the drone is aligned exactly over the chosen landing pad so that its feet end up sitting squarely on the perch. Otherwise, the drone could topple over or be unstable. Could be knocked over by…a bit of vibration? A gust of wind? A stupid bird? They held their breath.

"Wheels down." Ivan sighed, flicking the switch that turned off the rotors. He operated some of the controls, and the inner facade of the north wing came into view. He zoomed in on a window on the second floor—at that time just a dark rectangle. The angle of the view was a bit more oblique than what they hoped for, but they still had a pretty clear view into that window. "Good. We have eyes on Lao," he said, putting down the controller and flexing his fingers. Hands still shaking.

The three of them looked at each other, nodded, and finally started breathing again. Looking again like the three old men—flesh and blood—that they were rather than silhouettes of men frozen in time in the act of staring at the screen of the controller. Like some kind of Giacometti[58] figures.

---

[57] **Birdwalking**: A meandering from topic to topic as in a free-flowing conversation that follows seemingly random associations.

[58] **Alberto Giacometti:** A Swiss sculptor, painter, draftsman, and printmaker (1901–1966), famous for his cast bronze sculptures that depict a man in midstride—notable for capturing a sense of motion frozen in a moment.

Junjie patted Ivan on the back and muttered, "Good job, pilot."

Ivan nodded with relief. "Phew! I spent the last month or so doing little else than screwing around with drones. Flying them is actually a lot of fun—once you get a hang of it. Who says old dogs cannot learn new tricks? But this was…challenging." he concluded, a big grin blossoming over his face. "The rest is a cakewalk," he added sarcastically.

They retreated into the room, and Ivan gingerly placed the RC controller on the desk, next to the unfurled rolls of the building floor plans that Junjie had spread out there. These were marked to show the location of what they started referring to as "baby drones"—big Xs in red pen standing out against the black and white of the architectural drawings.

Junjie, his detectives, and a nephew that Junjie recruited, staged them inside the building earlier that day. It turned out that this was not as hard as they feared.

Their target—the Provost's building—housed the apex of a huge administrative organization that managed the university with its thirty-six thousand students, three thousand faculty members, and four thousand administrative staff. Most of the administrative and academic functions were distributed across the twenty-five-odd different colleges and faculties and were physically located in the hundreds of buildings scattered across the one-thousand-acre Tsinghua University urban campus. Provost's building was reserved for the top tier of that vast organization: the president, the party secretary, a few of the provosts, and senior-most administrators and deans, along with their personal staff. And for the business office that controlled more than a $4 billion endowment fund and oversaw the most important commercial activities of the university. And for meetings with the select prestigious visitors and partners. It was meant to be a showpiece of a world-class university. Hence, the use of architectural style intended to make it unique and notable, leveraging an interesting blend of modern glass and steel and classical brick and mortar, and with a traditional Chinese garden in the center.

They knew all this. From what Junjie told them. From the various blogs that Junjie translated for them. And they knew that they needed a plan—a pretext—for entering the building and doing what they had to do. They could not really just saunter in and leave a bunch of drones here and there throughout the building. But that is exactly what was needed…

So Junjie's nephew, who also happened to be an engineering student at Tsinghua, found a fellow student who was working as a part-time intern in the Provost building. With WeChat[59] and other social media and the digitally chatty generation of students, it wasn't too hard. He approached her with a made-up story that they were preparing a kind of a surprise for the Moon Festival. Supposedly, some of the engineering labs were planning to display a swarm of drones. Supposedly, a demonstration of a project that they were working on. The drones were supposed to be like indoor lanterns that would come together from all parts of the building form a flock and fly in a preprogrammed pattern of dancing lights. And supposedly they wanted to do this demo during a Moon Festival reception that the president of the university was apparently hosting in the west wing.

EXHIBIT 10.1   <u>Drone SWARM</u>

Precisely defined, drone swarms are "multiple unmanned platforms deployed to accomplish a shared objective, with the platforms autonomously altering their behavior based on communication with one another. Each individual drone is not controlled in itself but instead it shares a collective, distributed "brain," travelling in leaderless "swarms," members of which can adapt to changes in drone numbers and remain co-ordinated with their counterparts.

From: e.g. https://en.wikipedia.org/wiki/Perdix_(drone)

---

[59] **WeChat**: a Chinese multipurpose messaging, social media, and mobile payment app developed by Tencent. It was first released in 2011 and has since become one of the world's largest standalone mobile apps.

The intern understood, happily agreed to help a fellow student, and readily swore to secrecy, promising that she would not say anything to anyone until at least the following week. Supposedly to preserve the surprise effect. And, supposedly, to avoid any potential embarrassment if the demonstration had to be aborted—since the engineering labs were still working out the bugs. Supposedly. So she agreed to leave a few small drones unobstructed in selected cubicles and, in fact, helped identify suitable places in the open offices and the conference rooms. Most willing and helpful.

That gave them four active drones in the building: two in the second-floor open-office space in the east wing, one in a big glassed-in conference room in the north wing, and one on the first-floor open-office area. And a handful of dummy drones that they did not intend to fly but had scattered around the building to obscure the real ones and to mesh with the story. And a cover that was good for a few days.

The plan was that Junjie's nephew would get back to the helpful intern on Monday and tell her that the demo was aborted and that she might as well keep the drones as a gift of thanks. And ask her to keep quiet about the whole affair in order to save them the embarrassment of having to publicize the failure. Something that they thought all Chinese students would readily relate to. And, just in case, on Ivan's stubborn insistence, Junjie's nephew used a fake name and WeChat ID for the whole caper. So that the drones could not be traced back to him. Just in case.

Junjie's detectives placed two more baby drones in the west wing reception area. They apparently enjoyed hamming it up and pretended to be two country bumpkin visiting professors from the Agricultural University in Gansu province. They took turns putting on a Columbo[60] act, asking all sorts of questions of the staff at the reception desk. Questions that clearly seemed stupid to the urbane

---

[60] **Columbo**: An American crime drama television series starring Peter Falk as Columbo—a seemingly inept but wily homicide detective. Columbo trademarks included his rumpled beige raincoat, unassuming demeanor, irritating cigar smoking, apparent clumsiness, and relentless questioning usually preceded by a catchphrase, "Just one more thing."

receptionists—but who were too polite to brush them off. But sufficiently distracting so that one of them could discreetly stow away a baby drone in a display case at the far end of the hall while the other one asked yet another irritating question.

The hard part was placing a drone inside Lao's office suite. After many discussions and considering several different schemes—some quite farfetched—they ended up with a ploy that they thought was most likely to work.

Ivan dubbed it the Trojan horse[61] and waffled on excitedly about Greek mythology.

Junjie found this to be inane and irritating, thinking, *Who cares about the frickin' Greeks at a time like this? C'mon, Ivan*! He might have even said it aloud.

Their ploy was for Junjie to give a present to Professor Lao. Junjie confirmed that this would be appropriate for the season and a natural gesture of respect for the old professor. Certainly an act that happened to go so well with their cover story.

They placed a box drone on top of a fancily wrapped moon cake in a bright-orange cardboard gift box. The round lid-less gift box was decorated with seasonal messages in beautiful Chinese calligraphy and loosely covered with orange crepe paper—making a sort of a muffin top on the box. It looked very fancy. It took Junjie a few hours of online searches until he found just what they needed. Seasonally bright-orange cardboard gift box of the right size. Moon cake that is larger than the box drone and beautifully decorated and packaged—but not in tin shells or tin foil—to avoid interference with electrical signals. The lightest of the crepe papers—but not transparent...

---

[61] **Trojan horse**: Any trick or stratagem that causes a target to invite a foe into a securely protected place. The term is derived from "The Iliad"—an ancient Greek epic poem that describes a ten-year siege of the city of Troy. Ultimately—the ten-year war resulted in a stale mate, and the Greeks constructed a huge wooden horse, hid a select force of men inside it, and pretended to sail away. The Trojans, thinking that the Greeks have left, pulled the horse into their city as a victory trophy, thereby bringing the secret Greek force inside the impenetrable walls.

EXHIBIT 10.2 **Box Drone**

A kind of drone that has a lightweight cage to protect its rotors. Common feature for many hobby type of drones equipped with a camera – for aerial selfies and the like

 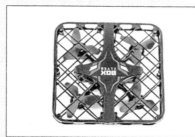

They assembled and reassembled it many times and convinced themselves that the ploy just might work. They also included a card from Junjie that conveyed his best wishes for the Moon Festival and added a cryptic note about drones being modern-day lanterns. Just in case…

Corny, Junjie thought, *but hey, it is the best idea so far. The only idea…*

Junjie took it that afternoon to Lao's office—at a time that he knew the professor was out—and asked his ancient secretary to give it to Professor Lao. He tried to appear earnest. Anxious to please the professor. He made her promise to be very careful with it and to give it to the professor only on the eve of the Moon Festival. Not before. She gave him a grandmotherly smile—in as much as she could manage a smile at all—and assured him that she will do as he asked. And he watched her carefully place the gift box on one of the shelves in her anteroom that guarded the door to Lao's office.

Phew! Junjie thought and left as fast as politeness allowed.

Altogether, not as hard as they feared. Considering… Easier than they anticipated.

Seven active drones that they distributed throughout the building earlier that day. Corresponding to the seven spare channels that their RC controller had. Corresponding to the seven numbered red Xs marking the location of the baby drones on the architectural plans.

"All right, let's do this," Ivan said, sitting down at the desk with the controller in front of him. Biting his lips, flexing his fingers, and drawing in a deep breath—probably to muster the focus and the emotional energy that he needed for the next step.

Junjie pulled up a chair, opened his laptop, and placed it on the far end of the desk.

Aki was standing between the two of them, holding the architectural drawings.

"Number 7," Ivan said, selecting an appropriate channel on his controller and toggling one of the switches. A fuzzy image of something that was not readily discernable popped up on the display screen.

Aki placed his finger on one of the red Xs on the architectural drawing that corresponded to the specific baby drone. This one was on the second floor of the east wing office area. They felt that that particular location was least critical for their plan and therefore started with this drone. Practice run.

"Remember," Ivan reminded them, "three minutes flying time, max."

Junjie brought up the timer app on his laptop and said, "Tell me when."

"Now," Ivan said, toggling another switch.

Junjie started the timer.

The screen on the RC controller displayed a blur of colors and shapes... In a few seconds, presumably the time that the drone took to rise above the partition in the area it was stashed in, an image of the open-office space came into focus. A sea of typical cubicles, dimly lit by the usual office night lights.

Ivan operated the joysticks as they watched a 360-degree scan of the office area. He fiddled with the controllers, and different parts of the large room came into view as the drone flitted about the open space. He then landed it on top of a filing cabinet in one of the cubicles and flicked the switches off, saying, "Done!"

"One minute and thirteen seconds," Junjie said, jotting it down on a pad of paper first and then typing it into his laptop.

Ivan sat back and heaved a sigh. Aki and Junjie also slumped from their tense positions, smiling in relief.

"I'll be damned. It frickin' works," Aki exclaimed, pumping his fist and slapping Ivan on the back.

They followed a similar procedure with the other three drones that were parked in the various locations in the open-office areas. One—number 4—placed on the first floor of the east wing did not respond. The camera seemed to work, but it would not fly. One—number 2—placed in the conference room on the second floor was entirely unresponsive. Dead.

"Okay," Ivan sighed putting down the controller. "So?"

Earlier, they had agreed on their respective roles.

Ivan was "the pilot."

Junjie was the "power manager." They knew that battery life was a key limitation, and their inner engineer told them not to trust the built-in power indicators. Notoriously nonlinear, they said. So his job was to keep track of the power usage rate—especially the flight times—of each of the drones. Earlier, they pored over the detailed specifications for the drones and defined a power budget to cover the operation of the cameras and the transmitters for the next few days, which left them with enough battery life for four minutes and forty-eight seconds flight time. But—like good engineers always do—they felt that they should reserve about 20 percent safety margin to account for variables that they knew mattered to battery life; things like ambient temperature, picture granularity, Wi-Fi traffic, frames per second rate, and any other unpredictable factors. Which, with rounding gave them the three minutes flight time budget.

Junjie, of course, made a spreadsheet to keep track of the cumulative flight time and camera-on time for every drone. He even proposed that they should hook up his laptop directly to the RC controller to improve the accuracy and automate the process. But frustratingly, Aki and Ivan thought it would add unnecessary complications. *Probably right*, Junjie conceded grudgingly.

Aki was to be the "flight manager." His job was to identify the suitable observation spots for each of the drones. Places where they would park their eyes—the drones. The initial flights were meant to not just verify the operational status of each of the baby drones but also to survey the various areas and give him a view of the layout.

"So?" Ivan repeated. "We have two drones down. One has probably been flipped on its back or something. Helpless—like a beetle. The other—I don't know. Maybe someone took it. But we have two left. So Aki where do you want them?"

"They have one minute and forty-seven seconds, and two minutes and thirteen seconds flight time left," Junjie added.

"Hmm. With only two drones left, I would think we want them monitoring the hallways in the north and south wings. That would leave us entirely blind for anything that may be happening in the east wing—upstairs or downstairs. But...," Aki rationalized and trailed off. He then asked Ivan to rewind the video and they reexamined the view of the hallways of the two wings.

"Ha! Good thing that this is a show-off building," Aki exclaimed. "See all the display cases next to the conference rooms? Taller than an average cleaning lady with a duster, I would think. And nicely positioned to monitor the traffic in the hallways... Why not park our eyes on top of those?" He sketched the position of the selected cabinets on the building floor plan.

Ivan and Junjie shrugged and nodded. *As good a spot as any other.*

Before parking the drones on their final observation posts, Ivan flew them around the open-office area again. With onboard drone LED lights flashing on and off. In an erratic pattern. Trying to attract as much attention as palm-sized drones could. For as long as the budgeted battery life allowed—with Junjie counting down the remaining flight time. Then they parked the drones and verified that the cameras had a good view of the hallways. Ivan activated the camera, and they waited.

Nothing.

If there were CCTV cameras anywhere and if anyone was paying attention to them, somebody should surely come by to check out those strange lights dashing about. But nothing...

Next, they needed to wait till 2:00 a.m. Twenty minutes.

One of Junjie's detectives has been schmoozing the university security staff ever since they took on the case and seemed like he has even managed to get friendly with some of the guards. He reported that the security protocol in Provost's building required the night guards to do a walk-around every three hours. In addition, there was an extra procedural step and the guard on duty had to lock the doors to all the outer offices at the end of every day. And, apparently, the building had no-go zones that were off-limits even to the security staff—mostly the inner offices. All supposedly because the templates for final examinations were stored there, and the university had some bad experiences in the past with students stealing the questions. Hence, the duty in Provost's building was different from other buildings and was quite unpopular among the guards. Apparently, it was hard to get a nice snooze when you had to do a walk-around through the whole building every three hours.

The next round was due at 2:00 a.m. They needed to wait for the night guard to leave his post in the west wing before they flew the two drones that were stashed there. They stared intently at the screen. And yes, the picture sent at 2:09 a.m. clearly showed a uniformed man coming down the hall of the south wing of the building.

They repeated the procedure with the two drones in the west wing with Ivan operating the controls, Junjie tracking the flight times, and Aki tracing their position on the floor plan. They ended up parking them on top of similar tall display cases with a clear view of the north and south elevator doors and the wide marbled flights of stairs. Before parking, they repeated the erratic flight pattern through the cavernous west wing with the lights flashing on and off.

Judging from the frozen grin on Ivan's face, that was the part that he enjoyed the most, Junjie noted. *A bit perverse*, he thought. *At a time like this?*

All in under six minutes that they expected the night guard would take.

From their perches, the two drones sent back the pictures of the guard returning from his walkabout, slowly ambling over to the reception desk, sitting down in a comfy chair…and duly dozing off. Nothing else.

Ivan again replaced the controller on the desk and slumped in his chair. A break!

"Looks like no special security systems in the building," Junjie opined thoughtfully. "This has got to be good."

"Maybe...," Aki said, fetching three glasses from the drinks tray. He poured some whiskey that he dug out of the hotel minibar and passed the drinks around. "We need it," he said. "This is tense... Nerve-racking shit."

They toasted each other in silence.

A little bit bleary-eyed, Junjie noticed. "Only one more to go," he said to pep up all three of them. "The last one."

The day before, they played quite a lot with the drone in Lao's gift box—the so-called Trojan horse. They tried flying the drone out of the gift box with the crape paper draped over it. But that did not work so well. Sometimes the paper would get caught in the blades and kill the drone. Sometimes the drone could not shake the paper sheet off, leaving it blind. They finally decided that powering the propellers, fired off in few short successive bursts, tended to work the best. The drone's propellers seemed to create an updraft in an enclosed space—which blew the crape paper off the box. But sometimes it wouldn't. Probably depending on the way that the crape paper was positioned. Maybe also depending on ambient conditions like temperature and humidity. They were not sure.

But this was a critical drone—the one that was supposed to give them eyes into the anteroom of Lao's office suite. They needed this one to work.

"Well, no time like now," Ivan said bravely, drained his glass, sat up, selected the appropriate channel, and gave three successive pushes to a control button. Nothing. The picture the drone was sending back was pitch-black fuzzy nothing of inside the gift box. Three more bursts. Nothing.

"Well, shazbat!"[62] Ivan muttered. "We are trapped?"

They looked at each other, at a bit of a loss.

"Press on," Junjie said. "No choice. Keep trying. We have nothing to lose by running the battery flat. It is that or Lao gets a drone with his moon cake."

---

[62] **Shazbat**: Expletive from the eighties sitcom *Mork & Mindy*, where it was used by Robin Williams's character Mork the alien. Generic swear word.

Ivan nodded and repeated the maneuver. Three bursts. And three more…and the picture turned dim gray.

"Aha!" Ivan exclaimed. Relieved. He very carefully pulled on a joystick and the view of Lao's anteroom, lit by the drone's LEDs, came up on the screen as the drone cleared the rim of the gift box. "Aha!" He flew the drone around the office and landed it on the secretary's desk. After a short discussion, they parked it on the top shelf behind the secretary's chair with a clear view of Lao's inner door. And with a view of the crepe paper on the floor. The theory was that the secretary would assume that there was some kind of a draft from the AC system or something. Anything. Hopefully, she would just stuff it back in the box and forget about it.

Ivan put the controller down and powered everything off. "I think this calls for another round," he said. "And then bedtime, gentlemen. I am old. I need my beauty sleep."

"Damn!" Junjie exclaimed. "You do deserve it. In fact, you deserve two rounds," he joked. "This was…something else."

"Yes, good job," Aki added.

All three of them were relieved. They congratulated each other with friendly backslaps and handshakes.

Phase 1, done…

It was 2:45 a.m.

Ivan Jovanovic
Tuesday, September 10
Holiday Inn, Haidian District, Beijing

Ivan was up again at 5:30 a.m. He did not trust himself to do it properly the night before—without at least a couple of hours of sleep. He made himself a cup of coffee, sat down, hooked up his laptop to the RC console, and initiated a macro[63]—an operating protocol for the system—that he wrote, and rewrote, over the last few days. He

---

[63] **Macro**: A saved sequence of commands or keyboard strokes that can be stored and then recalled with a single command or keyboard stroke. In a way, a very simple program…

made sure that it worked correctly while finishing his first cup. The routine put the five remaining baby drones distributed inside the building, and the mothership drone parked on the roof, into a time-lapse mode—where each would take its turn to wake up, activate its camera, take and transmit a picture, and then go back into sleep mode. This conserved battery life and, depending on the selected frequency of the cycle, was an adequate monitor of the activities in the Provost's building.

He then went back to bed with the screen of the laptop split into six fields, each displaying an update sent every minute by a corresponding drone. He preferred storing the data on his laptop rather than the phone in the mothership drone. This saved battery life and ensured that the phone memory was not overloaded.

At 7:45 a.m., he was woken by knocking on his door. It was Junjie and Aki, bearing gifts of coffee and breakfast: eggs, bacon, and toast. Ivan quickly got dressed, and they distributed themselves around the desk, eating their breakfasts, sipping coffee, and staring at the screen, mostly in sullen silence. Groggy and grumpy.

Three tired old farts, Ivan thought. *Operating on only a couple of hours of sleep is clearly not for us. Anymore. Might have been okay when we were students of twenty—staying up before an exam. Might have been okay when we were young engineers—pulling all-nighters for some chip tape out.[64] But definitely to be avoided now that we are what...fifty, sixty...ugh...almost seventy.*

He felt sluggish. Slow of mind and body.

He typed a few commands on his laptop and replayed the saved sequence of images with the time stamp starting at 5:32 a.m. and blurring forward to the current time. As expected, the early sequence revealed nothing at all. It was only the change in the lighting from predawn grim gray to a bright yellow of a sunny morning that revealed the time-lapse nature of the pictures. The activity seemed to pick up after about 6:00 a.m.—mostly the cleaning crew doing its chores—jerkily scurrying in and out of the various rooms, vacuum-

---

[64] **Tape out**: A procedure used to release a chip design to manufacturing, and specifically the final step in the design of integrated circuits, at which the chip design is checked and sent to the fabrication facility.

ing the hallways, dusting the window sills, and the like. At around 7:30 a.m., the activity picked up with early starters streaming into their offices and cubicles.

Ivan put the camera in Lao's anteroom into real-time video mode. The picture was slightly distorted due to its wide-angle setting—but clear. Lao's secretary was prompt, of course, and was in her office by the official start time of 8:00 a.m. She noted the sheet of orange crepe paper on her desk and looked at it somewhat puzzled, and the three of them held their breath as she scanned the office. She then gingerly took down Junjie's cake box from the shelf and covered it with the crepe paper. As they expected—hoped—that she would do.

She then went about what they assumed was her daily routine: turned on her computer, unlocked Lao's office, got some tea from the kitchenette down the hall, collected and sorted the mail, straightened random stuff on her desk, checked her computer and phone—presumably for messages—and the like. Going about her normal day...

Professor Lao came in at 8:47 a.m. They caught sight of him on the west hall camera, then on the camera in the hallway of the north wing, and finally on the live feed in his anteroom. He seemed to exchange a few words with his secretary and promptly went to his office, closing the door behind him.

Ivan put the camera in the mothership drone into video mode, and they watched Lao through the window. The camera on this drone was of the highest quality, equipped with a 10× optical zoom and with a resolution that allowed considerable scope for incremental digital zooming. Ivan played with the controls, and Lao's unexpressive face, absentmindedly picking at his ear, appeared on the screen. With excellent clarity. They watched as he settled in at his desk, pulled open his top drawer, and fiddled with some switches on the electronic panel that Junjie described as something that looked like it was made in 1950's Soviet Russia. Presumably placing an order for his morning tea or coffee. He then seemed to be thumbing through the files in the lower right-hand drawer, pulled out a thick-bound report, and started reading. Seemingly going about his normal day...

By 9:30 a.m., the activity in the building appeared to have settled into a steady pattern with random people coming and going into the building and through the hallways that they had monitored and Lao and his secretary seemingly occupied with whatever they were doing at their desks.

"So?" Aki questioned. "Now what?"

"Now we watch," Ivan responded simply, reverting the system into the two-minute refresh time mode.

He got up to tidy his suite, dumping their breakfast things in a trash can, and generally setting things in order. He knew that he was probably too fussy—some would say borderline OCD[65]—but he just could not feel comfortable and think straight with things messy and out of order. He, of course, also had to make the bed in the bedroom of his suite, fold his clothes, and tidy the bathroom.

"I am tired. Need more coffee," Ivan declared. "We can review the recordings later."

So Aki and Ivan showered, got dressed, and met up with Junjie in the coffee shop of the hotel.

Before leaving his room Ivan, of course, took the precaution of stowing away his laptop and the RC controller into his carry-on bag and locking it. He knew that all the pictures would be stored on the phone in the mothership drone and that he could download them whenever he chose. He left the full trash can outside his door and also hung the "Do Not Disturb" sign on the knob—just in case.

They got their coffees and gathered around a table to make the plan of the day. They thought that it would be good to get out of the hotel for a while. All they were doing is staring at the stupid screen at the not-so-interesting goings-on in the Provost building. They also agreed that it was a good idea to keep up the appearances and to stick to their plans as dictated by the cover story. This was supposed to be their free day—no meetings—and Junjie promised to organize a tour of interesting sites in Beijing for them.

Junjie looked over the list of the proposed tours put together by his admin and suggested that they drop most of the tourist traps—

---

[65] **OCD** (obsessive-compulsive disorder): A mental disorder in which a person feels the need to perform certain routines repeatedly. Some common compulsions include hand washing, cleaning, checking things (e.g., locks on doors), repeating actions (e.g., turning on and off switches), ordering items in a certain way…

like the Great Wall of China, the Summer Palace, the Forbidden City, and the Beihai Park. After a short discussion, they agreed that shopping was no fun without their significant others, and he scratched out the Nanluoguxiang district and the Bell and Drum Towers. Finally, he suggested they go to 798 Zone[66] in the Dashanzi Art District.

This turned out to be an excellent choice, and they spent a few hours wandering the eclectic area with its collection of the various modern and traditional exhibits, studios, galleries, and curio shops.

It also turned out to be an excellent diversion from what was really on their minds. They did not talk about it, but each one of them was all too aware that this was the proverbial eleventh hour. That soon—in a day or two—they would be faced with making the ultimate decision. To go in or not. To actually do something real and dangerous. Everything they did up to that point in time was just planning and preparing. Quite safe and perhaps somewhat abstract. Ivan's phase 1. Now they had to make a decision about phase 2. So far, they avoided facing that decision. Procrastinating. And hence, they did not talk about it. Instead, they meandered around the area, seemingly focused on the exhibits.

Ivan felt a bubble in his stomach reminiscent of the feeling he had before the exams, back in his university days. He suspected that underneath the stolid silence Aki and Junjie were equally anxious.

By midafternoon, they were getting tired and settled in a nice modern-looking restaurant—for a rest and a late lunch / early dinner. Junjie was excited to show off the international—and somewhat unexpectedly hip—side of Beijing and chose an establishment that served some of the local microbrews rather than just the standard mass-produced Yanjing or Tsingtao beers. He ordered a round of Slow Boat's Monkey's Fist IPA to go with generous portions of fries and sausages. Somehow very un-China.

After a while, Ivan ventured, "I've been thinking…"

"Uh-oh, never a good sign," Junjie interrupted jokingly.

---

[66] **798 Zone**: A complex of fifty-year-old decommissioned military factory buildings that have been converted into exhibition center of Chinese culture and art. It has become the heart of the world-famous cultural and creative industries area—the Dashanzi Art District of Beijing.

"Maybe so. But beer always helps." Ivan grinned. "Excellent beer by the way. And outstanding sausages. You just do not think of sausages and China in the same bite."

Then he began by holding up four fingers and saying, "We have four problems to solve."

"How do you mean four?" Aki questioned.

"Well, like the good engineers that we are, we have to break down a complex system into its individual components. It seems to me that the lowest-level subcomponents of our particular problem—the phase 2—are problem 1, getting into the building, problem 2, getting into Lao's anteroom, problem 3, getting into Lao's private office, and problem 4, getting into Lao's desk."

Ivan then reached into the man-purse that he carried about with him—whenever he was not lugging his normal computer bag. He had it hanging off a long leather strap slung diagonally across his shoulders in the manner popular among European men. For his essentials, he explained defensively when Aki and Junjie teased him about it: passport, phone, money, and the like. He retrieved a neatly folded copy of the overview page of the architectural drawings of the Provost building and wrote in the four challenges in big capital letters. For emphasis.

After a pause, he said, "And I guess we should not forget…" and added, "problem 5, getting out to his list."

"True enough," Aki nodded, "so?"

"So nothing… Just saying. Breaking it up like this allows us to focus on each step. I do not think we should contemplate going in until we have a specific solution for each of the subproblems. Makes sure that we don't forget something…" Ivan shrugged and trailed off.

"Brilliant," Junjie inserted, somewhat sarcastically. "Shall we head back?"

After finishing the beers and sausages, they headed back to the hotel and congregated again in Ivan's suite. They downloaded and reviewed the recordings: nothing in the jerky goings-on typical of time-lapse photography that caught their eye. Just random people going about their random business.

At 5:30 p.m., Ivan again put the cameras in Lao's anteroom and on the roof into video mode, and they settled in to watch the end-of-the-day routine. The secretary left promptly at 6:00 p.m. At 7:32 p.m., they watched Lao pack up his desk. He then collected his schoolboy bag, walked out, and locked his office door behind him. The other cameras captured him shuffling down the hall of the north wing and then out of the building. Presumably on his way home for dinner.

By 8:00 p.m., the building was mostly empty, and they saw the guard doing his end-of-the-day-rounds, making sure that the outer doors to all the office suites were locked, turning off unnecessary lights in the conference rooms, and the like.

By 8:30 p.m., the last straggler left, and the building seemed to settle in for the night.

"Tsinghua is clearly not a 996[67] organization," Junjie commented sarcastically.

Ivan put the system back into two-minute time-lapse mode. They stared blankly at the screen—not so much to see what was going on there—but more just as a focal point for their eyes. Ivan's mind was a bit blank, and he was guessing that Aki and Junjie were feeling similarly numb.

Maybe we are just tired, he thought. *Or maybe it is the usual posthigh blues. Parking the drones was a high, and watching the boring goings-on is not...*

Then it hit him. "Wait," he exclaimed and replayed the sequence from the morning time.

"See it?" he asked triumphantly.

"Wha—"

"That crepe paper was on the secretary's desk this morning. See," he said, pointing it out on the screen. "I am sure that last night it was on the floor."

---

[67] **996**: A term used to describe the work schedule practiced by some companies in the People's Republic of China. It derives its name from its requirement that employees work from 9:00 a.m. to 9:00 p.m., six days per week. A number of Chinese internet companies (e.g. Alibaba, JD.com, Pinduoduo, Huawei, and TikTok...) have adopted this system as their official work schedule. Critics argue that the 996 system is a flagrant violation of Chinese law that specifies a forty-hour workweek (8:00 a.m. to 6:00 p.m. with two-hour lunch, five days a week).

"Yeah," Aki confirmed. "Now that you mention it, you are right. Definitely."

Junjie nodded.

"The most likely explanation is that the cleaners were in her office. Our time-lapse camera in the anteroom missed it, which means that the cleaners were in there for a bit less than two minutes. Which may not be all that surprising. Empty out the trash cans, straighten out anything out of line, maybe run a vacuum—and done..."

"She did not seem to be all that disturbed by it," Junjie observed, beginning to catch Ivan's drift. "Implying that the cleaners come in regularly."

"Right! Therefore, the cleaners probably have the keys to all the office suites," Ivan asserted excitedly. "Which—if you think about it—would make a lot of operational sense. They do their stuff before anyone comes in, so they must have the keys." Then he added, in tones that made it sound like it was a very significant insight, "First, law of office security, no one ever worries about the cleaners."

Aki and Junjie nodded. That did make sense. Obvious and not particularly remarkable, though.

"They must have the keys to Lao's suite too. Maybe in a locker somewhere—along with the cleaning supplies, and such like? Cleaners normally do not take home their mops and stuff. Maybe they leave the keys behind too? So"—Ivan faced Junjie, finally getting to his point—"do you think that your detectives might be able to, er, borrow a set of keys for the offices in the Provost building? From one of the cleaners?"

"Oh, I get it. Okay. Let me check." Junjie pulled out his phone, dialed, had a lengthy conversation in Mandarin, and hung up. "They will try. Said to give them a day or two."

"Right." Ivan looked at Aki and Junjie and then held up two fingers for emphasis. "Problem 2 solved!"

He retrieved his copy of the architectural drawing from his man-purse and wrote "cleaners' keys" next to the line item about getting into Lao's anteroom.

"Definite progress," Junjie said, making a thumbs-up sign. Obviously feeling good.

"Let's not count the chickens yet," Aki warned. Cautious, as always.

"Maybe so," Ivan declared. "But right now, I need to go to bed. I had only a couple of hours last night."

Ivan Jovanovic
Wednesday, September 11, AM
PUMCH, Dongcheng, Beijing:

Ivan woke up early again. With a familiar tight lump in his throat—a feeling that he dreaded—and with his heart beating sporadically.

"Shit!" he muttered to himself. He knew instantly what was going on. He had arrhythmia—a chronic disorder that in his case led to atrial fibrillation.[68] A condition where his heart got all confused—sometimes skipping beats, sometimes beating faster as if to catch up, sometimes beating extra hard, and sometimes hardly beating at all. Very disquieting feeling. But supposedly not dangerous—as long as he did not remain in this arrhythmic state for too long.

He immediately pressed his fingers on the carotid artery in his neck to check the pulse. *Yup. It is real. Shit! Shit! shit!* He was not imagining it. He was out of sinus.[69] Arrhythmic.

This happened to him once in a while. *It's probably the stress and lack of sleep this time*, he thought. *C'mon, Ivan, when are you going to realize that you are an old man and that you need to behave like one?*

He never quite nailed down a definitive cause-effect relationship for these episodes, but he believed that they occurred more fre-

---

[68] **Atrial fibrillation** (AFib or AF): A quivering or irregular heartbeat (arrhythmia). Although atrial fibrillation itself usually isn't life-threatening, it is a serious medical condition that sometimes can lead to blood clots, stroke, heart failure, and other heart-related complications. At least 2.7 million Americans are living with AFib and the usual indicators include age, blood pressure, obesity, European ancestry, hyperthyroidism, etc....

[69] **Sinus**: A rhythm of the heartbeat. Sinus node creates an electrical pulse that travels through a heart muscle, causing it to contract. Sinus node is a sort of natural pacemaker.

quently when he got too tired, was overly stressed, drank too much coffee or too much booze, or did something else to excess.

He staggered to his travel bag where he kept his meds and retrieved two bottles. He knew that the whole problem was a kind of a miswiring issue that resulted in an errant signal due to some electrical leakage path in his heart. Basically the signal that ordered the top chamber of his heart to beat, leaked to the bottom part of the heart, inducing it to squeeze when it should not. And he interpreted the purpose of the meds in the same way. One pill that he called "threshold tweaker" that was supposed to decrease the sensitivity of the receptors so that the bottom part of his heart would ignore the leaked signal. And one pill that he called "attenuator" that was supposed to reduce the amplitudes of all the signals, hopefully leading to the errant signal becoming undetectable.

Simple electronic engineering solutions, he muttered to the room at large while swallowing the pills. *Implementation in a human body on the other hand—quite amazing...*

He went back to bed, knowing that now he just needed to wait. Usually, it took a couple of hours. Normally, if the arrhythmia persisted, he would double his dose and wait another couple of hours. If it persisted beyond that time, he knew he should go to a hospital. But that has happened to him only once—years ago—before he and his doctor developed the current pill-in-the-pocket medication regiment.

He knew all this and lay still and stiff in bed, feeling the pulse on his neck. Waiting for the meds to kick in. Trying very hard to ignore the voice in his head that was screaming that something was different. He told himself that he may be imagining it. To wait a bit and see. He told himself that there was not much he could do about it anyway. Not to make a fuss. He told himself to check his pulse again. Make sure...

His heart was beating at an extreme rate. He did not really need to feel his pulse to know this. There was a painful tightness in his chest—not just the usual lump in his throat. There was an unusual ache in his arms and legs. And his breathing was abnormal. Unusual. He was also sweating and felt nauseous—but that could be just because he was scared.

Finally, that voice in his head forced him to listen. *Ivan—you are having a heart attack!*

Oh shit! Now what?

He had made some preparations—in his head—about what to do in case of a heart attack. Something one does. Especially if oldish and with a cardiac condition. Like people who live in California have a plan in case of an earthquake. Or Floridians for hurricanes... He has thought about it. But he never imagined that it would happen to him when he was in a hotel in Beijing. None of the scenarios and responses that he played in his mind applied. Except for one overriding factor: he needed to get himself to a hospital. ASAP.

Hospital? Here? Do they have hospitals here? Do they take foreigners? How does one call an ambulance here? Is it 911? Something else? Would they speak English? I doubt that the 911 operators in the States speak Chinese. Concierge downstairs? He should know.

In desperation, he called Aki's room. He felt like he needed help. Someone to figure out how to call an ambulance. And somebody to give him a validating push. Calling an ambulance was such a disruptive action that his psyche—normally conditioned to being unobtrusive—required permission for such a drastic and bothersome action.

"Yeah...," Aki responded, clearly only half awake.

"Er, Aki, I think, er, that I am having a heart attack..."

"What the fuck?" Aki was awake now. "Did you call an ambulance?"

"Er, no... I am not sure I know how. Could you? And I don't want them here, in my suite. All the gear... It will look suspicious. Maybe I should come to your room?"

"Ivan, you are an idiot. I will be there in a sec."

He was there in a few minutes. To shut Ivan up, he put away the RC console in the drawer desk. And the EMTs, clad in neat blue uniforms, arrived in about ten minutes, wheeled him out on a stretcher, and told him—in pretty good English—that they are taking him to

Peking Union Medical College Hospital.[70] In the ambulance, with the sirens blaring, they seemed to do the kind of stuff that is shown on TV dramas. Hooked him up to an IV. Oxygen mask. Maybe an ECG. Or so it seemed to Ivan. He was a bit hazy, and everything was a blur to him.

They were met at the hospital by a Chinese doctor who looked to Ivan like he was barely out of school. A Dr. Mao—judging from his name tag—who started asking him questions in excellent and unaccented English. Which compelled Ivan to focus on describing his symptoms and explaining that he did have an AFib condition and that he took Metoprolol and Flecainide. Dr. Mao listened to his heart, nodded knowingly, issued a series of orders in Mandarin, and Ivan was duly transferred to a hospital bed, hooked up to all sorts of machines, given a few shots through his IV drip, and told to wait.

In a bit, Dr. Mao returned, told him that they have administered several drugs whose names meant nothing to Ivan, and said that if his heart did not return into a regular sinus soon—within fifteen minutes—they would have to defibrillate him to force a normal rhythm. Dr. Mao called it "zapping," assured him that it was safe, and asked him to sign some forms. He might have even said that it was fun.

Funny guy!

Ivan did as he was told. He phased out then—maybe due to the meds, maybe just as an escape from the terrifying situation, maybe as a consequence of the heart attack. The way he figured it, he has done all that he could, and the situation was out of his hands now.

He found out later that just before they were to zap him, his normal rhythm returned. In the nick of time. He did seem to recall that they wheeled the machine with the familiar paddles up to his bed, that Dr. Mao was rubbing the paddles together, that the nurse

---

[70] **Peking Union Medical College Hospital (PUMCH)**: One of the most popular international hospitals in Beijing. It has one hundred special sickbeds reserved for foreigners and is often used by Americans and Europeans in need. PUMCH is recognized as a world-class institution with two thousand beds and four thousand employees. Founded in 1921 by Rockefeller Foundation, named the "Anti-imperialist Hospital" during the Cultural Revolution, PUMCH is currently affiliated to both Peking Union Medical College (PUMC) and Chinese Academy of Medical Sciences (CAMS), and is regarded as one of the best hospitals and most prestigious teaching and research institutions.

said something, that there was some excited chatter in Mandarin, and that they then administered some more drugs, and...evidently, very fine sleeping drugs. Ivan did not remember anything after that. He was out of it for a few hours.

Later, as he was regaining consciousness and trying to piece together what happened to him, Dr. Mao came by and explained that Ivan did have a mild heart attack—probably triggered by the arrhythmia—but that his heart was back to functioning properly, that his blood pressure and pulse rate were normal, and that it was all over. He then asked a bunch of questions and administered a series of the usual awareness and motor control tests and eventually stated that everything seemed okay and that there were no signs of a stroke. He indicated that Ivan should stay in the hospital for a day or two. To complete further tests and make sure his heart was undamaged. And for observations to make sure that they did not miss anything. He even joked that Ivan should definitely take advantage of the savings, as a private and fully equipped and staffed suite in the hospital—including meals—would cost him only $225 per day. Cheaper than his hotel.

Funny guy!

And that was it. A nurse came by, had him fill out all sorts of forms and questionnaires—in English even—that addressed everything from dietary preferences to religious practices, and he was eventually safely ensconced in a private suite on the sixth floor.

To Ivan, it felt like a lifetime has gone by, but it was just 2:00 p.m. Only a few hours since that scary realization in his room that morning.

Aki and Junjie materialized then—wearing expressions that communicated a mixture of anxiety and relief, fear and joy, concern... They flooded him with questions about what happened, how he felt, what did the doc say, and so forth.

But the last thing that Ivan wanted to do then was to talk about any of that. He hated people fussing about him. He hated being the center of attention—always preferring to be the observer rather than the observed. Probably something about the way that he was brought up. A good Pioneer[71] never made a fuss about himself. He was embarrassed by his episode, felt guilty for causing problems, and needed to deflect attention to anything other than himself.

Besides, focusing on the fact that he just had a heart attack frightened him, and he needed to run and hide from that reality.

So he thanked Junjie and Aki for their concern and quickly changed the subject. He might have even asked them to leave the topic alone because it scared the shit out of him and there was nothing that he could do about it anymore.

Instead, he wondered if they could get a spare laptop for him so that he could patch in to his own machine to manage the drone cameras. He explained that since the console must stay within range of the mothership drone, it had to remain in his hotel room and that his laptop hooked up to it as a master controller must also stay tethered to the console and that therefore he would need an extra laptop to patch in in order to resume data gathering and control. He then went on fussing about having to avoid Wi-Fi connections on either end, as those tend to be least secure. Especially in hotels. That he needed a hard wire connection—Ethernet or something—perhaps through the cable for the TV. That he was not sure that he could implement a patch since some of the apps that he normally used may not be operative behind the Great Firewall of China.[72] That...

He was rambling on and on.

---

[71] **Pioneer**: A member of an organization for children operated by a communist party in many ex-communist and socialist countries—including Yugoslavia. Typically, children would enter into the organization in elementary school and continue until adolescence—when they could join the Young Communist League. The Pioneer movement was analogous to the Scout movement in the west but was positioned to be more prestigious and was far more political. Pioneers wearing a red neckerchief as a distinguishing part of their uniform were routinely featured in parades or other state sanctioned ceremonies.

[72] **The Great Firewall of China** (GFW): A combination of legislative actions and technologies enforced by the People's Republic of China to regulate the internet. GFW modifies search results, blocks access, and/or slows down traffic to selected foreign websites and mobile apps (e.g. Google, Facebook, Twitter, Wikipedia, etc.). In order to be allowed and accessible on the internet in China, foreign companies are required to adapt to domestic regulations and often have to remove content deemed offensive.

"Ivan," Junjie exclaimed, "forget about all that. You just had a bloomin' heart attack."

"Yeah, so? I am fine now—all that is behind me. Knock on wood," Ivan asserted, rapping his head with his knuckles—his usual superstitious habit. "Let's move on and do what we came here to do," he added, looking at them significantly and perhaps pleadingly. In his mind, he was yelling, *Drop it, guys! Please.*

"Ivan, you are an idiot. Forget about the fucking project. We will abort it," Aki said incredulously. "After a heart attack? With you pretty much disabled...," he added in gentler tones.

"Disabled?" Ivan retorted—almost yelling—and clearly quite upset. "Your nose is disabled. I am fine. Let's do what we came here to do," he insisted. This time, he even said aloud, "Drop it, guys! Please. I do not want to talk about it."

Aki and Junjie eyed him suspiciously—probably unsure whether Ivan was serious or if it was some kind of an act or maybe it was his meds talking. But the more they tried to talk him into sitting back and resting—which they thought would be the right thing to do—the more agitated and intense Ivan got. In the end, they had to accept that Ivan was actually serious and, for whatever reasons, just wanted to get on with it.

So they agreed—maybe just to calm him down—and patiently listened as Ivan told them what he needed and what they had to do with the console and the laptop in his hotel suite.

Junjie went down to his car and retrieved his own "dark" laptop—one of the machines that Ivan got for them for their clandestine project. He gave it to Ivan, saying that, per Ivan's fascist and neurotic instructions, he always carried it about with him and never left it in the office or home. He even got an HDMI[73] cable that Ivan needed—apparently something that the hospital staff had in a box of random stuff that patients left behind. Seemingly, Ivan was not the

---

[73] **HDMI** (high-definition multimedia interface): An audio/video interface standard for transmitting video and/or digital data. HDMI port is available in most modern TVs and laptops and can be one of the ways of accessing the internet through the cable TV network.

first patient who wanted a wired connection to the internet from his hospital bed.

At that point, a nurse came in to check up on him, followed by a staffer that brought his lunch. So Aki and Junjie announced that they would go out, get some lunch, set up the gear in Ivan's hotel room, and return in a couple of hours.

Junjie Wu
Wednesday, September 11
Ani's Italian Experience, Chaoyang Park, Beijing

Aki and Junjie left the hospital in a bit of a daze. Ivan's heart attack was shocking. And very sobering. Frightening. The kind of an event that made both of them stop and think. About the ephemeral nature of life and what is important.

But outside, it was a beautiful, sunny, cheerful day. Kind of a day that fills one with joy. In contrast to their mood. Bright and warm, not too hot or humid.

Junjie—feeling a need to appreciate it—declared that they should eat somewhere with outside seating and said that that he knew just the place. "To celebrate life," he said. "And to celebrate that we don't have a dead or a disabled Ivan on our hands. It could have been so much worse. We got to feed the good karma."

"Amen," Aki added.

They drove in silence—each somber in his own thoughts. Presumably reflective and musing on life-or-death kind of topics. Or perhaps just tired—after being rousted out of bed in such an abrupt way. The restaurant that Junjie chose had a large deck with outdoor seating under brightly colored umbrellas and with a view of a beautiful park.

After they settled in, Aki spluttered, "Wow, can you believe it? Ivan and his heart attack. Quite a…shock. Wow."

"Yes, it does make you think, doesn't it?" Junjie agreed. "But as they say, all is well that ends well. Seems like he is back to his normal self, 100 percent according to his doctor." he added the last bit to perk up Aki who seemed to be in a bit of a daze.

"Yeah. And he is like nothing has happened. Wants to go back to the project. Fretting about security and stuff..." Aki was shaking his head in disbelief.

"Yup, that is Ivan. He does get obsessive-compulsive sometime. But I suspect that it is also a kind of an escape for him. It is probably easier for him to fuss with the computers and things than to be lying there thinking about his bloody heart attack. Gives him space to digest things in his own time."

They both shook their heads and mumbled things. Still mostly inside their own heads.

But the wine, the lunch, the sunshine, and the setting worked their magic, and both Aki and Junjie gradually recovered and returned to everyday reality. Junjie said that he needed to go to the office to take care of some business and suggested to drop Aki off at the hotel. Aki said he would connect Ivan's laptop to the TV network as Ivan asked and that he would then review the status of the events at the Provost building. They agreed that they would meet up later in the afternoon and go visit Ivan in the hospital.

After finishing their wines and coffees and having procrastinated that luxury for as long as they would allow it—just as they were about to get up and go—Aki blurted, "I have made a decision... I am going to do it. I will be the one to go in."

"Huh? Er...," Junjie responded, obviously surprised. "Because Ivan had a heart attack?"

"No. I've been thinking about it anyways. Maybe his heart attack just forces me to get off the fence, so to speak. To focus on priorities. If I were to drop dead, I would not want Mary's memory of me to be tarnished by that dirt, and I would not want my BBI people to remember me as the guy who betrayed the trust they placed in me. So cleaning up my mess is important to me. Despite—or maybe because of—Ivan's heart attack. After all, like you said—he is okay. So—I think we should do it. And I think I should be the one to go in," Aki explained, now quite earnest.

They have not talked much about this specific part. Who exactly would be the one to actually go into Lao's office? They seem to have preferred to procrastinate on this—until the very last minute. Until they did decide to actually do it. *If* they decide to do it.

So far, the only thing that they have talked about was that they could not ask Junjie's investigators to go and steal Lao's papers. No matter how much more capable and adept they may be for that task. They agreed that it would not be fair. Possibly, it would put the detectives in too much danger with potential consequences that would have been unacceptable. They felt that breaking into Professor Lao's office—especially given his connections to the deep state—was a far more serious infraction of the law than swiping some plans from a library, borrowing some cleaners' keys, or placing some drones here or there.

If—God forbid—one of the detectives was caught in Lao's office, it would be a kind of offense that would for sure put them out of business and in China could very well earn them a quick bullet. Not to mention that if caught, they would lead the police to Junjie and therefore to Aki and Ivan.

On the other hand, if just Aki or Ivan or Junjie were caught in the act, they at least had a bargaining chip—their pinch point companies. And potential protective shield of foreign citizenship.

So they agreed that they would limit their requests from the good and willing private investigators to things that were either legal or had "plausible deniability" or were relatively minor infractions. Nothing that could be construed as an act against the state. Nothing that would be punishable by much more than a fine. Therefore, they shied away from doing what would have been the easiest for the three of them—to outsource the scary and dangerous part.

EXHIBIT 10.3   Capital Punishment in China

Capital punishment is a legal penalty in the mainland of the People's Republic of China. It is mostly enforced for murder and drug trafficking, and executions are carried out by lethal injection or gun shot.
The use of capital punishment is active in most East Asian countries, including Mainland China, Taiwan, Japan, North Korea, Malaysia, Thailand, Indonesia, Vietnam, and Singapore. England-based Amnesty International claims that Mainland China executes more people than all other countries combined, though other countries (such as Iran) have higher per capita execution rates.
From: https://en.wikipedia.org/wiki/Capital_punishment_in_China

A bullet fee is a charge/fee levied to the family of executed prisoners. Bullet fees have been levied in Iran, as well as in China, to the families of executed prisoners
From: https://en.wikipedia.org/wiki/Bullet_fee

Besides, they did not want to explain the entire affair to the investigators. This could put the individual detectives in an awkward situation—stripping them of that cover of plausible deniability and potentially obliging them to report whatever was overtly revealed to them. Thereby jeopardizing the entire caper.

And there and then—on that sunny deck of an Italian restaurant—Aki seemed determined, sounding very calm and sure of himself. "It makes sense," he insisted, in flat-level tones—stating facts. "We got to assume that somewhere along the way, there are CCTV cameras armed with facial recognition. Ivan is too foreign. Even if he did not have the heart attack and he was able, he would stick out like a sore thumb. Not good. Junjie, you, on the other hand, are too local. Easily recognizable, and they would ID you in no time. Not good. But to a casual observer, I could pass for a Chinese and so would not immediately draw attention. And facial recognition is not good with categorizing faces that are not well-represented in its training data set. I doubt that the Chinese authorities have used a lot of Greek Japanese in their training data. I could also wear a face mask, like people often do here when they are sick. And maybe wear glasses. Confuse the system more—just in case."

"Hmm, well…," Junjie said noncommittally. "What you say is true," he conceded, hesitating a bit, "but…"

EXHIBIT 10.4   Facial Recognition

A facial recognition system is a technology capable of identifying or verifying a person from a digital image. There are multiple methods in which facial recognition systems work, but in general, they work by comparing selected facial features from given image with faces within a database. It is also described as a Biometric Artificial Intelligence based application that can uniquely identify a person by analyzing patterns based on the person's facial textures and shapes.
From: https://en.wikipedia.org/wiki/Facial_recognition_system

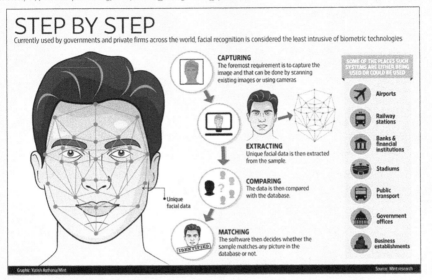

STEP BY STEP
Currently used by governments and private firms across the world, facial recognition is considered the least intrusive of biometric technologies

CAPTURING
The foremost requirement is to capture the image and that can be done by scanning existing images or using cameras

EXTRACTING
Unique facial data is then extracted from the sample.

COMPARING
The data is then compared with the database.

MATCHING
The software then decides whether the sample matches any picture in the database or not.

Unique facial data

SOME OF THE PLACES SUCH SYSTEMS ARE EITHER BEING USED OR COULD BE USED

Airports

Railway stations

Banks & financial institutions

Stadiums

Public transport

Government offices

Business establishments

Graphic: Yatish Asthana/Mint   Source: Mint research

In the US the technology isn't as effective at identifying people of color and women as it is white males. One reason for this is the data set the algorithms are trained on is not as robust for people of color and women. In addition, there are issues that can throw off the technology when a person changes appearance or the camera angle is not quite right. The technology is improving dramatically; according to independent tests by the U.S. National Institute of Standards and Technology (NIST) facial recognition systems got 20 times better at finding a match in a database over a period that covered 2014 to 2018.

"Besides, it is really my butt that is on the line. So it is only fair that I take the risk," Aki added.

"Well, my butt is right there next to yours," Junjie retorted. "Sounds like you were brooding on this for a while. Were you? You don't strike me like the type that makes a decision of this magnitude off the cuff."

"Maybe. Yeah, I guess…," Aki conceded, waving his hand as if to move off that topic and continued with what was really on his mind. "But I think we should do it tomorrow night. Not on Friday night."

"Oh! Why?"

"The offices will be just as deserted tomorrow night as on Friday. On the holiday eve, everybody goes home early. The difference would be that sneaking into the building tomorrow afternoon would be easier than any time on Friday. Tomorrow is a working day. There will be traffic there—people going in and out of the building and stuff. Friday—it will be a desert. How would I get in on Friday?" he explained.

"Hmm…rational," Junjie commented. "I was toying around with an idea of maybe using one of the side doors—not the main entrance. But those doors may be armed and might trigger a fire alarm. So…"

"Well, I thought that an easier way would be to just walk in tomorrow afternoon—during the business hours. Then do the classic thing and hide in the bathroom until everyone is gone. We have eyes in the building, and you—or Ivan—can tell me when the coast is clear. Or something like that…" After a pause, he added, "Besides, it is not like we have anything to gain by waiting until Friday night. I guess you guys were right, and it is unlikely that we would learn a lot by watching that building for much longer—especially during a holiday."

"Hmm, rational," Junjie agreed again. "Yes. I suppose we could also get one of the detectives to do a distraction act tomorrow PM so that you could sneak in unobserved. And getting out?"

"I thought I could wait until the guard does his rounds and just walk out. Again, we have eyes, so you guys could tell me when."

"Rational, I guess," Junjie repeated.

They fell silent. Seemingly just two guys sitting in a restaurant, enjoying the sun. In fact, examining the proposal in their heads. Looking for loopholes. And perhaps also regrouping and recuperating after the shock of Ivan's heart attack. Trying to get back into the groove.

"Okay. Seems like you have it all figured out. Let's run it past Ivan, but to me, it makes a lot of sense. You sure you are up for it? Gutsy move."

Aki just shrugged and said, "Someone has to do it."

Junjie did not say anything, but he thought, *Aki, you da man! No drawing of short straws or anything…*

Junjie knew that Aki must have been ruminating over this for days—since he was not exactly an impulsive type. And Junjie had to admit to himself, he did feel a sense of relief. *Phew, not me…*

Ivan Jovanovic
Wednesday, September 11, PM
PUMCH, Dongcheng, Beijing

When Aki and Junjie came to the hospital, they found Ivan sitting up with a laptop on the handy pullout tray that his high-tech bed was equipped with and with a bunch of wires running up to him and his laptop. He was off the IV drip, but there were about a dozen wires hooking him up to some kind of a monitor. And the laptop was connected to the power supply back of the TV and his phone.

He waved them in and said that they were just in time as he was about to activate the live video mode.

They asked about how he was feeling, what were the diagnoses and prognoses, and other such things, but Ivan just shrugged and gave monosyllabic answers to all the questions. Clearly still not prepared to talk about his health in general and the heart attack in particular.

Aki and Junjie pulled up chairs to either side of his bed and he reran all the time-lapse recordings. During their absence, he had clearly managed to connect to the RC console and the laptop in his hotel room and downloaded the info.

"Nothing notable there," said Aki, who reviewed the pictures earlier in Ivan's suite in the hotel. "Or at least nothing that I could see."

"Yeah," Ivan agreed. "Just the regular office shuffle. Lao did not seem to do anything while he was in the office. He was gone for a few hours—presumably for his lectures and/or student meetings and, I suppose, lunch. While in office, he just read the various papers stashed in that desk of his and stared out of the window.

"You know, some of that staring might have been him having a nap with his eyes open," Junjie commented sarcastically. "He is an old man. And we, Chinese, are almost as adept at it as the Japanese guys."

"But," Ivan ignored Junjie and held up a finger as if he had something important to say, "I played with some of the camera filters and image enhancement software and managed to zoom in on his reading material. If I make it out correctly—it is quite fuzzy—he is reading up on something called Design2Silicon."[74]

He fast-forwarded to a particular sequence of pictures, zoomed in, and pointed it out on the screen, saying, "What do you guys think?"

Aki and Junjie leaned forward, squinted, and nodded uncertainly. "Yeah, maybe..." It was blurry, and some guesswork was called for.

"Well, I looked it up—just in case that my reading is correct," Ivan continued. "Turns out Design2Silicon *is* a company. In our business even and based in the Bay Area. I don't know them, but on their web page, they claim to have some innovative model-based approaches for nanoscale device manufacturing... Some heavyweight industry veterans running it too. So I am guessing that they are what Lao would call a pinch point. Specialized. Unique. Just the kind of a company that he would want."

"Aha!" Aki exclaimed. "Excellent! That proves it. Shows that the papers *are* stashed in that office of his after all."

They looked at each other and nodded significantly, agreeing with Aki's observation. It was good to have a validation of what up to then has been an educated guess.

Junjie broke the silence that ensued, saying, "Aki thinks that we should do it tomorrow night—not on Friday. And he has volunteered to go." He summarized Aki's reasoning.

---

[74] **Design2Silicon** (D2S): A real technology company involved in the semiconductor industry. It is a specialized entity that would in the context be used here and be considered a prime pinch point target.

When Ivan looked at him questioningly, Aki shrugged and reaffirmed, "Someone has got to do it—and I think that out of the three of us, it should be me."

"I do not think that anyone should do anything—either tomorrow or on Friday," Ivan said dryly. "Not until we have a reasonable solution for each of the five problems. I suggest we focus on that for now." He was definite and sounded somewhat dismissive. Clearly not comfortable with Aki's proposal and not reticent to express his reluctance.

"Maybe so," Junjie retorted, "but I must say, I thought that Aki's rationale was spot on. So if we are to do this—if—tomorrow is probably the best day."

Long silence as the three of them digested this. There was tension in the air. They all knew that they must make that very fateful decision. Soon.

They sat in silence watching the screen with Lao and his secretary going through their end-of-the-day procedures. Much like the day before.

Then Ivan offered, hesitatingly, "I have been thinking. While you two were gallivanting out there"—the last with a grin, to lighten the atmosphere. "We do have a loose end of sorts. We were assuming—and now know—that the incriminating material would be in Lao's office," pointing to the screen—"And consequently, we were concerned about the security systems that they may have to protect it. But it seems like there is nothing there. Seems quite lax even for civilian-grade security. Apparently nothing sophisticated like CCTV cameras that are monitored in real time, motion sensors, electronic locks, or anything. Just a sleepy night guard and a slightly lame procedure for segregating private no-go zones with separate keys."

"Yes," Junjie exclaimed triumphantly. "So you agree. I said so last night. Or was it the night before? I knew it… All the more reason why we should go ahead and go in."

"Maybe that is perfectly normal for a typical office building," Aki commented thoughtfully, "There may be people working all hours—so some of the high-tech sensors you were worried about might not be practical."

"True," Ivan conceded, "but still, it does not seem to be appropriate for a place where you keep secret papers."

"I thought you said that this was Lao hiding under his cover of an unimportant old academic," Aki reminded them.

"Yes, but still. After some thought—I think it actually may make sense. I was too dumb to see it before. We focused on the word 'papers,' not on the word 'secret.' It struck me after lunch."

He went on to explain how the reports like the ones that Junjie got on BBI were probably not treated as Chinese state secrets. And that if they were, it would be unlikely that MSS would allow them out with no protection other than Lao's cover story.

"But," Ivan claimed, "those papers are presumably just a few reports on some *American* companies and some *American* citizens," emphasizing "American." "No biggie. Not *Chinese* state secrets. Maybe the methods as to how, and the reasons why, are, but the reports themselves are probably not. So it might have made sense to them to humor the old man and to just print out the reports for him. Even without any particular security in his office. The material may be sensitive, but even if it was to leak out—it would not compromise Chinese security in a major way. It might embarrass Lao, but not the state security organisms."

"So all your precautions and paranoia were excessive and unnecessary?" Junjie challenged somewhat testily. "Wish you listened to me a month ago—before making us jump through all the hoops and hurdles."

"Well, I hope so. Just saying…," Ivan reacted, feeling defensive. He was the designated paranoiac and felt responsible for all the obfuscation and precautionary moves that he has insisted on—sometimes quite inconvenient and expensive and often against the urging from Junjie and Aki. Especially from the impatient Junjie.

"All the more reason to bite the bullet and just do it. Tomorrow," Junjie insisted.

"Ivan is saying that the security system in the building may be primitive. But I agree with him that we still do have the five problems and need to know how to defeat each and every one," Aki summarized. "But much more importantly," he continued, "if what he says is right, another question is whether it is worth going in at all. Is there anything there worthwhile stealing?"

"What do you mean? Why?" Junjie demanded. Argumentative. *Like a cock ready for a fight,* Ivan thought.

"Well, if Ivan is right, the question is whether these reports—assuming we are successful at stealing them—are going to be sufficient to get Professor Lao to cease and desist. That was the original intent," Aki explained.

Ivan took a deep breath and said aloud, "Good point. I would think that a threat of leaking reports on multiple US companies, like the one on BBI, should be sufficiently compromising to him. I hope that *he* would think that they would be enough to get the FBI on his back. That is all we need. But Junjie knows Lao the best—so what do you think?" he asked, turning to face Junjie.

"Yeah," Junjie mumbled. "Probably. He did give the impression that he is very sensitive about keeping secret his pinch point strategy. So yeah, I guess that anything even remotely close to the topic would make him pause."

But Junjie did not look like he was really focused on what he was saying. He looked like he got some kind of a new idea. Like some realization percolated to his consciousness. He asked Ivan to replay the tapes of Lao and his secretary coming in the morning and leaving in the evening.

"There!" he exclaimed. "You see it?" He saw some kind of a discrepancy.

"What?" both Aki and Ivan responded. They didn't.

"Lao locks his door on the way out," Junjie explained, "but he does not unlock it on the way in. She does!" He was beaming. "So she must have a copy of that special key for his inner office! Either in her desk or her purse or somewhere."

They replayed the two scenes. Yes, Junjie was right.

"Problem 3 solved," Ivan declared victoriously, slapping Junjie on the back.

"Er, which was problem 3?" Aki asked.

"Getting into Lao's inner office. She must have that magic key," Ivan confirmed.

At that point, a hospital lady in a bright pink uniform came in, cheerily saying something in Mandarin and wheeling a tray with Ivan's dinner. She and Junjie had a quick exchange, and he translated that they can stay until ten in the evening and that they can bring up food from the cafeteria on the second floor.

"Good," Ivan declared. "Excellent. We can work here then—instead of you two pissing off to some odd place or other—supposedly to get food."

Junjie and Aki went downstairs and returned in a few minutes bringing up their dinners.

"Speaking of odd," Aki blurted, while unwrapping his egg rolls, "did you guys notice that Lao was messing with that electrical console in his desk before leaving? Tonight and last night. But why? Surely, surely, he was not ordering tea or buzzing his secretary at that time. You Junjie mentioned that this was what that console was for?"

"I thought so," Junjie shrugged. "I saw him use it to order tea. And I know he has an old-school buzzer for his secretary..."

Ivan stared at Aki trying to remember the scene that Aki was alluding to. "Good question."

They rewound the sequences and watched them again, this time, zooming in on Lao operating his console. Indeed, he did toggle several switches in the morning. They thought it was to order tea. And again in the evening, before leaving. On both days. But why?

"Do you think that this is some kind of an electrical lock for his desk? Maybe armed and alarmed?" Aki asked. "Maybe it is more than just the buzzer to the outer office?"

"If so, problem 4 is the gotcha. More than just finding a stupid old key to his desk somewhere," Ivan concluded.

Junjie and Aki left at 10:00 p.m. They agreed that all things being equal, Ivan would check himself out of the hospital the next day. And they would meet up in the hotel and make that ultimate final decision. Leaving it till the very last minute. But things were coming together.

Before they parted Ivan enumerated, "So problem 1, just sneak into the building and hide. Problem 2, swipe the anteroom key from the cleaners. Problem 3, get the key to Lao's office from his secretary.

Problem 4, still TBD. Problem 5, walk out while the guard is doing his rounds. Agreed?"

Aki Roussos
Thursday, September 12
Tsinghua University, Haidian District, Beijing, China

For sure, it was fucking nerve-racking. The scariest thing he has done in his entire life. Certainly not something that he expected he would be doing at the ripe old age of sixty.

What the fuck am I doing? Hiding in some frickin' toilet in China? Goddamn, shit, and fuck! What kind of an idiot am I? How did I get myself into this shit? The rants kept rattling on in Aki's head during those hours that he had to wait, sitting on the pot in the last stall of a men's room on the second floor of the north wing of Provost's building of Tsinghua University, in Beijing, China! *WTF!*

Although he had to admit—maybe to encourage himself—that up to then, things have worked out pretty much the way they hoped they would.

Junjie's investigators, bless their creative hearts, managed to obtain a bunch of keys—one of which was supposed to fit Lao's anteroom door. They said that it was a piece of cake. The detective that made friends with the guards has found out that the crew responsible for cleaning the Provost building were assigned lockers in the basement of a nearby tower block. When the investigators paid it a visit—at 2:00 a.m.—the basement was not even locked. According to the gossip that the friendly detective picked up, this was because some of the cleaners started earlier than the guards who were supposed to unlock the basement. Apparently, it was a common practice to leave the basement unlocked—probably not by the rule book but supposedly as a favor for some of the cleaners who had other jobs to run to. Possibly encouraged with some kickback.

"See? No one ever worries about the cleaners," Ivan commented when the detectives reported in. Somewhat smugly in Aki's opinion. *As if he discovered some hidden truth or something...*

So the investigators just needed to find out which of the crew did the Provost building and their corresponding locker numbers. Easy. Picking the lockers was apparently trivial for them. The plan was that they would borrow the keys now and return them over the weekend. Make the cleaning lady believe that she just mislaid them—if she missed them at all.

Whether for superstitious reasons,[75] or just as a coincidence, the cleaner that they targeted had eight rings of keys with eight keys per ring. Very helpfully, the key rings had plastic tags with handwritten building numbers, so finding the appropriate ring for the Provost's building was trivial. The keys on the particular ring that they "borrowed" were individually identified with dots of different colored nail polish. But this must have been a code that was private to the particular cleaning lady.

Aki—hunkered down in his bathroom stall—felt in his pocket. Yes, the key ring with the eight door keys was there. Just as it was a minute ago—when he last checked.

I'll just have to do it by trial and error. Not too bad though. Only eight tries at worst. With a 12.5 percent probability of success on the first try. But cumulative independent probabilities... So on the second try, it would be one in seven chance—14.3 percent probability. On third, it would be one in six—16.7 percent... He did the head math automatically—perhaps to fill in the time.

That morning, Aki and Junjie met in Ivan's suite, and they watched and recorded the two live feeds of the secretary's and Professor Lao's movements as they came in that morning. Ivan joined in online from the hospital—all bright and cheery, saying that he was as good as new, and that in effect nothing has happened and that therefore they should not talk about his so-called heart attack anymore. He insisted that they promise to not bring it up. Taboo subject. Thank you very much... And he indicated that he will check himself out of the hospital later in the day and join them in person in the afternoon.

---

[75] **Superstitious reasons**: 8 is the most favored number in modern China due to its association with wealth and luck. In traditional Taoist culture, 8 was associated with wholeness and completeness. In modern China, 8 is associated with wealth.

Stubborn fool, thought Aki. *But he must have his reasons…*

Junjie was right. The secretary again unlocked the door to Lao's inner office in the morning. And the day before, Lao definitely did lock it in the evening. They noted with glee how she took—and replaced—the key from the upper right-hand drawer of her desk. But on reviewing the sequence from the previous days, they noted with distress that she locked her desk and placed that key in her purse.

Junjie was apparently thinking about that overnight and came up with an encouraging observation—that it was possible that there would be only a limited number of different keys to Tiantan desks—like the one that she had.

"Tiantan Furniture Company cannot possibly be using different locks for each and every desk that they make. These types of desks are all over China. In every government office. Must be millions of them. They cannot possibly have a million keys," he rationalized.

He called his detectives, they made some inquiries, confirmed it, and then proceeded to buy the six types of keys that were common to all the classic Tiantan desks manufactured after the year 2000. Seemingly, a standard practice for the cost-conscious companies who liked to leverage economies of scale.

Aki—still hunkered in the bathroom with his legs going a bit numb from lack of circulation—felt in his other pocket. Yes, the other key ring—this one with six almost identical desk keys—was there. Still…

Hopefully, one of the six will work. With 16.67 percent probability on the first try…20 percent on the second try…

They spent a major portion of the morning reviewing Lao's manipulation of that electric console that was built into the top drawer of his desk. Recording, zooming in, playing back in slow motion, and using all sorts of filters and other image enhancement features that the fancy camera offered.

Junjie is right, Aki thought at the time, *that console does look like it was made in the fifties with Russian kind of technology. Just lacks something made out of cast iron or concrete…* Worn-out wood panel with three rows of old-school toggle switches. An old-style small red-light bulb in the middle below the last row—probably indicating that the power was on. Big screws in the corners probably holding it all together.

It definitely looked like Lao toggled the switches in the top row of the console before starting his workday. He did not seem to mess with these particular switches—the ones in the upper row—during the day. Even when he left the office to go to the bathroom or his appointments or whatnot. But he did again manipulate them in the evening before quitting time.

Evidently, judging from the immediate reaction in the ante-room, one of the switches in the third row was a buzzer for the secretary. And one—also in the third row—seemed to be for ordering tea. Just as Junjie said. It was not clear to them what the other switches may be for. Maybe just dummies? Maybe some code? Maybe to arm or disarm an alarm of some kind?

They reviewed the videos a number of times, debated, and finally agreed that the daytime configuration of the switches in the top row was: ON-ON-OFF-OFF-ON-OFF-OFF-OFF. And judging from the recording from the previous days, the consensus for the nighttime setting was ON-ON-ON-OFF-ON-ON-OFF-OFF. Junjie noted that it was the opposite of the daytime setting read backward (i.e., the reverse of the morning code read right to left). Very clever of him to spot that. Probably easier for Lao to remember a single code and a rule rather than having to memorize two independent codes.

But it was hard to say for sure. Lao's hand obstructed the view some of the time, and the way the light shone made it hard to be 100 percent sure. The camera was pretty much at the limit of its resolution, and the images were quite grainy at the required magnification. And the drone's position on top of the fart fan was not ideal—the angle was a bit too oblique.

They debated about moving the drone to give the camera a better view into Lao's office or, more specifically, into his drawer. But they discarded the idea as too risky. Someone was bound to notice a drone flying about during the day. They could potentially move it that night—but that would mean that they would need to delay everything by a day. So they agreed that they would have to go with what they have got—their shared best guess.

Well—not a guess—more like best interpretation. Fingers crossed.

They broke for lunch, and since Ivan was scheduled to complete his checkout procedures only after lunch, Aki and Junjie drove to the hospital to join him there—like the evening before. Over lunch, they speculated and eventually concluded that it was probably a key code for some kind of an electrical lock for his desk. It was the most reasonable explanation.

"Maybe that is his answer to the problem of the limited number of keys to the Tiantan desks," Junjie speculated although Lao's desk—made out of rich rosewood—was a cut above the run-of-the-mill kind that the secretary had. "Electrical lock. Likely even armed and alarmed. Sly old bastard. Probably a thesis project for the class of '58 or something like that," he joked sarcastically. "Back then, it must have been the height of technological achievement. And by now, he may have a sentimental attachment to it," he sneered.

Or so they hoped—that it was just a locking mechanism.

They were not sure what would happen if the switches were not set correctly. Or if the power was turned off. The theory was that there was a single correct arming and disarming code. But they had no idea what would happen if neither of those two was entered and someone tried to open the desk. Maybe the mechanism would cease up for some set period? Maybe some kind of an alarm would be triggered somewhere—either locally or at the guard's desk downstairs or somewhere else? Maybe some kind of a trap would be triggered—say, a camera taking pictures of the office? They joked that maybe the office would self-destruct.

They favored the idea that it would probably trigger some alarm somewhere—but had no idea where and what the response to it would be.

"Yeah," Junjie opined, "the sly old bastard probably does have it wired for an alarm somewhere. It may look like a primitive old-school kind of a setup, but he is sneaky and is probably relying on it being underestimated. He is too cagey to do nothing at all. My opinion."

They fell silent. This was the moment of truth. No more procrastinating. They looked at each other searchingly. Questioningly. Weighing the risks…

"Yes," Aki spoke up. "I say I go in this evening. As planned." Very determined and resolute. "You guys can watch tonight's procedures," he added, "and if anything unexpected happens, you pull me out. That way, the worst case is just that I get caught in the building without authorization. So what... I am a dumb tourist. I was lost. I had a diarrhea problem. I fell asleep. Whatever..."

Ivan agreed about pulling him out—but still felt that it was too risky. He was fretting about problem 4.

"We always knew that the risks would not be zero," Aki insisted. "And even if something does go wrong, it is not exactly the end of the world. So maybe the code is wrong and the desk stays locked—I walk out. If some kind of alarm is triggered—I walk out. Anything else goes wrong—I walk out. I think that I would have a reasonable chance of getting away. Even I can outrun that sleepy guard." The grin on his face indicated that this was his sense of gallows humor. "Besides," Aki concluded with a shrug, "I think that if we consider everything—all the five problems—the overall holistic risk is at a minimum tonight. So I say we do it tonight—or not at all. And seems to me that we have come too long a way to choose to chicken out now."

Junjie nodded and said, "Sounds reasonable to me. I agree with Aki."

Ivan stared at Aki as if seeing him for the first time. Clearly deep in thought. "We do have a reasonable solution for each problem," he admitted at last. "Not a perfect solution and not zero risk by any means. But reasonable. And, Aki, you are right—if we are to do this, tonight is the time."

They sat in silence for a while—searching each other's faces for an answer. For some special insight. In the end, they agreed.

It was a go! For that evening.

Aki—still sitting in his bathroom stall—felt in his breast pocket for his wallet where he knew there was a slip of paper with the switch settings. Although these were also etched in his mind—1-1-0-0-1-0-0-0 and 1-1-1-0-1-1-0-0. He found it easier to remember it as a binary code than a series of ONs and OFFs. In his mind—perhaps to fill the time—he toyed with the numbers and converted the binary codes into decimals: 200 and 236. 310 and 354 in octal system. He wondered if the numbers had any meaning…

The part that Aki was most anxious about—entering the building unobserved—went smoothly. In fact, easier than he expected. For some reason, this was the part that worried him the most. He had nightmarish visions of being called out and ordered to stop—in full view of the people around. Sort of like being caught naked in public. But it went off without a hitch.

They targeted 5:30 p.m.—slightly before the rush of people that they thought would be exiting the building around 6:00 p.m. They thought that if he went in later, he would stand out too much. And if he went in earlier, he would have to spend that much more time in that bathroom.

He and Junjie were just leaving when Ivan came back to the hotel, saying that he finally managed to check himself out of the hospital and that he was ready to assume his post as the voice of the "eye-in-the-sky" monitor. Ivan made the air quotes and jokingly assured Aki that he will be there, watching and sharing his great pearls of wisdom every step of the way.

"God, help me," Aki responded in the same sarcastic humor tone. But inside, he did not feel at all like joking. He was nervous and scared.

Aki got ready in Junjie's car. He threaded the wire for the phone earbuds through the back of his black T-shirt: a trick for obscuring the earbuds that Junjie learned from his son—apparently handy when listening to music in boring classes. Besides, it kept the wires out of the way. They felt that using old-school wired earbuds would be more reliable and secure than a Bluetooth connection. He verified that the phone link to Ivan was live. They agreed that everything was to be done using only burner phones—three of which Junjie acquired last night. In fact, Ivan told him to leave his regular phone in the hotel. Just in case someone was tracking the physical location of his number. Leave no tracks. He pulled on a small backpack with all the goodies that they thought he may need and put on a fashionable patterned face mask that they suspected would add to the confusion of any facial recognition software. And he put on a baggy black hoodie, specifically selected for its zippered pockets, and pulled the hood over his head. A bit excessive for the balmy autumn evening, but they thought that it would not stick out that much. Today's teenagers always wore hoodies...

Junjie dropped him off a couple of blocks from the target, and he assumed what he thought of was a good grumpy-teenager slouch.

He walked staying as close as he could to the sides of the buildings—rather than crossing the wide-open plazas—making sure to remain on the shady side. And then trying to be as nonchalant as he could, he walked into the Provost's building. Not too fast but not too slow. Trying to look like he had some business to take care of. He walked in through the front doors that were welcomingly wide open, purposefully turned left, past the display cases, and scurried up the stairs, two at a time, and turned right—into the first men's room on the second floor of the north wing. Well-memorized route.

It helped that the receptionist was busy talking with someone who was pointing to something on the south side of the building. *God bless Junjie's detectives.* It helped that he did not encounter anyone on the way. And it helped that he was listening to Ivan on his earbuds—talking to him the whole way—with constant updates on the six live feeds from their eyes in the building. And with Ivan's random comments about this or that—which were sort of reassuring.

Best of all and very surprising to him—his chest did not explode. His heart was beating a mile-a-minute, but he made it. Grateful to be in the safety of the last stall in the men's restroom, behind a locked door. Alone. Catching his breath, wiping the sweat off his face. *Point of no return...*

"You all right there?" Ivan asked, probably in reaction to Aki's panting.

"Yeah," he hissed—although he did not need to whisper since Ivan could warn him when anyone was heading for the bathroom he was in. "Good job that I am hiding in a toilet. With my prostate, I would never make it anywhere else." He was only half joking, imagining the conundrum he would be in if he was hiding anywhere else and had to go pee. In fact—he did have to go. He had to go a number of times during those interminable hours.

He had to hunker down in there until everybody left the building and it was dark. That day, the sunset was due at 7:45 p.m. and moonrise at 10:30 p.m. They checked. So he expected to be released from his hidey-hole at around 8:30 p.m. or thereabouts. After the guard completed his 8:00 p.m. lockdown rounds and when it was the darkest outside. Assuming, of course, that everyone was gone by then and the guards were on schedule with their routine. And assuming that Junjie and Ivan did not see Lao or his secretary do something odd or unexpected.

The frequency of interruptions in his men's room increased around 6:00 p.m.—presumably people using the facilities before going home. Causing him to hold his breath until he thought he would explode. He knew that this was not necessary—but did it anyways. Felt safer.

Ivan informed him that the secretary has apparently done as she promised and has delivered Junjie's present to Professor Lao before leaving for the long weekend. "Good news," he joked, "seems like Lao likes it. He took it home with him."

"Humph!" was all that Aki managed as a response. *Wise ass*, he thought to himself.

Ivan informed him when Lao left the building and said that nothing at all seemed to be unusual or noteworthy. He also confirmed the security code for the desk. Aki checked it again against the slip of paper in his wallet. Yup. Same.

By 7:30 p.m., it was deadly quiet in his men's room.

By 8:00 p.m., he was bored enough to actually want to get out and get on with it. Get it over with. But Ivan just told him to sit tight. He said that the guard seemed to have started his rounds earlier than normal and that he has not returned to the front desk yet. He warned Aki to keep quiet while the guard was in the north wing. He reminded Aki that they do not have eyes everywhere in the building. That someone might still be in their office. Although Ivan reported that the scan from the mothership drone showed that all offices in the north wing were dark.

Aki was antsy and needed to do something. The temptation to check his phone for e-mails and fiddle with it was enormous. But

Ivan just told him to sit tight. Besides, Aki did not want to take chances on his phone running out of juice later in the night.

He wished he had brought some reading material. Anything… This sitting for what felt like forever in his stall, staring at the blank white door inches from his face was driving him crazy.

"All right, Aki. Ready? The coast is clear." Ivan's voice. "The guard is downstairs, so walk like a pussycat," he admonished.

"Fucking finally!"

He got up, staggered, and fell against the stall door, making quite a racket. His legs were numb and entirely useless. He had to patiently wait to regain the feeling in his legs and for the pins and needles to go away. Once the circulation was normalized, he pulled on the surgical gloves—the usual precaution against leaving finger-prints—and walked out of the men's room. Quietly. Making sure that the door did not slam or make any noise. He turned right. Past the first door on his right. Second door. Well-memorized route. Third door…

He took out the cleaning lady's key ring and started working the lock to the anteroom. First key? No. Second key? No… The fifth key did the trick. He slid into the anteroom and quietly pulled the door shut.

"Phew!" he sighed. His heart was again threatening to explode.

"You are safe now," Ivan cooed, trying to be encouraging. "It is okay to breathe."

Aki took off his backpack, pulled out the two towels he had there, and laid them at the bottom of the two doors to make sure that no light seeped out. He then turned on the lamp on the secre-tary's desk, retrieved the key ring with the desk keys out of his other pocket, and started a similar trial-and-error procedure. The third key worked. He retrieved the key to Lao's private door from the top-right drawer where the secretary left it.

"Good man! Problem 3 solved," Ivan cheered, clearly watching his every move via the camera in the box drone perched on the shelf behind him. "Ding, ding, ding! Congratulations, player. You have reached level 3 in this real-life video game," he joked.

Aki gave the middle-finger salute, but he knew Ivan was trying to help in his way. Maybe to reduce his stress level or to make him feel less alone.

He unlocked the door to Lao's inner office, turned off the desk lamp, and slipped in, quietly closing the door behind him. He retrieved a small penlight from his pocket.

"Wave hi. I have you on candid camera," Ivan joked.

Probably playing with the infrared camera, Aki thought automatically, knowing that it was too dark for a normal camera to work—especially from across the central garden and through the window.

Ivan then started humming the tune from *The Pink Panther*.[76]

Definitely irritating, Aki thought and groaned. But he knew that this too—the constant chatter—was meant to encourage him. Not just one of Ivan's dumb jokes.

He drew up a chair and gingerly pulled open the top drawer to reveal the electric console. He turned on the penlight and retrieved the code from his wallet.

"Uh-oh. Shit!" he swore. "Shit! Shit! Shit!"

"What? Uh-oh is not good. What's up?" came an instant response. Worried and concerned.

"The current setting is not ON-ON-ON-OFF-ON-ON-OFF-OFF!" Aki hissed, checking and double-checking the console. "Now what?"

"All right. Stop. Hands off. Sit back. Let's talk it through" came Ivan's voice. Very calm—not joking anymore. Commanding. Serious.

"First, what is the current setting? Let's record that," Ivan instructed.

"ON-ON-ON-OFF-ON-ON-OFF-ON," Aki read out slowly and deliberately, double-checking every switch position. "The last digit is wrong."

---

[76] *The Pink Panther*: A British American media franchise, featuring an inept French police detective, Inspector Jacques Clouseau (Peter Sellers), with series of ten comedy-mystery films released between 1963 and 1993. All the films, and the subsequent series of cartoons, featured a characteristic musical *Pink Panther Theme* by Henri Mancini.

"OK. So either Lao made a mistake, or he changed the code," Ivan began.

"Or we misread the switch position for the arming code," Aki heard Junjie commenting in the background. He must have gone back to Ivan's room.

"Possible… We were not so sure about the code for arming the system. The evening light cast a glare on his window that made it harder to see…," Ivan was rambling—thinking aloud.

"True," Junjie confirmed.

"I do not think that Lao changed the code," Ivan continued—calm and trying to be logical. "When you change codes, you write it down somewhere or do something different. Tie a string around your finger. Write it on the palm of your hand. Put a notch on your calendar. Something—anything—to remind you of the change. Lao did not do anything like that this evening. Junjie, do you agree?"

"Er, yes. I did not notice anything," Junjie confirmed, faint but clear in the background. "Nothing like that."

"So my bet is that this evening Lao just made a mistake," Ivan proposed.

"Okay. So?" Aki was at a loss.

"So if he made a mistake, then the system is now in some undetermined state. This was the part that we were uncertain about. What happens with an unknown entry… If it triggered some kind of an alarm, then something should have happened by now. The system entered this unknown state a couple of hours ago. So either the unknown state does nothing at all—unlikely but possible. Or it did trigger an alarm. Which was presumably registered somewhere. They may have called Lao at home, or the guard downstairs, to make sure that everything was ok. And back then—a couple of hours ago—it really was. Maybe that is why the guard started his round earlier than expected. And so they must have cleared the alarm. After all, it is a holiday eve. Who wants to go rushing to the university for what was probably a false alarm…," Ivan was voicing a stream of consciousness. Typical of him. Talking in clipped half sentences as he was processing thoughts and possibilities.

"On the other hand, if we made a mistake and misread the setting—possible—then the system is in a known armed state right now," he continued.

"Okay, so? What do I do?" Aki hissed. He was on verge of panicking. Confused and ready to run. Adrenaline pumping.

"So…hmm," Ivan continued as if he had not heard—cool and calm and trying to rationalize things. "Either way, I think that the best thing to do now is to put the system in the known low-risk state. Enter the disarm code. Assuming that he did not reprogram it, that is what Lao would presumably do tomorrow morning."

Silence. Everybody was unsure. Especially Aki. Alone in Lao's dark office.

"All right. This is what we do," Ivan came through, now sounding definitive. As if he reached a conclusion. Not the usual rambling and a disjointed stream of consciousness. "Let us make double sure. Belts and suspenders. Take your earbud out and put your ear to the desk. Enter the disarm code and listen. Listen really, really carefully. If the disarming code is correct, then the electronics will operate something that is ultimately mechanical in nature—and will open the lock. There should be some kind of sound. Tumblers rolling, solenoids switching. Something. If you hear anything—then I think we are good. The disarm code is correct."

"And if not?"

"Hmm…if not, we can either leave it as is and you get out now. Or take a chance and try opening the drawer. Which might set off an alarm and you would be shafted. But one step at a time. Let's cross that bridge if you do not hear anything. Agreed?"

"Makes sense," Junjie opined supportively.

Aki sighed and nodded. He was not in a state when he could trust himself to be logical and rational. He would trust Ivan's and Junjie's judgment. "Okay."

Holding his breath. He entered the disarming code—all digits but one. With his ear pressed to the cool tabletop, he toggled the last of the switches…

Yes, he heard a distinct click. Definitely. Very faint, but it was there.

He tugged the drawer tentatively…and it easily slid open on its gliders. *Ha! Open sesame!*

"It worked!" Aki sighed in relief and replaced his earbud.

"Lights off!" Ivan barked into the phone. "Guard coming down the south wing!"

"Oh fuck!" Aki swore. Ready to run. He must have set off an alarm. *Goddamn, shit, and fuck!*

"Wait, wait," Ivan instructed. "Freeze. I think this may be a coincidence. True, this is not his time for a routine check. But just look at him. Looks like he is walking—not running. There is no sense of urgency anywhere in his body language. I think this guy is just doing his usual—but out of sequence for some reason. I cannot hear him but looks to me like he is even whistling. And he is in the south wing, not even in your part of the building. Relax. Lights off, stay still and wait," Ivan commanded. "Lights off, stay still and wait," he repeated the order.

In some way, the commanding tone was reassuring for Aki. Being told what to do in a voice that communicated certainty. As opposed to what he was feeling right then: adrenaline-stupid.

Aki turned the penlight off. He held his breath and felt like hiding under the desk. Entirely unnecessary, he knew, but…

In about ten minutes, Ivan sighed, "All clear," and Aki went to work.

There were five thick, bound folders in that drawer along with a bunch of other papers distributed in the hanging file folders. He retrieved one of the bound copies, marked its place with a sticky note that he brought with him, and took it into the anteroom. He closed the door, turned on the desk lamp, and started photographing the pages with his phone. Just the table of contents and a random sampling of various pages. He repeated the sequence for all five thick reports. Always remembering to close the doors behind him. To turn the desk lamp off. To be careful to put each report back exactly where he found it. To collect his sticky note…

Perhaps unnecessary but erring on the safe side.

He repeated the process for a handful of other papers that he pulled from the various hanging file folders in the same drawer. He selected them more or less at random, as he did not feel like he had the time to read them. In fact, he was not sure that right then he could read at all. Adrenaline-stupid…

"You are doing great," Ivan encouraged him. "Time to start wrapping up, though."

They knew that the guard tended to do his rounds every three hours or so. So if he missed his opportunity to get out during the 11:00 p.m. round, he would have to wait till 2:00 a.m. Aki definitely wanted to get out at 11:00 p.m. Junjie was probably already at the assigned meeting spot—waiting for him.

"So what do you think?" Ivan asked.

"About?" Aki demanded—quite irritated. He was close to the end of his rope. Definitely ready to go and not up for playing twenty stupid questions.

"Do we put the switches in the position that Lao left them in or leave them in the current disarmed position?"

"Shit… Good point?"

"My two bits," Ivan suggested, "leave them in the disarmed position as they are now. Worst case, sometime—sooner or later—Lao will realize that someone messed with his desk. He will know that anyways in a few days. And by tomorrow, we should be clean. And hopefully out of the country. Alternatively, if we reset the switches in the position that he left them in, it could very well—probably—activate some kind of an alarm. Then the worst-case design is that you will get caught red-handed. It is unlikely that they would ignore an alarm for a second time tonight—no matter how inconvenient it may be. So I vote for door one."

"Okay. I cannot think anyways but definitely do not like the sound of being caught red-handed," Aki concluded. He just wanted to get out, ASAP.

He closed the drawers and focused on retracing his steps. Very methodically, with Ivan reminding him to lock the inner door, to collect the towels, to return the door key into the secretary's desk, to lock the desk…

When everything was done, Ivan even reminded him to collect the Trojan horse. At that point, the box drone came to life, took off from its observation post, and gently landed on the secretary's desk in front of him.

"Wise guy," Aki commented. He was sure that he could hear Ivan giggle on the other end of the line.

Easy for him—sitting in the hotel room while I have my butt in the sling here, Aki thought.

"All clear," Ivan declared, and Aki left the anteroom, locked the door, and scurried back into his bathroom. To wait for the guard's rounds. The last bit.

At around 10:50 p.m., Ivan came on again. "Uh-oh. Er, Aki, I don't know how to tell you this, but…"

"What? What now?" The cold fingers of panic were gripping him around the throat. Or so it felt to Aki.

"Looks like your night guard is the friendly type. Has a buddy over by the front desk. Looks like they are busy chatting. Maybe celebrating the Moon Festival. That is probably why the guard did a round early and out of order."

"Fuck!"

"Hang tight, dude. They cannot party all night. Just drop trou and be kind to your prostate man. Surely, you got to go by now…"

"The funny guy is back, I see."

It was not until 11:40 p.m.—felt like an eternity to Aki—that Ivan came back on and said, "Now! The friend is gone and the guard is doing his round. Steady, steady, pussycat."

Aki pulled on his mask and hoodie and exited the bathroom. He had about a two-minute window—while the guard was in the south wing—to get out, go down the stairs, and exit the building.

He had to concentrate to stop himself from running in as much as his old legs could run. He focused, took a deep breath…

The alarm sounded like an earsplitting 110-decibel siren. Like one of those air raid sirens was in his head. Later, when they talked about it, Junjie and Ivan assured him that it was just a regular door alarm. But at that moment, it sounded like a siren to Aki.

They talked about this. That the front door may be alarmed and that when he walked out, it may go off and bring the guard running back to the west wing. He was supposed to just walk out, turn right, and walk to the next building. No looking back. No running. No hesitating. Ivan urged him on.

He did note from the corner of his eye that the night guard did come running into the west wing hall and walked purposefully to the front door—only to find two young men talking very loudly about something or other in Mandarin. From what Aki overheard, stated in an unambiguous international language, the guard swore loudly at them, probably called them "drunk young idiots," and chased them away.

God bless those detectives of Junjie's, he thought to himself as he scurried in the darkness.

"Junjie, if you are listening, your detectives deserve a huge bonus. They have earned double their rate," he whispered while focusing on maintaining a steady pace and on not taking any shortcuts.

"I am here. Waiting for you," Junjie responded reassuringly—he patched in on the call from his car. "And yes, I hear you and am sure that Professor Lao will be happy to comply with your suggestion," he chortled.

Aki retraced the steps that he took seven hours before. As planned—Junjie was waiting for him in his car at the same spot where he dropped him off.

"Home free!" Aki sighed and sank into the seat of the car. In his entire life, he has never been as happy—or as relieved—to see a familiar car. A familiar face.

"Done! Go, go, go!"

Junjie Wu
Friday, September 13
Holiday Inn, Haidian District, Beijing

Aki just could not stop grinning like an idiot. He and Ivan exchanged high fives and handshakes and fist bumps and hugs and backslaps... Aki even did a little jig. Looked very funny—a short, normally serious, and somewhat stiff kind of a man dancing an awkward jig.

Junjie looked at them incredulously and yelled out, "Stop! Have you forgotten? Lao is going to go to his office tomorrow morning.

He always does. And he is going to figure out that someone was in his desk."

In the car on the way back to the hotel, when Aki told him about the decision to leave the switches in Lao's desk in the disarmed mode, Junjie realized the problem and how serious it may be for the three of them.

"C'mon. We are in trouble!" he hissed. "What are we going to do about it? You two may want to celebrate now, but we have a serious problem." He had to use harsh tones to bring Aki and Ivan back to earth. Unusually demanding of him. But he felt that he had to be very insistent. "Focus! We are not out of the woods. You wankers may think that you will get away tomorrow, but in fact, our butt is hanging out. We're in trouble. Snookered!"

Of course, Ivan and Aki knew that they left a loose end. They felt safe in the hotel—for the moment—and needed to blow off some steam. But they knew that there was a big problem. Junjie's harsh tones sobered them up and cut the urge to celebrate. Like someone poured a bucket of cold water on them.

"Junjie, you are right, of course," Ivan said in tones of a chastised child. So they gathered around the sofa in the suite. To deal with the loose end. Ivan slumped in an easy chair. Aki lying on the sofa. Junjie pacing around.

They knew that it was possible—perhaps even probable—that when Lao came into his office later the next morning, he would register the wrong setting of the switches on his desk console.

"Such a primitive and stupid system—and yet so damned insidious. The sly old bastard!" Junjie swore.

They knew that it would likely—surely—alarm Professor Lao. At the very least, it would give him pause. Given the alarm that they assumed was raised last night and the phone call that he presumably received—it was highly unlikely that he would not notice. He would realize that someone was in his desk. And then he would possibly… probably…certainly…react. Raise a red flag? Call his cronies in PLA or MSS? Activate the state's "autoimmune system." And, worst case, they would figure it out quickly and nab the three of them before they were ready.

Bloody hell! We are done for. Fully fucked! Junjie had visions of being arrested and dragged out of his home in front of his family. Of interrogation rooms. Of jail for the rest of his life. Of very public shame... *Bloody hell!*

Of course, it was possible that Lao would not notice or that he would just sluff the whole thing off. That he may think that he was confused. That he might have left the desk in a disarmed mode. It was possible.

But they decided that it would be foolish of them to count on it.

It was also possible that even if Lao did take it seriously, realistically he would need time to figure it out. Time to react. Time to figure out who to go after. He would have to do a lot of retracing to even begin suspecting the three of them... Hopefully, it would take him at least a few days. That would be enough time for the three of them. By then, they would be ready...

But they decided that counting on this possibility would also be foolish.

So they agreed that they had to sidetrack Lao. At least until Aki and Ivan were out of the country.

Junjie texted his detectives and asked them to keep an extra sharp eye on Lao in the morning—and to call him the moment Lao started for the university.

After some debate, they agreed that if—when—Lao did go to the university, then Junjie would have to intercept him. Take him out to some restaurant and keep him there. If necessary, take Lao for a walk in the park. Anything that would keep Lao out of that office of his at least until early afternoon. At any cost. It was the only way. It was imperative...

They brainstormed for a while and cooked up a precept for the intercept: that Junjie needed to give Lao an update from the last week's meetings in Taiwan and Shanghai. Urgent because he just found out about a weeklong trip to Japan that Feng organized as a surprise for him. Supposedly because she wanted some alone time for the two of them to talk through some family problems. Before they got too busy with school and work. Supposedly an offer that he could not refuse. Sounded reasonable to the three of them. Something that they thought any married man would understand. Plausible…

They realized that it was likely that later—once he figured out that someone was in his desk—this intercept would make Junjie stand out in Lao's mind. Junjie would be a prime suspect. Would not take a rocket scientist to put two and two together. Too much of a coincidence…

So after considering all the alternatives, they rationalized that the only thing to do would be to pull forward their entire plan. Junjie would share with Lao the threatening note on Sunday morning. Just prior to his flight to Japan. Preemptive move. Their original plan was that they would send those out in a week or so. But they had to pull it forward to Sunday morning in order to give Junjie some cover. They felt that this would presumably deflect the suspicion away from Junjie. And it should fibrillate Lao.

They did not like it, but they agreed that they had no choice. The new plan gave them no margin of error for things like unforeseen flight delays or God knows what else.

"Man, you will have to put up an Oscar-winning act," Ivan cautioned. "Tomorrow and on Sunday."

"Yeah, that will be tough," Aki echoed, giving him a supportive pat on the back.

Junjie just nodded. He knew this, and just thinking about it made him nervous. Knot in the belly kind of nervous. But it had to be done.

No choice. My turn to take the risk, he thought. *But let's please not dwell on it now.*

Then they focused on cleaning up after themselves. It was vital that there would be nothing there that would help Professor Lao. It was vital that they had at least—very least—plausible deniability. Nothing that would tie them to breaking into Lao's desk. No physical evidence. No loose ends. No tracks.

Of course, they also wanted to breathe a collective sigh of relief. Following the adrenaline rush of that evening—they needed some downtime. After all, it did look like the three old geezers just might have pulled it off. They went into Lao's office, got the evidence that they needed, and were safe in their hotel! But only for the moment. They were not done yet. They could not afford to relax even a little bit. So they encouraged and urged each other to stay focused. Just a bit more.

No, no celebrating yet…
The fat lady has not sung yet…
We are not free and clear yet…
Let's not blow it now…
It is too soon to say prayers of thanks…
So they focused on cleaning up the loose ends.

Aki copied the pictures from his burner phone onto several memory sticks. Via his dark laptop. One for each of them. And three more that they were going to FedEx in the morning—separately to various addresses abroad. They agreed that all they needed to do right then was to secure the data—and multiple copies of suitably hidden memory sticks were as good a way as any. They debated whether to risk e-mailing or FTP-ing the file to themselves or storing it in the cloud. But they decided against it. They reasoned that it was possible that there may be a sniffer[77] attached to their accounts, and if so, all they would be doing is alerting Professor Lao. Even if they used their covert identity and hardware, they would be just risking a leak without much to gain. They felt more secure staying off-line.

Aki then erased everything off the burner phones, took out the SIM cards, and snapped them in half. He even wiped the phones clean. No tracks.

Ivan focused on flying all the baby drones on whatever little power was left back to their staging areas: the various cubicles where the friend of Junjie's nephew deposited them. Hopefully, the friendly intern will collect them, take them home, give them away. Do whatever with them to make them disappear from the Provost building. He even flew the drones from the west wing up the stairwell and through the hallways to the open-office space in the east wing. It

---

[77] **Sniffer** (packet analyzer): A computer program or piece of computer hardware that can intercept and log traffic that passes over a digital network or part of a network. Sniffers can be used for theft or interception of data.

took him quite a while because, of course, he had to time his flights around the guard's walkabout schedule.

On the other hand, the mothership drone on the roof of the building was retrieved with a press of a button. It flew back on autopilot and faithfully hovered over Ivan's balcony. He just plucked it from the air and then disassembled it into its basic pieces. That drone had to be exported to comply with the Chinese drone registration rules. So he packed it carefully in his roll-on bag. But he erased the memory card and gave it to Junjie, along with all the various gizmos and accessories.

They had a bit of a discussion about what to do with the box drone that Aki brought back. In the end, they agreed that—if they really did get away with their ploy—they would have to preserve it as a memento. A trophy. And that they would argue later as to who gets to keep it. Having erased all the pictures from its camera, Aki gave the SD card to Junjie and packed the drone in its original box and stuffed it into his carry-on bag.

Junjie called the airlines and switched Aki and Ivan's flight to the next day as opposed to the day after. Surprisingly, this did not require any special pleas or fees, pressure or connections, or anything. Turned out that flights were not full on the day of the Moon Festival. He even made bookings for him and Feng to fly to Kyoto on Sunday afternoon— just to make sure that his story for Professor Lao would hang together.

He also brought a large trash bag and collected the architectural drawings, all the loose papers, the trash from both of their rooms, Aki's face mask, hoodie and gloves, flashlight and backpack, along with the burner phones, the memory cards, and the various other electronic gizmos. His task was to dispose of it all. Ultimately, they agreed that he would dump the hardware in the river on his drive home and dispose of the rest in various public trash cans. And return the keys to Lao's anteroom to his detectives. Excessive, they suspected. But no tracks. No loose ends.

By the time they were done, it was 2:30 a.m. They really needed sleep.

Especially Ivan, thought Junjie. *C'mon, the man had a heart attack a couple of nights ago*. But he was too afraid of Ivan's reaction to mention it.

Aki Roussos
Friday, September 13
Beijing Capital International Airport

In the morning, before checking out, Aki and Ivan FedEx'ed the memory stocks using the convenient facility at the hotel and then grabbed a late breakfast. They debated whether to take a taxi or the usual train—to beat a proverbial "hasty retreat" to the airport.

Then Junjie showed up at the restaurant—beaming with an unusual ear to ear smile.

"Junjie? What the heck are you doing here?" they demanded. He was supposed to be ready to intercept Lao. And instead, he was in the hotel restaurant. And smiling? Like an idiot.

"No worries. We lucked out," he reported, plopping down at their table. "My men reported that Lao is on his way to Shanghai. They saw him board the Jinghu[78] train about half an hour ago. Must be meeting with his son and family for the holiday. We are good. Till Monday at least."

"No shit?" Aki exclaimed. "Best news. Ever!"

"Lord be praised," Ivan intoned and crossed himself, only half in jest.

Junjie just beamed, but inside, he resolved to do something really, really good. *To complete the cycle of karma.*

"Man, now that *is* lucking out," Aki affirmed. He made a mental note to go to church even though he was not particularly religious. *Should light a candle for this.*

The three of them sat there, in that restaurant of the hotel, with the widest, dumbest grins. They lucked out! Back to plan A. No need for an Oscar-winning performance from Junjie. All was good…

So Junjie—rightly proud of his city—could not resist and gave them a bit of a whistle-stop tour of Beijing tourist stops that they

---

[78] **Jinghu** (Beijing–Shanghai high-speed railway): A high-speed railway link that connects the two major economic zones in the People's Republic of China. Constructed between 2008 and 2011, it is one of the busiest high-speed railways in the world, transporting an average of five hundred thousand passengers per day. Initially designed for a maximum speed of 380 kilometers per hour, the trains were slowed to 300 kilometers per hour (186 miles per hour), to reduce the operating costs.

missed out on. And then a ride to the airport. It was a holiday and the traffic was reasonably light. And they decided that the forty-five-odd minutes of private time in his car would be welcome. More than welcome. They then allowed themselves some self-congratulating handshakes and backslaps. Finally. And they even traded jabs and jokes about each other's behavior—steering clear of Ivan's heart attack and anything else that might have been too serious.

They teased Ivan about his inane jokes and incessant talking the evening before...

"Hey, sorry. I cannot help it," Ivan protested. "When I am nervous, I either fall asleep or babble and make stupid jokes. My coping mechanism. My ex assured me that this was one of the reasons for our divorce. Apparently, my nonstop yakking and witty jokes just did not go down well while she was giving birth to our kids... Go figure." Then after a short lag, he added defensively, "But I am told that it is a kind of a defense mechanism used by intelligent people."

They joked about Aki's legs going numb due to his long session on the pot...

"Man, I suspect that my butt is still blue," Aki grumbled. "You try sitting on a pot for three hours, too damned scared to move or even just wiggle. But let me tell you, my bladder has not been this drained in years. Despite my enlarged prostate... Very nice."

They laughed about Junjie's intent to charge the cost of his brilliant detective company to Lao's M&A account...

"Seems only right and fair," he rationalized, trying to make a serious face. "Besides, Lao would suspect something was wrong if I did not have big expenses." He smirked.

Just three old geezers laughing and joshing in the car. Like they were teenagers. By then, of course, they were more than just any three old geezers—they were more like comrades in arms.

In between the antics—in the few minutes of seriousness that they could muster—they confirmed the next meeting that they would have—in Montenegro. With all the drama of planning and pulling off their caper, they have not had much of a chance to discuss and define a plan for the next steps. Perhaps they did not quite dare to plan for success. So all they did is agree on how—if—they would connect afterward...

And now they—Aki and Ivan—were in the American Airlines lounge of the Beijing Capital International Airport. Waiting to board their flight to Los Angeles. In about an hour. And Junjie was presumably home with his family—preparing for the celebration of the Moon Festival.

Two weeks ago—although it felt like a year ago—when Ivan was making the travel arrangements, the thinking was that they would treat themselves and splurge on business class seats. They thought that either they would be successful—in which case they deserved a celebratory treat, or their ploy failed—in which case they would need solacing, or they would be in jail—in which case it just would not matter. So they were taking advantage of the airport business class lounge and the amenities there: free drinks and snacks! Ivan suggested a round of brandies even though that was not one of those free drinks. Aki protested that it was too early in the day but relented. And they settled in one of the lounge booths.

The last hurdle that they worried about—clearing the passport control—was not a problem at all. Standard and usual. They worried about being picked up at the very last minute. *Please step this way, sir.* Like those scenes in the movies.

But evidently, Lao was in Shanghai, and they were free and clear. Nothing was amiss. No one was looking for them. Even the drone packed in Ivan's suitcase did not draw any attention. Nothing. They just stamped their passports and completed the export paperwork for the drone. Phew.

"Relax, dude… It is over," Ivan urged with one of his ear-to-ear grins smeared across his face. But even while saying that, he—perhaps instinctively—did his superstitious "knock-on-wood" gesture and rapped on his head with his knuckles.

"I am going to relax when we land in LAX. Not before," Aki responded tersely.

In his head, however, he allowed, *Ivan is right. Everything has worked out pretty much as well as could be expected*. But he did not want to jinx it and celebrate too early. *Wait until we at least enter international airspace…*

The Sting

Junjie Wu
Monday, September 16
Tsinghua University, Haidian District, Beijing, China

Junjie was at the Provost's building at 8:00 a.m. sharp. He caught Professor Lao's secretary just as she was coming into work and insisted that he just had to see the professor as soon as possible. That it was urgent. No polite greetings or exchange about the holidays or anything. He even forgot to thank her for delivering the moon cake to the professor.

"Professor Lao is not here yet," she replied in her matter-of-fact unflappable way. "He went to Shanghai over the holiday weekend, so he may be late this morning," she added with her best version of a kindly smile. She seemed to like Junjie—maybe because of that moon cake present for the professor. Or maybe just because women liked Junjie.

I bet this is as talkative as the old bat gets, Junjie thought. But he thanked her politely and assumed a seat in her anteroom. To wait—fidgeting only a bit under her stern gaze, busying himself with his mobile phone.

Professor Lao shuffled into the office at 9:30 a.m.—truly late by his usual standards.

"Junjie? What—"

"Professor, I need to see you. Now!" Junjie knew that he was a bit impolite with his insistence and urgency. But he did not need to summon up much of his supposed acting talents for this part. He was genuinely anxious to get this over with.

"All right, all right, young man… Come in," Professor Lao responded, unlocking his door and waving him into his inner office. "What is so urgent?" he asked, closing the door behind Junjie and slowly making his way toward the big desk.

"Er, Professor, I received this last night," Junjie blurted, sliding the printouts of an e-mail and its attachments toward Professor Lao. The alarm that he expected he was exuding was only partially an act. He was really quite concerned about Lao buying it… This was critical. Everything depended on it…

The e-mail was short and simple.

> To: JUNJIE WU, CEO, CHARM INC.
>
> WE KNOW EXACTLY WHAT IS GOING ON. WE KNOW THAT YOU ARE A PART OF A PLOT TO ILLEGALLY ACQUIRE US COMPANIES WITH SPECIALIZED AND PROPRIETARY SEMICONDUCTOR TECHNOLOGIES. WE HAVE PROOF. SEE THE ATTACHED SAMPLE DOCUMENTATION.
>
> STOP! CEASE AND DESIST RIGHT NOW. TERMINATE ALL EFFORTS TO ACQUIRE BBI. NOW. OR ELSE WE WILL
>
> a) INFORM THE FBI OF THIS PLOT. IF WE DO, THEY WILL BLOCK THIS AND ALL OTHER SIMILAR TRANSACTIONS. YOUR NAME WILL BE PUT ON THEIR BLACKLIST, AND YOUR COMPANY WILL BE PROHIBITED FROM DOING BUSINESS IN THE US AND WITH ANY OF THE US-AFFILIATED COMPANIES.

b) INFORM *THE GUARDIAN*[79] NEWSGROUP.
IF WE DO, THEY WILL PUBLISH AN
EXPOSÉ THAT WILL OUT PROFESSOR LAO
AND EMBARRASS THE GOVERNMENT OF
THE PEOPLE'S REPUBLIC OF CHINA.

The attachments were four files containing photographs of the table of contents of reports on Best Blank Inc., ProPlus Solutions Inc., PDF[80] Solutions Inc., and Design2Silicon Inc.

Professor Lao took the papers and carefully examined each page. He may have paled a bit—but Junjie was not sure of this. Outwardly, Professor Lao did not seem to react. He just asked in his usual controlled and unhurried way, "When did you get this…and who from?"

"The e-mail arrived last night. I saw it this morning. I have no idea who this mlhztkyu@guerillamail.com may be. What does it mean?" Junjie hoped that he was communicating concern, worry, confusion.

"I will need your laptop, and maybe we will be able to find out," Professor Lao responded. Calm and measured. "We will need to keep it for a week or so, I expect," he added.

He reread the e-mail. Probably just to get more time to digest it. Finally, he concluded pensively, "As for what does it mean, well,

---

[79] **The Guardian**: A British daily newspaper founded in 1821 as *The Manchester Guardian* and a part of the Guardian Media Group. Notable recent scoops include the following:

- In 2011, phone-hacking scandal that led to the closure of the *News of the World*, one of the highest-circulation newspapers in history.
- In 2013, secret collection by the Obama administration of Verizon phone records and subsequently the exposure of the entire PRISM surveillance program as leaked by the former NSA contractor Edward Snowden.
- In 2016, an investigation into the *Panama Papers*, exposing then Prime Minister David Cameron's links to offshore bank accounts.

The Guardian has been named "newspaper of the year" four times, most recently in 2014, for its reporting on government surveillance.

[80] **ProPlus** and **PDF Solutions**: Two real US technology companies entirely unconnected to the fictional story here; other than that they are specialized entities that would be considered pinch point companies in the context used here.

it sounds like we have a leak somewhere. Seems like someone knows about the pinch point strategy." Junjie got a feeling that the last was not really meant just for him. It was Lao thinking aloud.

"What do I do, Professor?" Junjie asked in what he was hoping would be worried and even frightened tones. He did want Lao to assume control and to give him the inescapable instructions. His cover. "I am very worried, Professor. If I do get blocked out of the US-controlled market, I am dead. Out of business. And what do I do about the BBI acquisition?"

"Nothing," Professor Lao responded. "Carry on with your CHARM business as always. As for BBI, wait for a bit. Procrastinate for now. Do nothing until you hear from me."

Good. Excellent, thought Junjie, *excellent. That is exactly what I wanted you to say, you old bugger...*

"But, but," Junjie protested aloud, seemingly concerned about their project, "we are on the path to close the deal in a couple of weeks. Everything is pretty much set... Final review, final signatures, transfer of money...and done. We have the closing meeting set for the twenty-seventh."

All this was, in fact, true. As a part of their cover story, they have agreed to meet and close the deal at the end of the month—in fact on Ivan's turf in Montenegro, of all the places. Most of the arrangements were already made.

"No! Do nothing for now. Do absolutely nothing until you hear from me," Professor Lao repeated. Quite firm and insistent. This was meant to be an order, not the pearls of wisdom that he delivered in that slow monotone of his. "Give me your laptop, please," he added.

"Er, all right, Professor," Junjie conceded. Obediently and maybe somewhat sheepishly. He retrieved his work laptop that by sheer force of habit he took home over the weekend and had with him that Monday morning.

Professor Lao did not get up to escort him out of his office, as was his usual habit. He looked absent—like his mind was elsewhere. And very concerned as he pulled the top drawer of his desk open...

Junjie Wu
Friday, September 20
CHARM Inc., Haidian District, Beijing, China

Junjie was surprised—shocked even—to find Professor Lao at the reception desk. Lao has never been to CHARM offices before. He somehow looked even smaller than usual—maybe more bent over. But perhaps Junjie was imagining it.

The visit did catch Junjie off guard, and inwardly, he did have to scramble to collect himself. A thought flashed through his mind that this might be one of those final confrontations—prior to an arrest. Like in the old detective movies. He had to focus to tamp down the idea—and all the fear that it elicited—and to carry on with his role. But he did cast a quick glance around the reception area to make sure that there were no goons waiting to nab him in case he decided to run for it. *No, no one suspicious…*

"Ah, Junjie. I have brought your laptop back," Professor Lao began.

"Professor. Come in, come in. Please come and sit in my office. What can I do for you?" he ushered the old prof in and asked his admin assistant for a hot drink tray.

They settled in his office, and after the admin left, Lao first asked, "Is your office secure?"

"Secure? How do you mean?" Junjie responded, genuinely puzzled.

"No bugs? Surveillance or such devices?" Lao clarified.

"Good god, Professor, I suppose so. I have no idea why anyone would be interested in bugging us. I don't really know, but I suppose so," Junjie protested. But inwardly he thought, *Aha! The old bugger is nervous. Good!*

"Good, good." Professor Lao nodded. "I have been feeling insecure in my office of late," he added in a way of an explanation for his question. "I am even not sure about our Liuxiaguan Teahouse."

"Bloody hell! Really? Why, Professor? What is going on?" Junjie demanded, trying to look as surprised as he could manage.

"Well, it turns out that there was a break-in in my office. Sometime during the Moon Festival weekend. We are still trying to trace down when exactly it happened and who did it. But evidently, they seem to have copied some of my papers…compromising our pinch point strategy." Professor Lao seemed depressed. Dejected. Somehow the aura of his usual gravitas seemed to be cracking. Maybe somewhat hunched into himself.

Junjie was concerned that this might be a ploy. A trap. He felt—perhaps imagined—like he was under a microscope. That Lao may be telling him this to gauge his reaction. *Possibly*? So he focused very hard on maintaining his composure and stance. He felt like he really had to sell his act. In a show of deep thought, he cupped his mouth with his hand and looked away—at a spot on the floor. As if trying to contain himself while digesting the news. But, in fact, to make sure that his eyes did not reveal anything.

"So that e-mail I got maybe a part of—"

"Probably," Professor Lao interrupted. "And it seems to be entirely anonymous. The techies at…er…the government offices tried to trace it back to the sender. It turns out that the e-mail address was ephemeral—self-destructed after use." Professor Lao used the term in English—probably because it may be new and strange to him. "And," he continued, "the IP address is equally untraceable. Apparently, they have used some kind of a VPN with a Tor wrapper. I am told that this constitutes a dual level of protection that is hard to decipher. The techies said that it cannot be traced based on only four e-mails. They said that they would need ongoing traffic and some kind of a continuous handshake to even have a chance of tracing the geographic location of the sending device…"

EXHIBIT 11.1 **Internet Anonimity & Privacy**

There are multiple ways of achieving privacy, anonimity and untracability on the internet, so that the content of a message remains private and/or the author of a given message remains unknown and unidentifiable.

1. Obscure sender identity: for examply by blocking the caller ID number on a phone or by scrambling the e-mail address (e.g. Guerilla Mial: https://www.guerrillamail.com/)
2. Obscure sender's IP address (Level 1): by using a VPN (Virtual Private Network) which encrypts an internet connection and routes it through an intermediary server. Many commercial VPNs share a common IP addresses accross multiple VPN users connected to the same server. This adds a significant layer of anonymity and makes it difficult to trace any activity back to a single user. (e.g. Express VPN: https://www.expressvpn.com/hide-ip)
3. Obsucure sender's IP address (level 2): by routing a message through multiple layers of servers where each layer adds a different IP address and often a different level of encryption (e.g Tor: https://www.torproject.org/ originally developed for and by the military to enable secret communication across the internet. Now a volunteer organization)

Tor Network Nodes

| You | Guard Node | Relay Node | Exit Node | Internet File |

4. Encryption: a process that encodes a message using an algorithm to scramble the data, so that it can be read only by users who have a key to unscramble the information. (e.g. Gihosoft: https://www.gihosoft.com/file-encryption.html)

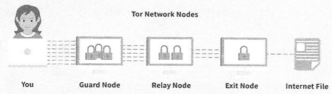

5. Ephemeral messaging: use of messages that self-destruct after a set period of time leaving nothing to trace (e.g. Snapchat: https://www.snapchat.com/)
6. Some combination of the above, depending on the nature, purpose or the content of the message)

NB: some of these methods and techniques have been associated with nefarious use of the internet (e.g. sexting, on-line bullying, hacking, use of the darknet…), i.e. more than just for the purposes of managing users' privacy.

"Four?" Junjie asked. "So my e-mail was not the only one?"

"Yes. Three other…er, colleagues…of yours received identical e-mails, sent in an identical way, at the same time," Professor Lao clarified.

"Wow!" Junjie was speechless. Or tried to be. Long silence—as if internalizing the revelations and focusing on managing his emotions. "I am sorry…," he began, as if not sure what to say.

"I have brought your laptop back," Lao interrupted, probably in a show of confidence and control. "Use it as you would normally.

In case that they are monitoring your e-mail traffic. If you receive another e-mail or any communication that is suspicious, let me know immediately." After a pause, he added, in maybe somewhat confidential tones, "Er, just between us, you may want to be careful about, er, personal communications that might be embarrassing. Our techies have told me that they are sniffing your laptop. Whatever that may mean. But apparently, it will help them trace back the source of the e-mails in case you receive further contacts."

This confidence surprised Junjie. Of course, he knew that the MSS would monitor his laptop. Surely, they have also bugged his phone and every other device—probably including his so-called smart fridge and doorbell. Ivan certainly warned him about that. Many times. But it was surprising that Professor Lao would tell him this overtly.

On the other hand, maybe it is a ruse, he thought. *Tell me something that appears confidential—but is, in fact, obvious—in order to win my trust? In hope that I may let down my guard and slip up? Maybe? Be careful Albert...*, he cautioned himself.

"All right, Professor" was all Junjie said. After a short pause, he added the obvious question, "And what shall I do about BBI?"

"Well, good question. We do need you to maintain an open channel to Aki. Perhaps you could leverage your personal relationship to find out if Aki received any contact—a warning like yours or something. Our techies are pretty sure that he has not—at least not on devices and accounts that they know about. Which would be very puzzling. Why contact you and not him? Maybe the people behind this are, in fact, Chinese? Maybe all this is some kind of a local political game? Internal struggle in the Party?" Professor Lao let the questions hover in the air.

Aha! Junjie noted the reference about the techies and Aki. *They are tapping Aki's computer and phone! Probably did so in the past as well. Ivan was right*!

"But on the other hand," Lao continued after a short pause—as if refocusing on the here and now, "the techies don't know what they don't know. So maybe you could feel Aki out to see if he has been contacted somehow? Use your personal relationship. Talk to him. Look for any telltale changes in body language."

"All right, Professor. But our relationship is purely business. Ever since, er, you know…," he trailed off.

Junjie was winging this part, but he could not imagine having a great personal relationship with someone who tried to blackmail him, so he thought it would be safest to present a cold and distant relationship with Aki.

Uncomfortable silence.

"And I have done as you told me," Junjie picked up the thread, "and have not talked with Aki at all this week. The moment I do, he is bound to have questions about the acquisition. Our target closing is in a week. What do I tell him?" Junjie was leading the prof to the answer that he wanted to receive. A black-and-white answer that would give Junjie the cover that he needed.

"Tell him that there has been a snag with the funding. Do not tell him about the e-mail. See if you can extend the term by about a quarter," Professor Lao instructed, sounding definitive. Not at all uncertain about that part.

"A whole quarter? That is a long time, Professor," Junjie warned. Looking dubious.

"Well, yes. I know. But the threat of exposure has got the Leadership quite worried." Professor Lao paused for a while, as if weighing how much to share with Junjie. He nodded imperceptibly and carried on. "They are not too concerned about the threatened FBI contact. The Leadership feels that our link to the deals involving a few American companies is easily denied. What they seem to have is not really proof of anything that the Chinese government may have done. Not too compromising. And ultimately, all that would happen is that those specific deals—and the front men who were exposed— would be blocked. That could be spun in the media and could be made to look like a part of the trade war. Not too damaging…"

Before Junjie could protest that such "blocking" of this front men would be devastating to his reputation and his business, Professor Lao continued, "But, on the other hand, even if all that was leaked is the reports on the target pinch point companies, the

Leadership is very concerned about an exposé in the press. The press would not require much more proof to publish a story. Especially *The Guardian*. And a story may alert various western governments to carefully examine all transactions that we have in flight. It may jeopardize several larger deals. In EU. And in Japan, as well as in the US. It may give President Trump an excuse for further sanctions against Huawei. And it would definitely tarnish our image that we have been building up in the world. So the Leadership wants to lie low for a while. They do not want to risk that kind of exposure. Too much to lose. So yes, maybe a quarter delay. Until some of these other deals are consummated. Until we are more certain about what exactly has leaked out and what is going on."

"Wow!" Junjie mumbled, concentrating on looking worried. "Aki may not want, or be able, to wait that long. He may want to pull the plug on the whole deal," he cautioned.

"Possibly... It would be best if you stayed in contact with him as much as possible. In a while—a quarter or so—we may be able to move ahead. Not all is lost. I am not sure that whoever is behind this knows of all the pinch point projects. In a while, we may know more and may be able to move ahead with some of them. Not all is lost... Besides, as you know, we do have ways to convince Aki to, er, cooperate."

Junjie swallowed hard to stop himself from reacting to Lao's reference to the dirt for blackmailing Aki. All he said was, "All right. I will try. So you don't think that we should cancel that meeting in Montenegro? It was meant to be the final review as well as a bit of a ceremony. Wives and families..."

"Probably. It would be best if you maintained as good a relationship as possible," Lao repeated.

"All right, Professor. But I must tell him now that there is a snag. ASAP. That the deal is off. You cannot hide a surprise like this and hope to maintain a relationship."

"Yes, yes. You should. Definitely. That would also give the appearance of compliance with the dictate of that e-mail. In case they have a way of monitoring your progress on that front. Probably safest if you do tell him that the deal is off. Yes, go ahead, Junjie. For now. But see if you can maintain the relationship. BBI would be such a good pinch point to have. Go to Montenegro. Keep the door open. Informally. Not on paper. Just between you two. In fact, a meeting in Montenegro, with wives and family, may be perfect. Do it. Not all is lost... I am old, and I know that one always has to be patient."

"All right, Professor."

Junjie now did have to focus on maintaining his acting skills. In reality, he really wanted to jump up on his desk and whoop like a cowboy. He—they, the three old geezers—have got everything that they hoped they would get. A reprieve. A delay that is requested by Lao himself. Of at least a quarter. Without directly confronting Lao or overtly challenging the system. Without exposing or compromising themselves. And Lao seemingly has no idea.

Ha! Good to see you squirm, you old bastard...

But instead, he focused on maintaining a somber expression, looking worried and concerned.

Aki Roussos
Saturday, September 21
Sunset Cliffs, San Diego, California, USA

"Well, I'll be damned," Aki muttered, shaking his head. "We did it! Fucking amazing."

He was at his thinking bench. Enjoying the sights and sounds, but not really appreciating them as much as he normally would. He was there for a different reason—a private celebration of sorts. And maybe to thank the gods for the good outcome of their crazy, crazy enterprise.

On the way to his spot, he even did stop by a church—St. George Serbian Orthodox Church in Pacific Beach. It was on his way and close enough in terms of feel and traditions to his own Greek Orthodox Church. He was not religious, but he did like the traditions. And it made him feel closer to his roots—to his father. So he lit a couple of candles[81] for his parents and placed them in the "for the deceased" tray. And he lit three candles in the "for the living" tray to commemorate his gratitude for the safe return of the three geezers. *Can't hurt*, he thought.

After their regular Red Lion videoconference the day before, he knew that they did it! When Junjie told them that the deal was off. Officially due to some funding issues. But unofficially—indicated by a fleeting thumbs-up gesture that Junjie flashed—due to their ploy. *A celebration is merited*, he thought.

It worked! It fucking worked! I'll be damned! Aki found it quite hard to contain his exuberance. And relief.

Mary, of course, saw that he was all amped up and excited and asked him about it last night. He just told her that he was very pleased about some prospects at work—their usual code for "don't ask"—and changed the subject. He couldn't really share the whole saga with her—even though he ached to. She knew some of the basics, of course—that he was intending to sell BBI and that they have hit a snag of some kind and were trying to work it out. But as usual, she did not seem to care that much about the details of his work life.

Maybe someday? Maybe at least a part of the story, he thought to himself, feeling the usual sense of guilt for keeping an important part of his life away from her.

He did not know the exact details of last week's events in Beijing—he will find these out the following week when they gather in Montenegro—but he knew that all was well with Junjie.

He, of course, did know all about the e-mails that Ivan sent to Junjie and another three Chinese businessmen involved in Lao's pinch point takeover game. They talked about that, and Ivan suggested that it would be best if they did not show their whole hand.

"The goal here is to fibrillate Lao. To make him worry. To make him think that we might know more than we do. To make

---

[81] **Lighting Candles** (in Christian Orthodox Church): It is customary that upon entering an Orthodox Church (Greek, Russian, Serbian…) candles are lit at designated spots. Prayers for God's mercy, protection, and gratitude are accompanied by lighting candles for the living while prayers for God's compassion and eternal salvation are accompanied by lighting candles for the deceased.

him unsure. But not to totally defeat him. We want him to believe that he still has a chance so that he treads very carefully. He should feel like he can still cut his losses. If he thinks that all is lost, he may want to lash out. So let's feed him just enough to make him worry," he rationalized, in his typical game theory[82] approach. "Four e-mails should be a number big enough to stop Lao from pinning the blame on any one person. Enough to give Junjie cover—at least for a while. But also a number small enough to let Lao think that some—at least one—of his projects may still be viable," he said.

"After all, we named this phase 'messing with Lao's mind' for a reason," he added with a grin.

Ivan was clearly enjoying this part of their ploy. Relishing it, it seemed to Aki.

To further confuse matters, he purposely mixed up some of the targeted companies and the Chinese acquisition agents that they sent e-mails to. "Let Lao think that we are confused," Ivan said. "That some of our intelligence is garbled."

When they returned from China—and after they sobered up following all the celebrating that they did on that return flight—they parsed through their treasure trove: the pictures that Aki took. It was pretty much what they expected. Other than that, there were five—not three—acquisition projects in flight, targeting five separate pinch point companies. Four in the US and one in the UK. With five Chinese businessmen pawns—like Junjie. And five key people in the target companies—like Aki. They did not have all the information— since Aki more or less randomly sampled the reports from Lao's desk. But they had enough to infer who the players are. And the rest they could fill in by simple Google searches and such like.

They also discussed whether to contact Professor Lao directly or not. Ivan kept saying, "Less is more in this game." He rationalized

---

[82] **Game Theory**: A theoretical framework for mathematical modeling of social situations among competing players. Game theory is the science of optimal decision-making of independent and competing actors in a strategic setting where the decisions of one player affect those of the others. The key pioneers of game theory were mathematicians John von Neumann and John Nash, as well as economist Oskar Morgenstern.

that the more things that they send out, the easier they make it for the Chinese geeks to track them down.

"Still a paranoiac, I see," Aki teased him.

"Oh yes. Always. Once it gets in your blood, you can't shake it off. Besides, it is not over yet, so we cannot let our guard down. Why send six e-mails when four will do? Lao will find out everything anyways, so a separate e-mail to him would just give them an unnecessary data point. Besides, let *him* wonder why."

They also debated whether to wait till the end of the week to send out the e-mails as they originally planned or to move ahead as soon as possible. They rationalized that the sooner they do it, the easier it would be for Junjie. Besides, they thought that there was nothing to be gained by procrastinating. So they sent out two threatening e-mails past Sunday night and two the following day. "A nice present for Junjie," Ivan joked.

They held their breath in hope and anticipation for a whole week—not sure what may be going on in China. It was nerve-racking. Killing. With worry about Junjie and his family and God knows what else. It was not like they could ping Junjie to find out. Ivan insisted on absolute and total silence.

Until Friday. Well, Saturday, Junjie's time. Until that Red Lion videoconference when Junjie told them all they needed to hear.

It fucking worked!

After a respectful half an hour of reveling in amazement and gratitude, Aki sort of shook himself to the here and now and tried to pull himself together.

Archimedes, pay attention! You are off the hook just for a quarter or so. You must focus and use the time wisely—or it will all be for naught.

Yes, he knew that Lao was off his back for a quarter. But that did not mean that he won't return. So Aki knew that he had a limited time to put that distance that they talked about between himself and BBI. Distance that would, presumably, shelter him from blackmail and possibly ensure the independence of BBI.

In between all the excitement and the preparation that they did in Beijing, Junjie mentioned that his plan for distancing from the company was to convert CHARM into a worker-owned co-op.

Junjie said that he was taking this approach mostly for political reasons—but that he also felt that it was the right thing to do.

That got Aki thinking. He did not need to worry about the political reasons that Junjie feared—but worker-owned co-op was a slick idea. And maybe the right thing to do for BBI too.

So he spent most of the past week poking into that. Partially to stop himself from exploding from worry about what may or may not be happening in Beijing. But partially because he really warmed up to the idea.

He consulted with a lawyer that a friend recommended, who diligently listed his exit options. The usual.

EXHIBIT 11.2   **Exit Strategy & Ownership Transition**

In general there are three traditional ownership succession strategies for private companies:
1. *sell to an outsider: competitors, private equity (PEGs), suppliers, collaborators, individual investors, etc.*
2. *sell to an insider: company's current partners, employees or current owner's family members*
3. *"till death do us part": i.e. continue as owner – possibly nominally only – forever*

Possible mechanisms for selling to emplyees include:
- *Employee Stock Ownership Plans (ESOP)*
- *Worker-Owned cooperatives (CoOp)*
- *Employee Ownership Trusts (EOT)*

From: https://www.nceo.org/articles/ownership-transitions-esops-other-strategies

Formulating a CoOp & Support Mechanisms (e.g: Project Equity)
Transition to broad-based, democratic employee ownership.
- *support selling business owners to assess fit with this approach,*
- *support the sale of the business,*
- *support transition to employee ownership and an effective ownership culture.*

Our services can be customized to the specific needs of a business, but core offerings are.
- *Financial feasibility: Can this option work financially for you and your business?*
- *Employee engagement: Employee ownership 101 training for you and your employees*
- *Deal structuring: Developing deal terms and structure, helping line up financing*
- *Employee ownership design: Developing the details of the cooperative or other democratic governance structure*
- *Ownership culture training and consulting*

From: https://www.project-equity.org/

Option one: IPO?[83] Aki discarded this option immediately. It would be an elegant way to raise the capital that BBI needed, but he knew that it would take too long. Much longer than a quarter. Besides, it seemed to him to be a process where the bankers—not himself—were in control.

Option two: Sell to a competitor or a client? Aki discarded this too—due to all the reasons he mulled over while thinking about the offer from CHARM. Before that turned nasty.

Option three: Sell to an insider? He liked the sound of that. Not an insider as in family or partners but an insider as in his colleagues and the people he worked with for the last thirty years. And it would presumably make any attempts at blackmailing him rather useless—since he would not be the owner, chairman of the board, and the CEO anymore.

So he did a bit of a search and found companies who actually specialize in assisting with that kind of a transition. From a founder-owner to the worker-owners. He liked that. He reached out to a few of these companies and met with some. To get educated. Familiarized.

He has not yet pulled the trigger, but he was pretty sure that he would engage with Project Equity—one of those outfits that seem to specialize in exactly what he was looking for. And who seemed to understand his care for the BBI people.

Yes, he would convert BBI into a co-op—American-style.

Maybe he would not be able to get the top dollar that he would get by selling to an outsider. But he would get enough. Enough for him and Mary to live comfortably. Very comfortably.

Raising the capital that BBI needed for the expansion of the EUV capacity—the damned expensive Actinic Blank Inspection[84] tools—may be tricky, but he believed that it could be done. After all, BBI was a viable, profitable, and stable business. Maybe, following the conversion, they could tap some of the very cheap sources

---

[83] **IPO (Initial Public Offering)**: A process of offering shares of a private corporation to the public in a new stock issuance. Public share issuance allows a company to raise capital from various investors in an open market.

[84] **Actinic Blank Inspection**: See exhibit 11.3 below.

of money that the Japanese government reserved for the indigenous companies? After the transition, BBI KK—a Japanese worker-owned co-op—could very well qualify. Probably?

Yes, he liked that.

Archimedes, do it! He urged himself.

He spent another hour or so enjoying his thinking bench. The sun has set, and it was dark—but he could still smell the seawater and the kelp and hear the breaking of the waves on the rocks below. Daydreaming about that all employee meeting when he would announce his plans to make all his people owners of BBI. Maybe he could stay on in some kind of an advisory or consulting role for a few more years. To guide the new entity and to help pick his successor. Maybe halftime? And maybe he and Mary can rekindle what they had all those years ago.

Yes, he liked that.

Part 5

EPILOGUE

Thursday, September 26
Kotor, Montenegro

"It is a tradition. You must at least try it," Ivan insisted.

They were in Kotor—a little town on the coast of Montenegro. In a café named Forza in the main piazza of the old town. The piazza looked like a set from *Merchant of Venice*. Old white stone buildings with red-tiled roofs, green wooden shutters, and tiny wrought-iron balconies, decorated with flowering plants. Multicolored and irregular slate stones paving the piazza, all worn smooth with the wear and tear of the centuries. A few people ambling along in the morning sunshine.

They agreed that instead of canceling the Red Lion "closing meeting," they would instead leverage the arrangements already made and have a nice vacation. In Montenegro. Ivan's so-called "neutral turf." After all, everything was pretty much already paid for—by Professor Lao's M&A fund. That made it all that much more enjoyable. To spend some time, to close the loop on all the loose ends, and to celebrate their crazy achievement. On Lao's money, to boot!

Aki and Mary, Junjie and Feng, and Ivan and Irina.

Feng—Junjie's wife—was a very personable and warm Chinese lady. Full of energy and enthusiasm. Very chatty. One of those people whom others were instinctively drawn to and who seemed to immediately form friendships. Very funny because her English was tinged with a Bostonian accent—apparently because she went to school there. Art History in Boston U. Junjie met her while they were both living in the States. Ivan even attended their wedding. But that was years ago, and Ivan had to admit that he could not recognize her—that it was like meeting her anew.

Irina—Ivan's girlfriend—was a beautiful Russian lady. Blond and with striking eyes that seemed to change shades from deep blue to gray—depending on her mood. Nice, quiet, polite, and giving an impression of being somehow shy. Maybe withdrawn into her shell? Maybe coy. Aki and Junjie immediately agreed—and announced—that she was too young and beautiful for someone like Ivan. She seemed to like that—her eyes sparkled turquoise—but Ivan protested and said that she sold her soul to the devil and was in fact older than she looked.

They all arrived the previous evening and were staying at Ivan's. In his family house that was supposedly a few hundred years old. A house with three-foot stone walls that apparently kept the inside cool in summer and reasonably warm in winter. Walled tiled courtyard with a seating area shaded by an old vine plant held up by a wooden trellis. Even an old water well and an underground cistern for storing rainwater that Ivan said was nowadays used only for keeping the watermelons cool in the summer.

Ivan welcomed them with just wine, cheese, and bread, showed them to their rooms, and insisted that they all go to bed early, as the activities would begin only in the morning.

Then in the morning, he made them ride bikes to the town—about five miles up the coastline of the bay. The bay was truly amazingly beautiful. More like a fjord than a regular sea bay—with steep barren mountains lining the edges of this complex of inlets of the Adriatic Sea. It gave an impression of a mountain lake, with clear azure water coming right up to the roadway that Ivan said was built by Napoleon. Picturesque houses lining the coastline, surrounded by all sorts of trees and bushes. Birds chirping. Smell of the sea. Few boats gliding lazily across the mirrorlike water. Amazing.

"Wars were fought here over whose cream cakes are the best," Ivan joked, "and I am definitely in Mishko's camp." He was making them all eat a raspberry-filled cream torte with their morning coffee. He called it the breakfast of the champions.

"What is Mishko?" Aki asked.

"The owner of this place. And the author of absolutely the best cream torte in all the bays of Kotor—and possibly in the whole world. I have tested them all and can definitely vouch for these," Ivan explained with a ridiculous ear to ear grin on his face.

"Cream cake seems a bit heavy to me," Mary ventured, eyeing the cream torte suspiciously. "I am more of a fruit-and-granola-breakfast kind of a girl. Maybe a yogurt."

"Absolutely not! This stuff is fluffy and light. Positively healthy. Fruit and dairy food groups included. Try it," he insisted.

They did. It *was* good. Very good. In fact, irresistible. Went down easily. With the coffee. And with just sitting in the café, people-watching the colorful pedestrians and enjoying the warm morning sunshine. Occasionally, Ivan waved and exchanged a few words with some of the passersby that he happened to know. He even introduced them to a man that dropped by to chat—a Jovan Ivanovic[85]— who also happened to be an engineer working in the chip industry in America. But up in Los Angeles. He said that they jokingly call each other "negatives"—as in the negative of old black-and-white films—due to the mirroring of their names: Ivan Jovanovic and Jovan Ivanovic.

"Good. Now that the healthy breakfast knocked out all initiative to do anything at all—we can blend with the natives and do what the locals do," Ivan carried on. "Mostly nothing," he clarified.

"But that would be such a shame," Feng protested. "I want to explore this place. It is beautiful. You said about a thousand years old. I want to walk around and explore the side streets, climb the walls, go to the museum, and see the sites..."

"And shops," Irina inserted...

"Yes, yes. There will be plenty of time for that. Later," Ivan explained. "But as they say, in Rome, do as Romans do. We now have to go back home and sit about. Maybe another coffee. Or a spritzer. We must spend at least an hour or two staring at the bay—to make

---

[85] **Jovan Ivanovic**: A common Serbian name and a protagonist in *Between the Titans*—another novel by the author involving engineers, some drama, Kotor...

sure it doesn't go away. It is an important duty, and we must do our share."

Ivan was a bit manic with the excitement of being in Kotor. Irina just nodded politely—probably used to Ivan's antics—and assured them that it was useless to argue with him when he got like this.

But he was right. Sitting in front of his house—right on the water—staring at the bay. All the anxiety to do things, all the worries and concerns, seemed to melt away. Magically. There was just the bay. The mountains. The warm sunshine. The mix of the aromas of laurel trees, oleander bushes, and the sea. The chirping of the crickets. The lapping of the sea. Hypnotic. There was just the now.

Hours passed. When they got hungry, they walked over to the neighboring village and had lunch: a mixed sampler of local fresh seafood—squid, fish, prawns, mussels. With potatoes and swiss chard. And Montenegrin white wine. They teased Irina about the surprising amount that she could put away—but she just smiled, said it was good, and contentedly picked all the bones clean, heads and tails included.

After, they enjoyed a siesta. And post siesta coffee with some gelato… Another tradition, apparently.

With Ivan continuously prattling on about the place, its history, its people…

The sun set around 6:00 p.m., and Ivan started making an excuse that the tradition here is that the men take care of business after dark and that they needed some time.

"Wow! Finally. You guys have been amazingly good so far," Mary commented, maybe a bit dryly. "It must have been killing you to refrain from talking about your technology and business stuff. A whole day. And there are even three of you here."

"Yes, I was surprised too. A whole day and not a word," Feng added. "Normally, after half a day, he starts making me listen to his technology mumbo jumbo," she said, pointing at Junjie and feigning a sleepy face.

"Well, let's let them have some time. Or they may get the shakes and other withdrawal symptoms. In Russia, we know that it is dangerous to take the vodka away from the men *all* at once," Irina said.

"You have to water it down gradually," she explained. She then suggested that they walk over to the restaurant at the end of the village and bring dinner home. "And maybe have a glass of wine while there," she smiled, adding, "it is a lovely place... Come."

And they went off—an American, a Chinese, and a Russian woman—laughing about how woody and inept their men were, how they seemed to have a one-track mind, and exchanging all sorts of stories of various faux pas. Seemingly a universally shared take on the social skills of engineers.

"All right," Ivan said when they were alone, "so?"

"What? You want me to tell you what happened in Beijing," Junjie asked feigning shock and surprise. "Out here? In the open? Aren't you worried about someone listening?" in an obvious jibe at Ivan's paranoia.

"You must be joking," Ivan responded in a show of incredulity. "This tiny village is the most secure place on the planet. Everybody here knows everything about everyone. You cannot even fart without the local rumor mill broadcasting it throughout the bay. If there was anything like an outsider anywhere within ten miles—we would for sure know it."

He was only half joking. Before Junjie had a chance to speak up, he added, "But seriously... As a last act of my duty as the paranoiac in chief, I do think that we must agree to never ever talk about what happened. Let us face it. Secret police everywhere are the same—they are an organization that is paid to never forget. The MSS for sure has open files on us by now. Possibly the FBI too—since they are sure to be watching whatever the MSS is doing. And once they have a file—every bit and detail that comes their way gets recorded. They never forget, and the file will never be closed. So we must continue the same practice as up to now. We never ever talk about this—except maybe only to each other and always just face-to-face. Never on the phone, in an e-mail, or even on paper. You do not know who may overhear what, how it could be used or misused, or whatever. So for the sake of our continued safety, for your families, we just got to agree to never talk about it. What happened—never happened. We always stick to the cover story. BBI abandoned its CFIUS appeal because CHARM walked away. Nothing else. After tonight, there is only one thing to say. Nothing happened."

Aki and Junjie stared at him for a long while as if to make sure if he was serious or joking. He was serious. After some thought, they nodded and said in unison, "Agreed. Nothing happened."

Junjie then brought them up to speed about the events in Beijing. About Lao's confusion and the apparent concern of the government regarding an exposé in the press.

"That was genius, by the way," Junjie commented. "The bit about *The Guardian*. That seems to have them more scared than the FBI."

"Just lucky." Ivan shrugged it off. "Even a blind squirrel gets an acorn every now and then."

"So," Junjie concluded, "it seems that we did it. Seems like we are free and clear. For at least a quarter. I have been told—ordered—to lay off BBI. The pressure on you, Aki, is off. For now, at least, we have undone all the harm. Everything. And through all this, I seem to be coming off smelling of roses. Looks like Lao is apparently convinced that I was a good boy. Otherwise, he would not have let us come here. Let alone, pay for it." He smirked and paused for a second. "You know, I was not sure that we could do it. I really had my doubts—but seems like it worked. Gentlemen, thank you. You are the greatest." Junjie made a point of formally shaking hands with Aki and Ivan and then raised his glass in a toast. "To the geezer heroes."

They drank up and talked about their progress with their long-term plans. The final phase of their caper.

Aki thanked Junjie for the idea about converting a private company into a co-op and described his intentions to engage with Project Equity to structure that kind of a transition. He was hopeful that it could be implemented within a quarter or so and that he would end up in some kind of a part-time advisory role to ensure continuity. Evidently quite pleased and excited about it.

Junjie shared his progress as well. He had broached the subject with TEL—who indicated that they might be interested in investing in CHARM. He was also excited about using the threat of being blacklisted by the FBI as a cover for his conversion of CHARM into a co-op. He thought that Lao would buy that. He thought that Lao might see it as a way of cutting his losses—distancing CHARM from Junjie, who was, as far as Lao was concerned, compromised. "Who knows, he might even actively support it. Another side benefit of that brilliant e-mail threat," Junjie said with a devilish grin.

They sat in silence for a while—enjoying the rich and very fruity homemade wine that Ivan got from a neighbor. Enjoying their success. Enjoying the tranquility of the bay. And heavenly silence interrupted only by the gentle lapping of the bay against the shore.

Then Aki brought up the topic that was on his mind for a while—almost as an afterthought. "So now that it is all done and once we have secured our companies, should we not tell the feds about the pinch point thing? Don't we have a, er, a civic responsibility to do that?"

"No, no, and no!" Ivan surprised them by slapping the table, startling Junjie and Aki and making them jump. "What we did, we did to save your companies and to protect the independence of our industry. Not to take part in the trade war. I, for one, absolutely refuse to participate in any activity that limits access to the technology. On anyone's side." Before Aki or Junjie had a chance to comment, Ivan continued with equal passion. "I really do believe that our technology is a gift to mankind as a whole. It has precipitated a renaissance like the world has never seen before. Everything has changed—virtually overnight. I am old and remember very well the way the world was just yesterday. Before the internet and the access it gave us to virtually all the knowledge of humankind. At our fingertips. Before the supercomputer in our pockets that we call a phone and the access it gave us to each other. Person to person, anytime, anywhere on the planet. The amazing miracle of today's technology is tenuous—like a seedling that just took root. It must be nurtured and treated with respect—not taken for granted. Sure, in the beginning, America—and its armed forces—provided a lot of seed capital that was needed to incubate the technology. And I believe that the army and the nation have got ample returns on their investment. But from the beginning, the intellectual contribution was international. From the very onset, the minds that conceived and developed the technology—the early pioneers[86]—came from all over. Europe, India, China, Japan—and America too. There is a Jagadish Bose and Jayant Baliga from India, Van Neumann and Andy Grove from Hungary, Mohamed Atalla from Egypt, Dawon Kahng from Korea, Leo Esaki and Masatoshi Shima from Japan, and so on, for every Shockley, Kilby, Gordon Moore, or Robert Noyce from America.

"So it seems to me that semiconductor technology is the intellectual property of mankind as a whole. It should not belong to any one nation. For sure, the dragons—the various countries and special interests—will vie to dominate it. Let us not kid ourselves. For every Professor Lao in China, there is a guy in America, or Russia, or wherever, that is also plotting to own the technology. Trying to dominate the industry. Trying to divide it up and segment it into bits and pieces that they can control. Trying to bottle it up. By equally illegitimate, or for that matter, even by legitimate means. But that does not make it right. The technology should belong to everybody. Especially now that it has matured—thanks to the contributions over the last half century or so from all across the planet. I believe that a study of history—big history[87]—shows quite conclusively that humanity has made the greatest leaps forward when people and ideas come together and interact. That is the strength of our species. Hence, helping that process of interaction is the greater good. And conversely, building walls—around technology in this case—is evil. And evil should be stopped. So I believe that what we did was a small strike for the greater good. And conversely, contributing to the trade war—on anyone's side—would be a strike for evil." Then, almost as if to explain, he added, "I do feel like I have been very fortunate—privileged even—to have been a part of the industry. For that oppor-

---

[86] **Semiconductor Technology Pioneers**: A random selection of some of the prominent names that made the semiconductor technology what it is today...

[87] **Big History**: An academic discipline that examines history from the Big Bang to the present. Big History resists specialization, and searches for universal patterns or trends. It examines longtime frames using a multidisciplinary approach based on combining numerous disciplines from science and the humanities and explores human existence in the context of this bigger picture. It integrates studies of the cosmos, Earth, life, and humanity using empirical evidence to explore cause-and-effect relations.

tunity, I am grateful, and I feel a responsibility to do everything I can to help protect it. It is a duty imposed by the privilege."

Aki and Junjie just stared at Ivan in amazement. This passion from Ivan caught them by surprise. Especially given the setting. The peaceful bay, the silence of the evening disturbed only by a few crickets and birds. And then Ivan's big speech—delivered with such conviction. A contrast. A surprise. They were shocked.

"Wow, Ivan!" Aki blurted. "Where the hell did all that come from?" After a pause, he added, "Don't hold it all in. You know, it is bad for you." A joke trying to lighten the atmosphere that has just gotten so serious.

Ivan caught himself and mumbled, "Sorry, guys. I guess I do feel strongly about this."

"But you are right," Junjie piped in. "I hate to use formal terms, but I applaud everything you just said. I, too, believe in the virtue of globalization."

"Really," Aki ventured. "I normally do not have much time for all the political crap—just busy taking care of my family and my business I guess—but I believe that recently a lot has come out about the negative sides of globalization. That it is not all a bed of roses. That there is a dark side…"

"Dark side?" Ivan reacted—again passionate. "Dark side! No, no, and no. We—as species—have never had it so good. If you take any objective metric—health, longevity, infant mortality, literacy, quality of life, anything—the world is better off now than it has ever been. Ever! At the level of the entire humanity. For Christ's sake, we have more obese people than starving people on the planet. First time ever. Sure, if you segment us into various pockets, you can find some subset of the population that may not be as well off. But as a whole, there is no doubt that globalization has been excellent for our species.

"Even for a subset, I believe that we are fooling ourselves. Nostalgia tends to paint a false picture, and various demagogues claim that globalization has made the people of America, or Europe, worse off. But if you look at it objectively, that is not so. People talk about our father's generation being able to afford the American dream—a house and a car and so on. But those guys tend to gloss over the fact that over the last fifty-odd years our definitions and expectations have also changed. Ballooned. Of course, the house now must have a bathroom for every bedroom and a den and a game room and a two-car garage. Of course, you got to have at least two cars, and each must have an air-conditioner and an infotainment center and God knows what other gizmos. The number of people who could afford the house or the car of the 1950s has grown in America and Europe—not shrunk. I think that social studies have shown repeatedly that we tend to measure our well-being in relative terms. Am I better off than my neighbor, not am I better off than my father or grandfather? I believe that all metrics show that we are in fact better off than our fathers and grandfathers. No doubt about it. But over the last half century or so of globalization, some segments of the population have grown less rapidly than other segments—and so they feel left behind.

"We do not have more than half of the world's population that is on the brink of starvation to remind us that they are doing okay. Fodder for the demagogues. But the fact is that in absolute—not relative terms—globalization has made us all better off. Besides, in principle—in terms of cosmic justice—I do not understand why some worker in China or India or Bangladesh deserves a job any less than some other sod in Europe or America. Those guys also have families to feed. The way I see it, if they can do the same job, with the same quality, as an American or European worker for less—then power to them. In fact, I believe that an argument can be made that altruism that is baked into all our genetic makeup dictates that what globalization has enabled is the greater good. Globalization has enabled the lifting of millions—no, billions—out of poverty, ignorance, and starvation at the price that some people in the richer world have had their standard of living improved by only a percent or two, as opposed to the 5 or 10 percent growth that their parents' generation has enjoyed. Arguably. No, to my mind, globalization has been a force for the good of the species. The greater good."

Aki and Junjie again just stared. Where did all this come from?

"Geez, Ivan. Is it the water here? Or the wine," Aki wondered. "What's gotten into you?" This was not the Ivan they were used to.

But before they could take it any further, their "better halves" arrived back. Laughing and seemingly happy with their evening. Maybe it was that wine that Irina mentioned? Or the company? Or the place?

They brought back supper that they shared on the porch—mixed grilled meat with just bread and chopped onions and a tomato salad. Smelled good. Tasted better. They stayed up eating, sipping the dark red Montenegrin wine, chatting easily, and sometimes just sitting there looking at the starry night. They went to bed late.

The next day, Ivan organized a boat tour of the four bays. Spectacular and memorable. But even in the middle of that historical and natural splendor that is rightly one of the UNESCO World Heritage Sites,[88] Aki and Junjie were sitting in the back of the boat, talking quietly with each other.

"Yeah, back then—when I started," Aki was saying, "it was all about the quartz. Getting the glass right was the name of the game. Now—it is all different. To outsiders, it feels like it is the same thing—just mask blanks. But EUV masks are entirely and totally different cattle of fish than the traditional ones. And, man, you won't believe it, just the inspection of the photomask blanks—to make sure that there are no defects—requires a piece of equipment that costs tens of millions of dollars. You got to scan the mask blank with an EUV laser and image the defects. Actinic Blank Inspection. And BBI needs a couple of them in order to scale up the production of EUV blanks. Major bucks! Almost equal to our annual revenue. Just for the stinkin' inspection. I mean, it doesn't help you actually build anything."

---

[88] **UNESCO World Heritage Sites**: A list of landmarks, selected by the United Nations Educational, Scientific, and Cultural Organization (UNESCO) for having cultural, historical, scientific, or other form of significance, which is legally protected by international treaties. The sites are judged to possess "cultural and natural heritage considered to be of outstanding value to humanity."

EXHIBIT 11.3   Actinic Blank Inspection

Actinic: of, relating to, resulting from, or exhibiting chemical changes produced by radiant energy especially in the visible and ultraviolet parts of the spectrum. From: https://www.merriam-webster.com/dictionary/actinic

In Photography: *to distinguish light that would expose the monochrome films from light that would not. A non-actinic safe-light (e.g., red or amber) could be used in a darkroom without risk of exposing (fogging) light-sensitive films, plates or papers. From: https://en.wikipedia.org/wiki/Actinism#Photography*

In chip manufacturing: *Actinic inspection of masks in computer chip manufacture refers to inspecting the mask with the <u>same wavelength of light that the lithography system use</u>.*

Inspection of photomask blanks for EUV Lithography requires identification (and isolation) of any imperfection that would impair the performance of the mask – before the cost of making of the mask ($M's) is Incurred.
With 13.5nm (EUV) light even nm size defects matter, even if they are buried 20 or 30 layers deep in the reflective coating.

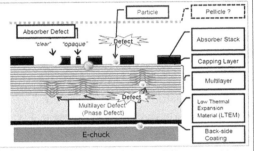

Actinic Inspection requires a 13.5nm light source. (see Exhibit 1.6)

It is Complicated!
The equipment is complicated! And Expen$ive

"Really?" Junjie was surprised. "No way. Can't you build some kind of a test wafer to give you an electrical readout?" He seemed to be working on some kind of an idea.

Mary, Feng, and Irina exchanged glances, shrugged, and laughed, saying something like, "Engineers will be engineers."

Sometime Later

Mr. Mori Hashimoto, a single forty-three-year-old resident of Yokohama, Japan, and a waiter in a local restaurant, has won the big prize of the Nenmatsu Jumbo Takarakuji end-of-the-year drawing run by Japan Lottery Association. The ecstatic, and possibly slightly inebriated, Mr. Hashimoto has been quoted as saying, "I did not know what to do with a tip that this gaijin left in our restaurant... So I bought a lotto ticket..." The winnings are expected to be over one billion yen. Mr. Hashimoto expressed intentions to continue with his normal life, including the job at the Marine Rouge Tour boat restaurant and lounge—but only after a short vacation that he plans to take in Hawaii and Las Vegas.

*****

CHARM Incorporated, a technology company based in Beijing, China, specialized in metrology tools and services for the semiconductor industry, has announced a new product line based on MEMS technology. The new product line is specifically defined to fully characterize the various packaging technologies and to implement semiconductor-grade process control techniques at packaging-grade cost structure. "Advanced Packaging is a vital and a rapidly growing segment of the semiconductor industry that has traditionally been underserved by the equipment and technology services companies," said Dr. YuYan Zhao, a VP in charge of Marketing and Business Development and the current acting CEO. "We think that this is an excellent opportunity for a company like CHARM and are pursuing it with all our energies," she said. This is the first new product announcement since the change in management and corporate structure at the company. It appears that the new team is pursuing unique opportunities with the same vigor and innovative spirit that characterized the past management.

*****

Dr. Ivan Jovanovic, a thirty-five-year veteran of the semiconductor industry, has fully retired from the technology field and has even shut down his consulting business. His San Diego City business tax has certainly not been paid up. He shares his time between San Diego, California, and Kotor, Montenegro, and seems to be managing his various disorders well even without a workplace to go to. He has been active in the new Amateur Drone Pilots of America (ADPA) campaign to legislate dedicated airspace for drone flying in urban areas. He is quoted as saying, "We need a place where we can legally practice our art with no fear of harassment from the misinformed public or misguided authorities." Some people close to him say that he has cut down his coffee intake to only two cups per day and supposedly enjoys a short nap every afternoon—apparently under doctor's orders as a preventive measure against a recurrence of a heart attack. The rumors that he is trying to embark on a new career as a writer of fiction, supposedly working on a novel about three old engineers pulling a heist in China, are totally unsubstantiated.

*****

Irina Yerpilova, a Russian native, naturalized US citizen, domiciled in the Bay Area, has recently been seen in Shoreline Park. She is quoted as saying that on that day she has seen two large snakes, a rabbit, and many pelicans, ducks, and geese.

*****

Following a recent meeting attended by the Chairman, the Prime Minister, and the other five permanent members, the Standing Committee of CPC has reaffirmed the Party's commitment to the "Made in China 2025" policy initiative. In an unusual display of openness, a short official statement has been issued to the press, emphasizing the importance of the initiative to the overall economic growth of the People's Republic. This has triggered rumors of increased government spending on the Chinese semiconductor industry and the associated infrastructure, and funding of phase 3 of the Big Fund is believed to be imminent. Reliable sources that wish to remain unnamed indicate that the committee has expressed a preference for large and visible projects. A comment along the lines of "The committee will fund mega-projects that the Party can proudly point to—something that the people can see—in order to justify the large investments," has been overheard. Apparently, the CPC believes that visible high-tech projects are an especially valuable way of demonstrating the superiority of the Chinese system during stressful times, for political and social morale reasons, among others. Another source has clarified, in an off-the-record statement, that the Committee has decided to abandon all other projects that divert the focus from the important primary activities. It was clarified that even the projects that might have made technical or economic sense but that did not meet these new political objectives would be aborted. No official mention has been made of the trade war with the US.

*****

After a long and distinguished career at Tsinghua University, the esteemed and highly respected professor Lao has retired. He seems to have just disappeared with the gossip alternately speculating that he has moved to Shanghai to be with his son, that he has died, that he has gone to live a hermit's life in the Gobi desert, that he has relocated to Hainan Island—sometimes called Chinese Hawaii. No one seems to know for sure. One of the last official acts of the venerable professor was to sponsor Dr. Junjie Wu for a post in the Electrical Engineering department of Tsinghua University. He even made a special point of singling out Dr. Wu in a speech that he made during a dinner that his current and past students organized to mark the occasion of his retirement. In a cryptic reference that no one quite understood and that may, in fact, be due to the amount of alcohol that was consumed, he is quoted as saying that he knew that Junjie was responsible for the break-in but that he nevertheless wished Dr. Wu all the best in dealing with the antibodies.

Professor Lao also seems to have been retired from all other posts and positions, sometimes rumored to be connected with the secret police. Supposedly, this was because it was believed that he has become a potential leak of sensitive information. The Leadership apparently concluded that he was compromised and wished to distance itself from any connections with him. One of Professor Lao's last acts as a person of influence was to support the transition of CHARM Inc. into a worker-owned co-op entity. He was even rumored to have been present at the ceremony that formalized the transfer of the ownership.

*****

Sing, a stuffed panda—supposedly the property of Dr. Junjie Wu— has been placed in a shoebox, stored on the upper shelf of a closet at an undisclosed address in Beijing, China. It is said that his travel days are over—most likely due to its poor state of health.

*****

Dr. Archimedes Roussos has retired from his post as the CEO and chairman of Best Blanks Incorporated—a company that he started thirty years ago in a small warehouse in Sorrento Valley, San Diego, and that has become a major player in the niche market for manufacturing photomasks for the global semiconductor industry. After failing to merge with CHARM Inc., due to the objections raised by the Committee for Foreign Investment in the United States

(CFIUS), he has sold his interest in the privately owned entity to a Trust Corporation owned by the current employees of the company. The restructuring of a private company into a co-op was noted in the press as it resulted in a relatively rare entity—a multinational worker-owned cooperative. Following a review by the Ministry of International Trade and Industry (MITI) of Japan, the restructured BBI KK has qualified for the low-interest loans offered by the Japanese government to stimulate its domestic industry, and has been rumored to have made major capital investments. Dr. Roussos is quoted as intending to dedicate his time to his family and various private pursuits, including learning to play the piano. He hopes to continue as a part-time adviser to BBI for a few more years and has therefore declined all invitations and bookings for piano recitals.

*****

A woman in a white dress has been seen buying a glass of wine at a bar in San Francisco International Airport. It is believed that it was a glass of chilled white Sauvignon Blanc wine from New Zealand Marlborough Valley—probably Kim Crawford, 2018. Possibly Whitehaven? Or Starborough?

*****

After a successful career as an entrepreneur in the electronic technology industry, Dr. Junjie Wu has sold his last company, CHARM Incorporated, and taken a post at his alma mater, the Tsinghua University. He has retained only an informal advisory position at CHARM—a company that he started up seven years ago and that he has recently restructured into a co-operative entity, majority owned by its employees, fronted by Industrial and Commercial Bank of China, and minority owned by Tokyo Electron Ltd. of Japan. In his new role, Dr. Wu is rumored to be currently working with the appropriate organs of the government of the People's Republic of China to obtain funding for his research focused on automating visual inspections in semiconductor manufacturing. He has been quoted as stating at a recent industry group gathering that automation of visual inspections is a huge opportunity since it represents a major portion of the overall cost structure of Integrated Circuits. He claimed that this is a relatively new area of research where China could not only assume a leading position but could even dominate. He has apparently mentioned the possible use of Artificial Intelligence and specialized test vehicles…

*****

Mr. Kaito Suzuki, a man in his late teens and a member of a Yankii motorcycle gang in Nagasaki, on the southern island of Kyushu, has been arrested by the local police for random acts of vandalism. Among his personal possessions were found a set of old photographs that he claims are of his mother (now deceased) and father (unknown). The Yankii motorcycle gang began as a youth movement that much of Japanese society still associates with juvenile delinquency. They embrace punkish rebellion and are often associated with Japan's infamous motorcycle gangs, "speed tribes" known as bōsōzoku. The group adopted the moniker "yankii," probably due to the general impression of vulgarity and gaudiness associated with Americans or American popular culture.

*****

ASML (Advanced Semiconductor Materials Lithography), a multinational company headquartered in Veldhoven, Netherlands (number of employees: >23,000 (2019), 123 different nationalities), and a sole provider of the EUV lithography tools, has reported excellent results for 2019 with thirty EUV scanner units sold. ASML has also expressed a very bullish outlook for 2020 and beyond with orders for eighteen EUV machines from TSMC alone, the world's largest foundry, already on the books. ASML's new Twinscan NXE: 3400C EUV scanner model, listed at US$125M each, has demonstrated satisfactory results with a throughput of more than 170 wafers per hour (at Dose: 20mJ/cm2, die size: 26 × 33 mm, 96 shots). The new scanner uses Cymer's new 340W light source, which enables higher performance. It is rumored that Peter Wennink, ASML president and chief executive officer since 2013, has been seen rubbing his hands in glee.

*****

Mrs. Feng Wu, the spouse of Dr. Junjie Wu, has been seen at the Beijing Museum of Art, hosting the opening ceremony of a visiting exhibit named "Montenegro: small in size only." The exhibit will be on a tour of five major cities in the People's Republic of China over the next twelve months.

*****

ProPlate, a small San Diego company specialized in custom gold plating services, has issued a quote for a private one-off job to plate a toy box drone. The quote explains that the process of plating such a complex shape consisting of compound materials would necessarily have to be implemented in two separate steps: first to deposit a conducting film—possibly nickel—on all the surfaces and second to electroplate a film of gold. A handwritten note at the bottom of the quote indicated that using just spray paint would be a lot cheaper and easier. "Duh!"

About the Author

Riko Radojcic is a lucky man who has been blessed with a fulfilling life rich in its diversity. He was born in what was then a poor post-war Yugoslavia and enjoyed a very happy and secure early childhood there. When he was twelve his father took a job with the UN World Health Organization, and Riko spent his teen years in East Pakistan (Bangladesh now), Nigeria, Kenya and Tanzania, observing both, the demise of the colonial Raj, and some harsh Third World realities. He completed high school in Swiss private schools—a polar opposite of the Third World—which gave him a peek into the lives of the one-percenters. He then moved to Manchester, UK, where he witnessed the bleak circumstances of the working class in the heart of the then-decaying industrial England. He earned his BSc and PhD degrees in Electronic Engineering and Solid-State Physics there, and after a couple of years of working in England he immigrated to the US. Riko and his then-wife settled in the San Diego area, where they brought up their three wonderful children, and he got to experience the American Dream—yet another polar opposite. He enjoyed a rewarding and a very stimulating career in the semiconductor industry, working in a variety of technical, managerial and business development roles. His professional life exposed him not only to the amazing wonders of the silicon chip technology, but also gave him an opportunity to travel internationally and to interact with people from very diverse and multicultural backgrounds. After 35+ years in the world of high tech and engineering management, Riko retired and is now trying to be a writer. Always more comfortable as an observer than the observed, as an analyst than a participant, he is trying to bring to life the magic of technology, the reality of the high-tech industry, and some of his diverse life experiences through storytelling...

Other books by the Author:

FICTION			
Between the Titans	Fulton Books	2020	ISBN 978-1646541775
MANAGMENT			
Managing More-than-Moore Integration Technology Development	Springer	2018	ISBN 978-3-319-92700-8
TECHNICAL			
More-than-Moore 2.5D and 3D SiP Integration	Springer	2017	ISBN 978-3-319-52547-1
Stress Management for 3D ICS Using Through Silicon Vias	American Institute of Physics (AIP)	2012	ISBN 978-0735409385
Three Dimensional System Integration	Springer	2011	ISBN 978-1-4419-0961-9
Guidebook for Managing Silicon Chip Reliability	CRC Press	1999	ISBN 978-0367400064

CPSIA information can be obtained
at www.ICGtesting.com
Printed in the USA
BVHW071319010621
608546BV00001B/54